THE NOTHING MAN

C.J. PETIT

Printed in the United States of America

First Printing, 2020

ISBN: 9798662923584

TABLE OF CONTENTS

PROLOGUE

May 11, 1868
St. Charles, Missouri

Charles Collins climbed the steps to St. Ann's Orphanage, entered and walked past the empty reception desk before heading for the office of Albert Flannery, the headmaster.

He didn't knock but just opened the door then closed it behind him as Mister Flannery looked up from the form he was completing.

"Mister Collins, I've been expecting you," he said as he set down his pen.

"I need at least four. If you can give me six, then that would be better. I don't want any younger than six."

"Alright. I'll have eight boys brought in and you can choose."

Albert then stood and left his office as Charles Collins took a seat. He was a 'boy finder' for Abbott Glass and Bottle Company. He was surprised that Flannery would have eight boys. He'd cleaned him out six months ago and had almost had to take two of the small ones. He must have gotten an overflow from the state's orphanage. He may be a boy finder, but he'd take girls if need be. They may not have the strength of the boys, but their smaller hands were more dexterous and were better at cleaning the bottles.

When Albert returned ten minutes later, he led eight boys of various ages and heights into the office and closed the door. Without saying a word, the boys stood in a line and seven of the eight had their eyes on the floor but the one second from the left end of the line glared at him.

Charlie stared back at the boy remembering him from the last time he'd come to find some workers. He had been too small then and was only marginally bigger this time, but his arrogance marked him as trouble, so Charlie was going to leave him again.

After he'd selected six of the larger boys, Albert Flannery pulled him aside, pointed at the angry youngster and said, "Can you take that one? He's been giving the staff a hard time. You won't have to pay for him."

Charlie Collins glanced back at the boy before nodding and replying, "Alright. We'll drive that rebelliousness out of him."

He then pulled out thirty dollars and handed it to Mister Flannery who then returned to his chair behind his desk and watched the boys being led away.

There was nothing illegal in anything that either man had done. Society expected the boys to be productive members and not leeches sucking blood out of the orphanage that was supported by citizens. Now those seven boys would be working and becoming useful.

————

September 8, 1878
Abbott Glass and Bottle Company
St. Louis, Missouri

Number 207 climbed the rickety ladder to the top of the noisy steam engine with the bucket of grease in his left hand. The ladder's rungs were getting close to breaking under his weight, but he wasn't about to fall and give them the satisfaction. His hands were too big to do the bottle cleaning and he had caused too much trouble to be carrying the crates of finished glassware any longer, so he expected that he'd be thrown out sooner than when he was supposed to leave. He'd managed to become as big a nuisance as possible, but all they had done was to assign him to ever-increasing dirty and dangerous jobs probably hoping that he would have a fatal accident, but he wasn't about to let that happen.

Since he'd arrived at the factory more than ten years ago, they had tried to humble him and to drive out his anger, but he refused to buckle. At first, they had put him in the floor with all of the bullies who had tried to beat him into submission. They'd almost succeeded, but it was then that #207 had discovered his natural ability to defend himself. He'd suffered a lot of punishment at first, but even as he worked the factory floor, he continued to improve his skills. By the time he'd been there a year, even the bullies had left him alone. He'd never used his prowess as a fighter to become a bully because that wasn't his nature. He didn't like anyone forcing their will on him and he wasn't about to do it to others.

He'd survived ten years of work and torment, but his attitude hadn't changed. Now he was assigned to grease and oil the engine that turned the belts and gears that moved the bottles and glass across the factory floor. What made it so dangerous was that the engine was always running when he had to smear the grease on the rollers and wheels. One slip would cost him a finger or a hand and then the fall would kill him. He'd almost fallen the third time he'd had to grease the steam engine but had realized that because no one else would do the job, he could take his time.

He had just smeared a handful of black grease on the top roller when he glanced down at the immense factory floor. There were rows of tables and benches covered with glassware and bottles that were manned by children. Walking down the aisle was the hated foreman, Jed Bristol. He carried a long hickory switch that he used to keep his young workers in line and #207 had felt its wrath many times over the years.

As he watched, a young blonde-haired girl of about ten knocked a green bottle from her table and when it hit the floor, the neck snapped then the body of the bottle shattered. Mister Bristol whirled around as the girl hurried from her chair then around the table and began to pick up the sharp shards of glass.

5

The foreman marched back to the girl who was on her heels picking up the broken pieces and pulled his switch from his belt as his face contorted in anger.

Number 207 knew that the girl was about to suffer severe punishment for the accident and what little patience he had disappeared. He dropped the bucket of grease to the floor twelve feet below and began to clamber down the ladder. By the time he reached the floor and made it past the hot steam engine, he could see that Mister Bristol was already at work, snapping his hickory switch on the girl's back as she cowered in pain and fear. He could already see streaks of blood on her faded yellow dress.

He wiped the grease from his hands as he angrily strode toward the scene. He didn't pay any attention to the children behind the worktables as they stared in disbelief. He clenched his fists as his fury reached mammoth levels. All those years of mistreatment and undeserved punishment had finally exploded inside.

The foreman's switch was high over his head for another blow when he spotted #207 approaching and could see the anger in his eyes and his fists clenched for a fight. He wasn't afraid but saw his opportunity to finally make that boy pay the ultimate price.

"You're gonna pay now, boy!" he snarled as he turned away from the girl and toward the hated boy.

Number 207 never said a word but continued to close the gap.

When he was four feet away, Mister Bristol's switch whistled as it arced through the air and lashed the boy's left shoulder. The foreman then made the mistake of thinking that the boy would flinch or grab his shoulder in pain which would give him the chance to begin a series of blows, but that didn't happen.

After feeling the sting of the switch, #207 lit into Mister Bristol with ten years of pent up rage. He didn't let the bigger foreman even bring his arm back for a second whip as he reigned blow after blow on the man. His fists flew making the foreman step back to avoid the surprise assault. But he had stepped back too quickly and slipped on the damp floor just as the boy struck him with a hard shot to his chin.

Jed Bristol fell onto his back with his hickory switch still clutched in his right hand and fell onto the broken glass that he'd prevented the girl from picking up. He screamed in pain which brought the two guards from the doorway to his aid.

They soon grabbed the boy's arms as the foreman returned to his feet. He wanted to whip the boy to death, but everyone was watching, and the guards had him under control, so he had to be satisfied with getting rid of him.

"Get out of here, boy! You ain't comin' back and you can't go back to your comfy bed either. You're nothin' and will always be nothin' until the day you die."

Number 207 still didn't reply as he continued to glare at the foreman.

Before the guards took him away, he turned to his left and saw the blue eyes of the girl as she said, "Thank you."

It was the last thing he would see of the Abbott Glass and Bottle Company as he was unceremoniously tossed out of the building and left on his own.

Number 207 glanced back at the two guards at the door then walked quietly into the night.

———

April 19, 1880
T.L. Wilson Gymnasium
St. Louis, Missouri

Ned stared at his opponent and then glanced at Tom Proctor, his manager. *Why had he scheduled this man?* Bill Noble was about Ned's size, but his conditioning looked less than what one would expect of a bareknuckle fighter. He looked more like a bank clerk as he stood on the other side of the ring. But Tom wasn't watching as he meandered among the crowd making bets as he usually did.

THE NOTHING MAN

This would be Ned's forty-third fight since he'd started his career as a fighter. He'd lost three of the first six, but only one since then and that was to a much larger man. The man facing him looked as if he shouldn't even be a spectator. Ned knew that he'd make short work of it but suspected that Tom would want him to let the challenger get a few shots in to make it look good. He suspected that if he was lucky, Tom would be able to get odds of eight to one for the bank clerk to beat him. It was a far cry from the even odds that he usually managed, and that was what bothered him. *Why was he betting at all when he would only make a dime or so for each dollar he bet?*

Ned was already well known in the St. Louis circuit and in his last fight against an equally skilled opponent, Tom was still only able to get even money. Ned guessed that the only way Tom would make any money on this fight was to wait until the third round. They had only instituted rounds a few months ago ostensibly to give the fighters a chance to breathe, but the real reason was for the bettors to continue to place their wagers as the fight progressed. If Ned let the man last and put on a good show, Tom might get halfway decent odds after the second round.

The starter walked to the middle of the ring and Ned stepped toward the center as did his opponent.

As he and Bill reached the middle, the starter loudly cried, "Gentlemen, toe the line!"

Ned's clenched fists snapped to a defensive position near his chin and he let Bill have his first blow. He swung a weak roundhouse left that smacked into Ned's shoulder before Ned snapped a hard jab into his chest, knocking him back a step.

Ned could hear the crowd exhorting him to finish Noble off quickly, but Ned did no such thing as he let Bill take another shot. Again, he used his left and popped an ineffective uppercut into Ned's elbow.

Ned quickly popped Bill with two successive jabs which seemed to take the wind out of him, and Ned realized that he wasn't going to be able to carry his opponent even if he tried. So, once the other man stabilized on his feet, Ned waded in preparing to finish him off.

Suddenly, Bill Noble swung a right at Ned's head which he ignored as none of Noble's other punches had much of an effect. But when his fist struck, Ned was stunned. He felt a lot of unexpected power in the punch that started his ears ringing and made him stumble to his left. Then Bill Noble hit him in the side of the chest with another crushing right which sent Ned to the floor.

He could hear the boos and jeers as he tried to regain his feet wondering what had just happened. As he tried to focus, he caught sight of Bill Noble as he stood over him and noticed a dark cylinder in his right fist. The man was carrying an iron cylinder! *Why hadn't Tom spotted it when he'd inspected his opponent?*

As much as he tried, Ned couldn't regain his feet. He heard the referee call the fight and then all hell broke loose. He was pretty much ignored as the men began a wild melee over the upset. Ned tried to find Tom Proctor but didn't see him anywhere.

They had to clear the ring for the next fight, so someone helped him to his feet and helped him to the locker room. As he walked, his sense of balance began to return so when he reached the locker room, he was almost himself again.

"Where's my manager?" Ned asked loudly, but no one was there to answer him.

He took a deep breath then walked to his open locker and began to change. He realized what had happened. Tom Proctor had set him up. The odds were so bad now that there wasn't much more money to make on him. Tom had scheduled the nobody opponent and then probably even provided him with the iron plug. He probably paid the man twenty dollars to get in the ring and another thirty if he won while his manager would make hundreds on the bets. It would be one last killing with Ned Boyd before he found another talented young fighter.

Ned hung his bag of gym clothes over his shoulder and left the back door of the locker room rather than facing the losing gamblers out in the gym.

He entered the dark alley and began heading for the roadway when he finally found his manager. Near the end of the alley, Tom Proctor was facing four angry men who had obviously discovered that the fight had been fixed and wanted their money back...with interest.

Ned slowly walked closer to the scene still unsure if he would help his traitorous manager. He could have simply turned the other way and let Tom deal with the angry men he'd cheated, but Ned had been cheated much worse and wanted to extract his own payment.

As he drew closer, he noticed that one of the four men was brandishing a knife at his manager and could hear their threats as Tom begged for understanding. Ned was almost ready to help the bastard when he heard him blame Ned for the unexpected loss which made any further debate unnecessary.

When one of the four men confronting his manager spotted Ned, he pointed and shouted, "You! You owe us money, too!"

Ned didn't slow down but angrily replied, "The hell I do! That bastard cheated me worse! I don't care what you do to him!"

Tom then turned and spotted Ned and knew he was going to die.

"Ned! I didn't cheat anybody! That feller just got a lucky punch!"

Ned stopped when he was three feet behind his manager and stared at the angry men and asked, "How much did each of you lose on the fight?"

The amounts varied from five to twenty dollars, so Ned turned his eyes to Tom and said, "Give each man his money back and another five dollars. Then we'll talk about what you did."

"I told you, Ned. I didn't do anything. You're my boy, not Bill Noble."

"You're supposed to inspect him before the fight, Tom. Did you do that?"

"Sure...sure, I did. He was clean."

"You didn't notice the iron slug in his right hand?"

Tom glanced back at the man with the knife as he tried to make an excuse. He didn't think that Ned had seen it.

Ned didn't wait for an answer but quickly asked the man with the knife, "If he give you your money and another five dollars will that satisfy you?"

"I reckon."

Ned then glared at Tom and said, "Give them the money, Tom or I'll beat it out of you."

"Alright…alright," his manager said as he rammed his hand into his right jacket pocket and pulled out a crumpled mass of currency.

After counting out each man's payment, the knife-wielder slid his blade back into his belt and said, "You're lucky Ned came by, Proctor."

The four men then turned and walked away, leaving Ned alone with his manager. Tom may have trained him how to fight but didn't have Ned's skills or his youth. His twenty years of toeing the line had left him arthritic and almost feeble.

Before he could return the money to his pocket, Ned said, "Give me the rest, Tom. You owe me for the beating I took so you could bet against me. I won't charge you for saving your skin."

Tom slowly handed him the fistful of bills which Ned stuffed into his pants pocket.

"I'm sorry, Ned. It's just that I wasn't makin' any money from your fights anymore."

"You were making the ring fee and even if you were only getting even odds, you'd still make money. You just wanted to make a killing and almost got me killed in the process. I'm leaving you, Tom. You're not my manager anymore."

Tom was startled and snapped, "And go where?"

14

"I'm going to fight my way across Missouri and then Kansas. Where I wind up isn't your concern. If I were you, I'd leave St. Louis. I imagine those four boys weren't the only ones who were a mad enough to slice you up."

"I can take care of myself! You go ahead and leave. Without me you ain't nothin!"

"Another man told me that last year. Maybe you're both right. Maybe I am nothing, but even nothing is better than what's waiting for you."

Ned then strode quickly past his manager and then out of the dark alley into the gaslit streets of St. Louis. Within five days, he headed west never to return.

CHAPTER 1

November 12,1881
Hays City, Kansas

Ned strode into the back room of the Corncob Saloon to meet their local champion, Big Jack Cooper. He outweighed Ned by a good forty pounds and had never lost a match. Ned had beaten men like him before, but he'd lost some, too. It all depended on speed and the absence of cheating. He'd been victimized by a few fighters who'd used all sorts of ploys to gain an advantage and one had almost cost him his life when a compatriot shot him from the shadows with an air gun.

He heard hisses and boos when he passed through the crowd of spectators and scanned them for any men who would provide Big Jack with assistance but doubted they would be there because men like his opponent didn't think that they'd need any help.

Ned had been fighting his way west since leaving St. Louis and had made a decent amount of money and too much of it had been by taking a beating against bigger, faster opponents. But he'd gotten better with each of those defeats and learned lessons about men that served him well.

Tonight's match would be the second he'd fought since arriving in town four days ago and it was only after he knocked out Mac Poteet in the first minute and broke his nose that they asked him to go against Big Jack Cooper.

Ned reached the open area of the room where he took off his coat and just tossed it onto the floor near the first line of men. If someone walked off with it, they'd just get his coat. It would be a cold walk back to his hotel room, but hopefully, he'd have a pocketful of cash when he left.

There were no real rules in most of these matches other than no punching below the waist. For some reason, hitting a man in the crotch was deemed to be too much of a sin even among the unsophisticated crowd and Ned appreciated it. It had happened to him more than once anyway and he understood all too well why that rule existed, despite its somewhat lax enforcement.

Ned studied his massive opponent as he removed his shirt to display his impressive physique, probably as a way to intimidate the newcomer. Ned wasn't intimidated, but he did admire Big Jack's muscular torso and thick arms. He was going to be a tough nut to crack, but it he was able to put him down, then Ned would be paid a healthy one hundred dollars. He'd only been stiffed twice in his fights and he'd learned to read the promoter to see if that was likely after he'd been stung the second time. Joe Gilligan, the promoter who had set him up for both fights, had paid him his twenty dollars for knocking out Mac Poteet, so he didn't worry about not being paid for beating Big Jack. All he had to do was win, which wasn't going to be easy.

Joe Gilligan walked to the line with his smoking cigar clenched between his teeth and his bowler hat pulled down heavily onto his head and waved the two fighters in.

Ned stepped forward and stared into the cold eyes of Big Jack Cooper who was still trying to put the fear of God into Ned.

Ned didn't give in to Big Jack's tactics and glared back at him as they each approached the line. Ned didn't bother doing a quick inspection of his opponent's fists for any secreted metal as he usually did because he didn't think that Big Jack's large hands needed any help. As it was, the inspection was unnecessary for an altogether different reason.

When both fighters stopped, Joe Gilligan said, "Alright, show me your palms."

Ned was surprised because he hadn't made that request in the last fight but figured that it was probably just because of his quick elimination of Mac Poteet and some of the bettors had suspected that Ned had cheated.

Ned spread his fingers wide and held out his hands as did Big Jack.

Joe looked at their hands then pointed at the chalk stripe on the floor and said, "Alright, gentlemen, toe…"

Before he finished, a loud voice shouted, "Hold it right there, Joe!"

Ned and everyone else turned to the voice and there were groans from most of the others as an older man wearing a badge stepped out of the crowd. He was wearing a Colt, but it was in his holster as he strode toward the two fighters and the promoter.

"I warned you about this, Joe. I don't care if you have your fights and even do some wagerin', but you can't be doin' it on a Sunday. You know that."

"Hell, Gal, the only ones to care about it are the ladies' guild and the preachers."

"That may be, but it's still the law in this county and you know better. Why didn't you just wait until tomorrow?"

Ned was annoyed for having the fight stopped because he'd just reached his maximum state of readiness and his adrenalin was pumping, so he whipped around and stared that the old lawman.

He locked his angry eyes on the sheriff and snarled, "Just let me finish off Big Jack and then I'll take my money and leave your righteous town."

Ted Galloway looked back at the young fighter and asked, "Who are you?"

"My name is Ned Boyd and you're not stopping me from making my living."

The sheriff smiled and pushed his Stetson back on his head before saying, "Now, son, don't be so all-fired mad. I'm just askin' Joe here to postpone your match 'til tomorrow. You can get your butt whipped on Monday just as good as on a Sunday."

Ned bristled and snapped, "I don't intend to get my butt or anything else whipped by Big Jack and after I'm done with him, maybe you'd like to toe the line against me."

The sheriff tilted his head slightly then scratched his bearded chin and replied, "Now, Ned, that just wouldn't be fair; would it? I'm an old man and here you are a strappin' young buck."

"If you don't want your old butt whipped by this strappin' young buck, just let us fight."

"That ain't gonna happen today, Ned. So, why don't you just pick up your coat and head back to wherever you hang your hat."

Ned was beyond annoyed and made the mistake of suddenly pushing the sheriff with both hands. As the old lawman stumbled back, he stepped forward to take a shot at the sheriff when everything went black.

———

Ned slowly opened his eyes and felt his world spinning when he lifted his head. He dropped it back down and asked, "Where am I?"

Sheriff Galloway turned and looked through the bars at his prisoner before standing and walking around the cell and entering the open door.

He looked down at Ned and replied, "You're where you belong, son. You're in jail and when you can think straight, I need to get your particulars for my report."

Ned didn't try to sit up again but asked, "What happened? Why am I in jail?"

"You don't recall pushin' me and gettin' ready to strike an officer of the law?"

"Yeah, I remember that but how did I wind up here?"

"You didn't see one of my deputies and he gave you a love tap with his Colt."

"What happens now?" Ned asked as he slowly sat up and swung his legs to the floor.

"Well, it's still Sunday, so I reckon you can head back to the saloon and get yourself drunk before you leave town."

"I don't drink."

"Now that's a surprise. Fellers like you seem to live in the sad side of life and I figured you'd be all hell and gone when you weren't fightin'."

"I make my living by fighting and if I drank or imbibed in tobacco, then I wouldn't be able to stay in the game very long."

The sheriff pulled a stool over to the cot and sat down across from Ned before asking, "I got your name, but where are you from?"

"I grew up in St. Louis and started fighting professionally when I was sixteen."

"And your folks were okay with that?"

Ned paused, then replied, "I didn't have any folks. I was an orphan."

"They gave you your name?"

"No. I don't even remember the name they gave me at the orphanage. It was John, Joe, or maybe Jacob, but most of the time, they called me 'boy' or 'kid', or something else."

"When did you pick out your name?"

"When I started fighting. I needed a name, so I made one up that suited me."

"Well, Mister Boyd, now you got me curious. Why'd you choose Ned Boyd for a moniker?"

"After I was taken from the orphanage when I was around six years old, I was sent to a bottling factory where I was assigned a number. I was #207 while I worked there."

"They gave you a number instead of a name? Why did they do that? Why didn't they just keep callin' you what name the orphanage gave you?"

"At first, I thought it was just because they didn't want to bother, but after a while, I learned that they didn't want us to think of ourselves as people. They wanted us to be more like slaves."

"Even slaves got names, son. I never heard of things like that before. But you didn't say why you chose that name."

"After working in that bottle factory for almost ten years, I felt like I was nobody and would never amount to anything. When I saw the supervisor whipping a girl for dropping a bottle, I attacked him and then after the guards came and threw me out of the factory and banned me from going back to the dormitory, the supervisor yelled at me and told me I was nothing and would always be nothing. So, when I began fighting, I took the name Ned Boyd, which was as close as I could get to Nothing Boy."

"Was it that bad in that factory?"

"There were days when it wasn't so bad, but it was all I knew."

"Is that why you're so damned mad all the time?"

Ned lifted his eyes to look at the sheriff before answering, "I try not to be that way, but I just fly off the handle too fast sometimes, especially when I'm all set to fight. You showed up at a bad time, Sheriff. I'm sorry for what I did, but it's just the way I am."

"You don't have to be that way, Ned. You never had a girlfriend or another feller to be your pal?"

"No. I can't. I didn't even know where or when I was born, so how could I ever amount to anything or be just a regular person?"

"So, after you leave Hays City, where will you go?"

"I've been traveling west since leaving St. Louis and intend to keep going until I reach San Francisco."

"Then what are you gonna do? Are you finally gonna settle down or are you just gonna turn around and start fightin' your way back to New York?"

"I don't know. I don't think that far ahead."

Sheriff Galloway looked at Ned for a few silent seconds before saying, "That's a bad thing for a man to do, son. You look like you're about eighteen or so and a young man should be able to have some idea of what he'll do with his life by then."

"I may be eighteen, but I've never had a past or a future. There's no point."

"Now that kinda attitude will only get you in trouble. Have you ever been arrested?"

"No, sir. This is the first time."

"No, it's not, 'cause you ain't been arrested. After my deputy put you down, we just carried you here 'til you woke up. You're free to go, but I'd like to talk to you for a bit, if that's okay."

"I owe you that for what I did and not locking me up for a month."

The sheriff snickered before saying, "That sounds fair. So, aside from your fightin', do you know how to do anything else? You sure talk like you're smart."

"I learned a lot since I left St. Louis, but I always talked like this when I wasn't spitting mad. Mainly I learned about men and how to tell if they're trying to cheat me or if they'll play fair. I can read their eyes and almost follow their thoughts."

"You ever fired a gun?"

"No, sir. I never even owned one."

"How'd you get all this way without any protection?" the sheriff asked in disbelief.

"I take the trains or stagecoaches if the tracks aren't going where I want to go."

"Are you tellin' me that you never even rode a horse?"

"Of course, I've ridden a horse, but I don't own one. To me it was just an unnecessary expense."

Sheriff Galloway spent almost a minute just thinking before he said, "Ned, you don't seem like a bad kid and I reckon there's a lot more good in you than even you figure you got. What I'd like to do is offer you a job as one of my deputies."

Ned's eyes widened as he sharply asked, "Are you serious? Why in God's name would you even think I could be a deputy sheriff? I can't shoot a gun and am far from being a decent horseman. I don't have any of the skills needed for the job."

"You have two of the most important things that a good lawman needs, Ned. You're an honest young man and what really is even more necessary, you know how to read men. Too many young men are headstrong and pull their pistols before tryin' to understand what's goin' on. Me and my other two deputies will work with you on the shootin' and the horse ridin' and we'll show you about trackin' and all the other things you'd need to know."

"Why would you even make the offer, Sheriff? I tried to slug you."

The sheriff laughed and said, "Maybe it's 'cause I was askin' for it. Anyway, what do you say?"

Sheriff Galloway's offer had come out of the blue and Ned had to take a while to try to weigh the advantages of staying and learning a new way of life versus following his previous unknown path. His biggest concern wasn't the dangers involved or even staying put which would be something he hadn't done since leaving St. Louis. His only real worry was the barriers that he had built since the day he'd been assigned #207. He'd never allowed anyone past those walls and didn't know how he'd react if he did. The sheriff was the only person he'd ever told about his past life and even now, regretted letting it out. But still, the idea of learning new survival skills was a great incentive. There had been times on his long journey west where he'd wished that he did have a pistol and the territories between Kansas and California were even more lawless. He didn't know how long he'd stay in Hays City, but he wanted to learn.

It took Ned almost two minutes of mental debate before he replied, "Okay, Sheriff. I'll take your offer."

Sheriff Galloway grinned and said, "That's fine, Ned. I'll introduce you to your fellow deputies tomorrow when I swear you in. By the way, my first name is Luther, but nobody calls me that. Even my wife and young'uns call me Gal."

"Okay, sir. If it's okay with you, then I'll head over to hotel to get some cash and then go to the café for supper."

27

"Nope. You'll come home with me and have supper with me and the family. It's Sunday and my Retta always cooks too much on the Sabbath."

Ned felt the heavy doors to his barriers slam shut but the sheriff had been kinder to him than anyone else he'd met and probably had less reason to be that way, so Ned smiled awkwardly before standing and saying, "Okay, Gal."

The sheriff stood and smiled at Ned before saying, "Let's go and fill our bellies, Deputy."

————

April 2, 1883

"Gal, why are you retiring? You're still in good health and the county needs you," Ned asked as he sat in front of the sheriff's desk.

"That gunfight really spooked Retta, Ned. She didn't say much but I could see it in her face. If you hadn't put down Baxter, I would have been a goner."

"You've been in worse situations than that, Gal. Why is this one any different?"

"It was different because I didn't see it comin'. I knew George Baxter and never reckoned he'd pull a gun on me. I almost saw that .44 headin' right between my eyes and it gave me the willies. I'm not quick enough anymore, Ned."

"You don't have to be quick, Gal. You don't even have to wear your pistol anymore. Everyone in town respects you and so do all of us. We can handle the bad troubles."

"I know you can, Ned. You and the boys are doin' a fine job and I can't tell you how proud I am of how much you changed since I dragged you to the jail. That was the second best decision I ever made after asking Retta to marry me."

"I'm forever grateful that you did, Gal, but please reconsider your decision. You know that if you retire that they'll appoint Bill Reasoner as sheriff, and he has none of your compassion or common sense."

"Ned, would you rather see me shot after I screw up again?" Gal asked quietly.

"That's a low-down question to ask, Gal. You know the answer. Do you have enough money to get by?"

"We're fine. You forget that Retta's family owns the Slash W and we'll move out there in a couple of months after we get another house built."

Ned knew that there was no point in arguing, so he just nodded and asked, "Are you going to start riding herd on cattle now?"

Gal laughed and replied, "No, I'll do some things but I'm not about to become a cowhand. What are you going to do if they do appoint Reasoner?"

"I'll see how it goes, but if he's as bad as I suspect, I'll pull up and head west."

"You're not going to go back to bareknuckle fighting; are you?"

"No, sir. I'll use the tools that you and the boys have given me. It might be as a lawman, or I could go the bounty hunter route."

"I wish you'd stay, Ned. Our Millie is getting pretty fond of you."

"I know and she's a nice girl, but even though you've given my life a new purpose, I'm still not able to be a husband and father. How can I even fill out a marriage license when I don't have a real name, date or place of birth or even my parents' name? What kind of a woman would trust a man who had spent brawling for most of his life?"

"None of those things matter, Ned. Lots of men and women have the same problem with not knowing their parents and you weren't brawlin', you were fighting as a profession."

"Maybe, but I guess I still feel like my life was nothing but a void until I came here. That's going to take more time to erase, Gal."

"You think too much, Ned. You always have."

Ned smiled at his boss and friend before standing and heading out to the front office to tell the other deputies that he'd failed to get the sheriff to change his mind. They knew that if Ned couldn't talk him out of it, they had no chance. They all knew that Nate was as close to a son as the sheriff ever had.

————

It didn't take long for Nate to discover that the new sheriff was, if anything, worse than he'd expected. It was just two months later that he pulled up stakes and after an emotional parting at the Galloway home, he mounted his brown gelding and rode west out of Hays City for parts unknown.

May 23, 1886
Eight Miles Southwest of Laramie, Wyoming

Rich Hooper stared between the trees at the approaching rider and asked, "What do you think, Bob?"

Bob Allen snickered before replying, "He looks like some mean old sheriff or maybe a killer bounty hunter, Bill. I think we outta plug him."

Rich turned to his partner and said, "I was just askin' if we should go out there or just wait for him to pass by."

"I know. I was just funnin' with ya. He's probably only got a few bucks on him anyway, but his horse ain't half bad. We could use some more ammo too."

"Alright. Let's mount up and pay him a visit. Check on his hammer loop. If it's off, I'll plug him right off. If it's not, then I'll distract him, and you shoot him."

"Good enough," Bob said before he reached for his saddle horn and stepped into his stirrup.

They walked their horses out of the trees and turned them north to head toward the cowhand who was leading a steer.

Nate Manning spotted the two men and didn't react at all. He was only four miles from the Step R fences and the steer was wearing the brand, so he was where he was supposed to be.

When they were close enough, he slowed and then stopped his brown gelding and sat back in the saddle. The steer began grazing as the two riders continued to get closer.

"Howdy!" Bob said loudly with a grin when they were thirty feet away.

"Mornin'! Where are you boys headed?" Nate asked.

"We're ridin' to Laramie, but I think we got kinda turned around a bit. Can you tell me how far off we are?"

Nate twisted in the saddle then pointed to the northeast and said, "It's about two hours that way."

Bob had noted that the cowboy's hammer loop was in place, so he wasn't a threat even if he knew how to use that Colt.

"You gotta run that wanderin' critter back to the ranch?" Rich asked.

"Yes, sir. I figure the boss will want to send him to the railroad stock pens pretty soon. This one seems to make a habit of runnin'."

Rich laughed then quickly pointed and exclaimed, "Who's that?"

Nate didn't bother turning, but before either Bob or Rich could even think of going for his pistol, he had his Colt cocked and pointed in their direction.

"With your left hands, slowly pull your pistols from your holsters and drop them to the ground."

"What do you think you're doin'?" shouted Rich as he held his hands up at the elbows.

"I'm taking you two boys back to Laramie and turn you over to the sheriff."

Rich then shook his head and laughed before asking, "You're a bounty hunter?"

"It's one of my jobs."

"How'd you get that pistol out so fast? You had it strapped down."

"The hammer loop is only held in place with a couple of loops of thread. I can draw it just as quickly with the loop on as I can with it off. I just have to make sure it doesn't snag."

"Just wonderin'."

"Well, now you know. Drop those pistols."

"Alright," Rich said before reaching across with his left hand and slipping his pistol from his holster and dropping it to the ground as Bob let his fall to the dirt.

"Now slide your Winchesters out and let them fall."

After the two repeaters flopped to the ground near the revolvers, Nate said, "Now I need you both to back your horses another fifty yards or so."

As they began backing their horses, Nate kept his gelding moving at the same pace while keeping his Colt pointed at them.

After they stopped, he had them dismount and lay on their stomachs where he bound their wrists.

Twenty minutes later, Nate was leading the steer and the two outlaws back toward Laramie. It was two more hours before he left the two men with the sheriff and then dropped off the steer at the butcher. He'd bought the animal the day before and made a deal with the butcher that he'd get a steak every other day for a month in trade then headed for his office.

When he arrived in the back of #207 Kansas Street, he dismounted and led his horse into the small barn in back and began to unsaddle him. He had dropped off all of the outlaws' things including their horses with the sheriff. It wasn't necessary, but he tried to keep a good working relationship with Sheriff Scott and his two deputies. It wasn't a bribe, but he didn't advertise it either.

He entered the back of the house and dropped his saddlebags on the floor near the door and hung his hat on the nearby peg before placing his Winchester in the gun rack.

"That you, Nate?" Ike Parker yelled from the office.

"I was when I left yesterday," Nate said as he strode down the hallway to the office area at the front of the house.

Ike set down a letter he'd been writing when Nate entered the office and plopped down in the chair next to the desk.

"I assume you found those two."

"It wasn't really that hard. They hadn't gone that far. I left them with the sheriff along with their gear."

Ike nodded then said, "We have another client. He said he'd stop by tomorrow."

"Does this new client have a name?"

"He has a name and the biggest ranch in the county."

Nate's eyebrows arched as he asked, "Fred Miller needs something? Did he say what it was?"

"Nope. He seemed a bit anxious, though."

"Anything else happen in the past two days?"

"That last reward on Lou Wanamaker showed up at last. I don't know what took it so long. I left it on your desk in the box."

"Okay. How's Alice doing?"

"She's happier now that the morning sickness is gone but she wishes the baby was in her arms rather than in her tummy. Now she keeps asking me if she's getting fat because she's eating so much."

"And you say?" Nate asked with a slight smile.

"I tell her she's even prettier than she was on our wedding day. I think she's just fishing for compliments, but I like to make her smile."

"You always do, Ike."

"She was with the midwife when I left. Have you met her?"

Nate laughed then replied, "Now why would I need to meet a midwife? I don't believe that I'm expecting."

"She hasn't been in town very long and Alice really likes her. I was just wondering if you'd seen her around."

"Nope. Where did she come from?"

"Some town in west Kansas. She's pretty young to be a midwife, and I don't think she's ever had a baby. I don't even think she's married."

"Is that a hint, Ike?"

"Not from me. You should come over for supper sometime. Alice has her stop by all the time and she helps a lot with the chores, too."

"That's okay, Ike. I'm pretty set in my ways."

"Alice likes you, Nate. She just thinks you shouldn't live alone."

"Tell her I appreciate her concern, but I'm comfortable with the way I live."

"I know, but I don't think Alice is ready to give up."

"That's your job to convince her. Did Fred Miller say what time he was going to come by?"

"Just in the morning. He showed up about two hours ago."

"Alright. I'm going to fix myself something to eat. Why don't you head home and take the rest of the day off? It's slow and I need to take care of some paperwork."

"Are you sure? I have to finish this letter to Mister Crump. He still hasn't paid your fee for tracking down his embezzling partner."

Nate rose and said, "Go ahead and finish your letter and post it on your way home. I'll see you in the morning," then headed for the hall as Ike returned to writing.

As he walked to the cold room to retrieve a big jar of pickles, Nate wondered what Fred Miller needed. It had to be personal because he'd be visiting the sheriff's office if it was criminal in nature.

He threw together a quick ham and cheese sandwich and pulled one of his favored sour pickles from the jar. Some men had a sweet tooth, but Nate had a sour tooth. He loved the big sour pickles that could make his eyes water but didn't care for dill pickles at all. He was grateful for his strong stomach that could tolerate the vinegar and all of the other spicy concoctions he sent down there.

After he finished his quick lunch, he returned to the office and searched in box where he found the last reward voucher. He folded the voucher and slipped it into his jacket pocket and headed for the door. He'd deposit the voucher and swing by

T.F. Green's Dry Goods and Greengrocer to pick up some more food and a couple of other items that he needed. He didn't have a lot of expenses as his solitary life wasn't conducive to an extravagant lifestyle.

———

He returned to his house late that afternoon and returned to his desk to review some paperwork. But as he sat behind his desk staring at the sheet of paper in his hand without seeing it, he wondered what Fred Miller needed. His ranch was enormous and encompassed at least forty square miles of Wyoming. He ran over six thousand head of cattle and employed almost twenty ranch hands along with another ten or twelve employees to maintain his large remuda and his household.

Nate had a basic knowledge of his family makeup but not the details. He knew he lived with his wife and had at least three sons and two daughters and that one of the daughters was married. After that, he didn't know much about the spread or its owner. Whatever he wanted, it had to be private and he began to think it had something to do with his unmarried daughter. He couldn't recall her name and had only met her twice in Laramie. She was a handsome young woman with long black hair and dark eyes. She wasn't very tall, less than five and a half feet and seemed pleasant. He doubted that it had anything to do with his wife as she wasn't about to cheat on the man. He did know that Fred Miller was a hard man who expected even his suggestions to be followed to the letter. He was one of the few men in Wyoming that could have the governor do his bidding.

So, whatever he wanted, it would be both private and urgent. Nate assumed that what he needed wouldn't be illegal in nature as there were other men in town who called themselves detectives but were really nothing more than guns for hire. His curiosity was beginning to imagine all sorts of things, but he knew that he'd have to wait until the morning to get his answer.

He let out a long breath then began to read the letter. It was just a sales pitch from the Winchester Repeating Arms Company trying to get him to buy one of their new models, but Nate wasn't interested, so he tossed it into the trash can without crumpling. He'd stick with his '73 and doubted if the newer model would give him any great advantage.

After clearing out his box of incoming mail and notes, he returned to his bedroom to get some reading done before turning in for the night.

He was still curious about what Fred Miller wanted when he finally drifted off to sleep three hours later.

———

By the time Ike entered the office the next morning at eight o'clock, Nate was already at his desk reading his copy of *The Laramie Bugle*.

"Morning, boss," Ike said cheerily as he removed his hat and hung it on the coatrack near the door.

"Good morning, Ike. How's Alice?"

"She's fine. Mary said she's doing really well."

"She's the midwife?"

"Yup," he replied as he took his seat behind his desk.

"You said she was new here. How did Alice find her?"

"When she arrived in town, she met with Doctor Armitage and after he'd talked to her, he recommended her to three of his patients, but only Alice agreed to let her be a midwife. I guess it's because they're so much alike."

"She can't be a midwife without doing something else. Do you know what she does besides acting as a midwife?"

Ike shook his head before replying, "I didn't ask. Why are you asking? Have you heard something?"

"No, I didn't even know that she was in town. I guess it's just my suspicious nature."

"I'll ask Alice when I get home. Now that you mention it, I haven't seen her anywhere else."

"What does she look like? Maybe I've seen her around."

"She's about five and a half feet with an oval face, blonde hair and blue eyes. She's almost as pretty as my Alice."

"Then I'm sure that I would have noticed her if I'd seen her around town. I wonder if she's hiding from someone."

Ike laughed and said, "Nate, you are the most untrusting man I've ever met. Maybe that's why you're so good at what you do."

"Maybe. Pretty young women don't stay unnoticed for very long around here. I'm surprised that I haven't heard about her from anyone else."

"You should accept Alice's offer to come to supper to meet her, Ike."

"First, I need to learn whatever mission Fred Miller is bringing to us. I don't think it's all that legal, so I may not be going anywhere."

"Do you have any idea of what it is?"

"I have a feeling it's about his younger daughter. I can't think of anything else that could be happening out on his ranch that couldn't be handled by the sheriff."

"I guess we'll have to wait for him to show up. Maybe he's found somebody else to do the job if it's nasty work. You've had others show up and ask you to drygulch somebody."

"I know. I guess my reputation isn't as good as I try to keep it. It's alright, though. It makes some of those bad men think twice about shooting it out."

Ike didn't have long to compose a reply when they heard a horse arrive outside, and he looked out the window. Fred Miller had arrived.

As he entered the office, Nate rose from behind his desk and said, "Good morning, Mister Miller. Ike said that you'd stopped by. Have a seat and tell me what you need."

Fred glanced at Ike and then said, "This is very private, Mister Manning."

Nate nodded to Ike who rose from his chair and grabbed his hat before leaving the office.

Once the door was closed, Nate returned to his seat as Fred Miller removed his Stetson and sat down on the other side of the desk.

"Three days ago, one of my ranch hands, Toby Halvorsen, ran off with my younger daughter, Ruth. I want her found and returned."

"How old is she?"

"She just turned nineteen. Her mother is very upset and so am I."

"She's an adult by law, Mister Miller. If she decided to elope, then she can do that legally without your permission. You may not agree with it, but there's nothing you or I can do about it."

"That may be, but what I want you to do is to find her and talk to her. I need someone to convince her of the mistake she's making and get her to return before she marries that cowhand."

Nate leaned back and replied, "How could I convince her? What argument could I use?"

"Just tell her that she's breaking her mother's heart."

"Couldn't you do that?"

"No. She's a rebellious girl and I have no idea where she went. That's why I'm here. I expect your discretion in the matter and hopefully you'll be able to find her quickly. Your reputation is that you can track anyone as well as any Indian."

"I'm not that good, but if you want me to find her, I'll do that."

"Thank you. When can you get started?"

"I can leave in the morning. Don't you want to even hear my fees? I think that they're reasonable, but some balk. I charge ten dollars a day with a minimum of a hundred dollars and a maximum of two hundred. I'd be surprised if I can't find her in two or three days."

"That's fine. Let me know when you return and hopefully, it will be with my daughter."

He then stood, shook Nate's hand, pulled on his hat and left the office while Nate still stood behind his desk.

He remained standing until Ike returned and took the same chair previously used by Fred Miller.

Nate waited until the rancher had ridden off before sitting down and saying, "It's pretty much what I expected. He wants me to find his younger daughter who eloped with some cowhand."

"What are you supposed to do when you find her?"

"That, my friend, is the interesting question. He told me that I was supposed to convince her to return to his ranch because she broke her mother's heart."

"That's not gonna work."

"I know that and that's what has me snockered. I know that I won't have any difficulty in finding her and her boyfriend, but the question is what he really expects out of the job."

"You don't think he wants her back?"

"Oh, no. I'm sure that he does. It's just a question of how he gets her back. He didn't ask me to shoot the cowhand who ran off with her and that surprised me. Men like Fred Miller don't like it when someone makes them look bad and that cowboy made him look bad. He may want his little girl returned, but he'll want that man punished even more."

"Why didn't he say that?"

"Because he's probably asked someone else to do that. Whoever he asked probably wouldn't be able to find her, at least not quickly. He expects me to find her and then after I leave, someone else will take out her boyfriend before they get a chance to get married."

"But if you know that, doesn't that make you an accessory to murder?"

"Yup. But unless I'm just being overly suspicious again, I don't think he'd want to risk me going to the sheriff either. I imagine that once I find them and I'm heading back, his backup man will drygulch me and then go shoot the cowboy. He'd save my fee, too."

Ike blinked then asked, "What are you going to do, Nate?"

Nate grinned and replied, "Lead the second man on a wild goose chase and then go find out from the couple what really happened. He'll have to stay reasonably close to make sure he doesn't lose me, and I intend to surprise him. What I do with him will depend on the circumstances and who he is."

"What are you going to do today?"

"Find the clues to where they went. It won't be hard. Most folks think finding somebody always means following a trail, but most of the times it's asking questions of the right people. So, I'm going to head out in a few minutes and start asking questions. Then I'll come back and start getting ready to leave in the morning."

"Well, just keep me informed."

"I always do, Ike."

Nate then rose, pulled on his hat and left the office to begin his search for Ruth Miller. He started by heading to the nearest livery, Livingston's, which was the one he used when he needed his horses shoed or needed a new one.

Paul Livingston hadn't been able to help him at all, so Nate walked down to the S&R Livery on Third Street and again received no answers.

When he asked John Brinker in the Brinker Brothers Livery, he hit pay dirt. He told Nate that four days ago, Toby Halverson had three horses shod and bought a pack saddle.

After that visit, Nate headed for the land office in the Albany County courthouse. He didn't expect to find anything, but he hoped that what had driven the cowhand's decision to elope was that he'd bought some property and wanted to start his own place. He wasn't sure he would have enough money but

47

suspected that Ruth Miller might be providing the bulk of the purchase price if he had and that might have what pushed her father too far.

Ten minutes later a happy Nate Manning headed back to his office. Toby Halverson may not have bought any land, but his parents must have owned a small ranch about twelve miles southeast of Little Laramie which was just twenty miles southwest of Laramie. Little Laramie was in neighboring Carbon County, but the ranch was southeast of town and was in Albany County which was why he found the record. But finding the deed had been so simple for him to find out where they were that he wondered if the whole story wasn't a ploy to make him a target. But he didn't believe that Fred Miller had any grudges against him. Fred wanted him to find his wayward daughter but probably arranged for someone else to kill him for a different reason.

He swung by the railroad station on the way back and asked the ticket agent if he'd had any young couples buy one-way tickets in the past four days and received a negative response.

When he entered his office just ninety minutes after leaving, Ike looked at him and said, "Back so soon?"

Nate hung his hat and replied, "It was pretty easy to find unless they went somewhere else. Maybe they went to Cheyenne to get married first, but I don't think so because they wanted to be alone. Unless I'm wrong, they just rode out of Laramie with their pack horse early in the day and headed straight for Little Laramie where the cowboy's parents own a small ranch southeast of the town."

"Are they still there?"

"I don't think so. It was overdue in taxes and will be up for auction soon. It's kind of a bad place to build a ranch. He'd still need money to fix it up and pay the taxes if he intends to stay there with his girlfriend."

"Where would he get enough to do that?"

"I imagine that Ruth Miller took some of Fred's loose cash with her. Maybe that's why her father is so mad, but he didn't mention it."

"He didn't seem mad to me."

"Trust me. He was mad. I'm just wondering why he couldn't find her as easily as I did or why he didn't give me any more information other than the cowhand's name. This case is as smelly as five-day old fish."

"Are you still going?"

"Yup. I may be a suspicious character, but I'm even more curious."

"You could be making a really bad enemy, Nate. Maybe you should forget about this one."

"I already told him that I'd do it. Besides, if he doesn't use me to find them, he'll send someone else."

Ike shook his head but knew that he wouldn't be able to change Nate's mind.

"What can I do to help?"

"Just mind the store, Ike. I don't think I'll be gone that long. It'll be interesting when I return, though."

"That is an understatement. What if Miller doesn't like what you tell him?"

"I'm sure he won't be happy to see me at all, but I'll figure out a way to break the news."

"Did you want to come over for dinner tonight? Mary White will be there."

Nate could sense a potentially dangerous situation that had nothing to do with guns and replied, "I think Alice is already overworked, Ike. Tell her I appreciate the offer, but I need to work some things out before leaving in the morning."

"Okay, I'll tell her, but she'll be disappointed, Nate."

Nate then stood and headed back to his bedroom to begin packing for tomorrow's departure. It wouldn't take long. His saddlebags always contained enough trail food to last three or four days and the other essentials for living outdoors including a backup shaving and sewing kit, a compass and spare ammunition for both his Winchester '73 and his Colt.

He selected a pair of spare britches, two shirts and two union suits along with four pairs of heavy socks and set them on the dresser. Even though it was already late spring, it could still get chilly so he hung his heavy jacket on his bedpost just so he wouldn't forget it. He'd made that mistake once before and wasn't about to repeat it.

Ike left the office for lunch before he finished his preparations and as he made his own lunch, he wondered if he should have accepted the invitation to have dinner with Ike and his wife even if she was trying to fix him up with her midwife. It was his curiosity about the mystery woman that made him debate his decision to turn down the invitation.

He was chewing on his chicken sandwich when he concluded that it really didn't matter. He was sure that he'd meet the unseen young woman sooner or later and would be able to ask some well-disguised questions to learn more about her past. He didn't want Alice to be placed into a bad situation at the worst time. He liked Ike's wife and wished that he could experience that kind of relationship but knew it wasn't possible. It was the main reason that he had never accepted their dinner invitation after the first one because he admitted that he was jealous of his secretary and his cute wife. They seemed so happy when they were together even now that she was carrying her heavy load.

Nate was ready for an early departure when Ike returned to the office and before he even hung his hat, he said, "Alice was a little more than just disappointed when I told her that you wouldn't be coming to dinner."

"Was that because she was planning on trying to harness me to her midwife?"

"Probably. Are you ready to go tomorrow?"

"Yup. I'll be taking the buckskin mare."

"On a job? I thought you always took the brown gelding because it wasn't so easily spotted."

"That's the idea, Ike. I reckon that I'll be followed, and I don't want him to lose me."

"Oh. I guess that makes sense then," he replied, then asked, "Remember when you asked me what else she did to make money? Well, I found out that she does housekeeping. Alice told me that she doesn't charge us for the work and won't charge us for acting as a midwife. That surprised me and I don't understand why she would do that. How can she make a living?"

"That is odd. You know, I was thinking of hiring a housekeeper to stop by once a week or so to keep this place shipshape. Maybe you could ask her if she can fit us into her schedule."

"That would make Alice happy."

"I'd be hiring her to keep the house and office clean, Ike, and not as a wife or a mistress."

"You shouldn't make that claim so quickly, Nate. She's a pretty girl and seems really nice, too. You could do a lot worse."

Nate didn't answer but just shrugged and pulled out his logbook. He'd neglected to annotate the particulars of the takedown of Rich Hooper and Bob Allen. His logbook was really a ledger that listed the rewards, but also contained the details of the capture. It provided him with a base to improve his methods. It also tracked expenses, so he always knew almost to the penny how much money he'd made each month and what his current balance was in his account at the Laramie State Bank. His biggest expense was his secretary's salary, but that annual expense was usually covered in his first capture each year.

He probably could function without Ike, but when he'd first arrived in Laramie three years ago, he found that he'd sometimes lose clients when they couldn't find him, so he'd hired Ike Porter. Ike didn't even own a gun, but he was a good clerk and was pleasant to have around.

Nate put away the pen then waited until the ink was dry before he closed the logbook and slid it back into the drawer.

He then stood, grabbed his hat and as he headed for the door, he said, "I'll be back in a little while. I just thought of something that I forgot to do."

Ike waved as Nate left the office and headed back to T. F. Green's to pick up a little something for Alice to let her know that he really did appreciate the offer to come to their house and share their dinner. He knew what she and Ike would soon need but wasn't quite sure what to pick from the shelves.

After he entered the store, he turned down the second aisle to visit an area that he never thought he'd use. He walked all the way to the end of the aisle and stopped when he spotted the baby items. He selected a stack of diapers and then looked at some baby nightshirts and was debating about a color when he heard light footsteps approaching from his right, but he didn't turn to see who it was as he selected two of the yellow nightshirts.

He saw a woman's hand reach for a pair of baby socks, so he finally turned and found himself looking into the blue eyes of a young woman who he was sure was the mysterious midwife, Mary White.

"Do you have pins for those diapers?" she asked.

"Um…no, ma'am. Do I need some?"

"Doesn't your wife have any?"

"I'm not married, ma'am. These are for my friend's wife. She's going to have a baby soon."

"You must be Nate Manning. I'm Mary White, Alice's midwife."

"I kind of guessed who you were. There aren't many folks around Laramie who I don't know and I'm sure that Ike mentioned that I hadn't seen you before."

"He did, but I try to stay busy. I sew, do housework and my midwife duties."

"Where are you staying?"

"I have a room at Winchell's Boarding House."

"I was talking to Ike a few minutes ago and he mentioned that you did some housekeeping and I was going to ask you if you had any room in your schedule for my house and office. I'm out on jobs fairly often, so I don't keep the place as clean as I should."

"My Wednesdays are free. How often would you want me to stop by?"

"Once a week should work."

"That's perfect. I charge three dollars a day. Is that alright?"

"That's fine. Do you know where my office is?"

"Yes. Ike mentioned it."

"Good. Can you start this Wednesday?"

"I can. Do you need any help in buying something for Alice?"

"I'd appreciate it. I know she'll need diapers because there never seems to one around when you desperately need one. At least, that's what I've heard. What else should I buy?"

"Well, she'll need some pins and I was going to buy some socks. You already have two nightshirts, so I think you're alright."

"Thank you, ma'am. May I ask you something that you may consider too personal, so you don't have to answer if you'd rather not."

"You want to know how I became a midwife at my age because most midwives are much older and have had children of their own."

Nate smiled and said, "Pretty much."

"I'm not married and when I was fifteen, I began working in a doctor's office as a nurse assistant. By the time I became a nurse, I had helped deliver four babies and started working as a midwife. It doesn't pay much and its inconsistent, so I do the other jobs to provide a steadier income. Does that answer your question?"

"Yes, ma'am."

"Call me Mary, Mister Manning. You'll be seeing me more often now."

"Thank you, Mary. Call me Nate."

She smiled up at him and said, "If you really want to make Alice smile, buy her one of those cradles. She doesn't have one yet and is a bit concerned about it."

"I'll do that. Thank you for your help, Mary."

"You're welcome. I'd better get back to help Alice. She's pushing herself too much."

"That's what I told Ike."

"It's been a pleasure talking to you, Nate."

"It was nice to meet you as well, Mary," Nate replied before she smiled once more then turned and headed back to the front of the store.

Nate took a card of diaper pins and set them on the top of the diapers and nightshirts then set them in a nice maple cradle and carried them to the front of the store. He watched Mary White leave the store as he set his items on the counter.

Ted Green smiled at him and said, "Having a baby, Nate?"

"If I was, I sure wouldn't tell you, Ted. These are for Alice Porter."

"That was her midwife who just left, but I reckon you know that."

"I just met her. She seems pleasant."

"Real pretty, too. You oughta do something about that, Nate."

"So, everyone tells me."

Nate paid for the order and didn't need anything bagged, so he carried the cradle and its contents down the boardwalk and received a few curious looks and heard even more chuckles as he walked along.

He walked into the office and as Ike watched with raised eyebrows, Nate set the filled cradle on his desk and said, "This is a peace offering to Alice."

Ike looked at the selection inside the cradle and asked, "How did you manage to buy the right things, Nate?"

"I had assistance in making my choices. You'll never guess who I met at Green's."

"Fred Miller?"

"How would Fred Miller know anything about babies? I met Alice's elusive midwife, Mary White. We chatted for a few minutes."

"So, what did you think?"

"She seems pleasant," he replied as he took a seat.

"That's all that you're going to say? Did you like her?"

"It doesn't matter what I think of her, Ike. It's what Alice thinks that's important. Speaking of Alice, why don't you head home and help her and Miss White? It's quiet now and I don't think we'll have any clients until I get back."

Ike grinned and said, "I'm not going to look a gift horse in the mouth, boss," before he stood then quickly walked to the coat rack, took his hat and pulled it on before returning and hefting the cradle from the desk and after Nate opened the door, Ike grinned at him and scurried through.

Nate watched him leave with a smile on his face. Ike was only a year younger than he was but sometimes Nate thought of him as a son because he was so full of life. His Alice was a lot like him, and he wondered if each of them added to the others almost constant optimism.

———

At five o'clock, he locked the front door of the office and headed to the kitchen where he put some kindling into the cookstove and set it on fire. After tossing in some firewood, he closed the firebox door and filled the coffeepot with water.

As he waited for the water to heat, he continued to plan for tomorrow's departure. Little Laramie was to the southwest, so he'd ride east out of town until the road made its long turn to the northeast where there was a good-sized forest. He'd enter the trees and wait for up to an hour to see if he was being trailed. If he wasn't, then he'd cut across the road and ride cross country to Little Laramie. It would add a few more hours to the ride, but he wasn't in any rush. If he wasn't being followed, he'd have to come up with a different theory for Fred Miller's secret motive.

The best way to answer that question would be if he was being followed, which he suspected was more likely, and was able to ask the man who trailed him. A lot depended on the man who was doing the following. Some men were more easily persuaded to talk than others. Regardless of who he was, Nate would have his Winchester trained on him when he approached him. He'd have a few questions for him before he decided what to do with him.

He poured himself a mug of coffee and then began gathering food and hardware to cook his dinner. He was a fairly accomplished cook compared to most men and now he had a few weeks of nice steaks coming and he'd have the first one tonight.

CHAPTER 2

Early the next morning, Nate had the buckskin saddled and his trusted Winchester in its scabbard before he returned to the office to wait for his secretary. If Ike was later than usual, which was understandable given the condition of his wife, then he'd leave before he had a chance to talk to him. He was still curious about the midwife and would like to satisfy the remaining questions before he rode out of town.

He was sitting at his desk reading Dickens' *Great Expectations* by the time Ike entered the door then quickly set aside the book and waited for him to hang his coat and hat.

"You're still here, Nate?" Ike asked as he walked to his desk.

"I'll leave shortly, but I was curious if you found out any more about Miss White."

Ike was grinning as he sat down and asked, "I thought you weren't interested?"

"I hired her to clean our office and the house on Wednesdays, Ike, so I wanted to make sure that she was trustworthy."

"You said you thought she was nice when you talked to her, so why wouldn't she be trustworthy?"

Nate felt the need to leave tugging at his mind, so he quickly said, "I guess it doesn't matter. We don't have anything worth stealing here anyway."

"I'm sure that she'll do a good job and won't walk off with one of our desks."

Nate laughed more for his own answer than because of Ike's remark, but stood and pulled on his hat before saying, "If I'm not back when she shows up to clean, pay her for a month in advance. Okay?"

"I'll do that, boss. Good luck."

"I'll see you when I return," Nate said before turning and heading down the hallway and soon exited the house.

He mounted the buckskin mare and walked her out onto the main street but didn't make a show of scanning the roadway for any potential followers. He imagined that if there was someone assigned to tail him, then he'd wait in a business and watch him leave town before taking to the street.

Nate left Laramie heading east and after thirty minutes, left the buildings behind and disappeared down the road. The thick pines were mostly on the north side of the roadway as the train tracks needed the room on the south side. The trees picked up again a hundred yards or so on the other side of the rails, so it was as if some giant thumb had followed the shining ribbon eliminating any trees on either side.

He never checked his backtrail as he continued to ride. Nate wanted to get far enough from town before he disappeared, and it had to be in a spot where his follower wouldn't be surprised not to see him. He rode for another twenty minutes before the road made a sharp northern turn and Nate continued for about a hundred yards before entering the trees and heading back toward the road before the sharp curve began.

He pulled the mare to a stop when he was still about thirty feet from the end of the trees and pulled his Winchester. He cocked the hammer and sat back in the saddle to await his unwanted companion. There could be other traffic on the road, and he'd wait until he identified the man before making his appearance. He knew most of the men who would be likely to take the job, but it was still possible that he was reading this all wrong and it was really exactly what Fred Miller had described. He simply doubted if that was true.

Nate had been waiting for ten minutes of the thirty he was going to allot to just sitting on the horse when he heard hoofbeats coming from the west. He smiled as he waited to find out who Miller had hired.

As the rider passed on a dark red gelding, Nate wasn't surprised at all, but walked his mare out of the trees and as soon as he reached the road, he nudged her into a medium trot and just before the man turned at the sound, Nate brought his Winchester level and the rider pulled up.

"Howdy, Stubby. What brings you out here this fine morning?" he asked loudly as he kept the mare closing the gap between them.

Stubby Nicks knew he'd been had but tried not to show it as he grinned and asked, "What's with the hardware, Nate? I was just heading to Cheyenne."

Nate pulled closer to Stubby and stopped the mare a few feet away before saying, "Well, I'm going to delay you for a little while, Stubby. I want you to slowly pull out your pistol with your left hand and just drop it to the ground."

"C'mon, Nate? Why are you gonna make me do that to a perfectly good Colt?"

"Just do it, Stubby. You can clean it later."

Stubby paused for a few seconds then reached across with his left hand and pulled his pistol free and let it fall to the ground.

Nate then released his Winchester's hammer and pulled his own Colt before sliding his repeater back into its scabbard.

He glanced at Stubby's rig and asked, "Well, Stubby, that's something I didn't expect to see you carrying."

"What do you mean?"

"I can see your Winchester on the right side, but that's not a repeater on the left side; is it?"

Stubby shrugged but didn't answer before Nate continued.

"I didn't even know you had a Sharps rifle, Stubby. I don't suppose that one has a telescopic sight on it; does it?"

Again, Stubby didn't answer the question because he knew that there was no excuse that he could make that Nate would believe.

"Okay, Stubby, I want you to walk your horse another fifty feet and dismount, then step away from your horse another twenty feet."

Stubby didn't argue but nudged his horse away from his fallen pistol and then stepped down after he'd moved the required distance.

Once Stubby was on the ground and far enough away from his horse to prevent a sudden attempt to get to his Winchester, Nate dismounted and let the mare's reins drop before walking closer to Stubby.

"Alright, Stubby. Let's have it. Why are you following me? I have a pretty good idea, so don't hold back."

Stubby sighed then answered, "Fred Miller asked me to follow you and let him know where his daughter is. He figured you might just warn her and tell him you couldn't find her and her boyfriend."

"Really, Stubby? Do you really think I'm that stupid? You're carrying a Sharps rifle with a scope and I'm not even sure that you've ever used one. The only reason for a scope is to do some long-range hunting and you aren't going to be looking for any elk. What was your job, Stubby? Were you supposed to shoot me before or after you shot the kid who ran off with Miller's little girl?"

Stubby licked his upper lip as he tried to come up with any way of avoiding having to face Fred Miller and admit he'd been outsmarted. He knew that Nate was pretty tight with Sheriff Scott, so he was sure that this job was over before it started.

"What if I tell you what I was supposed to do? Are you gonna kill me and bury me in the trees?"

"You know better than that, Stubby. I am going to relieve you of your new Sharps and your ammunition and then I'll empty your Winchester and your Colt and take all of those cartridges. You can go back to Laramie and tell Fred Miller what happened, but that wouldn't be a good idea; would it?"

"No."

"What I'd recommend is that you head back to Laramie then make a sudden change in residence. Take the train or ride to Cheyenne. It's a nice town and I'm sure you can set up there, but if I see you in Laramie when I return, it won't work out well for you. I'll be seeing Fred Miller myself and I'm sure he'll be surprised to see me. After I talk to him, I'm sure that he'd send someone to find you and ask for his Sharps back if not ask for something else like your head."

Stubby was already making plans to follow Nate's advice when Nate pulled Stubby's repeater and after having him step back even more, quickly began cycling the lever spitting cartridges onto the ground before sliding the empty weapon back into its scabbard.

He then walked to the other side of the horse and removed the heavy scabbard containing the scoped Sharps rifle and set it gently on the ground near his mare before he returned to Stubby's Colt and snatched it from the ground. He pulled the hammer halfway back, opened the loading gate and began rotating the cylinder letting its cartridges drop to the ground.

"You had all six cylinders filled, Stubby," Nate said as he returned and handed the empty pistol to its owner, "Planning on doing some serious shooting?"

"Now what?" Stubby asked without answering.

Nate then untied Stubby's saddlebags and lifted them from his horse and set them near the Sharps.

"Okay, Stubby, you can mount and ride back to Laramie now. You can refill your Colt with the spare cartridges on your gunbelt, but I wouldn't trust it to fire right after being dropped

67

into the dirt like that. I'll keep your saddlebags and I hope you didn't have anything valuable inside."

Stubby was about to protest but needed to get started back to Laramie. He knew he'd never be able to run Nate Manning down, especially now that he had the Sharps. He'd been right that he'd never fired it before, but he had used a telescopic sight before. It didn't matter now. He had to get into town and prepare to head east again. Cheyenne was sounding pretty good right now. Besides, he'd never had to answer his question about what Fred Miller had really asked him to do. Maybe he should stop by and tell Fred anyway. He might be able to get paid just for letting him know. He'd think about it on the way back to Laramie.

He mounted his gelding and without saying another word, set off at a fast pace back toward Laramie.

Nate watched him until he disappeared and was pretty confident that he'd follow his fatherly advice to leave Laramie. He knew that Stubby wasn't afraid of him, but he was damned sure afraid of what Fred Miller would do to him.

He picked up the saddlebags and opened the flap on the left one. He found two boxes of .44s and two boxes of .45-100 cartridges for the Sharps. He whistled when he pulled one of the long, deadly cylinders of brass and lead from the box and knew that he would have never heard the report from the bullet that killed him if he hadn't trapped Stubby. Other than the ammunition, that saddlebag held all of his personal items and a half-bottle of whiskey. The other saddlebag had a spare set of clothes and two towels along with some paper sacks with some cold chicken and bread. It looked pretty good, so Nate was glad for the menu change before he hung the saddlebags over his shoulder, picked up the Sharps and moved them to his buckskin. After everything was lashed down, he gathered all of the .44 cartridges from the ground, made sure they were clean, then put them in the saddlebag with all of Stubby's ammunition.

He mounted his mare, crossed the road then walked him over the tracks and after another hundred yards, he turned west to ride south of Laramie until he reached Little Laramie.

His eastward excursion may have cost him time, but it had saved his life. Now he needed to discover what was really going on and expected he'd discover that when he found Toby Halvorsen and Ruth Miller.

As he made his way at a slow trot through the rugged country, he wondered if they were married already. If they were, then they'd be in serious trouble if they stayed where he expected to find them because he knew that Fred Miller would find them sooner or later and he was even more sure that Fred Miller wasn't going to be happy when he saw Nate ride onto his ranch after he returned and was still breathing.

———

It was getting late in the afternoon by the time Nate rode the buckskin into Little Laramie. It was a sad idea to start the name of any settlement with that adjective, but this town earned it. At its peak, the population was under a hundred and he doubted if sixty called it home now. He could understand why the Halvorsen's ranch had failed, even if it was larger and had perfect grazing land.

He didn't stop in town because he only had another four hours of daylight and hoped to find the missing couple today, if possible.

Nate had spent the rest of the ride thinking about the situation and what he would do when he found Halvorsen and Miss Miller if she was still a miss and not a missus. A lot depended on their story, and he admitted to hoping that they were star-struck lovers and wanted to start a new life together. He just hadn't seen that happen very often, especially not when either or both sets of parents were dead set against it.

Even more critical to his future was how he would deal with Fred Miller when he returned. He couldn't just pretend as if he hadn't found the couple because just his appearance would negate that angle. If he'd just turned around after confronting Stubby, then he could have just confronted Miller and refused to continue with the job, but then Miller would have sent someone else anyway.

Above it all, he still had no idea why Fred Miller wanted to have him find the cowboy and then have him and their finder

70

assassinated. Was Stubby supposed to then return Ruth to the ranch? He couldn't imagine that Fred wanted her to embarrass the family by having her show up at the door again. Nate suddenly began to think that maybe Stubby was supposed to eliminate all of them. He'd shoot Nate first, then the cowhand and then Fred's daughter. It made more sense than anything else. Nate would be the hardest kill, then the only other real threat, the cowhand, would have to be shot before killing Ruth Miller. Nate shuddered at the thought, but even after it dawned on him, he couldn't imagine any father sending someone to kill his own child.

By the time he spotted some buildings on the horizon in the low sun, he had stopped trying to come up with a motive until after he'd talked to the couple. This was going to be a tough nut to crack ever since Fred Miller decided to pay him a visit.

As he approached the tired ranch, he spotted smoke coming from the cookstove pipe in the dilapidated ranch house. It wasn't that big, and the barn was in even worse shape. He couldn't see any horses anywhere, but they could be in the barn, so it wasn't a big concern.

He turned down the overgrown access road and headed for the house but continued to scan the ranch for any signs of activity. He finally concluded that if the couple wasn't inside, then Halvorsen's parents would be and he might be able to get some information from them about where the young elopers had gone.

Nate walked the buckskin to the front of the house and pulled up just in front of the low porch before he shouted, "Hello, the house!"

He leaned back and waited for someone to open the door and after a minute of sitting, he thought that the couple might be otherwise engaged and was about to shout again when the door flew open and banged against the wall.

He assumed he was looking at Ruth Miller, as a pretty young woman with long dark hair stepped out with fire in her eyes. He hadn't seen her often enough to be sure.

"Who are you and what do you want?" she asked loudly and with vigor.

"I'm Nate Manning. Are you Ruth Miller?"

"I am, but you didn't say what you were doing here."

"Your father asked me to find you and Mister Halvorsen."

"I thought so," she replied but didn't ask him to step down.

Nate didn't see her boyfriend and hoped he wasn't behind one of the windows with a rifle, but he could tell that she wasn't pleased to see him.

"Miss Miller, may I step down so I can speak to you and Mister Halvorsen?"

Ruth stared at him for another thirty seconds without answering before she finally said, "You can dismount, but you can't talk to Toby."

Nate didn't ask why he couldn't talk to her lover but nodded and stepped down before tying off the buckskin on the hitchrail.

She turned and walked inside leaving the door open, so Nate stepped onto the porch, removed his hat and entered the room, but still left the door open in case he had to make a hasty exit.

The furnishings in the front room were sparse and Ruth Miller took the better of the two chairs, so Nate walked to the other chair and carefully lowered himself into the seat, half-expecting it to collapse under him.

Before he could ask about Halvorsen, Ruth Miller snapped, "I suppose you're here to take me back to my father's ranch."

"He asked me to come and talk to you to try to convince you to return, but I explained to him that as an adult, I couldn't force you to do anything. If you want to stay with Mister Halvorsen, then I'm not going to take you anywhere."

Ruth Miller's demeanor suddenly became much less combative as she quietly asked, "He sent you knowing that you wouldn't try to take me back against my will?"

73

"Yes, ma'am, but there's a lot more to it and I'm not sure what it is. I was hoping that you and Mister Halvorsen could help me solve that mystery."

"I'm sure that there is some hidden motive because my father always seems to have one, but I'm afraid that you can't get any information from Toby."

Nate thought that Fred Miller had contracted with yet another killer who had done the same investigative work as he had and beat him to the Halvorsen ranch, so he asked, "What happened? Did someone else find you before I did?"

"What are you talking about? No one found us until you rode to the house. Toby left me this morning. I thought that my father had this all timed to have you arrive as soon as he abandoned me."

Nate leaned back in the chair and said, "I have no idea why he'd leave, Miss Miller. Would you please just tell me why you left the ranch with Halvorsen. I need to have some idea what is happening."

"You really don't know? What did my father tell you?"

"He told me that you ran off with Toby Halvorsen and he wanted me to find you and tell you that you were breaking your mother's heart and ask you to return. I didn't believe that was what he really wanted, but that's all I know."

"If you knew that he wanted something else, then why did you take the job?"

"I thought about turning it down, but I knew that if I did, he'd just hire someone more unscrupulous to do the job. So, I thought if I found you, I'd just tell you what he said and warn you that it wasn't safe to stay here because he'd find you soon enough."

Ruth Miller nodded before saying, "Alright. I'll have to trust you because I really don't have any other choice. The basic fact that I ran off with Toby to marry him is true. I was infatuated with him and my father was dead set against it. My mother told me that he didn't love me but just lusted after me.

"I was too naïve to see it and believed his words of love. When my father laid down the law and said he'd fire Toby if I didn't break it off, I took a thousand dollars out of his safe and Toby and I ran away. He said we could hide in his parents' old ranch, so we came here. I asked him why we just didn't take the train to Denver and disappear, but he said that he'd never look for us here and it was closer.

"I guess my infatuation clouded my judgement, so I agreed. We'd taken three horses from the ranch and after we stopped in Laramie and bought some supplies, we left town and rode here. That's when everything changed."

"How so?"

Ruth sighed and replied, "He kept telling me that we'd get married as soon as we cleaned up the house and settled in, so as far as Toby was concerned, we were already married and he convinced me to consummate the marriage. I'll admit that I didn't object. In fact, I'll be honest enough to admit that I wanted it as much as he did. Then after he deflowered me, he became more possessive and demanding. I almost didn't recognize him. He made me clean the place while he just watched me. Whenever he wanted me, he just took me.

"For the next three days, he bedded me so often that I was barely able to walk. Then this morning, he simply said that he had to go into town and saddled both horses and the pack horse and rode away. It wasn't until I saw him head south rather than toward town that I realized he wasn't coming back. He left me about half of the food and supplies but took all of the money that I'd stolen."

"Why would he go south if he told you he was going into town? There's nothing south of here except mountains and forests."

"I don't know, but I was so upset at him at the time that I didn't pay much attention."

Nate thought about it for a little while then asked, "When you arrived here, did you stop in Little Laramie?"

"No, we came from the direction of Laramie and bypassed the town. Why?"

"Maybe he didn't want to be seen in by someone he knew. It's the only thing that makes any sense to me."

"He did say something like 'it's better if we head straight to the ranch', but I thought it was because he wanted us to be alone."

"Speaking of that, what were you going to do now that you were alone?"

"I wasn't sure yet. I was trying to come up with a plan, but the town is too far away to walk and even then, I don't have any real skills other than the one that Toby taught me after we arrived."

"Then why were you so hostile towards me if you needed help?"

"Because I knew you'd been sent by my father and I'm not about to let him rule my life anymore. Can you imagine what he'd do to me if I returned after taking his money and embarrassing him as I did? It would be even worse if he knew what Toby had done. What if I'm pregnant?"

Nate blew out his breath and said, "You were right to be worried, Miss Miller. I was pretty confused about your father's motives for asking me, but now I'm beginning to see the light. I don't believe that your father wanted to ever see you or Toby Halvorsen again."

Ruth's eyes widened as she asked, "Why would you say that? He didn't ask you to kill us; did he?"

"No, but I was supposed to find you. Your father asked me to find you, but his instructions for what to do after I did weren't in keeping with his personality. He sounded almost forgiving and considerate and I know he possesses neither of those traits. So, after he left, I thought about it. As I told you, I only took the job because I believed that he would hire someone else to do whatever he wanted done if I turned him down."

"Why didn't he just hire someone else in the first place?"

"He must have thought it would take a long time for someone else to find you. He knows my reputation and like many people, he believes that finding someone means tracking them across uninhabited lands. But it's rarely like that, especially in the beginning of a case. You find out as much background as possible and then ask folks questions. It may come to tracking, but in your case, it was much easier. He probably thought that I'd have to pick up your trail and chase you down."

"But if he hired you to find us and you told him that you'd just talk to us, then why do you think he would kill us?"

"After I left Laramie this morning, I rode east, not toward Little Laramie. I even rode my buckskin because she's more easily seen. I expected to be followed and after I was well out of town, I ambushed the man he'd sent to follow me."

78

"You killed him?" she asked sharply.

"No, ma'am. I put him under my Winchester and took away all of his ammunition and the sniper rifle he was going to use to kill Halvorsen. I think that once I found you, he'd kill me first and then Halvorsen before taking his time with you. His name was Stubby Nicks and he's a bounty hunter too, but he's got a seedier reputation. I let him go and suggested he move to Cheyenne rather than facing your father's wrath."

"Are you sure that was his plan? Even for my father that sounds almost unbelievable."

"No, I'm not positive because at the time, I thought that Stubby had been sent to shoot Halvorsen and after he eliminated me, he'd take you back to the ranch. It wasn't until you told me that you'd taken that much money and that you weren't going to be welcomed back that I realized his full intent. I could be wrong, and if you'd prefer, I can take you back."

"No!" she quickly exclaimed, "I'm not going back there! Ever! I think you're right about what he was planning to do even if it's difficult for me to accept."

"Then we have both have a problem, Miss Miller, although I'll admit that yours is much worse than mine."

"Why do you have a problem?"

"Because I'm not supposed to be alive. Your father will be expecting Stubby Nicks to return with the news that no one is left to talk about what happened. I assume that your father told him he could keep the money you took, the horses and the sniper rifle as payment."

"And have his way with me as a bonus."

"Before he killed you."

"I'm not sure my problem is worse than yours."

Nate smiled before asking, "You have no money, no support and no way of leaving, and you think my problem is more difficult to solve?"

"I think so. Now that you're here, I believe that you can help me solve my problem."

"You want me to track down Toby Halvorsen."

"Yes. Can you do that?"

"I'm sure that I can, but what do you expect me to do with him after I find him?"

"I'd like you to turn him into a steer, but I'd be satisfied if you gave him the same treatment you gave to the man who was following you. I'll even pay you out of the money that he stole from me that I stole from my father."

Nate had to smile as he replied, "You don't have to pay me, Miss Miller. Your father is going to pay me for finding you. He'll just be a bit more reluctant and I'll have to come up with a way to have him give me dollar bills instead of a bullet."

Ruth smiled back and asked, "How long will it take for you to find him?"

"It depends on whether he stayed riding cross country or headed for the nearest train station. I'd guess that he'd be riding because he has the three horses and supplies, so he'll take his time and might head for Cheyenne. He might just be watching the ranch house from those trees right now and waiting for you to leave so he can come back here."

"You don't think he's really out there; do you?"

"It's not likely, but it is possible. I'll know soon enough."

"When will you leave? There's not much daylight left."

"I know. I was planning on starting early in the morning. I can't track him at night."

"Will you stay with me tonight? Even though Toby treated me like a whore, I don't like being alone."

"You're going to be alone after I leave, Miss Miller."

"I know, but I would appreciate at least one night where I could sleep peacefully."

81

Nate smiled then said, "I'll go take care of my horse. I'll be back in a few minutes."

Ruth smiled back then stood before saying, "I'll cook dinner."

"Thank you, ma'am," Nate replied as he rose then walked out of the open door onto the short porch where he pulled on his hat before untying the mare.

He led the mare into the shabby barn and began to plan for tracking down Toby Halvorsen. He suspected that the ranch hand thought he was home free once he left, so he wouldn't be in a rush. The question was where he was headed. The fact that he'd ridden south at all meant a lot. If he had just told her that he was going into town, then he could have headed that way until he was out of sight then shifted northwest skipping the town and kept going until he reached the railroad. She wouldn't have known he wasn't coming back for hours. Nate just had a hard time trying to figure out where he could be going because there was nothing south of this ranch other than the Rocky Mountains. He would have to turn east or west before going back north. His choice of that direction made it more likely he was in those trees watching the house and waiting for Miss Miller to walk to Little Laramie. If he was, then Nate's already low opinion of the man would sink even lower. *How could any real man watch the woman he professed to care about walk to a town with no money and no prospects?*

He was unsaddling the mare when he stopped and tried to picture the map of the area. Halvorsen surely wouldn't risk heading east back toward Laramie where he was known, so after riding south, he probably turned northwest toward Cooper's Creek. It was a bigger town than Little Laramie and he might stay there for a while until things calmed down. If he continued north, he could just take the train west. Once he boarded a train, he would be gone and there would be no purpose in following him after that. He suspected that Miss Miller had maybe another four days of food left and if he tried to track Halvorsen on the rails, it could take weeks.

By the time he finished with the mare to return to the house, Nate decided that he'd track Halvorsen for about a mile to make sure that he wasn't just waiting to return, then he'd had to Cooper's Creek directly and ask if anyone had seen him.

Before he was even halfway to the house, Nate turned and walked south away from the barn to pick up Halvorsen's trail. It didn't take long and after finding the three sets of hoofprints, he stopped and stared at the tall mountains to the south that continued along a southeast to northwest line and even with the thick forests that stretched before them, he was almost certain that if he followed this trail in the morning, it would shift to the northwest after entering those trees.

He looked west and decided that tomorrow, he'd forget about the tracks altogether and head for Cooper's Creek. He wouldn't go through Little Laramie just to pick up the road but would go cross-country and maybe even pick up Toby's trail before reaching the town.

Nate then turned and began walking back to the house with his new Sharps in his hand. When he'd taken it from its scabbard, he wasn't surprised that it was almost new and when he opened the breech, found a cartridge inside which was usually a bad idea with a single-shot breech loader. It wasn't the kind of weapon one used for sudden defense, so it wasn't even necessary.

He opened the back door and entered the kitchen, not bothering to use the one step. Once inside, he found Ruth Miller at the cookstove frying a piece of meat that he couldn't identify by the smell.

After leaning the Sharps carefully against the wall, he took off his hat and tossed it onto the table before taking off his gunbelt and hanging it on the knob of one of the chairs.

"What are you cooking, Miss Miller?" he asked as he began stroking the pump.

"Rabbit. After Toby ran off, I found a jackrabbit in the barn and killed it with an old pitchfork."

After filling two old tin cups with water and setting them on the table, Nate took a seat and said, "I found his trail heading south, but I know he can't keep going in that direction. There aren't any passes that he could take, and I don't believe he'd dare to show in face in Laramie. Tomorrow morning, I'm

84

planning on just riding cross-country to Cooper's Creek. I suspect he may be hiding out there for a little while. If not, then he took a train and we've probably lost him."

She turned and asked, "You're going to give up if he takes the train?"

"Yes, ma'am. If he was a wanted man, I'd follow, but you don't have much food or a horse, so unless you can find a whole passel of rabbits, then you'll be hungry in four days or so. If I took a train to go after him, I probably wouldn't be back in a week. Knowing that, would you want me to keep after him if I don't find him tomorrow?"

"I suppose not. What will I do if you can't find him?"

"We'll worry about that when it happens. What are you going to do if I do bring you back your money and horses?"

"I haven't decided yet, but I'm not going back to my father's ranch. Especially not after what you told me."

"I've only met your father a few times and I know that he's a rich and powerful man. What else can you tell me about him?"

She flipped the meat over before she replied, "He's an arrogant, selfish man who will stop at nothing to keep that power and his reputation. That's why I was so anxious to run away. Well, that and I was smitten with Toby Halvorsen. My father always dominated the house and the family. I've never heard him apologize, even when he was wrong. He never beat my brothers or anyone else in the family because it wasn't necessary. He would stare us down and terrify us with just that look."

"Does he do anything illegal?"

"I don't know. I don't think so, but I wouldn't be surprised, either. He thinks that he's above the law. On the ranch, he is the law."

Nate put his elbows on the table and rested his chin on his hands as he thought about what he would do when he returned to Laramie and how he could handle Fred Miller…if he could.

Ruth filled two plates with the rabbit that had been cooked with onions and hash browns that she must have made earlier then set them on the table before placing some cutlery where it belonged.

When she sat down, she picked up her fork and asked, "Have you ever been smitten, Mister Manning?"

Nate was lifting his forkful of meat from the plate, so he paused and replied, "Not really. I like women, but I've never gotten to that stage."

"That's sad; don't you think?"

Nate swallowed his mouthful then answered, "I don't think so. Look what happened to you because you were smitten.

86

You're stuck out here in the middle of nowhere with no money and little food."

"But I'm not having to put up with my father anymore and now I have pleasant company. I'll get over what Toby did to me, but I'm not about to give up hope for finding love."

"Ah, you're a romantic, Miss Miller. I'll bet that you read a lot of those spicy novels."

Ruth held up a finger then after chewing, she swallowed and smiled before saying, "I guess I am and I'm not ashamed to admit it. I may not read spicy novels, but I do read books about heroes and heroines. I think that you're a hero, Mister Manning."

"I'm hardly that, ma'am. I hunt down criminals for the rewards on their heads and when I'm acting as a detective, I snoop around documenting infidelity or financial shenanigans."

Ruth laughed then said, "If you aren't a hero, then why didn't you shoot the man who was going to kill you?"

"There was no reason to shoot him. The smart thing to do was to scare him into leaving town."

"That's what I mean. You have honor, Mister Manning. All heroes have honor."

"I just try to do take the smartest path. It has nothing to do with honor."

"Oh? Then why did you agree to find me in the first place? Wasn't the smarter path to decline the assignment? You chose to accept it just to keep someone else from killing us; didn't you?"

"At the time, I just suspected that Toby Halvorsen would be the target."

"That's even more honorable, sir. If you'd done it to keep me from being killed, then I could assume an ulterior motive, much like the one that Toby hid from me."

Nate finally just shrugged and finished eating his dinner while Ruth continued to smile as she ate.

When he finished, Nate picked up his place setting and carried it to the nasty-looking sink near the pump and began to wash his plate when Ruth walked close and set her plate next to the sink.

"Why didn't you let me do the dishes?" she asked.

"I'm accustomed to taking care of myself. I do my own cooking and laundry, too."

"Really? I think you'd make an amazing husband, Mister Manning."

"No, I wouldn't. I'm gone a lot and I'm a very private person which can be very annoying to most women."

"You don't seem that way to me. I think you're a very personable man and I like having you around."

Nate was getting uncomfortable with the way the conversation was headed because it was beginning to appear that Ruth Miller was exchanging the runaway Toby for him and that would make everything much more difficult. He wished he'd invented a girlfriend, but it was too late.

Over the years, he'd invented and continuously refined a fictitious family and homelife, but he'd never bothered creating the long-lost love back in his hometown. The one woman he could use to deflect the attentions of the women who tried to get too close. It was a startling omission and one that he'd need to correct if he hoped to successfully avoid Miss Miller. He wished he could be rude to her, and he would have had no problem before taking on that deputy sheriff job in Hays City. Now he was so accustomed to being polite and friendly that he found it difficult to revert to his angry persona.

He finally replied, "I just try to be polite, Miss Miller."

"Call me Sissie. My middle name is Cecilia, but I only let people I like call me Sissie. My parents, brothers and sisters all call me Ruth or worse."

"I assume that Toby called you Sissie?"

"No, he called me all of those endearing names like sweetheart or darling after we decided to run away. After we arrived, he began calling me a lot of other things. May I call you Nate?"

"That's fine," he replied, "I want to get an early start in the morning, so I'd better turn in."

As Nate turned to leave, Ruth quickly said, "There's only one bed. I don't mind sharing because I would feel so much safer having you close."

Nate couldn't afford to have Ruth Miller become infatuated with him, and he was certain that it would be because she had been treated so shabbily by the man she had expected to marry. He knew that if he gave in to the temptation, and it was definitely a strong temptation, he would be hurting her as much as Halvorsen had done. He may not consider himself the hero that she obviously did, but he surely didn't want to become a heel, either.

"Sissie, I don't want to risk becoming too familiar, so I'll just bring my bedroll into the room and set up on the floor. Besides, I've spent all day in the saddle and I'm not exactly pleasant to be within smelling distance."

She nodded and in a subdued voice said, "Alright. I guess that'll be okay."

"I'll go and get my bedroll."

"I'll be under the blankets, so you won't be embarrassed."

"Thank you," Nate replied before walking out the back door.

As soon as he'd gone, Ruth quickly turned and trotted into the bedroom and pulled back the blankets before she sat down on the edge of the bed and took off her shoes. She hadn't worn any stockings since she and Toby had arrived and after the second day, she hadn't bothered wearing any bloomers at Toby's insistence.

She slid her dress over her head and smoothed her camisole before slipping beneath the blankets and pulling them up to her chin. There was no need for a lamp as the window allowed the light from the half-moon to provide ample illumination.

When Nate walked into the room, he was relieved to see Ruth beneath the blankets with her eyes closed, so he spread out his bedroll a few feet away then took off his boots and shirt, but left his britches on rather than risk exposing himself to Ruth. He did have a bare torso, but she wasn't looking.

He laid down on the bedroll and pulled up his blanket rather than sliding into the bedroll. It gave him two layers of rudimentary softness and it was his preferred method of sleep when on the trail unless it was cold.

He suspected that Ruth Miller might try to join him after she thought he was sleeping, so he decided that he'd talk her to sleep first.

"Sissie, I've been thinking about a way to solve both of our problems after I catch up with Toby."

"You have?" she asked from her side of the darkened room.

"I'm still working on it and it will depend on your ability as an actress. Have you ever put on a false front to convince your parents to get something you wanted?"

She laughed and replied, "All the time. At least until I was fully grown. Now it doesn't work as well as it used to."

"That's okay. What I may need from you is a masterful performance worthy of any stage actress to make this work and I'll have to do my part, but I'm used to it."

"What is your plan?"

For almost thirty minutes, Nate outlined his thoughts and answered her questions. Just discussing it seemed to change her mood and focus as she became excited at the prospect. Even Nate found himself becoming more enthused and confident that the scheme might actually work, but there were a lot of variables. It would also depend on Miss Miller not becoming too enamored of her rescuer.

By the time that the long session of planning and modifying had finished, Ruth Miller was thinking only of how she would be leaving this place of her humiliation and not of the man who would be instrumental in the process.

Nate heard her soft breathing and knew he was safe, at least from the much more pleasant threat presented by Miss Miller. Finding Toby Halvorsen was the next step and then, if he found the cowhand, then the much more difficult part of the plan would begin.

CHAPTER 3

By the time Ruth opened her eyes in the morning, Nate and his bedroll were already gone from the room.

She sat up, rubbed her eyes and stretched before loudly asking, "Nate? Are you still here?"

Nate was at the cookstove and shouted back, "In the kitchen, Sissie. I'm cooking breakfast and then I'll be on my way."

Sissie bounded out of bed, pulled on her shoes then quickly slipped her dress back on before hurrying out of the room and down the short hallway.

"I'll be right back," she said as she scurried out of the back door to use the privy.

Nate had just glanced at her as she passed as he was still modifying the complex plan which would begin when he left the ranch house. He'd bring all of his guns because he might need them and hope that Ruth would be safe. He began to rue not having a shotgun in his arsenal. If he did, he could have left it with her in case Toby decided to return and Nate missed seeing him. It was possible because he thought that Miss Miller was a very desirable young woman and a cowhand, even one who'd treated her as badly as he had, would let his urges overpower his logic. Besides, he would think that she was still alone.

He had the plates of beans and ham on the table when she returned and then took a seat.

He poured two cups of coffee and set them near the plates before joining her and saying, "I'm going to be riding almost due west and hopefully I'll pick up his trail before I reach Cooper's Creek."

She had a mouthful of beans and nodded as he began to eat then after she swallowed, she asked, "How long will you be gone?"

"I'll try to get back before nightfall. If I can't find him in Cooper's Creek, then I'll come back, and we'll have to modify our plan."

"I hope you catch up with him. When you return, I'll love to hear the story."

"Sissie, do you have a gun?"

"No. Toby had a Winchester and a pistol, but he took them both with him. I can't shoot anyway."

"You were raised on a ranch and don't know how to fire a gun?"

"No. My father insisted that his daughters act like fine ladies and not tomboys."

Nate shoveled in a big slice of ham as he looked at Ruth and tried to see Fred Miller anywhere in her appearance. Maybe she was more like her mother, whom he'd never even seen, but she didn't have any facial or personality traits of her father that he could see.

"I've met your sister and brothers occasionally, and you're not similar in appearance. Did you ever notice that?"

"Of course, I did. My hair is a light brown and except for my mother, they all have a darker shade. I don't have their square face, either."

Nate didn't want to press the issue and began to wonder if her father's plan to have Stubby follow him and eliminate his daughter wasn't based on an entirely different reason than her elopement. Maybe it was the final straw that he'd been harboring for years knowing that some other man had fathered Ruth with his wife. If there was time maybe he'd broach the subject, but now he needed to get in the saddle and ride to Cooper's Creek.

He quickly finished his breakfast and coffee before standing and saying, "I'll leave the cleanup to you this time, Sissie. I'm on my way and I should see you before the sun goes down."

She stood and as Nate stepped toward his coat and hat, she cut him off and hugged him before saying, "Stay safe,

Nate. Don't risk getting shot just to get the money back. We can come up with some other way out. It's not worth it."

He stepped back, smiled and said, "You need a horse, ma'am. I'll be fine."

He donned his jacket, pulled on his hat and snatched the Sharps before heading out the door. He didn't look back as he strode to the barn and after putting the rifle in its scabbard, led the buckskin from the barn, mounted and waved to Ruth Miller before riding south around the barn and then turning west at a medium trot.

Ruth still had her right hand in the air as she watched him disappear, then slowly lowered it, turned and entered the ranch house. She was alone again but hoped that he would find Toby soon and return.

Nate didn't bother looking for a trail at all for the first half an hour because he doubted that he'd find it. He did look back at the fading ranch to make sure that Toby didn't suddenly appear from the trees. He knew the area reasonably well, so he was heading directly toward Cooper's Creek, but it was far from a straight line as he followed the tortuous path dictated by the harsh terrain. He figured that if he kept this pace, he'd arrive in Cooper's Creek in the early afternoon. Whether Toby Halvorsen was there or not was the big question.

He'd ridden almost two hours and had been studying the ground since the ranch disappeared from view when he spotted Toby's trail. It wasn't that difficult to find because he was leading two horses. The trail looked remarkably fresh and Nate wondered if Toby hadn't been watching the house waiting for Ruth to leave and only departed this morning. But if he had, then he would have seen him arrive and that thought abruptly changed Nate's plans.

He slowed the buckskin and began scanning the visible landscape for possible ambush sites. If Toby had seen him show up at the ranch house, then he'd know that he'd been sent by her father. That would make Toby nervous and see Nate as a threat, so if he'd waited until sunrise to leave those trees, then he'd be checking his backtrail and wouldn't risk going into town. His best bet would be to set up and wait for his tracker to arrive, just as he had done with Stubby, only Toby wouldn't just talk to him.

Nate had dealt with ambushes often since he'd been a deputy sheriff and some had been deviously arranged, but he didn't think that Toby had the mindset of an outlaw. He'd just find a good hiding place and wait with his Winchester. Nate guessed that after he'd set up his ambush location, Toby would wait for a couple of hours and if no one showed up, he'd resume his ride. He wouldn't have the patience of a killer and Nate was hoping that he didn't have the soul one, either. Killing another man in cold blood took a level of moral disconnection that most men didn't possess. In Toby's case, Nate assumed that even as cruel as he'd been to Ruth, he still would find it difficult to shoot a man without warning.

He had the buckskin at a slow trot as he continued toward Cooper's Creek, following the trail left by Toby Halvorsen. The droppings by the horses showed that he was very close now and his examinations of possible ambush sites grew more intense.

He rode for another twenty minutes after first picking up the trail and knew that he was more than halfway to Cooper's Creek when he thought he spotted a hint of movement about four hundred yards ahead at his one o'clock position. Nate didn't stare at the spot and he didn't pull his Winchester. There was no point at this distance. Besides, he wasn't going to be the one to initiate a gunfight. He only wanted to talk to Toby and was betting that the ranch hand wouldn't take advantage of it.

———

Toby Halvorsen cursed as he waited in the rocky gap with the three horses. He'd set up over an hour ago and began to think that the man who had shown up at the ranch house wasn't coming at all. He thought that he would be busy becoming acquainted with Ruth rather than coming after him. He should have left her a horse so she could ride into town, but then he'd risk that she would have send a telegram to the county sheriff.

Now he was trapped. He had his Winchester cocked and ready to fire, but he'd never shot a man before and wasn't sure if he could do it, but he felt that he had no choice. He'd

99

stay hidden now and wait until the rider was close before popping out and shooting him. Maybe he'd just shoot the horse and when it threw him, he'd take the opportunity to make his escape. Without a horse, the man couldn't follow him.

Toby was still deciding how to eliminate the threat when he heard the first echoes of steel horseshoes on rocks. The man was getting close now.

He gripped his Winchester and took a breath as he prepared to step outside and fire.

———

Nate had spotted a horse's tail when he passed a hundred yards, so he was certain that Toby Halvorsen was preparing to drygulch him. He could have pulled his Winchester and waited for him to appear, but he didn't want to kill the man and then have to bring his body into town and face all the questions and paperwork. He needed to return to Ruth so they could get started back to Laramie.

He pulled the mare to a stop and shouted, "Toby! I know you're in those rocks and you have no place to go! My name is Nate Manning and I'm a bounty hunter, so I'm a lot better with my weapons than you are. I only want to talk to you and if you peek out from behind your rocks, you'll see that my hands are empty."

Toby was startled at first before fear took command of his senses as he listened to what the rider said. He'd heard of Nate Manning and although most of the stories portrayed him as a stone-cold killer, he knew that he really had no choice. He had to take him at his word or engage him in a gunfight that he knew he would lose. His first worry was that Manning had his rifle aimed at the edge of the rock where his face would be when he took that peek, so he dropped to his heels and duck-walked toward the edge of the rocks.

When he reached the last slice of granite, he pulled off his hat and peered around the sharp rock and saw the bounty hunter on his horse with his empty hands in the air. He was surprised and briefly thought of shooting his horse, but it was Nate's reputation that kept that thought as just a passing idea.

He shouted back, "Alright! I'm coming out!" then pulled on his hat, stood up straight and stepped around the rock.

Even though Toby still had his cocked Winchester in his hand, Nate started the buckskin forward at a walk without pulling his pistol. He kept his eyes focused on the ranch hand as the gap closed. He still doubted that Toby would try to shoot him, but he was ready to grab his Colt the instant Toby tried to lift his repeater.

It was a nervous minute and a half for Toby as Nate approached, but he didn't move a muscle, knowing that there was no point.

Nate pulled the mare to a stop thirty feet away and said, "Set your Winchester down, Toby. We need to talk, and we can do that much better if we eliminate the chance that one of us gets spooked."

"Alright," Toby replied as he released the Winchester's hammer and leaned it against the nearest boulder.

Nate then dismounted and led his horse closer to Toby then stopped when they were standing face to face just six feet apart.

Nate began the conversation by saying, "Miss Miller isn't very happy with you, Toby. You not only left her, you took her money and all the horses. All you left her was some food and supplies that would only last her a few days."

Toby had no excuse or argument, so he just nodded.

After not hearing a response, Nate said, "You do know that I could have easily tracked you and killed you at my convenience; don't you?"

"Yeah. I know."

"But I didn't do that because I only shoot men if I need to. Now what you did to Miss Miller was unacceptable and you should face some measure of punishment for it, but I don't have the time to run you back to her father's ranch. I have other reasons for not returning with you. Do you know what they are?"

"No. Why did he send you after me if you aren't going to bring me back?"

"First, I want to know why you did it. Why did you take her away from the ranch and have her steal the money, then take her here just to abandon her?"

Toby rubbed the back of his neck as he stared at the rocky ground without answering for almost a minute. Nate had asked the question because he wanted to know if Fred Miller had any hand in the plot to send his daughter away to eliminate her.

Toby finally replied, "I was kinda sweet on her and she told me how she really wanted to get off the ranch and away from her old man. I told her that I'd take her away, but we needed money so I could find us a new place to hide out. She got the money and then I kinda borrowed the three horses. We lit out in the dark and bought some supplies in town before riding out here to my folks' old place."

"Then why did you abandon her and leave her in such a bad spot? You didn't even leave her some of her own money."

Toby then began scraping the ground with the toe of his right boot in a rhythmic arc as he answered, "I said I was sweet on her 'cause she was real pretty and all, but after we, um, did it, then she reckoned that we'd live there and I didn't want to stick around 'cause some of the folks in town didn't think too highly of me or my family. After a few days, I figured

I'd just go off on my own. She coulda walked into town and some feller would probably marry her."

Nate was about to start preaching at Toby for his selfish behavior but knew it didn't matter now. He had to get back. At least Fred Miller hadn't been involved in the elopement, which he hadn't expected anyway because if he knew where Toby was, he would have just sent Stubby directly to the ranch. He just had to be sure that it was all Halvorsen's idea.

"Okay, Toby, here's what's going to happen. I'm going to leave you with one saddled horse and the packhorse. I'll even give you fifty dollars to let you make your way out of here. I'll be leaving here with one saddled horse and over nine hundred dollars."

Toby stared at Nate as he asked, "You're lettin' me go?"

"I'm not about to kill you and I don't think you'll be hanging around Laramie anyway. I'm going to tell Fred Miller that you escaped, and you know what he'll do if he hears that you're nearby; don't you?"

"He'll kill me."

"He was going to kill you anyway. He hired me to find you and his daughter and told me that I was just supposed to convince her to return to the ranch, but he really intended to use me as a bird dog to track you down and had another man follow me to kill you. I double-backed and ambushed the man and send him away after disarming him, but you'd better understand just how serious Fred Miller is and if I were you, I'd make tracks."

"I will, and I appreciate you not killing me, Mister Manning."

"Just get the money and you can leave with the packhorse."

"Yes, sir," Toby snapped before quickly grabbing his Winchester and trotting back to the horses.

———

After watching Toby ride away and disappear in the terrain, Nate attached the saddle horse to the buckskin and mounted. He had nine hundred and some odd dollars in his saddlebag and was sure that he had seen the last of Toby Halvorsen.

He rode east at a faster pace than he'd used following the tracks and was almost regretting letting Toby escape without paying any price for what he'd done to Miss Miller. He hadn't even said to apologize to her for his behavior. He doubted that Toby even knew just how much he'd wounded the young woman beyond the hurt he'd inflicted on her by using her as he had and then abandoning her.

He still had a lot of details to iron out on the plan that he and Ruth had developed last night and had yet to address what would happen if the first part succeeded. He was already concerned that she might already believe that if it worked, the aftermath would involve a permanent relationship.

———

Ruth had spent the day while Nate was gone by mostly doing busy work like sweeping and doing her laundry in the leaking sink as best she could. She was worried that Nate wouldn't return at all, and not because he'd run afoul of Toby Halvorsen. She didn't doubt that Nate would have no problem dealing with her intended beau if he was able to find him. She thought that he might have to follow him much farther than he'd intended and might decide to take the train after all.

Even though she had already placed him in her pantheon of heroes, her limited experience with men led her to suspect that he might just leave her there. Even though he hadn't taken advantage of her obvious offer last night, she still wasn't convinced that he would return because the longer he was gone, the more she began to believe that there simply weren't any men who didn't have hidden schemes. She'd lived her entire life watching her father operate that way and then she thought that Toby would be different, but he'd been even worse. The only difference was that Toby wasn't as smart as her father. *Was Nate Manning really any better? What was he hiding?*

She was hanging her wash on the front porch rails when she looked toward Little Laramie wondering how long she'd wait before she had to make that long walk. She wiped her damp hands on her dress as she stared at the northern horizon imagining what would happen when she entered the town. She knew no one and didn't even have money to send a telegram or anyone she could trust to receive it, either. She never felt so alone, even after she'd seen Toby ride away.

Ruth was still staring when she picked up the slightest of movement out of her peripheral vision on the left and turned her head to identify it. Her mind had told her that it was probably just a coyote or some other critter, so she wasn't expecting to see what her eyes were telling her now. It was just past mid-afternoon, yet she saw a rider coming from the west leading another horse. His horse looked like Nate's buckskin, *but how could he be returning so soon?* He had said the earliest he would be returning would be after sunset.

She put her hand over her eyes to shield out the bright sun as she focused on the distant rider. He was still at least a half a mile away, yet her growing suspicions that she would be alone suddenly evaporated and were replaced with an explosion of hope and optimism.

———

Nate had seen her long before she spotted him and hadn't understood what she was doing at first but before she turned towards him, he figured out she was hanging laundry and smiled. It was an everyday task that seemed so out of place given her circumstances that it tickled his sense of humor.

When he saw her hand cover her eyes, he took off his hat and waved it high over his head to let her know that he wasn't an unknown wanderer or Toby Halvorsen. Then she returned his wave and he pulled his hat back on before nudging the buckskin into a faster pace.

After he returned, they'd spend the rest of the day smoothing out their plans which would start tomorrow.

————

After she had returned Nate's wave, Ruth hurried into the house to start cooking. She knew that he hadn't brought much food with him and she was sure that if he was returning this quickly, that they wouldn't need to conserve the food that she had in the house. She knew that they'd be leaving in the morning but was anxious to hear what had happened when he found Toby Halvorsen. The fact that he was only leading one horse back with him meant that he must have let Toby go with the other two. It was just a question of what else he was bringing with him; specifically, how much of the money he had taken back.

Nate was unsaddling the second horse when Ruth arrived in the barn and he turned when he heard her enter.

"Couldn't wait to find out what happened?" he asked with a grin.

"I'm not that patient. You obviously found him, so what did you do?"

Nate continued to strip the second horse as he told her what had transpired after he discovered that Toby must have been watching the house when he had arrived, because his trail was so fresh when he picked it up.

Before he even reached the point where he spotted Toby's ambush site, Ruth shuddered and asked, "Why was he watching the house? Do you think he was going to come back and hurt me?"

"No. I think he was waiting for you to leave and begin walking to town. I didn't ask because I wanted to start back as soon as possible."

She was still hugging herself as Nate continued the story and was brushing down the buckskin when he finished.

"Why did you give him any money at all? It wasn't his."

"It wasn't yours either, Sissie. I gave it to him to let him get far enough away so your father wouldn't bother trying to send anyone after him. I don't want him killed for what he did."

"Did he even say he was sorry for leaving me?"

Nate stopped and looked at her before replying, "I'm not going to lie to you. I don't believe he even considered it. But at least your father hadn't been the one behind his decision to take you away and it was only his own selfishness that made him abandon you."

"Is that any better than if my father had even suggested that he do this?"

"If he had been behind it then you would already be dead, and I wouldn't be talking to you. I'd be back in my office waiting for another job and talking to my secretary about his pregnant wife or their new midwife."

"You didn't tell me about him at all. You can do that later while we eat. I didn't leave much in the pantry if that's what you want to call it."

"That's alright. We'll be in Laramie by noon tomorrow."

Ruth nodded then sighed as Nate set the brush down, patted the buckskin on the neck and picked up the Winchester and the Sharps then walked with Ruth out of the barn.

As they walked, she asked, "Do you always do that?"

"Do what?"

"Talk to men who are trying to kill you?"

"If I can. I used to be a real hard case with an enormous temper. I'd fly off the handle if anyone even looked at me cross-eyed. I learned from a good man who put me under his wing that being angry all the time would probably get me killed before I was twenty. It took a while and his good nature to understand that lesson and I've lived by it ever since. Even in the business that I'm in, when I'm out there hunting dangerous men, I found that if I could get close and act as if I'm just a friendly cowhand, then I can usually talk them into giving up.

Of course, I talk them into it with the persuasion of a Winchester or Colt pointed in their direction."

Ruth laughed as they entered the back door and after Nate set the rifles against the wall and began to remove his jacket, Ruth asked, "How many men have you had to kill?"

He hung his coat then his hat and was unbuckling his gunbelt before he replied, "Including when I was a deputy, I've had to shoot six men and three of them died. Considering that I've captured another thirty-two, I think that's a pretty good record."

She began loading up their plates as Nate pumped some water into their cups and sat down at the table.

"Do you really think your plan will work?"

"I think so. If it doesn't then I may have to leave Laramie and probably head to Denver or someplace else."

She set the plates on the table and sat down before quickly asking, "You'd leave town? Why would you do that? You haven't done anything wrong."

"No, but if it doesn't work, then your father will put a lot of pressure on the local politicians to have me leave town, and that's only if I'm lucky. He could hire one of the more violent men to make me leave this life. Besides, I'm used to moving. I've never stayed anywhere else as long as I've stayed in Laramie. At least after I was sixteen."

"Where did you grow up?"

Nate almost gave her a truthful answer before he stopped himself and replied, "In a small town outside of Council Bluffs in Iowa. I was the fifth child of a family of farmers and the fourth son. I had three other siblings younger than me: two girls and a boy. I wasn't very fond of the life, and I tended to be a troublemaker, which didn't suit my father or older brothers very much. So, as soon as I could, I left the farm and started working my way west."

"Don't you miss you family?"

"Not at all. As I said, I was a real problem child and was angry at the world, so I knew they were more than happy to be rid of me."

"How did you make a living while you were making your way to Laramie?"

"Would you believe I was a bareknuckle fighter?"

"I can see that, at least if you were as angry as you say you were, but it doesn't show on your face. You don't have any broken bones and your nose is straight. Did you win a lot?"

"I won about ninety percent of my fights and a lot of the ones I lost were because the other man cheated or was a lot bigger. It was when was scheduled to fight a man in Kansas where I was tossed in jail and then befriended by the sheriff who changed my life. He retired and was replaced by a poor excuse for a lawman, so I left town and continued west."

Ruth was chewing as she gazed at Nate and tried to imagine him as a hellion and found it difficult. He always seemed so calm and in control of himself. When he'd ridden off to find Toby, even though he said that he wouldn't shoot him, Ruth found that hard to believe. He was a bounty hunter and they killed without mercy. Nate Manning was a very interesting and unusual man.

Nate took a sip of water before saying, "After we leave tomorrow, I don't think we'll have any problems on the ride. I only have one real concern that I haven't mentioned yet. I'm pretty sure that Stubby Nicks took my advice and is probably already in Cheyenne, but there is a possibility that he rode out to your father's ranch and explained what had happened. If he did, then there's a chance he and a few other men will be waiting for me to return and try to take a shot to keep me from reaching town."

"How can we avoid them if they're watching?"

"They can't be that close to Laramie or they'd have a better chance of being spotted, so either they hired someone to follow my tracks here or they'll set up an ambush a few miles outside of town along the roads. But as I said, that's not very likely. I'd give it a low probability that Stubby would even think of talking to your father and confessing that he was outwitted."

"But if he did, how can we reach town without being seen?"

"I have a back way that I've used more than once that no one else knows about. Once we're in town, then we'll head to my office using the back roads. I'll explain everything to Ike and then the next day, we make the ride to see you father."

"I'm still nervous about that, Nate. I'm not sure that I can convince him of the story."

"It's not much different than the truth, Sissie. Besides, I'll be doing most of the talking because you'll be too distraught over your treatment at the hands of the despicable Toby Halvorsen who was not the gentle person who had won your heart."

Ruth smiled then nodded before saying, "He did, you know. He could have just brought me here and we could have stayed and raised a family. I guess that he had other ideas and saw me as a stupid, naïve girl who would serve as his tool for robbing my father."

"I wonder why he was so reticent about going into Little Laramie. He said that the folks in town didn't think too highly of him and his family and I'm curious about why it was that way. It really doesn't matter, I suppose, and we're not going to go into town just to ask. But forget about Toby and everything else that happened. We need to review what we expect to happen tomorrow and the next day."

"Okay, but you still need to tell me about Ike and his wife."

114

"And their new nanny," Nate added as he smiled.

———

As the sun set, they moved into the bedroom and even though Nate was more comfortable around Ruth, he still wasn't about to join her in her bed, but that turned out not to be a problem.

After they'd set up in their separate sleeping arrangements, Ruth's focus was on what would happen over the next two days and not what might have happened the next few minutes, which suited and soothed Nate's mind.

Yet neither of them mentioned what might happen in three days because they may not be alive that long.

CHAPTER 4

Nate and Ruth rode away from the Halverson ranch early the next morning and Nate followed the same path he'd used on the way in. He didn't intend to follow it all the way to Laramie but would cut north about two miles west of town and take a more difficult but more secretive entrance.

As they rode, he scanned for potential ambush sites, but not any more than he would have normally. He still thought it was highly unlikely that Stubby had the nerve to go back to Fred Miller and tell him that he'd failed.

He and Ruth talked about many things on the ride, including her family and especially her father. Nate wanted to know as much about the man as possible when they met him tomorrow.

Ruth found herself more comfortable with Nate with each passing minute and was almost ashamed for lumping him with Toby and her father after he'd ridden away to find Toby.

It wasn't until after they'd ridden for two hours that Nate decided to ask the question about her parentage. He needed to know if that was the real reason for wanting to have her killed, if in fact that was Stubby's plan. He had reminded himself many times of the mistake he'd made by not giving

Stubby a chance to explain his mission. He was in a rush to find the couple, but that was no excuse for committing the error.

"Sissie, don't be offended if I ask you this question, but I'm still trying to understand if your father was intending to have you killed or just Toby."

"I won't be offended, Nate. You can ask me anything."

"Is it possible that your mother had an affair with another man, and you are the result?"

Ruth wasn't surprised by the question because of his earlier comments about the differences in her appearance compared to others in her family. Even though she'd noticed it before, she'd never really thought about it until Nate had mentioned it.

"I don't know," she answered, "It's possible, I suppose. I'm the youngest, but I find it hard to imagine that if my father found out that she'd been unfaithful that he'd still allow her to live on the ranch as his wife."

"I know. That's why I don't think it's likely, but what if the differences in your appearance put that thought into his mind. Maybe it simmered there for years and when you ran off with Toby, he thought it was almost proof of her infidelity."

"That's a real stretch, Nate."

"I know. I guess I'll just have to wait to see what his reaction will be tomorrow when we meet with him."

"I'm still nervous about that. I hope it turns out as you expect."

"So, do I. Just remember to stay out of sight until I pick you up in the morning. I don't want him to find out that you've returned until after I've talked to Sheriff Scott."

"I promise to stay invisible and I probably wish that I'd stay that way when we get to the ranch."

"I'm sure you do," Nate said with a grin as he looked at her.

He didn't think that the meeting with Fred Miller would be that dangerous. I might be after they left the ranch that the real threat would emerge. He'd be on pins and needles for at least a week and wouldn't be able to take any more jobs until he was satisfied that Ruth would be safe. He already considered her his responsibility now, but it could never be anything more than that.

They never saw any of Laramie's buildings before Nate turned them north and into the forest of pines that he'd passed on the ride west. There weren't any trails through the trees, but there were his marks that he'd carved on some of the trunks to let him know he was following the right direction. He'd created the personal path almost two years ago when he needed to find a fast way to disappear because an irate outlaw named Willie Leopold whom he had captured escaped from

118

jail and Nate was caught unarmed riding to Ike's house. He had turned and raced down the street past his office with the escapee hot on his trail and headed for the trees. After he'd disappeared into the forest, he slowed his horse and continued heading south trying to figure out a way to stop his armed pursuer because he suspected that the sheriff or his deputies would have to be careful entering the trees assuming they were chasing Willie.

He continued south and when he popped into the clearing, he pulled up again and looked behind him. He was surprised that Willie wasn't there yet and guessed that Willie must have thought he was armed and didn't want to find out the bad way. That gave him a little bit of time, so he turned his horse back into the trees and after fifty feet, stepped down and pulled his rope from his saddle and created as long a line as possible but just three feet above the ground. He mounted and stepped his horse over the rope and waited. He didn't hear Willie's horse but caught a flash of color about sixty feet away and swore loudly before he whipped his horse around and headed south toward the end of the path as Willie fired his pistol.

Nate didn't look behind him but headed for the open ground ahead and was already planning on making a hard right to head west when he heard a loud crash and then a scream from Willie's horse. Nate immediately turned his horse back into the trees hoping that Willie was down but was ready to bolt again if he found the outlaw on his feet with his pistol ready to fire.

It wasn't difficult to find the horse or its rider because of the cries of pain from the animal, and as he walked his horse closer, he found the horse writhing on the ground and Willie Leopold sprawled awkwardly on the ground nearby. He wasn't moving but Nate was concerned he might be playing possum as he approached. When he saw Willie's staring eyes, he knew that he wasn't faking death. How he died didn't matter. Nate dismounted and after taking Willie's pistol, he shot the injured horse and then undid his rope booby trap that had saved his skin. He vowed never to be seen without a pistol again as he shouted to the sheriff to let him know that Willie wasn't a danger.

Other than being told he couldn't get the reward twice for capturing the same wanted man, Nate let the sheriff and his deputy, who's mistake had given Willie the opportunity to escape, handle the cleanup. The next day, he returned and marked the path from the start of the trees, which began when his street ended to the clear land on the other side of the forest.

As they rode through the trees, Nate told Ruth the story and the advantage it now gave them. They'd be able to get to his house with a minimum of exposure to curious eyes.

"I wonder what Ike will say when he sees me?" Ruth asked.

"Whatever it is, it won't be nearly as bad as when I tell him what happened and what we plan to do."

Ruth smiled at Nate as they wound between the pine trunks and ducked from branches.

Nate knew that in a few minutes, they'd reach the edge of Laramie. Then he'd angle to the back alley that ran behind the houses and after a few hundred yards, they'd ride into his small barn behind his office. It was early afternoon and Nate was sure that Ike was at his desk. He wasn't going to demand that Ike and Alice hide Ruth for the night but would ask and then read his secretary's reaction. He didn't want to put either him or Alice at risk but didn't think it was likely. But if Ike thought that there was any danger to him or his very pregnant wife, then he'd have a second question that he hadn't mentioned to Ruth.

When the afternoon sun suddenly engulfed them, Nate shifted the buckskin to the east and with Ruth riding on his right to hide her as much as possible, they headed for the alley. He watched the road as they passed by and didn't see any onlookers, so he was reasonably sure that he'd be able to sneak Ruth into his house.

They turned down the alley and kept their horses at a walk as they passed by the backs of houses on both sides of the alley. He heard the typical sounds of lively households as they made their way but didn't see any faces.

When he spotted his barn, he felt a bit relieved and turned to smile at Ruth who was already looking at him with a big smile on her face.

After they entered the barn, Nate dismounted and waited for Ruth to step down. He then pulled off his saddlebags which contained the cash, then after he hung them over his shoulder, he slid his Winchester and the Sharps from their scabbards and looked at Ruth.

"Ready?" he asked.

"This is the easy one," she replied before they began crossing the narrow ground to his back porch.

He had to wait until Ruth opened the door before entering with his rifles. Ruth closed the door and looked around before she heard Ike shout, "Is that you, Nate?"

Nate loudly replied, "It's me. I'll be out in a minute as soon as I put my guns away."

"Okay, boss," Ike yelled back before putting away the book he'd been reading and picked up some correspondence from the box.

Nate put the rifles on the racks near the door. He'd never used the second or third racks, but now the two were holding rifles. He then removed his coat and hung his hat while Ruth removed her jacket and draped it over a chair.

He then looked at her, nodded and they stepped down the hallway to his office.

Ike hadn't paid much attention before, but when he heard the sound of more than one person walking toward him, he set the letter down then looked at the hallway just as Nate and Ruth stepped into the office and popped to his feet.

Nate quickly said, "Ike, I'd like you to meet Miss Ruth Miller."

"You found her and even convinced her to come back! How did you do that?" Ike asked excitedly before saying, "Oh, excuse me, Miss. It's a pleasure to meet you.

Nate held out a chair for Ruth and after she and Ike both sat down, he leaned against the desktop and said, "It wasn't that I had to convince her, Ike. There were a lot of unexpected developments after I left. Before I tell you about them, I need to know if you've heard anything about Fred Miller after I left."

"No, sir, not a word."

"How about Stubby Nicks?"

"Nope. Was he the one that followed you out of town?"

"He was. I ambushed him about six miles east of here and took the Sharps rifle with a telescopic sight that he had with him. It's in the kitchen. I sent him back to Laramie with a strong suggestion that he move to Cheyenne."

"He was going to kill Halvorsen?"

"I'm sure of that, but I think he was also supposed to shoot Miss Miller. Of course, he was going to put one of those .45s into me first."

"Why would Fred want him to kill his own daughter?" Ike asked with wide eyes.

"I'm not positive that was the plan, but it makes sense if you think about it. Why shoot me and then Toby Halvorsen and then either bring her back to the ranch or let her go? She'd tell the first lawman what had happened, and all hell would break loose."

Ike digested that information before asking, "What happened to Toby Halvorsen?"

"He abandoned Miss Miller at his parents old ranch house and took their horses and the only cash they had with them. I ran him down and took one of the horses and the cash back and let him go."

"Why did he run off after eloping with her?"

Nate looked at Ruth before answering, "Because he's stupid, Ike."

"What are you going to do now? If Fred wanted her killed, then she's in a lot of danger by staying here and so are you."

"I'll agree to both of your estimates of the situation, Ike. I have a plan to handle it. Tomorrow, after I talk to Sheriff Scott and let him know what happened, Ruth and I will ride out to her father's ranch and I'll tell him that Toby abandoned her, and I brought her back. I'm not going to mention the cash. Let him believe that Toby still has it, at least for now. Miss Miller is going to tell him that Toby threatened to hurt her sister if she didn't take the money and go with him. He'll know that it's a lie, but he can't dispute her word in front of me."

"But you can't leave her there!"

"No, I can't. We'll have to deal with that after we leave the ranch. I may even have to tell her father that I'll marry her, but whatever it takes, I won't leave her there. I think once she's in town, he won't dare do anything to her or to me. I'll hint that I have the Sharps that he probably gave to Stubby just to let him know that I understand his plot to kill us all. He'll be mad as hell, but he can't do anything. Or at least, I hope that he can't. Until we leave town tomorrow morning, I need to keep Ruth hidden."

"Are you going to keep her here?"

"I will if you'd feel uncomfortable hiding her at your place."

Ike paused then glanced at Ruth before saying, "I guess that's okay."

Nate smiled as he said, "No, that's alright, Ike. You have Alice to worry about. But how about this? Could you ask Miss White if she could stay in the house tonight to act as a chaperone? The last thing I need is to have Fred Miller accuse me of hanky-panky with his daughter."

"I'll do that, Nate, but weren't you already alone with her for a couple of days?"

"I was, but nobody here knows that. If she's in my house the gossips will notice soon enough."

"I'll ask her when I get home. I think she'll be there."

"Go ahead and take the rest of the day off anyway. If she agrees, just send her over. She might want to bring a travel bag for overnight."

"Okay, Nate," Ike said as he rose, then stepped over to the coat rack picked up his hat and pulled it on before leaving the office.

After the door closed, Ruth said, "Why didn't you accept his offer to have me stay with him and his wife tonight?"

"Because he was worried. I'm not about to put him and Alice into a situation that makes them uncomfortable. If Miss White agrees to act as a chaperone, then you'll have pleasant company for the night."

"I already have pleasant company, sir."

"Well, you'll be able to have a nice conversation about topics that are of no interest to men. How about that?"

"That's better. I'll go and start cooking. I don't know about you, but I'm starving."

"I could do with some food. I'll stay out here and mind the store and catch up on some paperwork. If you need to use the washroom, it's on the right as you go to the kitchen. There's a bathtub in there, too. You saw the privy in back, so that's all of the important things you need to know."

Ruth rose, smiled and said, "At least for right now," then walked down the hallway.

Nate watched her leave and wondered that when he told Ike that he'd tell Fred Miller that he would marry his daughter in order to get Ruth out of the ranch safely if she wasn't beginning to believe that it would happen. He could understand why she might think that way because she had so few options now.

He sat behind his desk and picked up a pencil and absent-mindedly began tapping it on the edge of the desktop as he finally shifted his mind to what would happen after they left the ranch. Ruth Miller may become a bigger problem than her father, but for a totally different reason.

Nate continued thinking and tapping for another three minutes before he sighed, tossed the pencil into the flat box on the corner of the desk and pulled out the envelopes that Ike had already opened and read their contents.

One was a request for employment which he tossed into the trash basket, the second was another advertisement, but this was from the Remington company which reminded him that he needed to buy a shotgun the next time he visited the gun shop. After dropping it in the trash, he read the last letter and this one intrigued him.

It was a long request from a recent widow living in Rawlins. After her husband of sixteen years had died from pneumonia, she took over the ranch's operation rather than let the foreman take charge. The foreman had been expecting a promotion if not more control and had been sent packing. She'd been running it for six months when a man arrived who claimed to be her husband's brother, who she believed had died during the war. He had a birth certificate and his army record to prove his identity, and she was worried that she would lose the ranch to the man whom she believed to be an imposter. The sheriff and the lawyer she'd hired had said that his claim was legitimate, and she asked if he could come to Rawlins and investigate the matter. She did add that if she lost the ranch, she might not be able to pay his fee.

He set the letter aside and took out a sheet of paper before opening a bottle of ink. He quickly wrote a reply accepting the challenge and said he'd be there within the week after he cleared up a current job.

He addressed the envelope, and after letting the ink dry, folded the letter and slid it inside. He'd drop it off at the post office in the morning when he went to talk to Sheriff Scott. He was pleased to have a normal investigation after the strange case that Fred Miller had delivered and was far from over.

He set the letter on the desk and headed for the kitchen where he found Ruth at the cookstove.

She turned and said, "Coffee is ready," so Nate continued to the cookstove and grabbed a towel before picking up the hot coffeepot then filled two mugs and set them on the table.

Ruth then brought two full plates and set them on the table before sitting down on the side closest to Nate rather than facing him.

As he prepared to fill his fork, she said, "You told me what Miss White did and what she looked like, but you didn't say much else."

"What do you mean?"

"Do you like her?"

"She seems quite pleasant, but I've only talked to her for a minute or so. Ike and Alice seem to like her well enough."

"Don't you think that it's strange that a pretty young woman suddenly arrives in Laramie as a midwife and isn't married yet?"

"You're a pretty young woman and you're not married, Sissie, and you're probably only a little younger than she is."

"But I grew up here. You said she came from Kansas. Is she running from someone? Are you sure that she wasn't married before?"

Nate set down his fork and said, "Sissie, Mary White is Ike and Alice's nanny and does housekeeping. I've hired her to clean this place once a week and she starts in two days. Why are you so interested?"

"What if I have no place to go after we see my father? I thought I could stay here, and I could do the cleaning and cooking for you."

Nate could almost hear his barrier doors close before he said, "We'll see what happens tomorrow before we have to worry about that. If you need someplace to stay, then you'll be able to stay here for a while. I'll be going to Rawlins soon to work a new case."

"You're leaving already?"

"In a couple of days. I'll take the train and I'll probably finish within three days or so before I return. It's not a dangerous job. It's to help a widow who might be being swindled out of her ranch."

Ruth didn't ask any more question but just ate her food silently as she slipped into a sulk.

Nate knew she was at least disappointed in his answer, but it was better to deflect any of her hopes now rather than let her become more dependent on him. Yet even as he looked at her, he felt empty for having been so callous despite his logic.

He thought he'd try to lift her mood and maybe dispel his own sense of guilt, so after taking a few more bites, he said, "Remember when I told you that my constant absences were one of the reasons that I'd make a bad husband? It's my job, Sissie. I'll try to make it up to you by offering you a warm bath. Would that help?"

She looked at Nate then replied, "A bath does sound nice."

Nate was relieved and smiled before saying, "Good. I'm almost finished and then I'll put on the pots of water on the stove and start filling the tub."

"Do you want to me to leave the water after I'm done?"

"Yes, ma'am," Nate replied before quickly finishing his dinner then picking up his plate, cup and cutlery and walking to the sink.

After washing the dishes, he began pumping water into two big pots and setting them on the hot plates of the cookstove before adding more wood to the firebox. He let Ruth wash her own dishes while he walked to the washroom and began pumping water into the tub.

When he returned, he sat down at the table to wait for the water to heat and Ruth asked, "What happened to the widow in Rawlins?"

131

"Her name is Agatha Swarthmore, and she's the owner of the Double 8 ranch north of the town. It's a huge spread that runs over five thousand head of cattle. Her husband died of pneumonia just before last Christmas and she explained that she had trouble with the foreman who was angry that she decided to run the ranch and not appoint him as ranch manager with an increase in salary and control over the ranch's finances. She fired him few months ago, and things settled down after she appointed a new foreman.

"Anyway, last month, a man arrived at the ranch claiming to be her late husband's long-lost brother. She was more than just shocked, she was horrified. As Wyoming allows women to inherit, she would still be entitled to half the value of the ranch, but that would mean that she'd have to share control of the ranch as well and she knows that he'd actually have more authority than she would."

Ruth was definitely interested and asked, "How can he claim to the unknown brother? Does he have documentation?"

"Not only unknown, but supposedly dead. She wrote that the brother, Finney Swarthmore, died in the Civil War. Yet he suddenly reappears and has a birth certificate and a copy of his army records to prove it."

"Didn't they get a telegram or something during the war to let them know he'd died?"

"I didn't get that much detail yet. But you can see why I'd find this intriguing. She stands to basically lose the ranch she'd built with her husband and she believes this man is a fraud but can't prove it. She's hired an attorney and both he the sheriff have investigated his claim and found it valid. My impression is that her lawyer is pressuring her to make a deal with the man or risk losing a lot more. She even said that she may not be able to pay my bill. It sounds as if I'm her last hope."

"Why did she contact you? Aren't there any private detectives in her town?"

"I guess not. She must have heard about me somehow. Anyway, this case is one of those that's almost impossible for me to turn down. I can't sit idly by and allow her to be cheated if that's what it is. I suppose it is possible that the claim is genuine, but the timing is too extraordinary."

"Will you be able to talk to the man and look at the documents?"

"I don't know. It'll depend on her lawyers and what rules they've already set up. But the longer I delay, the more likely it will be that she'll be forced to settle."

"I guess I was being selfish for wanting you to stay, Nate. I'm sorry I behaved so childishly."

"That's alright, Sissie. You've been through a lot in the past week and I can understand how worried you must be about what will happen tomorrow and after that. But remember that even after I'm gone, you'll have Ike out front in the office and Sheriff Scott won't let anyone bother you, not even your father. He's a good man and isn't afraid to stand up against the powerful to do what's right. He's got two good deputies, too. You'll be safe and I should be back in a few days."

Ruth smiled and said, "Thank you, Nate. That does make me feel better."

"Now go and get your things ready for your bath. The water will be ready in a few more minutes. The soap and towels are in the small cabinet under the sink in the washroom."

Ruth smiled, then stood and left the kitchen.

Nate watched her leave then after hearing her bedroom door close, walked to the washroom and began to fill the tub halfway with cold water from the pump. By the time that was done, he returned to the kitchen and began lugging the steaming pots of water to the washroom.

He was already sitting in the kitchen when he heard Ruth leave her bedroom, enter the washroom and close the door. He was just about to pump the pots full again to heat them for his own bath when he heard the front door open and close.

He stood just as he heard Mary White ask, "Nate? Are you here?"

As he walked past the washroom, he replied, "On my way, Mary," then spotted her in the office just before he left the hallway.

"Ike told me what happened and that you had asked me to act as a chaperone for the night. Is that right?" she asked as she set down her travel bag, removed her hat and hung it on the coat rack.

"Yes, ma'am. I really appreciate this, Mary. It's a very strange situation and I don't know how much Ike was able to explain because I only told him about half of it. Miss Miller is taking a bath right now, so I'll tell you the full story."

Mary removed her coat and hung it next to her hat before walking to his desk and sitting down on the client side.

Nate quickly sat in his swivel chair and asked, "How is Alice?"

Mary smiled and replied, "She's doing better than her husband. He's becoming more of a nervous wreck the closer she gets to her date of expected delivery."

Nate smiled back and said, "Ike's a very emotional man, but he's a good husband and I'm sure he'll be a good father."

"I think so, too. So, you'll need me to stay one night as a chaperone; is that right?"

"Yes, ma'am, although it might be two, if that's possible for you. I'll be taking Miss Miller to her father's ranch tomorrow and hopefully we'll be able to return later in the day. If things go as I anticipate, then I'll bring her back here and if that happens, I may need you to act as a chaperone tomorrow night as well. Would you be able to do that?"

"I have a cleaning job tomorrow, and I have to check on Alice, but I'll be able to stay tomorrow night and Wednesday I'll be staying here anyway because it's your first cleaning day."

"That's right. I lost track of time. I really do appreciate your help in this matter, Mary. I hadn't expected that Miss Miller would be returning with me or I would have made other arrangements before I left."

"That's understandable. So, tell me what happened."

Nate nodded and began narrating the story of the case beginning with Fred Miller's phony request. As he spoke, Mary listened intently with her blue eyes almost burning into his browns.

When he finished ten minutes later, Mary asked, "At the risk of sounding judgmental, why do you need a chaperone now as you've been alone with Miss White for two days out on that ranch?"

"Ike had the same question and it's a matter of reputation. When I was with her on the ranch, no one knew either of us was even there. Here, it will only be a matter of time before someone spots her and the gossip will begin. Miss White's reputation will suffer as a result."

"I would think that yours would suffer more. I'm sure that the gossip is already out about Miss White's elopement and her return without the cowboy will lead to some very salacious stories."

"That may be, but still, I think it would be a wise precaution to have a chaperone."

Mary smiled and asked, "Is that the only reason, Nate? Are you sure that you're not just a bit afraid of Miss Miller?"

Nate stared at her for a few seconds before smiling as he scratched the side of his jaw with his right index finger and replied, "Maybe just a little."

"And how much worse will it be if you have two young women in the house with you? You could have asked an older, married woman to act as chaperone."

"Um, I don't know any older, married women well enough to ask."

"Really? How long have you lived in Laramie?"

"Around three years."

"And you don't know any older, married women? How about older, unmarried women?"

"No, and before you take more time to expand your question, I don't know any older men, married or unmarried, either. I know Ike and Alice well, but I don't socialize, so I have no other acquaintances."

"Really? None at all? Why not? You seem like a very personable young man," she asked with raised eyebrows.

"No, I don't have any other close acquaintances. Between my investigative work and bounty hunting, I'm not here often enough to cultivate friends."

"That sounds like an excuse, Mister Manning. Did you have any friends before you came here?"

"A few, but after I left Iowa, I never stayed in one place very long."

"Ike told me that you grew up outside of Council Bluffs before you left your family farm. Is that right?"

"Yes, ma'am. I didn't have a lot of friends in school because I was a hothead and troublemaker. I didn't get along with my brothers or sisters that well, either."

Mary tilted her head slightly as she seemed to be studying him then said, "It still must have been nice having a big family."

"No, it wasn't. As I said, I was the black sheep of the family and tended to stay on my own and I'm sure that they had a big party after I left."

"Did your father punish you severely for your misdeeds?" she asked quietly.

"He used a hickory switch and I knew it well. My brothers rarely felt its bite. I guess that was my sole purpose growing up; to prevent my siblings from incurring my father's wrath."

Mary was about to ask him another question when the washroom door opened, and Ruth stepped down the hallway to the office.

When she appeared, Nate rose and said, "Mary, this is Ruth Miller. Ruth, this is Mary White and she'll be staying here as a chaperone to keep you safe."

Mary laughed lightly as Ruth walked into the office before saying, "I don't need anyone to protect me from you, Nate. We spent two nights together and I wasn't afraid having you sleeping in the same room."

Nate stepped over to Ike's desk and returned with his client chair and set it down on the side of the desk before saying, "I was just making light of the situation, Sissie. I know you weren't afraid. Have a seat and we'll explain to Mary what we'll be doing tomorrow. It's important that she knows."

"Alright," she replied before sitting down.

139

Nate could tell that the lighter mood that Ruth had recently achieved had disappeared and been replaced by a one that was less sulky but more defensive as if she was jealous of Mary White. Granted, Mary was a very pretty young woman, but Nate had expected that Ruth would be happy to spend some time with a pleasant woman of her own age. He hadn't expected the reaction he was witnessing, but maybe he should have.

He decided to ignore the change and began explaining to Mary what he hoped would happen tomorrow beginning with the stop at the sheriff's office before continuing on to the Lone Wolf ranch.

Mary listened intently and didn't ask any questions as Nate outlined his plan, and only when he finished, did she ask, "What happens if you're successful and Miss White's father agrees to let her leave?"

"She'll come back here until we can work out a more permanent arrangement."

"Then you may need me to act as a chaperone after Wednesday?"

"No. I'll be leaving on Wednesday for a few days or maybe a week to handle a job in Rawlins."

"Alright. Where can I put my things?" Mary asked.

"You'll be sleeping in the middle bedroom. It's across from the washroom. I'll show you and take your travel bag to the room."

"Thank you, Nate," she replied before they stood, and Nate walked across the office to pick up her travel bag.

Mary followed him to the middle bedroom and after he set her travel bag down on the dresser, he turned and said, "I really appreciate your help, Mary."

She smiled then glanced back at the door before stepping close and whispering, "Why is Miss Miller jealous?"

Nate shrugged then left the bedroom while Mary began unpacking her travel bag. He knew that Mary was right and felt as if the hallway walls were closing in on him as he headed back to the office.

He sat down behind his desk and smiled at Ruth before saying, "I feel better knowing you'll have someone here with you after I leave. That's assuming that your father doesn't have us shot before we even get to the house."

"You really don't think he'd do that; do you?" a startled Ruth asked.

"No, ma'am. I was just using absurdity to confirm my belief that everything will go as we expect tomorrow. I apologize for scaring you. It's just that I'm not accustomed to conversing with women. If you'd been a man, you would have laughed and suggested that your father may not shoot us, but he might tar and feather us before he hanged us."

Ruth smiled and said, "I'm sorry, Nate. I should have known that was your intention. I've been around men all my life and they do say things like that."

"Speaking of men, is there anything you can tell me about your brothers, brother-in-law or the ranch hands that could cause us trouble? Or are we only concerned about your father?"

"None of them would even sneeze without my father's permission."

"That's what I thought, but I wanted to make sure. So, we'll visit the sheriff and I'll post that letter to Mrs. Swarthmore then we'll ride to the ranch. We should get there by mid-morning and hopefully, we'll be leaving before noon. In celebration, I'll treat you to a steak dinner at the Richmond."

"Will Miss White be joining us?"

"No, Sissie. We'll stop on the way back."

Ruth smiled and asked, "Nate, what will you do with the money?"

"It's your money, Sissie. You'll need it."

"I won't mind if you keep it. You saved me, Nate."

"Your father is going to pay me a hundred dollars for completing the task he gave me and that's more than enough. As I said, you'll need the money."

"Alright, I guess it's okay."

Before Nate could invent another less stressful topic, Mary returned to the office and sat down across from Nate.

"You keep a very neat house, Nate. Why did you need a cleaning woman?"

"It's clean now because I haven't been living here for a few days."

"I won't have much to do on Wednesday. Did you want me to do your laundry?"

"No, that's okay. I'll handle it when I return. You and Miss Miller can spend the day chatting about whatever women talk about and maybe play checkers or chess. I have a set in my room but don't get to use it very often. I also have a bookcase that's not quite full and you're both free to browse."

"That will be a pleasant diversion. I'll take you up on your offer. May I borrow a book or two when I leave?"

"Of course. Consider it a small library where you aren't charged for overdue books."

Mary laughed and looked at Ruth as she asked, "Do you play chess?"

"No, but I'll play checkers if you'll stop by after Nate leaves me."

"I'll do that, but my schedule is surprisingly full, with my cleaning jobs and helping Alice."

"When is she due?"

"In two weeks, so I'm having to keep a close eye on her. Ike knows where I am, so if she goes into labor, I'll have to leave."

Nate listened to the two young women having a normal conversation and was relieved. He knew that Mary would be much more accepting of Ruth and her situation than Ruth would be having the pretty young blonde staying in the house. He just hoped it stayed that way.

———

Everyone had turned in and the house was dark as Nate laid on his bed and tried to think of anything that he'd missed that could create a disaster tomorrow. The only real hiccup he could imagine is if Stubby had told Fred Miller what had happened, and they were expecting him and Ruth to arrive at the ranch. It was a long shot for many reasons, but Nate knew he had to consider it. He had planned on bringing the Sharps with him as an unsubtle hint that he knew what Fred Miller had planned but decided that he'd stick with their modified plan where they would feign innocence. Either way, tomorrow would be an interesting day.

CHAPTER 5

Nate waited until Ike arrived the next morning before he and Ruth left for the Lone Wolf. It had been a busy morning getting ready for the confrontation and Nate made sure that he'd remembered everything, including posting the reply letter to Mrs. Swarthmore.

He wasn't concerned with anyone seeing Ruth now because they'd be riding out to the Lone Wolf within an hour, so he didn't think it mattered.

They turned onto Main Street and headed for the sheriff's office on the busy thoroughfare. No one paid any attention to them before they pulled up in front of the jail and dismounted. Nate was riding the brown gelding today and Ruth was mounted on the horse that she'd ridden out of Laramie. The saddlebag with the cash was back in Nate's office being guarded by Ike who had them under his desk.

They entered the sheriff's office and after Nate closed the door, he spotted Deputy Sheriff Bill Caruthers at the desk.

Bill looked up, smiled at Ruth and said, "Mornin', Nate. What brings you and Miss Miller to our humble shop this mornin'?"

"Is the boss in?" Nate asked as he looked down the hallway.

"Sure is. Go on back."

Nate nodded then he and Ruth walked past the three cells which were devoid of prisoners as it was the middle of the week. They were usually full by Monday morning.

After entering the sheriff's private office, Nate closed the door before removing his hat and sitting beside Ruth who had already taken a seat as Sheriff Scott looked at him curiously.

"What's going on, Nate?" he asked after Nate was seated.

"After we leave here, I'll be escorting Miss Miller back to her father's ranch."

"I heard that she ran off with some cowhand. Is that right, Miss Miller?"

"Yes, I did," she answered without hesitation or excuses.

"So, what do you need to tell me that worries you?"

Nate then quickly explained the circumstances that surrounded the unusual case and when he finished, he said, "I'm just telling you this in case anything happens to us at the ranch. I'll stop by later if we're okay. After that, Miss Miller will probably be living in town and I need to make sure that she stays safe."

146

"Okay. Feel free to mention that to Fred Miller."

"Thanks, Bart, that's all I need. I'm going to post a letter to a new client before we ride out there. I'll be heading to Rawlins tomorrow."

"Anything dangerous?"

"I don't think so, but you never know."

"That's the truth," the sheriff replied before Nate and Ruth stood.

Nate opened the door and walked behind Ruth down the hallway.

After they'd stopped at the post office where Nate posted the letter, they headed out of Laramie to make the ride to the Lone Wolf Ranch.

Nate had never been on the massive spread before and as they rode, he let Ruth explain the layout and point out landmarks. They were already on the ranch after forty minutes, but no buildings were in sight. It was a measure of the size of the property that the access road was almost two miles long and for all practical purposes, the entire length of roadway to Laramie was just an extension of that access road.

Before Nate saw the outline of a manmade structure, he heard the lowing of cattle and the distant shouts of men trying to move them. He scanned the horizons and didn't see any movement until he checked his three o'clock and saw dots about two miles away.

"This is even bigger than I expected," he said to Ruth who was more nervous than proud of what used to be her home.

"We'll see the ranch house in a few more minutes."

"Is it as big as the rest of the ranch?"

"It looks almost like one of those pictures you see of the old Southern plantations before the war."

"Minus the slaves."

"There is that, but most of the time, I felt like a prisoner if not a slave."

The grand house began to rise above the horizon before Nate answered, "Well, let's go see the king."

"He expects the same amount of deference that one would give royalty short of kissing his ring or bowing."

"I'll be polite, but I won't be subservient. I may not be constantly ready to fly off the handle, but I never was able to completely rid myself of that chip on my shoulder."

"Good. It'll be interesting to see how he handles it."

Nate glanced at Ruth and hoped that her at father didn't push it too far. He needed to be professional. After all, he'd just managed to do the exact task that Fred Miller had asked of him.

The mansion-like house kept growing ever larger as they continued riding and Nate began seeing people and horses moving about. There were two barns, two more smaller houses and two bunkhouses. He spotted an expansive corral filled with horseflesh and suspected that there was at least one more that was out of sight. Everything about the Lone Wolf was Texas-sized but in Wyoming.

They almost reached the front of the house without being noticed, or at least challenged, when the front door opened and two men stepped onto the front porch, but neither was Fred Miller. Nate was sure that they were Ruth's two older brothers, Jasper and Frank. He just didn't know which one was the older brother and Ruth had gone quiet. He took another glance at her and saw her face white with fear. *How could anyone be so afraid of her own father?* Of course, Fred Miller may not be her father and he had probably ordered her death, so maybe she had good reason for her terror.

He pulled up in front of the big porch and waited until Ruth slowly dismounted before he stepped down.

He kept his eyes on her brothers as he took her arm to help her up the six steps because he was concerned that she might stumble or even faint.

They reached the next to the top step before the taller brother said, "Well, look who's back. Did you scare you boyfriend away, Ruth?"

The other brother snickered before saying, "Our father will want to talk to you, Ruth. He's in his office."

Ruth didn't reply, so Nate said nothing as he could feel her already beginning to tremble. They stepped onto the porch and her brothers turned and entered the house in front of them. They followed and Nate closed the door before they passed through the foyer and entered a large, fancy parlor where her brothers sat down. Nate didn't see anyone else, so they hadn't been expected, but apparently some ranch hand had seen them riding in and told the boss that they were coming down the long access road.

Nate let Ruth guide him toward the office. The door was open and after they crossed the threshold, Nate closed the door and had his first look at Fred Miller since he'd given him the job. He wasn't surprised by the lack of a reaction as the rancher had time to prepare after he'd been given his short warning. Now it was time to see if the hard man would accept his story of ignorant innocence.

He held a nice leather cushioned chair for Ruth who slowly sat down and wasn't even making eye contact with her father as he stared at her. Nate found it very difficult to read the man as he had a perfect poker face. He couldn't tell if he was really surprised or angered by his daughter's reappearance.

He finally sat down next to Ruth and said, "As you can see, Mister Miller, I've done as you asked, but I didn't have to convince your daughter to leave Mister Halvorsen. When I found her, he'd abandoned her and then disappeared."

Fred finally spoke when he shifted his eyes to Nate and said, "He left her alone? Why didn't she send me a telegram?"

"She didn't have a horse or much else after he left. He only left her enough food for four or five days. I rode into Little Laramie and bought one for her to ride back. As it turned out, the one I bought was the same one that she had ridden out of the ranch. I guess that Mister Halvorsen sold it before making his escape."

"That bastard!" he exclaimed in a believable show of anger.

Nate was almost ready to believe that Fred Miller really hadn't intended to have Ruth killed and even began to wonder if he'd even contracted with Stubby Nicks to follow him. He was that good of an actor, but Nate didn't quite fall for his performance.

"I wish I could have tracked him down, but I didn't want to leave Miss Miller unprotected just to find him. I thought my first priority was to bring her back."

"I agree with you," he replied before looking at Ruth.

"Well, Ruth, have you learned your lesson? I warned you not to believe that man and so did your mother. You not only disobeyed us, but you stole a thousand dollars before you ran away. Are you spoiled?"

Ruth still kept her eyes down as she quietly answered, "Yes, Father. Toby took me several times before he ran away."

"So, you could be pregnant now; isn't that true?" he snapped.

"Yes, Father."

"Well, now that presents a whole new issue; doesn't it? You disobeyed, stole and ran away and now you shamed us even more by giving yourself to that boy. You didn't even marry him; did you?"

She whispered, "No, Father. He said we'd get married in town, but...," then stopped as she seemed to run out of breath.

Nate knew that she wasn't acting and didn't think she could keep going without breaking down. Her father was crushing her spirit.

Nate then attracted Fred Miller's attention by saying, "Mister Miller, my fee for the job will be one hundred dollars. I'll accept a check if you'd prefer. I can submit a written bill for my services if you'd like."

"No, that's not necessary," the rancher said before sliding his wallet from his jacket pocket and counting out five twenty-dollar notes and handing them to Nate.

After pocketing the cash, Nate asked, "What will happen to Ruth now?"

Fred's considerable eyebrows rose as he asked, "What do you mean? She'll stay here and learn her lesson."

"Mister Miller, I don't mean to intrude into family affairs, but since I found Miss Miller, I've come to respect her immensely. I know that she offended you and I can understand why you'd be upset, but in the short time that we were together, I understood just how much she wished to be on her own. Even though she'd been abandoned and had no money and little food, I still had to convince her to return with me. It was only my promise to her that she would have the option of returning to Laramie after I brought her to the ranch that convinced her to come back with me."

"What would she do in town? What if she's pregnant? I'd be the laughingstock of the entire county. They all know she ran away with that stupid boy."

"And they all know that I returned with her after we rode through town. I'm sure that the gossip tongues are wagging even more now that everyone knows that I spent some time with her even though I assure you that all I did was my job. There is no escaping the rumors and innuendoes, Mister

153

Miller, whether she stays with you or returns to Laramie. If anything, those whispers will fade much faster if she's in Laramie and becomes popular with the townsfolk, especially the women."

Nate still was trying to get a read on Fred Miller as he leaned back and either pretended or actually was thinking about what he'd just heard. The only thing that Nate was sure of was that Fred Miller must be one hell of a poker player.

After almost a minute of rumination, the rancher leaned forward and looked at Ruth.

"Do you wish to return to Laramie, Ruth?"

She finally raised her eyes to meet her father's stare and whispered, "Very much so, Father."

Fred grunted then looked at Nate and asked, "Where would she stay?"

"For a few days, she'd stay in my office and house. I'll be leaving to do another job tomorrow morning. After that, we'll figure out something."

"I'm not going to give her a penny. She's already cost me a thousand dollars and two horses."

"Can she pack the rest of her things before we leave?"

"Well, I have no use for any of her things," he answered, then looked at Ruth and said, "Go upstairs and pack your things."

"Yes, Father," she replied quietly before standing then leaving the office without closing the door.

After she'd gone, Fred Miller asked, "How difficult was it to find her?"

"I had a good guess before I left town, so it wasn't hard. I thought I had someone following me when I left, so I rode the wrong direction and lost him."

"Oh. That was fortunate. Why would someone be following you?"

"It's not uncommon in our business. Whenever I leave town, a competitor sometimes follows to see if I lead him to a man with a price on his head. I've had situations where they'll even try to drygulch me after I've captured the man, so they can claim the reward."

"Really? Did you recognize the man who was following you?" Fred asked, which was the first indication that he had sent Stubby after him.

Nate nodded and replied, "I'm pretty sure he was Stubby Nicks, and after I get back into town, I'll track him down and ask him why he was trailing me."

"Well, I'm glad you were able to lose him. You did a good job, Mister Manning, and I'm glad that I chose you to find her."

Nate smiled as he said, "I always try to do exactly as I'm directed by the client. In this case, it wasn't a difficult job at all. I'm pleased that everything seems to be working out when one considers the much worse outcomes that could have happened."

Frank Miller just nodded, then pulled a thick cigar from his drawer and asked, "Would you like a cigar, Mister Manning?"

"No, thank you, sir. I don't smoke."

"You're a smart man," he said before biting off the end and taking a match from the ceramic duck on the desk and lighting it.

As the rancher puffed his cigar, Nate was still trying to understand the man's motives for acquiescing so quickly to Ruth's departure. *If he'd sent Stubby to kill her, then why is he so willing to let her live in Laramie?* His unexpected reaction was setting off alarm bells in his head and he wished he could at least get an inkling of what to expect.

He thought that Ruth would take time to gather her things, so he asked, "How many cattle do you have on the Lone Wolf, Mister Miller?"

"The last count was just under twelve thousand."

Nate whistled and said, "I knew that you had a lot, but even I couldn't imagine that many."

"It took a while to build up the ranch to the size it is now, but I put in the work and the time."

"I guess that it took more than just work and time. You must have experienced a lot of hardships to overcome in the process. You probably had problems with Indians, rustlers and maybe even the government."

After blowing out a big smoke circle, Fred smiled and said, "You've got that right. It took a while to get those paper-pushing politicians off my back, but I'd rather face a whole passel of angry Cheyenne than a roomful of bureaucrats."

Nate laughed then asked, "How many hands to you have working on the ranch?"

"Not including the departed Toby Halvorsen, I employ twenty-four full time hands, two wranglers and two cooks. I have another sixteen employees to handle the other work on the ranch. It's almost a small town out here. I've got a blacksmith, a butcher and even a baker."

"That's more than some towns have, Mister Miller," Nate said as he watched the rancher grin at the recognition of what he'd created.

Nate wasn't sure if he'd wormed his way into the rancher's confidence enough to ask anything that could shed more light on his intentions because he didn't think that Fred Miller even confided his plans to his own sons before setting them in motion.

But before he could even come up with a vague question that might give him a clue, he heard Ruth step into the office and turned to look at her.

"I'm ready, Mister Manning," she said without looking at her father.

Nate stood then shook Fred Miller's hand as he said, "Good day, Mister Miller, and thank you for the business."

"Thank you for taking care of Ruth, Mister Manning."

Nate smiled then turned and took Ruth's arm and led her out of the office. He picked up her two heavy travel bags and didn't spend much time looking at her two brothers who were staring at them as they crossed the parlor and soon exited the big house. He strapped the two travel bags behind their saddles before they mounted and turned away from the house.

He wasn't worried about being shot in the back as they left the ranch because Fred Miller understood that everyone knew that he'd taken Ruth out to the ranch and if he didn't return, Sheriff Scott would make the Lone Wolf ranch the place where he'd start his investigation and unless he killed Ruth, he knew that she'd tell the sheriff everything. If her father was going to do anything, it would be after they returned to Laramie.

They still rode at a medium trot as they headed southeast on the long access road, and once they'd traveled a couple of hundred yards, he looked across at Ruth and asked, "Are you alright?"

She looked back at him and replied, "I'm not sure. I've never seen my father act that way. I expected him to be hideously angry and call me every slutty name imaginable."

"I've never met a man who was so difficult to read. For a little while, I almost began to believe that he hadn't sent Stubby after me. I'm still miffed at myself for not waiting for Stubby to answer my question. I was so damned sure that your father had paid him to trail me, so I'd lead him to you and Toby Halvorsen that I almost answered my question before I even asked. When he answered with something totally different, I just let it go."

"Do you still think that he sent that man to kill us?"

"Absolutely. Stubby may not have answered my question, but he didn't deny it either. Just having that scoped Sharps with him was proof. Even I don't have a sniper rifle. He tried to say that he was going hunting, but he never hunted since I've known him, and most men who do don't use something that fancy. I never did ask if you ever saw that rifle in the ranch house."

"I didn't, but that doesn't mean much. My father has two rooms that he doesn't let anyone else enter."

Nate's eyebrows peaked as he asked, "Really? Not even your brothers?"

"Not even them. I think one is where he has his guns, but I don't know what he has in the other room and I'm not sure that I want to know."

"It's still interesting."

"Maybe to you, but not to me. I'm never going back to that house."

"I noticed that your mother, sister and sister-in-law weren't there. Is that normal?"

"No. I imagine that once we were spotted, my father ordered them upstairs to wait until we left. I didn't see them up there, but I didn't go into any other rooms."

Nate nodded as they continued along the access road. They'd stop at the sheriff's office when they got to town and he'd let Sheriff Scott know what happened and his suspicions of Fred Miller's possible reaction to his daughter's unexpected return. The mystery of the two rooms only added to his concerns, but also increased the likelihood that he had provided Stubby with the Sharps. He wouldn't have bought it in Laramie unless he special-ordered it but would pay a visit to Jerry Hare at his gun shop to ask anyway. He might be able to get that done today but wasn't expecting to get any results.

They finally left the access road and entered the road to Laramie that only went to the Lone Wolf Ranch. As they rode along, Nate wondered who paid for the construction of the extra eight miles of access road for Fred Miller. Maybe it was some of those bureaucrats that he hated more than a passel of angry Cheyenne warriors.

As they rode, he would glance at a silent Ruth Miller who had her eyes focused straight ahead. She was no longer fearful, but she did seem distracted. He wasn't sure if it was for the same reason that had him concerned, or she was still thinking about the threat that she had envisioned in Mary White. He still had to deal with that issue but was already trying to take a different approach. At least he hadn't told Fred Miller that he would marry her. That would have made everything much more difficult. It was bad enough as it was.

Ruth finally spoke again when Laramie came into view, asking, "Are we going to have that dinner you promised me when we get to town?"

"Yes, ma'am. Right after we stop at the sheriff's office again to let him know that we're still alive and what happened with your father."

"So, the worst is over now?"

"I think so. It'll take a while for you to adjust to a different life after living all those years on the ranch, but I'm sure that you'll be much happier with your newfound freedom."

"And I still have his money. I thought he'd really scream about that, but he almost didn't mention it. Then he paid you, too."

"I know. That surprised me. Not the payment, but the lack of questioning about either the money or Toby Halvorsen's whereabouts. I expected a real grilling about why I didn't chase him down to recover the money. He already paid me for my minimum billing, so it wouldn't have cost him much to send me after him to recover the money. It's almost as if he knows that Toby doesn't have it."

"That's what I thought when I was able to pay attention. I was too disoriented most of the time."

"You did seem frightened out of your wits, Sissie, but you're better now."

"I am. And thank you for getting me out of there."

"You're welcome, Miss Miller."

Ruth smiled at him from across the way before Nate gave another check of their backtrail and saw an empty road for two miles. He really wasn't expecting Fred Miller to do anything and wished he hadn't mentioned that he was leaving town to do another job. It was information he didn't need to give him, and it was another mistake that was just as bad as not waiting for Stubby's answer.

———

After telling the sheriff about the meeting, Nate took Ruth to the Richmond Restaurant for a prime rib dinner. They were able to relax and have a pleasant conversation as they enjoyed the well-prepared meal and as they left the restaurant, Nate began to feel too comfortable around Ruth again and had to check that slide into a close relationship.

Before they headed to his office, Nate said, "I need to make one more stop and you're welcome to come along as it involves your father."

"Okay," she replied, "What is it?"

Nate pointed and said, "J. Hare, Firearms and Gunsmithing."

Ruth looked at him curiously before she understood what he would be asking.

They dismounted and entered the small shop that was filled with the odors of cleaning fluid, oil and gunpowder.

The gunsmith saw Nate enter and grinned as he approached the counter, "Finally getting a new Winchester, Nate?"

"Maybe. But while I'm here, I need to pick up a double-barreled twelve gauge and two boxes of buckshot and one of birdshot."

"Sure thing. I'm kind of surprised that you don't have one yet," he said as he reached behind him and lifted a shotgun from a nearby rack and set it on the counter before placing the three boxes of shells next to the scattergun.

"Jerry, have you ever sold a Sharps in the rifle barrel length with a Malcolm scope?"

"You want a scoped Sharps?"

"No, I have one back at the office. I got it from Stubby Nicks."

"Stubby? When did he get a Sharps with a scope? I only sold one in the past year and that one was to Amos Baker out at the Lone Wolf."

Nate said, "I guess Stubby bought it from him. Anyway, I keep getting advertisements from Winchester about their new models. Do you really see any advantage over my '73?"

"It depends on what you're using it for. The only advantage you'd get with the '76 is the greater power and range of the bigger cartridges. It doesn't have nearly the range or accuracy as that Sharps does but having a repeater that uses a rifle round rather than the .44 pistol round that your '73 uses might be worthwhile in your line of work."

"Okay, Jerry, you've sold me. What barrel lengths do you have?"

"I've got three in carbines, no rifles and one musket. The carbines are chambered for the .45-75 Express cartridge and the musket uses the .50-95 Express. That's the most powerful a round that Winchester makes right now."

Nate looked at the display as he said, "Let me have the musket and three boxes of the cartridges if you have them."

"I do, and I appreciate you taking them off my hands. I'll even toss in an extra box because I'm not selling them to anyone else anyway."

When he placed the new Winchester on the counter, Nate said, "Lord, that's a long barrel. It's got to be eight inches longer than my '73."

"Try ten inches. You have the carbine version, like most of them are. This one is going to be a bit awkward to pull quickly out of the scabbard, but it'll be worth the extra range, accuracy and power you'll get with the long barrel."

"If you say so. How's the balance?"

"It'll take some getting used to, especially when the magazine tube is full of those big cartridges. Do you want to load it and check out the balance now before you pay for it?"

"I think that's a good idea. Is it cleaned and ready to load?"

"That's an insult, Nate. Of course, it is."

Nate grinned and picked up the musket and felt its balance without any ammunition and thought it wasn't that much different from his '73. He began slipping the long 50-95 Express cartridges into the loading gate until the magazine tube was full and then tried sighting it and noticed the change. It was still manageable, but it wasn't nearly as quick to get sighted as the '73, but that wasn't its purpose anyway. He wouldn't replace his carbine, but it might be a good weapon to have with him.

He set the loaded Winchester on the counter then said, "I'll take it, Jerry. Let's add up the damage and then put everything into a sturdy bag that I can hang from my saddle horn."

————

After they had mounted and Nate had turned them away from the gun shop, Ruth asked, "Did you really go there to buy guns?"

"I told you I'd buy a shotgun, but the Winchester was a spur of the moment thing. I don't know if it's really necessary, but it doesn't hurt to have one and your father paid for it anyway."

Ruth smiled as they rode down Main Street then turned onto Kansas Street and rode behind #207 to the small barn in back.

After he dismounted, Nate took down Ruth's two loaded travel bags and said, "I'll take these inside for you and then I'll move the rest in after I unsaddle the horses."

"Thank you, sir," Ruth replied before they headed for the back door.

She opened the door and let Nate enter then walked in behind him, closed the door and stayed in the kitchen while he carried her bags into to her room.

Ike hopped to his feet and trotted down the hallway to find out what had happened and almost bumped into Nate as he exited the bedroom.

"Oops! Sorry, Nate," Ike said as he skidded to a stop.

"That's okay, Ike. I heard you coming."

"So, what happened?"

"Follow me out to the barn to help with the horses and I'll fill you in."

"Yes, sir!" Ike exclaimed as he and Nate passed through the kitchen.

Ruth almost went with them but headed to the table and took a seat then glanced down the hallway wondering where Mary was.

Mary had been tidying up the office when she heard them enter and continued to work as she felt that Ruth would be more pleased if she wasn't there. She was sure that Miss Miller was either smitten with Nate or viewed him as her savior and hero. She could understand both conditions, but that

167

would create tension as long as the three of them shared the house. Luckily, Nate would be leaving in the morning and she'd be gone as well. She wondered how Ruth would do on her own, even with the large amount of cash that she had sitting under Ike's desk.

Nate and Ike were unsaddling the horses after Nate removed the heavy bag with the two new guns and ammunition, which Ike didn't even ask about after seeing the two stocks.

Ike was unsaddling Ruth's horse much more slowly as he listened to Nate explain the meeting with Fred Miller.

When Nate began brushing down the brown gelding, Ike asked, "Why do you think that he didn't even ask about the money?"

"That's one of the big questions; isn't it? I just couldn't get a read on the man. If I wasn't convinced that he'd paid Stubby to kill me and at least Toby Halvorsen, I would have believed that he was just a caring father who was happy to see that his precious daughter had been rescued. He didn't even balk at my bill. The only time that I had a glimpse of the real Fred Miller was when he began chastising Ruth, but even then, it wasn't nearly the way she'd described him to me."

Ike finally began brushing Ruth's horse as he asked, "Do you think he's going to do anything?"

"I'm not sure. I just can't believe he'd buy what I told him. I may have a suspicious mind, as you point out to me regularly, but I know his is much worse. I'm sure he is aware that I know about Stubby because I told him that I'd been followed but lost the guy. He asked me if I recognized him and I told him I thought he was Stubby. But even then, he didn't give away anything. The man is the ultimate poker player."

"What are you going to do?"

"I'm heading to Rawlins tomorrow and see if I can help Mrs. Swarthmore with her problem, just as I planned. Ruth will probably be safe while I'm gone, and you'll be here during the days."

"Is Mary going to be staying here at night?"

"Only tonight to act as a chaperone. I can almost feel the ice between them, and it's all coming from Ruth. I think she's jealous that I invited Mary to stay while she's here."

"I can understand that, boss. They're both pretty young ladies and you're an unmarried man who's stuck in the middle."

Nate stopped brushing the gelding and held the brush against his hip as he looked at Ike and said, "I'm kind of glad that I'm leaving, but I wonder if you could do something while I'm gone that doesn't exactly fit in with your normal duties?"

Ike's eyelids narrowed as he asked, "Just how much out of line is it from my normal work?"

"Well, suffice it to say that it's something that Alice would be more inclined to do and has been doing it almost since I met her."

Ike scratched his ear and asked, "You want me to fix you up with Mary?"

"No, Ike. I want you to ask Deputy Caruthers to stop by sometime in the next day or two. Just tell him that while I'm gone and you're out of the office, Ruth needs to have someone watch over her."

"Are you doing some kind of matchmaking, Nate?" he asked with a grin.

"If I'm lucky. He's one of the few bachelors I know who I can trust, and I do want someone to give her some measure of security. I'll tell her when I get back into the house that I'm going to have one of the deputies stop by for that reason."

Ike chuckled before saying, "I never thought I'd see the day you'd do something like this."

Nate tossed the brush into its box and picked up his heavy sack then he and Ike headed back to the house.

When they entered, Nate lowered the bag to the floor and wasn't surprised to find that only Ruth was in the kitchen.

He hung his hat on the hook near the door as Ike walked down the hall to the office.

"All done?" Ruth asked as he walked to the table.

"Yes, ma'am. Now I've got to start getting ready for tomorrow's train ride to Rawlins."

"Oh."

He sat down across from her and said, "I was talking to Ike about the trip and the conversation with your father and I wanted to feel a bit better after I was gone, so I asked him to have one of the deputies stop by. Ike will ask him to watch over you while I'm gone. It's just overkill, but I'd sleep better."

Ruth then threw him off balance when she asked, "Why don't I come with you? You said it wasn't going to be a dangerous job."

Nate was disconcerted by the unexpected question and had to pause for almost twenty seconds before replying, "I said I didn't think it was going to be a dangerous job, but if you remember just before we were leaving the sheriff's office, even he said one can never tell what would happen when getting in the way of someone's scheme. It won't be a problem if the man's claim is genuine, but if he's trying to defraud Mrs. Swarthmore, then things can get dicey very quickly."

Although Ruth's hopes were dashed, she understood Nate's concerns and replied, "That's okay. I understand. Will I meet the deputy, so I know what he looks like?"

"I'm sure you will, but that will be after I'm gone. Besides, you already met Deputy Caruthers in the office when we met the sheriff. Can you put on some coffee while I go tell Ike that you'll be expecting to meet the deputy?"

"Alright."

Nate smiled before he stood and headed for the office feeling a bit like a phony, although he was honest about the reason that she couldn't accompany him on the job...or at least one of the reasons. It was the underlying wish that she'd meet some young man who would sweep her off her feet that made him feel dishonest. At least it appeared that Bill Caruthers was impressed with Ruth.

He entered the office and was almost startled to see Mary White because she was so quiet and hadn't come out to the kitchen when he returned.

Nate continued to Ike's desk and quietly said, "I told her about Deputy Caruthers stopping by, so she won't be surprised."

"Did you promote his attributes at all?" Ike asked with an impish grin.

"No, Ike. I felt bad enough even thinking about it."

172

"Why did you think about it, Nate? I thought you liked Ruth."

Nate was about to reply when he felt Mary's presence, so he just turned and walked to his desk where he took a seat to reread Agatha Swarthmore's letter to see if he could glean any more details about the situation.

Mary had heard the conversation, despite Nate's use of his conspiratorial low voice and had even more questions than Ike had. Mary knew that Ruth was well beyond the liking stage with Nate, and that was a dangerous situation. Her real concern was just the opposite of Ike's. She was worried that Nate may actually be considering Ruth Miller as a love interest, but his hushed conversation with Ike had dispelled that possibility.

She took three steps and sat down in the chair beside Nate's desk as he read the letter but didn't say anything as she just watched.

Nate soon began to find it difficult to concentrate with Mary sitting so closely and could almost feel her eyes boring into him, so he set the letter down and looked into those blue eyes.

"The office and house are almost clean enough to eat off the floor. I imagine that you're already bored."

"I'm not bored, but I was going to ask if you needed anything else done."

"I'll be packing soon for tomorrow's trip, but I can't think of anything else that's left to do."

"Ike said you bought more guns, yet you said that this job wasn't going to be dangerous. Why did you need more weapons?"

Nate was relieved that the topic was more innocuous than he'd expected. Ever since Mary had deducted Ruth's jealousy, he was worried that somehow, she'd see it as a challenge, even though she'd shown nothing but consideration towards him.

"I still don't think the next job will call for any gunfights, but when I found Miss Miller and had to leave to chase down Toby Halvorsen, I left her defenseless. She couldn't fire a pistol or Winchester, but if I had a shotgun, I could have left that with her. So, I decided to have one and bring it with me in case of any similar circumstances."

"Is that likely? Do you make it a habit of rescuing pretty young women?" she asked with a slight smile.

Nate quietly laughed before replying, "No, ma'am. She was the first and only young woman that I've removed from a bad situation but having the shotgun will be handy."

"When will you be leaving in the morning?"

"The westbound train departs at 9:40, so I'll have to leave here around eight o'clock."

"Do you think you'll be able to help the widow?"

"Honestly? If the sheriff and her own lawyer say that the man has solid documentation, then it will be difficult. I'll do some investigation when I get there and hope that I'll be allowed to question the man, although that may be difficult because Mrs. Swarthmore said that he had his own attorney. She's in a bad situation, Mary. If he's really her brother-in-law, she could eventually lose the ranch that she and her husband built up from nothing even though the brother had nothing to do with it at all."

"That's not right. I hope that you can find a way to prove that he's not the brother and he gets sent to jail."

"So, do I."

Mary was about to ask a more personal question when she heard Ruth's footsteps coming down the hallway and looked up as she entered the office and the two women shared a brief look. Mary could sense the hostility in Ruth's eyes and knew it would be a long night, but at least most of it would be spent in slumber and Nate would be gone soon after breakfast, as would she.

Ruth looked at Nate, smiled and said, "The coffee's ready, Nate."

Nate smiled back, then stood and after setting the letter back in the box on the desk, turned to walk to the kitchen when Ruth took his arm before they walked down the hall.

Mary walked behind them and had to keep from giggling.

Once in the kitchen, Nate walked to the cookstove to get the coffee and noticed that only two mugs had been set on the table, so he grabbed a towel to pick up the hot coffeepot, took down another mug, then filled it before carrying the steaming mug and the coffeepot to the table where he filled the other two and set the third mug down.

Mary sat down in front of the third mug while Ruth sat down across the table from her and grasped her mug with both hands. Nate set the coffeepot down, then hung the towel back on the hook before taking a seat between the two women.

After thirty seconds of icy silence, Nate said, "I was reviewing Mrs. Swarthmore's letter and it sounds like a lost cause, but I find it hard to believe that the man is who he claims to be. He supposedly survived the war and doesn't contact his brother for almost twenty years, then just months after Mister Swarthmore succumbs to pneumonia, he suddenly shows up. I understand that unusual coincidences happen all the time, but not in this case. What do you think, Sissie?"

Ruth hadn't been paying much attention as she was focused on Mary's presence, so when he asked, she blinked and looked at him before replying, "Oh. Um, I'm not sure. It sounds strange."

Mary then said, "Ike told me about it and let me read the letter. I hope you don't mind."

176

"Not at all. What do you think?"

"I'd be suspicious of the foreman who she fired. I know that he's not the missing brother, but maybe he had friends or family that he could set up to be the undead brother."

Nate nodded and said, "I was thinking along those lines, so I'll have to ask where the foreman went after he quit. She may not know, but some of the ranch hands might. The problem is that whoever the man is, he couldn't be anyone local, or even within a hundred miles around the town because he'd risk being identified."

"I hope that he doesn't get away with it, unless he really is the missing brother. That would be a disaster for Mrs. Swarthmore; wouldn't it?"

"It would be. She wouldn't be destitute, but she'd probably suffer enormous loss. If he wins his case, then he'd get half of the value of the ranch. I'd estimate the Double 8, including the cattle, is worth almost a hundred and fifty thousand dollars. But if he demanded the cash, she'd have to sell most of the herd to pay him off, and then she'd be stuck with her enormous ranch and not enough cattle to support the staff. She'd have to fire most of the ranch hands and after the man left town, she'd be land rich but cash poor. She would probably be devastated by the loss. I imagine that she's very attached to the property because it's the child that she and her husband never had. It was all that they created together, and it would be a wound that she'd never be able to heal."

Mary looked at the pain in Nate's eyes just from discussing the possible agony losing the case would cause to a woman he'd never met and wasn't surprised by his compassion.

Nate then smiled and after he took a sip of his coffee, he said, "Well, I just hope I can nail this bastard. It'll be very satisfying."

Ruth then asked, "Do you know Mrs. Swarthmore at all?"

"I've never met her or even been to Rawlins. I've heard of the Double 8 because it's almost as big as your father's ranch."

"How old do you think she is?"

"I have no idea. She was married to her husband for sixteen years, so she could be anywhere from thirty to sixty, depending on how old she was when she was married, but she doesn't have any heirs. She may have been a war widow when she married him. It'll be an interesting story, and not just because of the mysterious brother."

Mary then said, "I noticed that there are two stocks sticking out of that bag. One is the shotgun, so what is the second one?"

"Just another newer model Winchester. I figured I may as well have a backup."

"For a man who isn't expecting any trouble, you are certainly preparing for a war."

"It's always better to have too much firepower than not enough, Miss White."

"From what Alice tells me, you try to avoid gunfights if the other man pulls his pistol, so why would you need more firepower?"

Nate laughed then shook his head before replying, "You've got me, Mary. I just bought the new Winchester because I wanted it."

"I thought so," Mary said with a smile.

Ruth watched the easy banter between them and felt a surge of jealousy boil within her. She'd spent two nights alone with Nate Manning and she knew that it was only his noble character and concern for her recent soreness that prevented him from joining her in her bed. Now he was paying attention to the blonde woman and she didn't like it. *Was he ignoring her now because she'd been spoiled and might be pregnant because of it?*

Nate quickly finished his coffee then stood and after setting the mug in the sink, said, "I need to start preparing for tomorrow, so I'll take all that new firepower into my room and start packing."

Ruth looked up at him and asked, "Do you want me to cook supper after that big meal we shared?"

"No, I'll just snack later," he answered before picking up the heavy bag and heading to his room to start his preparations and feeling as if he was escaping from a collapsing cave.

He closed the door after he entered and after setting the heavy bag in the corner, sat down on the bed and took a deep breath before standing again and walking to his closet where he pulled out his extra set of saddlebags. He'd store his spare clothes and other personal supplies in this set and keep the ammunition and other hardware in the ones in the barn. He wouldn't be bringing any food with him, but he might wrap up a couple of sour pickles to enjoy on the four-hour trail ride to Rawlins. He hadn't had one since he left to find Ruth Miller and figured he'd grab one after he finished packing.

Ike had gone home, and the sun was low in the sky when he carried the new Winchester and his saddlebags out to the empty kitchen. Apparently, both women had adjourned to their bedrooms just after he'd gone.

He set the saddlebags near the door and leaned the Winchester alongside before putting the one box of ammunition for the new musket on the floor near the brass-covered butt.

He entered the cold room to get his pickles when he heard a door open and close and footsteps in the hall, so he assumed that Ruth was on her way. If it had been Mary who'd left her room, then he expected that Ruth's door would open soon afterward.

After taking three of the big pickles from a jar and putting the top back on, he exited the cold room and smiled at Ruth as she was about to sit down.

"Pickles?" she asked as she smiled in return.

"Yes, ma'am. I have a sour tooth that needs to be satisfied. I'll munch on one and wrap the other two to keep with me. I use waxed paper and then another layer of butcher paper to keep the moisture in."

As he took a big bite and walked to the table, she asked, "Are you going to send a telegram to Mrs. Swarthmore letting her know that you're coming?"

He sat down and replied, "Nope. I posted the letter earlier today and I doubt if she'll get it before I arrive. I'd rather that no one else knows I'm coming, so I'll be able to ask some questions in town before I head out to the ranch."

She glanced at the hallway, then leaned forward and said quietly, "I found out earlier that I'm not pregnant. I was so relieved!"

Nate smiled and replied, "That is good news. I don't suppose it will make any difference to your father though; will it?"

"Not at all. I'm just happy to know that Toby didn't ruin my life any more than he had."

"So, am I, Sissie. You deserve to have a happy life after having lived with that family all your life."

Ruth smiled, but hoped that she was right about her condition as her monthly wouldn't arrive for another week. She just didn't want that problem to drive him away before they had the chance to spend more time together.

Nate took another big bite of his pickle and his eyes began to water, making Ruth laugh.

"Why do you eat those things if they do that to you?" she asked.

"Because I like them, ma'am. Other men like their whiskey, or cigars like your father does, but I like sour pickles. I like them so much that I'll even resort to drinking the leftover brine in the bottle when there aren't any more left."

"You're kidding! How much do you drink?"

"Not much, but I will sip a good three or four tablespoons before my stomach objects."

"Doesn't it make you sick?"

"A lot less than those cowhands who imbibe the same number of glasses of rotgut whiskey. But I have had a few episodes where the sour pickles created an equally sour stomach that finally revolts to let me know that it wanted no more."

Ruth laughed again and reached across the table and placed her hand on his before she said, "I'll be here to make sure that you don't overdo it anymore."

Nate replied, "Thank you, ma'am," then after he popped the last of the pickle into his mouth, he slid his hand away then stood and walked to where the Winchester was leaning against the wall and picked it up.

He returned to the table, set the Winchester on the surface and sat down.

"All this talk about sour stomachs made me realize that I may need to feed my new gun's stomach. I wasn't sure if I filled the magazine tube and there's no sense in having a repeater if you don't have it fully loaded."

Nate knew that Jerry had filled the magazine but began levering out the cartridges and making a show of counting them as they were ejected onto the tabletop. When the last one popped out, he set the musket back down and began setting the .50-95s on the table in line.

"Those are bigger bullets than your other ones," Ruth said as she stared at the lineup.

"They're real rifle rounds while the ones for my older Winchester are really designed for pistols. But these are still smaller than the ones that I took from Stubby Nicks for that scoped Sharps that's in my bedroom."

"Really? Are you taking it with you, too?"

"No, ma'am. I'll take the two Winchesters and my pistol but leave the shotgun and Sharps here."

Nate began reloading the repeater as Ruth just watched as she'd exhausted her pretended interest in the gun.

After he'd returned the Winchester to the same configuration it had been when he'd used it as an excuse to leave the table, he carried it back to where it had been before regaining his seat.

"It's getting late, Sissie, and I need to get a good night's sleep before leaving tomorrow. I want you to stay here as much as possible until I return. I don't think your father or anyone else will bother you, and you'll have Ike or one of the deputies nearby until I return. That should be in less than a week."

"Can you send me a telegram before you leave to let me know you're on your way?"

"I'll do that. I'm sure you and Ike will have a lot of questions when I walk through the door."

"Unless it's a Sunday and then only I will be here."

Nate nodded as he smiled before he rose and said, "Goodnight, Sissie."

Ruth remained seated as she looked up at him and replied, "Goodnight, Nate."

Nate turned and left the kitchen and soon entered his bedroom and closed the door. He didn't bother lighting a lamp but quickly stripped off his clothes and boots, then slid between the blankets.

He heard Ruth return to her room and heard her begin to disrobe. He wondered why Mary had remained in her room and guessed that she was reading.

But as he listened and stared into the dark, he wondered what was wrong with him. He was in his own house and had a good-looking young woman in each of the adjoining bedrooms and here he was sleeping alone because he wanted it that way. He was sure that even with Mary next door, if he'd given Ruth even the tiniest suggestion that she join him, she wouldn't have hesitated.

Even as he asked himself that question, he knew the answer and it wasn't because he wasn't fond of Ruth or impressed with her or Mary White. If anything, the fact that he was fond of her was the reason that he was alone in his bed. And with Mary White making her own inroads into his inner kingdom, he began to feel that the only solution to his self-imprisonment would be to move on. It wasn't only the new sheriff that had made him leave Hays City. The more time he spent with Sheriff Galloway and almost felt as if he had a real family, the more enamored he'd become with his younger daughter, Millie. She had no reservations in letting him know of her feelings for him, and despite his constant adding bricks to his internal walls of protection, he felt himself sliding ever closer to having genuine feelings for her. When the boss announced his retirement, he'd used that as an excuse for not spending so much time at the Galloway home, but that excuse didn't last long. If the new sheriff had been a good lawman, then he had no idea how he'd be able to honestly explain his decision to leave Hays City. It was by the grace of God that the new man was incompetent and arrogant at the same time.

Even leaving was difficult as Millie had asked him to stay several times but he never explained why he couldn't stay maybe because he didn't understand himself. But like a coward, he left after promising he'd write to her, but after one letter he'd sent from Cheyenne, he hadn't contacted her again. He hoped that she'd found someone else and still felt the guilt of a coward and traitor to the best friend he ever had and the man who changed his volatile, angry life into a productive, calmer one. That letter was also the last time he'd ever used the name Ned Boyd.

Now he was in even a worse situation but there was one big difference. Here he had his own business and his own home. He was well-regarded by most of the townsfolk and the law. It had taken him a long time to build that level of respect, and it would all be gone if he left. *If he left, where would he go?* He couldn't go back to Kansas or even Cheyenne. He'd probably have to leave Wyoming altogether and maybe go to Denver.

He was still pondering the question when he heard Ruth climb into her bed and thought he heard her sobbing but wasn't sure. If he felt like a heel before, he felt like the entire boot now.

Nate had to shift his focus away from his past and present life, so he tried to concentrate on what awaited him at Rawlins and the Double 8 ranch. He was able to examine the problem for another twenty minutes before he finally drifted off to sleep.

CHAPTER 6

Nate thought that he'd be the first one up the next morning because he'd set his pocket watch's alarm for five o'clock, but when he awakened and slid out from under the blankets, he heard the light clang of iron on the cookstove and quickly dressed. He suspected that Ruth might have awakened earlier to press her case for coming along again.

When he quickly walked out of his bedroom, he was surprised to see Mary at the cookstove, and she turned and smiled at him.

"I'm a midwife and a nurse. I'm used to getting up early."

"I should have guessed that," Nate said as he hurried past to make it to the privy.

He stepped out into the cool air of the predawn and after his brief visit to the little house, he walked to the barn to begin saddling the brown gelding. He had the horse saddled, his '73 in its scabbard and the first set of saddlebags tied down after just fifteen minutes then attached a second scabbard for the new Winchester before heading to the house.

He quietly entered in case Ruth was still sleeping and was somewhat relieved when he entered to find that she wasn't up yet.

"I'll be back in a few minutes," Nate said as he softly stepped to the washroom.

He was able to wash and shave without disturbing Ruth then made another stealthy walk in the other direction. Having Ruth in the front bedroom was an advantage.

As soon as he reached the kitchen, he began setting the table with three plates and mugs in case Ruth suddenly arrived. As he laid the knives and forks nearby, he noticed that he wasn't worried about having Mary just a couple of feet away but was concerned about Ruth who was still in bed. He guessed that it was because Ruth was interested, and Mary was just doing a job.

After he sat down, Mary set the plates of scrambled eggs and sausage on the table before filling two of the mugs with coffee and sitting down opposite Nate.

"Are you all ready to go?" she asked before adding some salt to her eggs.

"Almost. I just need to take my second set of saddlebags and strap on my Colt. Don't let me leave the house without my pistol. Please."

Mary laughed softly then asked, "You haven't really done that before; have you?"

"I left the house once without it but had to turn the horse around and return to pick it up. I don't know why I just don't buy a second one and keep it in my saddlebags."

"Then you'd probably forget the horse."

Nate stifled a loud laugh and managed to keep it to a series of snorts before exchanging her salt for his pepper.

Nate finished salting his eggs and after taking a bite, he asked, "Where will you be going after you leave this morning?"

"I'll go and see Alice and after that, I have a cleaning job at the Butlers."

"Maurice and Jeanette Butler's house?"

"Yes. I guess he has enough money that he can afford to let his wife avoid such chores."

"That is an understatement, Mary. Just watch out for Maurice. He's got a reputation as a womanizer. He's probably paying you to clean the house as a bribe to keep his wife from divorcing him."

"I made that deduction about him the first time I was there. He made a fairly blatant suggestion about how I could make ten dollars each visit."

"Yet you still go there?"

"It's a job, Nate. You should know that there aren't a lot of places where a woman can make money, even if she's a nurse and a midwife. I just make sure that Mrs. Butler is there while I am. I think she's of the same mindset."

"How difficult was it for you to become a midwife?"

"That wasn't really my choice. I was offered the position of a nurse's aide which got me out of a bad situation, then I became a nurse and being a midwife was just part of my job."

"It must be a joy to bring new life into the world, but I imagine it can be devastating when something goes wrong."

She nodded and replied, "I lost one mother after she delivered a stillborn little girl, then I lost another mother, but her boy survived. It is very disturbing and after the first one where I lost both mother and child, I wasn't sure that I could continue to be a midwife. But Doctor Wilkens, who first started me on the path, explained to me that losing patients was just part of the job, but to concentrate on all of the successes."

Nate quietly asked, "Is that why you've never married? Is it because you don't want to have a baby and take that same risk?"

Mary quickly shook her head and answered, "No, not at all. I very much want to marry and have children, but I have my own reasons for waiting."

191

Nate was about to ask if she would tell him the reasons, but Ruth's bedroom door opened and she quickly walked toward the kitchen, ending the personal conversation.

After she passed with a smile for Nate and headed out the door, Nate said, "You are an interesting person, Mary White."

"I noticed that you consider me an interesting person and not an interesting woman, Nate Manning."

"All women are persons, Miss White, but not all persons are women. Forgive my use of the more inclusive noun."

Mary laughed before saying, "You're also a very interesting person, Mister Manning. Ike told me about your family in Iowa. One of these days, you'll have to tell me more about your childhood. Maybe that's what made you so interesting."

"How about your family, Mary? Were they interesting?"

"No, not at all," she replied just as Ruth reentered the kitchen.

Once she joined them for breakfast, the conversation shifted to talk about his mission in Rawlins which was fine with Nate.

By the time breakfast was over, he had to finish his preparations before Ike arrived and he was able to talk with him for a little while.

———

Nate waved to Ruth who was standing on the back porch as he rode away from the house. Mary had already gone to the Butlers and Ike had told him that he'd talked to Deputy Caruthers and he'd be stopping by in a couple of hours. Nate still felt guilty about setting it up, but he hoped that when he returned, Ruth would happily tell him that the deputy had asked to visit her.

As he rode to the train station, he scanned the traffic to see if anyone from the Lone Wolf ranch was hanging around, but didn't see any of them, nor did he see Stubby Nicks, so he assumed he'd gone. He should have asked Sheriff Scott to check on it, but it was too late now.

He checked the gelding into the stock corral and after getting his ticket and horse tag, he sat on the bench and waited for the westbound train.

Now that he was almost on his way, he was able to push the immediate issue with Ruth Miller out of his mind and focus all of his attention on the problems facing Agatha Swarthmore. He'd explained the case so often now that he didn't think that he'd missed anything. But then again, he'd forgotten to wait for Stubby Nicks' answer and now he'd forgotten to ask the sheriff about his wayward fellow bounty hunter. Maybe he was getting forgetful in his old age. He wasn't sure how old he really was, but guessed he was around twenty-four. Luckily, no one had ever asked for paperwork to confirm his birthdate. He'd chosen February 7 for the obvious reason as it would be written as 0207, the number he'd carried instead of a name for more than half of his life.

By 9:55, he was seated in the passenger car of the train as it barreled along the tracks toward Rawlins. There weren't a lot of stops along the way, just enough to fill up the locomotive's water tanks and sometimes top off its supply of coal.

―――――

The train pulled into the Rawlins station in early afternoon, and Nate was mounted and riding into town twenty minutes after it stopped. He rode to the closest eatery and pulled up before Phil's Diner and dismounted.

He didn't need to ask directions to the big ranch as he knew it was north of town and the only road headed that way was much like the one leaving Laramie for Fred Miller's massive ranch. He was planning on asking some of the locals about the situation, but even as he was finishing his lunch of a thick beefsteak and enormous baked potato, he decided that he'd probably just be wasting time that could be better spent talking to Agatha Swarthmore. He hoped it wasn't another mistake, but as soon as he finished, he dropped four bits on the table, pulled on his hat and left the diner.

Nate took one of the side streets to the north end of town where he spotted the roadway that disappeared into the horizon and headed that way.

After he turned onto the road, he picked up traffic going in the same direction about a mile ahead and soon identified that the traffic was a buggy and that meant it was either one of the legal eagles or the brother himself, so he picked up the pace to close the gap. Maybe he could talk to the lawyer or even the mystery man if he could get close enough to get his attention.

As it turned out, he was wrong on both counts. He'd cut the gap to just two hundred yards when the buggy stopped, and he saw a woman's head appear on the right side. He assumed he was looking at Agatha Swarthmore and hoped she hadn't returned from signing anything but doubted it, or she wouldn't have sent the request for him to investigate the stranger.

He slowed his gelding and soon reached the buggy then tipped his hat as he said, "Mrs. Swarthmore?"

"Yes. Are you Nate Manning?"

"Yes, ma'am."

"You responded quickly."

"I had just finished a job and found your request intriguing. I hope that you haven't agreed to anything yet."

"I haven't, but I'm getting pressure from all sides to do just that. Can you ride with me to the ranch house, so we can talk along the way?"

"Yes, ma'am," Nate replied before dismounting and lashing the gelding's reins to the back of her buggy.

After he'd clambered into the buggy, he had his first close look at Mrs. Swarthmore and estimated her age to be in the mid-thirties. She was still a handsome woman and he could already see the determination in her eyes.

"Why did you ask me to investigate the claim, Mrs. Swarthmore?"

"We don't have any detectives in town, and I heard about you from some of my ranch hands who'd visited Laramie. You have a good reputation, Mister Manning."

"Thank you, ma'am."

She snapped the reins and the horse began to move again before she said, "I just left my attorney's office. His name is Horace Woolford. We'd offered the man ten thousand dollars to renounce his claim on the ranch, but his lawyer rejected the offer and they're still negotiating."

"That's a lot of money to turn down."

"I thought so, but even that amount would require me to take out a mortgage on the ranch and then sell more cattle than normal to pay it off. Even though giving that scoundrel a penny really angers me, my lawyer and the sheriff both tell me that he has impeccable proof that he is my brother-in-law."

"Did you get to see this proof?"

"Yes, I saw it. He had a clear birth certificate, but his army records were in bad condition because he'd kept them with him so long."

"About that, Mrs. Swarthmore. Can you explain how you discovered he died during the war? Did you receive a telegram from the War Department?"

"No. I wasn't married to Leo until he returned from the war. He and his brother had a nice farm in Minnesota before the war and they joined up on the same day. I was just fourteen when they marched off and Leo promised to marry me when he returned. He returned in '65 and we were married, but he didn't know what happened to Finney for two more years. He knew that his brother had been captured at the battle of Fredericksburg but had heard nothing after that.

"Leo finally assumed that his brother had died in that horrible prison camp at Andersonville where he'd been taken because he would have returned or at least written to him. He didn't want to stay on the farm any longer, so he sold it and we took the train west in '72. We stopped here because he liked the land and its remote location.

"We built this ranch, Mister Manning. We suffered hardships and the loss of our three children, but the ranch thrived and now it's one of the largest in the territory. When Leo passed on in December, I was very distraught, as you can imagine. I had no more family to comfort me and I almost thought about selling the ranch rather than see the constant reminders of my loss. But then I almost heard Leo telling me that even though we had no children, this ranch was our dream and our creation. I can't sell it Mister Manning. If I have to lose all of the cattle, I won't leave. Do you have any children?"

"No, ma'am. I'm not married."

"That has little to do with fathering children, but if you did have children, you'd know how I feel about my ranch."

"That's what I expected you to say after reading your letter, ma'am. I'm not sure that I'll be able to help, but I'll do whatever I can to investigate this man's past to find a hole. When he arrived, how did he explain his absence?"

Agatha sighed then said, "Everything was coming back to normal after I fired the foreman because he wanted to run the place. He even suggested that I marry him, which really frosted me. I never liked the man, but Leo could handle him. Then out of the blue in early April, I had a visit from an attorney, a Mister James Chilton. He has an office in Cheyenne. Do you know him?"

"No, ma'am. I avoid lawyers if possible."

"As have I until Mister Chilton arrived with the man's claim."

"You have met him, though; haven't you?"

"Only in the presence of his attorney. He hasn't even come out to the Double 8."

"As an aside, can you tell me how you came up with the name?"

"I play the piano, and it was my husband's idea. It makes for a nice brand that's difficult to overbrand."

"Now back to your mystery brother-in-law. What was the story that he gave you for the missing years and then suddenly finding out about your husband's death?"

Agatha kept her eyes on the road as the buggy rocked along and replied, "He said that after he was finally freed from the prison camp, he spent almost two years in an army hospital recovering and when he finally returned to Minnesota, he found that we'd already gone and no one was sure where we were."

"Why didn't he write to you while he was recovering? Even if he was incapable of writing, he could dictate a letter to let you know he was alive."

"I asked him that and he said that he did send letters, but we never answered."

"After he found that you'd gone, where did he go?"

"He said he searched for us for a while before leaving Minnesota and heading west because someone had told him that we were planning on moving there. He said he thought we'd be farming again, so he headed down to Kansas and then spent years there, traveling from one town to the other asking questions. Then he said he finally gave up hope and settled in Hays City where he was living when Leo died."

"*Hays City?*" Nate asked sharply.

"Yes. Why does that seem to interest you?"

"I was an Ellis County deputy sheriff for more than a year in Hays City."

"Then maybe you've seen him there!" she exclaimed.

"It wasn't a big town, so if he was there for any length of time, then I'm sure I did. But if he just invented that story, he could come up with some reason why I might not have seen him before if I get a chance to ask him."

"I don't think that his attorney will even let you meet him. My lawyer told him that I'd sent a letter asking you to do an investigation and Mister Chilton made it clear in no uncertain terms that you would not be getting any information from him because he considered it an insult to his integrity."

Nate snickered then said, "I'm sure that's the reason why. But very few people know that I was in Hays City, so I'd like to keep it that way. What I'd like to do is get a look at the man without calling attention to myself. Do you know where he is staying?"

"They're both staying at The Rawlins House. It's a boarding house on the main street."

"Can you describe him?"

"He's an average-sized man with brown hair and is clean-shaven. The only unusual physical feature about him is that his face seems imbalanced."

"Imbalanced?"

"It's hard to describe, but it's not as if he's cross-eyed, but something doesn't seem right, and I can't pinpoint it. It would be easier to identify Mister Chilton, who wears his black hair slicked down and usually dresses in a dark suit and with a blue vest and a pocket watch and gold chain. They are never apart almost as if the lawyer is his bodyguard."

"Okay. Now about the foreman, whom you must believe is behind this scheme."

"I do."

"Do you know where he went after he left?"

"He said he was going to get a job on the Lone Wolf ranch out your way."

"Really? My last job was for Fred Miller, so maybe I've seen him."

Agatha turned to look at Nate and asked, "You did a job for him? Is he your kind of man?"

"I took the job to stop him from giving it to another man because of what I suspected he really needed done. I think he's a very dangerous man."

"So, do I. He's been a thorn in our sides for five years now."

"What has he done?" Nate asked hoping it was something illegal that would give him a chance to make life miserable for the arrogant man.

"Nothing serious, but he'll use his political friends to give him contracts that we should have gotten and even coerced the railroad to charge him less for shipping his cattle. If he wasn't so damned arrogant and aggressive, then we'd probably have twenty percent more cattle and a lot more cash in the bank."

"That sounds like things he'd do."

———

As they continued their buggy ride and conversation about the situation, back in Laramie, Deputy Sheriff Bill Caruthers arrived at Nate's office and dismounted.

When Ike had asked him to keep a watch over Ruth Miller and then suggested that he stop by to meet her, he was beyond simply being pleased. When he'd heard that she'd run off with Toby Halvorsen, he'd been more than just surprised. He had been ready to shoot the cowboy. It wasn't as if he believed that he had any real chance with the powerful rancher's daughter, but he, like many other men in town, had admired her from afar and thought that Halvorsen was unworthy of her. Now he would actually get a chance to not only talk to her but stay close for a few days and who knows what would come of it?

He tied off his horse and quickly strode to the front of the office, climbed the three steps and crossed the porch before entering.

Ike had seen him ride up and had to suppress a grin when he could see the obvious hope-filled haste in Deputy Caruthers' steps. He'd known Bill Caruthers since they'd been in school together and was only a year younger. He also knew that Bill had a soft spot for Ruth Miller, which wasn't unusual, so he hadn't mentioned it to Nate.

When Bill popped into the office, he spotted Ike smiling at him and pulled off his hat before saying, "Well, I'm here, Ike."

Ike didn't have to call Ruth as he heard her footsteps coming down the hallway and his smile grew even larger as he studied Bill's face rather than watching Ruth enter. Maybe Nate's little matchmaking scheme really would work.

After Bill's smile had expanded as large as physically possible, Ike stood and turned to Ruth before saying, "Miss

Miller, this is Deputy Sheriff Bill Caruthers. He'll be the one who will be keeping you safe while I'm out of the office and Nate is still out of town."

Ruth stepped close to the deputy and offered her hand as she said, "Thank you, Deputy. Please call me Ruth."

Bill shook her hand and almost stammered as he replied, "I'm pleased, pleased to meet you, Ruth. Call me Bill."

"Where will you be when Ike has gone for the day?" she asked.

"I thought I'd stay in the office until it's dark and then I'd just head back to my room at Mrs. Anderson's Boarding House. It's just on the corner of Kansas and Main Street. Is that alright?"

"That's fine. Personally, I think that Nate is just being overly cautious, but I do appreciate his concern. I'll cook supper for you as a sign of my appreciation for keeping an eye on me."

"I don't really need any rewards for it, Ruth. Just being able to talk to you and spend some time with you is more than enough."

Ruth smiled at him and said, "Well, I'll still cook supper. I have to eat myself anyway. So, I'll see you at five o'clock?"

"Yes, ma'am," Bill replied as he kneaded his hat's brim.

Ruth smiled once more before saying, "I'll see you then," then turned and walked back down the hallway and disappeared into her bedroom.

Ike grinned at Deputy Caruthers whose smile never left his face before he wordlessly turned and left the office.

As he mounted his horse and rode away, Ike was sure that Bill Caruthers thought he was on his way to visiting Miss Miller, but he wasn't sure that Ruth had seen him in that light. He'd get a better idea in the morning after they'd spent more time together.

————

Agatha Swarthmore's buggy rolled to a stop before her ranch house, which was large by most standards, it wasn't close to Fred Miller's enormous home, nor was it in any way ostentatious. Nate hadn't expected anything other than what he found after getting to know the widow better.

She stepped out and waited for one of the ranch hands to come and take the bridle of the buggy's horse as Nate walked to the back to untie his gelding.

"He'll take care of your horse, Nate," she said before he undid the knot.

"I appreciate having my horse unsaddled and cared for, but I plan on riding back to town in a little while, Agatha."

"You're welcome to stay the night, but I can understand that you'd prefer to begin your investigation."

"That's the plan, ma'am," Nate replied as the ranch hand led the buggy away.

He quickly got in step with Mrs. Swarthmore before they climbed the three steps to the porch and soon entered the house.

The more she'd told him about the entire episode, the more he was convinced that the man was a fraud. Proving it would be difficult unless he'd actually lived in Hays City, which could have been just another lie. Even if he did live there, he might not have been there in the year that Nate had been a deputy sheriff.

Aside from personal recognition, which was iffy at best, the only possible way to expose his ruse was to find a hole in his story that could be proven. Without being able to even meet the man, that possibility became distant if not impossible. He felt hamstrung by his inability to question any of the players on the opposite side of this drama, but he felt that he owed it to Mrs. Swarthmore even though he barely knew her. For some reason, he felt a kinship to the recent widow and didn't understand why.

She'd been happily married for sixteen years and built a very successful ranch. She seemed to share none of his empty background, yet he still felt as if he knew her well.

They took a seat in the parlor and her housekeeper and cook brought them coffee as they continued to talk about the brother and his attorney.

Agatha looked at Nate and said, "The man seemed to know all about Leo and his life since he had been a boy in Minnesota. It was a stronger proof than his birth certificate."

"I assume the foreman had been with you for a long time. Is that right?"

"Yes, for eight years. That's why he thought he'd be made ranch manager and thought I'd be willing to marry him and let him take charge of my life as well."

"Then he'd know all about Leo; wouldn't he?"

"Yes, I suppose he would."

"He had been gone long enough to thoroughly school this imposter in your husband's history. Did you try to trip him up with some details that the foreman wouldn't know?"

"Neither I nor my attorney were allowed to spend enough time questioning him and that was my fault. I was so angry and disgusted with the whole charade that I couldn't think straight, and I tended to insult him more than question him. My attorney spent most of the time trying to keep me under control. I'm a very spiteful woman, Nate."

Nate grinned, then after taking a sip of coffee, he said, "I don't think you are, Agatha. I can understand why you'd be angry, but I don't believe that it's even a small part of your personality."

"You haven't been around me long enough, Nate. Don't you ever get angry?"

"I was always angry at the world and everyone in it until I learned that it was self-defeating. I still carry a chip on my shoulder, but it's a lot smaller and I can keep it balanced."

"You'll have to explain how you did that when you have the time. I'm getting pressure from my lawyer to settle the case and after they rejected the ten-thousand-dollar offer, I'm sure that he'll expect me to settle for twenty thousand dollars. The way its headed right now, I'm not sure that they'd even accept that. I think they'll only be satisfied with half of the ranch."

"But they won't want the ranch itself; will they? They'll want the cash value of about seventy-five thousand dollars. Is that what you think?"

"Yes, and so does Horace. I know that there's no way that I can raise close to that amount, even by mortgaging the ranch. I'm sure you know that I can't sell that many cattle in one big move, especially in today's depressed market. I'd have to cut the price per head even more if I had to go that route. It would almost empty the ranch and it would be just as bad as if he decided to take control."

"I understand that, and whatever you do, even if they say that they'll accept twenty thousand, don't agree until I've had a few days to do some checking."

"I wouldn't have agreed anyway. I'd probably shoot the bastard first."

Nate grinned and replied, "If you're planning to do that, let me know and I'll take out the lawyer."

Agatha laughed and was immensely pleased that she'd sent that letter to Nate Manning, but still didn't believe that he'd find any way out of this dilemma.

Two hours later, after Agatha had insisted that he stay for supper, Nate was riding south on the empty road to Rawlins. He had enjoyed spending time with the widow and wondered why he had felt so comfortable with her. He knew she wasn't looking at him with any romantic interest, which would at least explain part of the reason for his relaxed conversations, but not all of it.

He tried to recall the last time he'd felt this way about anyone else and had to return to Hays City and the times he'd spent with Sheriff Galloway's family, at least before his daughter had shown interest in him. He suddenly realized that Agatha reminded him of the sheriff's wife and that cleared up the small mystery.

Even though it solved the question, it did present new questions about his current situation back in Laramie. He felt as if Ruth Miller was a threat to his privacy because he envisioned her almost as a twelve-point buck would look at a hunter pointing his rifle at him. He felt the urge to run and escape before feeling the impact of that bullet. He even considered leaving Laramie because of her growing affection. He knew it was irrational, but he understood why he felt that way.

He finally had to push away thoughts of what awaited him in Laramie when the first buildings of Rawlins rose over the southern horizon in the waning light.

He dropped off the gelding at the nearest livery to The Rawlins House and hung his traveling saddle bags over his shoulder and took his new Winchester with him as he walked to the boarding house where Mister Chilton and the imposter were staying.

After he entered the large house, he was met by the owner, a tall, thin man who introduced himself as Eric Lindstrom. After paying for three days, Nate was given a room on the second floor, but had missed dinner with the other guests, which wasn't unexpected because of the late hour.

He leaned his new musket against the wall near the bed before dropping his saddlebags on the floor and hanging his hat on the hook on the back of the door. Nate then ran his fingers through his light brown hair and took a seat on the bed rather than the hard, straight-backed chair.

He thought about going downstairs to the sitting room in the chance that he'd run into the lawyer and his client but was already too tired and wanted to see them when he had full possession of his faculties.

So, even though the sun was still above the horizon, he began to strip off his dusty clothes to get ready for bed.

————

In Laramie, Bill Caruthers left Nate's office after spending more than three hours with Ruth Miller. They had talked for a long time and she seemed very happy, so he believed that he'd made significant progress and hoped that tomorrow would only be better.

Ruth watched him leave and locked the front door before returning to the kitchen. She liked Bill Caruthers, but he wasn't close to the man that Nate was. What made it strange to her was that the deputy seemed to be interested in her as a woman while the man she really wanted didn't seem to see her that way at all. Maybe that was why he was so attractive to her. She still believed that it was his integrity and compassion that had kept him from joining her in her bed on Toby's ranch, but she began to have second thoughts about his real motives. Maybe he and Toby were somehow in this together and now he wanted to be rid of her because she might find out the truth. She'd ask him when he returned and see how he reacted.

After cleaning up, Ruth headed for her bedroom and then stopped and changed direction to go into Nate's bedroom. She had been tempted to inspect his room since she'd been alone in the house, but Ike or the deputy had been with her for most of that time. Now she was truly on her own and with the doors locked, no one could catch her snooping.

She began opening drawers and found nothing other than clothes before she moved to the closet. Again, she was disappointed because she discovered no personal items or memorabilia of his past. She walked to his gun cabinet and opened the one drawer beneath the racks but only found ammunition. She even looked under his bed but found nothing, not even dust bunnies. It was as if he had no previous life at all.

Ruth then left his bedroom and walked out to the office to rummage through his desk expecting to find some hint of his existence before he arrived in Laramie. She hoped to find a birth certificate or maybe even a marriage certificate from a deceased wife. She began imagining him weeping over his wife as she faded into death after childbirth even as she thumbed through papers and folders. But all she discovered were records of cases, business correspondence and some bills that clients had yet to pay.

She closed the last drawer in frustration and as she leaned back in Nate's chair, she lapsed into deep thought about the man she now loved. *What was his past? Was he some outlaw who was hiding under the guise of a detective and bounty hunter?* If he knew how outlaws thought and behaved because he'd been one, then maybe that was why he was so successful. Her nagging suspicions of his complicity in a plot with Toby were almost plausible if he was an outlaw.

Finally, she started laughing at the absurdity of the idea. *What outlaw would become friends with a lawman like Sheriff Scott?*

She rose and walked back to her bedroom and closed the door. After changing into her nightdress, she slipped beneath the quilts and hoped that Nate would be back soon.

CHAPTER 7

A fresh, clean Nate Manning left his room and trotted down the stairs to the first floor of The Rawlins House to have breakfast with the other residents hoping to meet Mister Chilton and his client.

He walked down the hallway to the dining room behind an older couple and after they entered, he paused at the threshold for just a moment to see if anyone else was at the table and was disappointed.

As he ate his breakfast, he paid little attention to what he was putting into his mouth as he focused on the doorway waiting for them to arrive, but they never showed.

Everyone else had already gone and he was alone in the room finishing his third cup of coffee before he accepted the fact that they weren't going to show up and wondered why they didn't. *Surely, they hadn't known he would be there, or did they somehow get word of his summons and almost instant arrival?* He swallowed the last bit of the cup's cold contents then left the dining room and returned to his room.

He buckled on his gunbelt, grabbed his hat then left the room and walked down the stairs before exiting the boarding house into a gray overcast. He was still thinking about the missing pair as he walked along the boardwalk toward the nearest place where they could have had breakfast if they hadn't used the boarding house's dining room, which they'd already paid for. Maybe they just wanted some variety in their morning meal and opted to spend some of the money they expected to defraud from Mrs. Swarthmore.

Nate wasn't sure his stomach could handle any more coffee as he entered White's Diner and scanned the customers. He spotted two men having coffee, but their backs were facing him, so he chose a table off to their right and headed that way. He noticed that both men were wearing dark suit jackets, so the odds were high that they were the men he was trying to find.

He sat down in the chair that would give him at least a silhouette of one of the men's faces and waited for the waitress to arrive. He figured he'd order some tea just to avoid an open rebellion by his stomach.

Before she arrived, he was sure that he was looking at Mister Chilton. Agatha's description was spot on and he could see the gold chain across his blue vest as a clincher. He just couldn't get a good look at the supposed brother.

After he place his order for a cup of tea, he tried shifting to the right slightly, but it didn't help. If they left, he'd probably get a glimpse but didn't want to make a show of tailing them out of the café.

As he waited for his tea to arrive, he tried to listen to their conversation, but couldn't pick up anything more than a stray word. They were talking in low, conspiratorial voices as one would expect from men trying to commit a complex scheme.

He smiled at the waitress as she set his cup of tea on the table and after she'd gone, he took a small sip as he tried to not stare at the lawyer and his phony client. It was difficult as he desperately hoped to get a good look at the man claiming to be Agatha's brother-in-law.

Nate was looking out the window to his right when he caught movement at their table and almost missed his chance to get a face-on view of the man. He shifted his eyes to his left just in time to look at the man's face who was already staring at him. For the briefest of moments, their eyes locked and then he turned away. They left the diner and Nate took another sip of the tea not really tasting it as he tried to place that face.

Agatha's odd description of his face being off-balance was strangely accurate. That short glimpse of his visage could only be described as slightly deformed, but unlike Agatha, his years of bareknuckle fighting had given him a much wider base of knowledge when it came to men with misshapen faces.

The man he'd just seen had one of those faces and then he made the leap to a face that he'd seen in Hays City. He remembered seeing the face for the first time in the back room of the Corncob Saloon just two days after arriving in town and then only for a few minutes after they'd been told to toe the line.

He had to remember the name because he'd had so few dealings with the man as a deputy sheriff. He'd knocked the man out and given him that unbalanced face when he'd mashed his nose to the side with a strong right.

Nate had long finished his tea as he tried to recall the man's name. He'd seen him around town fairly often, but never talked to him as he spent most of his time learning and working with the sheriff and other deputies. He had worked as an assistant to the blacksmith, which is why he'd tried his hand as a fighter believing that he had the strength to knock out other men, but he didn't have the speed or the skills. *Why couldn't he remember the man's name?* It was driving him to distraction as he stood, dropped a quarter on the table and picked up his hat before heading for the door.

As he stepped outside, he pulled on his hat and started walking toward the livery to pick up his gelding when he spotted the two men watching him from the doorway of the chemist. He managed to avoid taking a longer look as he continued to take long strides. He doubted that they'd follow him, but he realized that the man probably recognized him as well and that might pose a problem; the problem he'd hoped to avoid. The best he could hope for was that he had only tickled the man's suspicions and he hadn't made a firm identification. If he had, then it was far more likely that he'd have an easier time remembering his name than Nate had trying to recall the losing fighter's.

He hadn't seen a pistol on either man and suspected that they weren't carrying any because it was a scam and not a strongarm operation. But even as he walked toward the livery, in addition to his annoying inability to recall the man's name, he started to think of how someone from that far away had been chosen to fill the role of the missing brother.

The ex-foreman's last name was Strickland, but that name didn't ring a bell. He couldn't imagine the disgruntled former foreman asking a friend or anyone close to do the job. He'd have to use someone he could trust and that would probably be a relative. He'd ask Agatha where he was from to help solve that mystery, but the connection was irrelevant. Remembering the man's name was critical. If he didn't have the man's name, then he could always come up with a story, especially now that he might have identified Nate.

He didn't bother returning to his room to pick up his unused Winchester as he didn't expect any gunfire and his '73 was still with his horse. But as he turned toward the livery, he glanced behind him and spotted the two men just fifty yards away. They'd moved from the chemist's shop and were sitting on a bench in front of town hall pretending not to be watching him.

Nate entered the livery and found it devoid of humans, so he began saddling his gelding to make the ride to the Double 8. He may not have the man's name yet, but the fact that he had identified the man would be a great relief to Agatha Swarthmore. Hopefully, by the time he reached the ranch house, the name would come to him.

He was just tightening the cinch when the liveryman walked through the back door and said, "Howdy, young feller! Come to get your horse?"

Nate grinned at him and said, "Curses! You caught me trying to steal this animal!"

The liveryman released a deep belly laugh as Nate continued to prepare the mount.

When he finished laughing the man said, "That's right funny, mister. I ain't laughed that hard since Max Pollock was kicked in the butt by his own mare."

Nate started to laugh himself when he felt as if he'd been kicked in the butt by his horse. Mac Poteet!

He reached into his pocket, pulled out a five-dollar gold piece and handed it to the startled liveryman.

"What's this for? You're already paid up for a week."

"That, sir, is because you just prodded my stupid brain into remembering something that was hidden in its deepest caves."

He pulled on his left earlobe as he stared at the shining gold coin and said, "Well, I sure am glad I helped ya."

"So, am I," Nate said as he took the gelding's reins and turned to leave the barn.

He mounted outside the front of the livery and instead of turning west and passing the two men who were still on the bench, he turned east and rode out of town before circling around the edge and taking a back road to the northbound road to the Double 8. He still wasn't concerned about the pair who'd caused this problem, and while that lack of concern was well-founded, he'd neglected a critical part of their scheme.

The foreman, John Strickland, who had not only concocted the scheme and arranged to have Mac Poteet play the part of the long-lost brother, had also been living in Laramie rather than stay near Rawlins. He'd returned with the other two on the train and stayed in Laramie while they continued onto Rawlins. He hadn't contacted them since they'd separated and believed that there was no chance that anyone would recognize his cousin as he'd never been out of Kansas.

It was only when he had been in Laramie for two weeks that he'd learned that Nate Manning had been a deputy sheriff in the same town that Mac had called home that he thought that he might be a potential problem.

But after Nate had gone off on a job, he thought it that the remote chance that he'd see Mac had disappeared. Then just as the negotiations were progressing, he heard talk that Nate Manning was going to help Mrs. Swarthmore and he didn't have enough time to act before Manning left town.

He had been on the same train with Nate as it left Laramie and watched him leave and head north. He'd had to stay out of sight but last night, he'd left a note for Mac that a deputy sheriff from Hays City was in town helping Mrs. Swarthmore and that he was staying at the boarding house. He also said that he'd handle the problem the next time he rode out to the ranch.

After he'd left the note, he'd ridden out of town and set up his ambush sight halfway between the ranch and the town in a location he knew well. He expected to see Nate Manning ride by before noon as he was sure that he'd identified his cousin and would rush to tell the widow. Once he was eliminated, the scheme should be back on track.

———

As Nate rode unknowingly into an ambush, Ike was sitting at this desk when Ruth finally walked into the office after having her breakfast and then tidying up her bedroom.

Ike looked up at her and smiled before saying, "Good morning, Ruth. How are you this fine Saturday?"

She returned his smile before taking a seat behind Nate's desk then replying, "I'm fine. How is Alice doing?"

"Still complaining about the baby's refusal to leave its comfortable quarters."

Ruth laughed and said, "I hope I don't have that problem soon."

"I hope you don't either. How was Bill Caruthers?"

"He was very charming. He seems like a nice man."

"He is. I've known him since school days and never figured out why he was still a bachelor."

"That is surprising. I would have thought some girl would have set her cap for him by now."

"So, you like him?"

"Yes, I like him. Why shouldn't I?" she asked.

Ike replied, "No reason. I'm glad that you like him."

Ruth looked at him curiously and asked, "Why are you so happy that I like him?"

"Oh, it's not important. I'm just happy about it."

"Now you've got me wondering. What is going on?"

"It's nothing. Really."

Ruth stood and walked over to Ike's desk and stood over him as she again asked, "What's going on, Ike?"

Ike felt as if Ruth was a giant hovering over him with an enormous, sharp sword in her hand. He knew he'd shown too much enthusiasm for her positive replies to his questions and now he'd dug himself into a hole.

"Um, it's just that you're a wonderful woman and I was kind of hoping that you'd like Bill because he's my friend and he needs a good woman, just like my Alice."

"Oh, really? What you're saying is that I'm not good enough for Nate. Is that it?"

"No, no. That's not it at all. I was thinking about Bill."

"So, he's a better friend than Nate is?"

Ike had his eyes focused on his inkwell as his mind searched for an escape from this verbal maze it had created.

"No, Nate's my best friend, but he's not looking for a girlfriend and Bill really likes you."

Ruth pressed her interrogation to discover the reason for Ike's comments because, so far, he hadn't given her a plausible answer.

"Nate doesn't like girls. Is that what you're saying?"

"No. He like girls a lot. I'm sure that you know that. But, well…"

"He doesn't like me; is that right? Are you telling me that he doesn't want me to stay with him?"

Ike wanted to either scream or break down in tears as her pointed barrage of questioning continued to escalate.

He finally asked, "Will you please just let it go, Ruth? I was just happy that you liked Bill, that's all."

Ruth stared down at Ike and understood that she wasn't going to get her answer but would ask Nate as soon as he walked through that door. She didn't say another word before turning around and stalking back to her bedroom where she slammed the door behind her.

Ike let out a breath and hoped he hadn't caused more problems for Nate, but he was sure that he'd created a big one for Bill Caruthers. Tomorrow was Sunday and he'd be able to stay at home, but he'd be able to soften the blow for Bill when he arrived. Luckily, he only worked until noon on Saturday, so he pulled out his pocket watch and thought that maybe he'd sneak out an hour early.

———

Nate had turned onto the road to the Double 8 and had the gelding moving at a fast trot. He was excited to be able to tell Agatha the wonderful news that the danger was gone, and she wouldn't have to worry about losing the ranch or even a part of it. As he rode, he wondered if she'd want to prosecute the pair for their attempted theft. He knew it was against the law and that she would want to at least kick each of them where it hurt the most, but she may want to avoid the publicity of a trial. He wasn't sure how she would answer that question, but he was sure what her reaction would be when he told her who the man claiming to be her brother-in-law really was.

He still hadn't checked his backtrail because nobody would be able to catch up with him on the eight-mile ride anyway.

Less than a mile away, John Strickland had Nate in sight as he waited behind the wall of a shack that Leo Swarthmore had built halfway between the ranch and town in case someone was caught in a blizzard. He'd arrived at night and slept in the shack, so he'd been waiting since daybreak. He hadn't had to wait too long before he spotted Nate, and now he had his Winchester cocked and would hold his fire until the bounty hunter passed the shack just thirty yards away. He didn't expect to miss with his first shot, but he would probably be able to get off a second one before the ex-deputy was able to get his Winchester out of his scabbard.

Nate had noticed the shack on his trip to the ranch and again on the way back because keen and continuous observation was one of the learned skills that kept him alive. He saw it on the left and was about to change his focus when he took a second look and noticed that the door was half-open. It hadn't been that way when he'd passed by yesterday, but it was now.

It wasn't likely that some critter had opened the door, so someone must have gone inside to get something. He hadn't asked Agatha about its purpose because they had much more immediate topics to discuss.

He was about to forget about the minor discrepancy when he saw a horse's tail swish out of the deep shadows behind the large shack. That was a not something he could ignore. He didn't change the horse's speed but pulled his Winchester from its scabbard and cocked the hammer. The shack was less than fifty yards off the road, but the question was whether whoever was there was waiting for him or not. He couldn't imagine how they could have known he was coming, but both Mr. Chilton and Mac Poteet seemed to have expected him as they weren't having breakfast in the boarding house, so maybe they had hired someone.

Whatever the reason, he needed to play this smart. He was about two hundred yards out and still didn't see anyone, but he might be inside the shack watching him approach, or he could be on the north side hidden from view.

What he did know is where his horse was, and Nate decided that was where he'd go. He'd turn off the road when he was a hundred yards away and ride straight at the shack keeping his Winchester aimed at the half-open door. If the man was inside and Nate was the target, he'd pick up movement and fire. If he didn't see anyone, he'd ride to the back of the shack and the man's horse. That's where it would get dicey. If he wasn't inside the shack and he wasn't sitting on his horse, he'd be waiting on the other side and would know that Nate was there. That meant Nate would be more vulnerable because the shooter could circle around and come at him from behind while Nate waited for him to show himself.

He reached the hundred-yard mark and shifted the brown gelding toward the shack and had his Winchester's sights trained on the door opening.

John Strickland had heard his approach and didn't notice any shift in the direction as he waited for Nate to pass by in front of him.

After he was within fifty yards, Nate took the gamble to forget the possibility that the man was inside the shack. He hadn't met anyone with that kind of patience. But what he did do after shifting toward the horse behind the shack was to create a way of keeping his surprise advantage. He was certain that the would-be assassin would soon hear his brown gelding's hoofbeats behind him and would have to change his plans.

Almost as soon as Nate changed his approach, John Strickland recognized that Manning must have seen his horse and was trying to get behind him. He quickly turned and then stepped along the shack's northern wall with his Winchester aimed at the corner.

Nate slowed the gelding when he was just fifty feet from the shack and slipped out of the saddle onto the ground as his horse continued to the back of the shack.

He trotted toward the shack and slipped inside without touching the door lest the shooter hear a likely squeal from the hinges. As soon as he was in the small dark interior, he stopped and faced the northern wall that was invisible to him as he rode toward the ranch. He saw a shadow slowly moving past the thin gaps between the worn-out boards and knew that the assassin was heading toward his horse and would soon know that Nate wasn't in the saddle.

Now he had a moral decision confronting him. There was a remote possibility that the man wasn't trying to kill him at all but may have just been worried about a stranger riding out of town. *Did he shoot the man or wait?* If he shouted a warning, the man would be able to drill a lot of holes in those walls before Nate got a chance to return fire.

He decided to wait to see what the man did when he found two riderless horses behind the shack. It wasn't a real decision and he felt a bit stupid for making it, but he still waited as he tracked the man's slow advance to the back of the shack.

John Strickland was listening intently for the sound of Nate's horse as he neared the back of the shack. Now he faced the question of whether or not to stick his head out to see if he was there. He'd lost the sound of the hoofbeats and could almost feel the man's Winchester's sights aimed at that suddenly frightening corner. If his horse wasn't back there, he would have just jumped into the saddle and made his break, but he couldn't do that now. He slid the tip of his tongue across his upper lip then backed away from the threatening edge of the shack. He'd assume that Manning was there and decided that he would come around behind him.

He slowly backstepped but knew he couldn't waste much time, so as soon as he was a few feet away from the back edge, he turned and walked faster but quietly toward the road and once he reached the eastern edge with the door, he swung around the front with his Winchester ready to fire at any motion, but no one was there.

His nerves were being ratcheted higher with each step as he stalked past the door to take a quick peek at the southern side of the shack. He didn't expect to find Manning there, but it was a chance that he'd have to take.

Nate had seen him walk past with his Winchester cocked and leveled but still didn't recognize him, which wasn't exactly unexpected. He slowly stepped closer to the door and still had the shooter in his sights when the man stopped.

Nate settled his sights on the man's back and shouted, "Drop it!"

John Strickland was startled by the unexpected warning and instead of freezing, he turned, and his repeater turned with him.

Nate didn't wait to see the muzzle of the man's Winchester, but as soon as the barrel began its sudden arc towards him, he fired.

The .44 left his carbine and drilled through the right side of John Strickland's chest just in front of his bicep, punching though is right lung and lodging in his heart. He continued his spin and corkscrewed to the ground letting his Winchester fall against the edge of the door.

Nate quickly stepped out of the shack as Strickland's blood poured from his chest before he shuddered and stopped breathing.

It had been a long time since he'd gotten into a gunfight, if this could be called one, and even longer since he'd had to kill a man. He only hoped that he hadn't made a mistake.

He leaned his Winchester against the wall before stepping close to the body and dropping to his heels.

He rolled him onto his back and checked his pockets but found nothing. He stood then picked up both Winchesters and stepped around the body and headed to the horses.

When he reached the two animals, he found the man's black mare tied to a heavy peg in back of the shack and after sliding both repeaters where they belonged, he opened the saddlebag on the right side of the mare and began emptying its contents.

There was nothing unusual in that one and nothing that identified the man, so he walked around the mare and opened the second saddlebag and that one produced a veritable treasure trove of information.

At first, Nate thought all he'd found was the man's dirty clothes until he realized that they were the clothes he'd worn before arriving at the shack. Inside those pockets he found some cash, a used train ticket from Laramie to Rawlins on the same train he'd used, which bothered him more than it should have. He found the man's wallet with more cash and a business card for Robert M. Chilton, Esq. who practiced his profession in Dodge City, which was the next big town to Hays City in Kansas.

Two other valuable items that he found in the saddlebag were a notepad and pencil. He wasn't initially impressed with that find until he carried them out to the sunshine and tilted the pad slightly and saw the depressions from a recent note. He tried to read the words, but only got a few letters before sliding the pad and pencil back into the saddlebag. He'd shade the page to reveal the writing when he got to the ranch and bring the body with him to see if Agatha could identify him. He suspected that he was the angry ex-foreman, but he could be another disgruntled ranch hand that had left around the same time. She had told him that three others had drifted away after the foreman left.

His greatest concern in his job as a bounty hunter was hearing that brief question, "Who is he?", and hoped he didn't hear it when Agatha looked at the body.

It took him about forty minutes to get the body over his saddle and tied down before he mounted his gelding and rode away from the shack to finish his violently interrupted ride to the Double 8.

————

As Nate regained the road, Ike checked his watch for the eighth time since Ruth had returned to her bedroom and thought it was close enough to noon, give or take ninety minutes, and began to organize his papers to prepare for his hasty departure.

Since she'd slammed that door, Ruth had been sitting on her bed fuming over what she had soon surmised that Ike was revealing with his questioning. It sounded as if he expected Bill Caruthers to begin courting her and at first, she thought it was because Ike thought she wasn't good enough for his friend. But then she began to believe that Nate had asked him to set it up because she didn't believe that Ike would do anything without his boss's say-so. *How could she have been so foolish again?*

Once she shifted to that line of thought about Nate's intentions, she began to merge it with her earlier suspicions that maybe Nate Manning hadn't rescued her at all but was in league with Toby. After all, she'd never seen this Stubby character and she hadn't been there when he'd 'captured' Toby Halvorsen, either. All she had was what Nate had told her and now he was gone to allow the deputy to become close to her.

Ruth had been played as a fool by Toby Halvorsen and wasn't about to be duped again. Her previously discarded conspiracy theory that Nate was in cahoots with Toby to get her to steal money from her father was taking hold of her imagination. She even suspected that somehow, her father was the instigator of the plot to get her away from the Lone Wolf ranch.

Even as Ike was putting papers away, her racing mind assembled more pieces of the disjointed plot. If what Nate had suggested when he first found her, that she was the product of her mother's affair with another man, then that would be a motive for the entire scheme. Her father wanted her gone, but probably couldn't have her killed because her mother had probably gotten wind of the plot and while not being able to prevent her being taken away, demanded that her daughter be unharmed.

She giggled before she whispered, "Unharmed, Mother? I was raped more than a half a dozen times before he left!"

But why bring her back at all? Proof! Her mother needed proof that she hadn't been killed. That was why she'd been brought to the ranch and why her father hadn't exploded as he had. *But why had Nate demanded payment if he'd already gotten half of the thousand dollars that she'd stolen?* Then she realized that she'd never really seen that money, which made sense because he said he had it all, but if he'd shown it to her, then she would have seen much less.

233

Her entire theory was gaining solid ground as she answered her own questions. It would explain why her father hired Nate in the first place. He had a better reputation than others in his business and she'd be more likely to believe his story. But if he was part of this conspiracy, then her father must know that he would agree to do it. That meant her father knew something about his past that was less than reputable.

Who really was Nate Manning? He said he grew up in a small town outside of Council Bluffs, Iowa, but he never told her the name. She could ask Ike but thought that he was in on the big secret and wouldn't tell her anyway. She had to figure out a way to disprove his story.

She revisited their conversations and remembered that the one part of his life that he repeated often was how he changed from an angry young man to a much more thoughtful person after he was taken under the wing of the sheriff in Ellis County in Kansas. He'd told her his name and that he'd retired, which is why he'd left, so she had to assume that he'd still be in Hays City. She smiled as she remembered his name: Sheriff Luther Galloway. Nate had told her that he wasn't even a Lutheran, which is why his Christian name had been so easily recalled.

Ruth's only remaining question was the reason why he now wanted the deputy to show interest in her. She could understand why the deputy wouldn't need any urging, *but why did Nate set it up?* That may have been the easiest part of the puzzle to solve. He couldn't marry her and spend so much time with her that the secret would eventually be exposed. He

234

even mentioned that he might be leaving Laramie probably because he expected the plot to be revealed. She did give Nate the benefit of believing that he hadn't known what Toby did to her, and that was only because he hadn't used her like her supposed boyfriend had.

Ruth finally let out a long sigh now that she understood everything. She was sad for losing her image of the heroic, noble Nate Manning, but the anger that replaced it was more than enough to make it insignificant.

She was still sitting on the bed deep in thought when she was startled by Ike's call from the office. She hadn't heard what he said, but now she wasn't worried about him, Nate or that deputy.

She stood and walked to the door and opened it much more gently before walking out to the hallway and heading to the office.

"What did you say, Ike?" she asked as she entered the front room.

Ike was relieved she didn't have a knife or a long hairpin in her hand as he stood with his hat in his hand and replied, "I just said that I'd be heading home. I only work half-days on Saturdays, and I'm all caught up. I need to check on Alice, too."

He was disjointed when Ruth smiled and said, "Well, you'd better go and do that, Ike. Be sure to tell Mary White to take care of her, too."

Ike paused for three or four seconds before saying, "I'll do that. I'll see you on Monday, Ruth. Maybe Nate will have solved Mrs. Swarthmore's problem and will be back by then."

"I'm sure he'll handle it just as he helped me. Oh, and tell Deputy Caruthers that I won't need watching any longer."

"What? But Nate won't be happy to hear that. What if your father sends someone to hurt you?"

"My mother wouldn't allow that to happen. Just tell the deputy that he is no longer needed."

"Alright. If you're sure."

"I am. Goodbye, Ike."

"Goodbye, Ruth," Ike said before pulling on his hat and leaving the office in a very disagreeable and confused state.

Ruth watched him walk away and locked the office door before quickly turning and heading back down the hallway and continued until she exited the back door and quickly strode to the telegraph office.

———

After Ike told a crestfallen Bill Caruthers what Ruth had told him, he left the sheriff's office to go home and would ask Alice and Mary's opinions about what had just happened with Ruth. She'd been so angry over what he considered normal questions about whether she liked Bill or not and then she was so pleasant just a couple of hours later.

He wasn't sure if Alice would be able to figure it out, but Mary had spent much more time with Miss Miller and seemed to be able to understand her better than even Nate had.

———

Nate was approaching the Double 8 ranch house and was sure that Agatha had been told of his arrival by one of the ranch hands because he'd seen one of them rush into the house. That guess was confirmed as he drew within a hundred feet of the front porch and Agatha stepped through the door and waited near the steps.

He slowed the gelding and then stopped before dismounting and tying him off under the watchful eyes of Agatha Swarthmore and probably a few of the ranch hands. She never said a word as he mounted the steps to the porch.

When he stopped a foot before her, he quietly said, "Agatha, I hope that you can identify that body that's draped over the saddle."

"That looks like John Strickland. How did that happen?"

Nate exhaled in relief before replying, "I need to get the body back to Rawlins and talk to Sheriff Blount. He was planning to ambush me on the ride from town. He was hiding behind that halfway shack and it was only because I noticed that the door was half open that I was able to avoid getting bushwhacked."

"I can imagine why he would do it, but how was he even here? Someone would have spotted him."

"I'm pretty sure he was on the train that I took from Laramie. I found a ticket in his wallet."

"Is that good enough proof that Leo's brother isn't who he claims to be?"

"Probably not, but that wouldn't be necessary anyway. I'm sure that the reason he tried to shoot me because he was worried that I'd identify your fraudulent brother-in-law."

Agatha's breath quickened and her eyes widened as she quickly asked, "Did you? Did you recognize him?"

Nate grinned before answering, "Yes, ma'am. That imbalance you noticed in his face was because I broke his nose more than four years ago in Hays City. His name is Mac Poteet."

"Can you come into the parlor and explain everything before you go back to town?" she asked excitedly.

"I need to get something out of his saddlebags first, then I'll join you."

"Hurry," she said before turning and entering the house leaving the door open.

Nate trotted back to Strickland's mare and pulled the notepad and pencil from the saddlebag then quickly walked back onto the porch and entered the house.

When he found Agatha, she was sitting on the couch and obviously wanted him to sit beside her as he explained what he'd discovered, so he removed his hat as crossed the parlor floor and took a seat.

She glanced at the blank pad of paper in his hand and suspected that it there had been a sheet removed from the pad which contained incriminating evidence that Nate would soon reveal.

Nate held the pad and pencil in his left hand as he began to explain what had happened beginning when he had returned to Rawlins yesterday evening. The fact that the two men had avoided going to breakfast in the boarding house was his first indication that they had known he was there, even though he admitted that he couldn't figure out how they could have known unless someone had sent a telegram from Laramie before he left.

By the time he reached the shootout, Agatha was bouncing inside. She would keep her ranch and those two bastards

239

would go to prison. All because she had written that letter to the incredible young man sitting beside her.

After he'd told her about his search of Strickland's saddlebags, he finally paused in the narration to see what had been written on the page that had been removed.

He set the edge of the pencil's exposed lead then gently began shading the paper and the message slowly began to release its secret.

"Well, isn't that enlightening," Nate said as he read:

Mac:

I followed a man who used to be a deputy sheriff in Hays City. He was hired by the widow to investigate your background. He even got a room in the boarding house. If you can identify him, try not to be seen and I'll take care of him when he leaves town to tell Agatha Swarthmore the news. He'll never get to expose you. Once he's gone, we'll be okay.

J.S.

"I can't believe that he found out about you. How did that happen?"

"I guess he was waiting in Laramie and heard about me. Nothing else makes sense and I feel a bit foolish for not noticing him at least getting on the train. I usually pay more attention than that."

"So, what are you going to do next?"

"As I told you, I'll take the body back into Rawlins and go around the back of the jail. Then I'll tell Sheriff Blount what happened, and we'll have a chat with the two men. Before I go, I need to know if you want to have them charged with attempted fraud."

"Of course, I do. They tried to ruin me and steal the only thing that mattered to me anymore."

"That's what I expected. That'll mean that I'll have to stick around for the trial."

"You can stay here and fill me in on all the details and that other case with Fred Miller that you'd mentioned."

Nate nodded then replied, "I'll do that, ma'am. I'll be back before sundown."

"I'll be sure to have a good supper waiting for you when you return."

"Thank you, Agatha," he said before standing and adding, "I'll have more stories about how they reacted to the news and being tossed in jail."

Agatha smiled and rose from the couch before Nate turned and pulled on his hat before leaving the house.

He mounted, then waved to Agatha before turning his horse and the body-laden mare south to make the ride into Rawlins.

241

———

In Hays City, Luther Galloway and his wife Betty were reading in the parlor when there was a loud knock on the door jamb of the open front door.

Luther looked up from his book and saw Chuck Arnaud at the door and said, "Come on in, Chuck. Got a telegram for me?"

Chuck walked into the room and as he held out the yellow sheet, replied, "Yes, sir."

Luther took the message, unfolded it and a look of puzzlement crossed his face as he read its contents.

He handed it to his wife and asked, "Have you ever heard of this feller before?"

Betty read:

LUTHER GALLOWAY HAYS CITY KAN

MAN NAMED NATE MANNING WANTS TO MARRY ME
UNSURE OF HIS BACKGROUND
SAYS HE KNEW YOU
IS THIS TRUE
PLEASE REPLY SOON

RUTH MILLER 207 KANSAS ST LARAMIE WY

"No, I don't know anyone named Manning. The closest I can get are the Manleys over on Hickory Street."

Luther took the telegram back and then picked up a pencil from the side table and wrote his reply on the back before handing Chuck two quarters.

"That should cover this short message, Chuck. Keep the leftovers for a tip."

"Why thanks, Sheriff!" Chuck exclaimed before taking the reply and dashing back out of the house.

The echoes of his hurried footsteps had barely died down when his wife said, "That was a strange one, Luther."

"That's what I was thinking. I wonder why that feller claimed to know me. I'm not exactly a household name up in Wyoming."

"Maybe he came through town and thought that you would provide him a good alibi for whatever scheme he's hatching to delude this poor girl."

Luther shrugged and said, "Maybe I should have asked a question rather than just sending that short answer I gave her," then opened his book and continued reading.

———

Nate reached Laramie in the middle of the afternoon and rode around the western edge of town to avoid being seen by either of the two men. He soon reached the back of the jail and dismounted, tied off the gelding and walked through the alley to the boardwalk then turned and soon reached office door.

He walked inside expecting to see one of the two deputies and was surprised to find Sheriff Mitch Blount behind the desk.

The sheriff looked up, then sat back and said, "I heard you were in town to do an investigation on behalf of Agatha Swarthmore, Mister Manning. What brings you by this afternoon?"

Nate removed his hat as he stepped closer to the desk then took a seat before replying, "I finished my investigation, Sheriff."

"Already? That's surprising because I would have thought it was your job to expose the brother as a fraud. How could you have done that in such a short time? Or did you discover that his claim was valid? He would have paid a handsome fee for you to confirm his story."

"I'm sure he would, but I've never spoken to the man or his attorney, and there isn't any point now. He is a fraud, Sheriff, and I can prove it a lot easier than you might have expected."

The sheriff's expression showed his surprise as he asked, "How can you do that? You haven't even seen the documentation he had with him, including a birth certificate, his army record, and even affidavits from folks he'd known for years."

"I can do it, Sheriff, because as soon as I saw his face, I recognized him from the time I was a deputy sheriff in Hays City in Kansas. Actually, it was just before I became a deputy sheriff. I met him briefly before I knocked him out in a bareknuckle fight. His name is Mac Poteet."

"Are you sure? Do you have any proof?"

"I can send a telegram to the retired sheriff of Ellis County, Luther Galloway, but that won't be necessary. After I identified him, I headed out to the Double 8 to tell Mrs. Swarthmore. About halfway there, a man tried to drygulch me, but I was able to get him first. His body is over his horse in back.

"I didn't recognize him, so I went through his things and I found a pad with blank pages, but the top sheet had impressions from a note he had written. I shaded the sheet and read the note which corroborates my story. I then brought the body to the ranch to see if Mrs. Swarthmore could identify the man and she told me that he was the foreman who tried to move up the ladder before she sent him packing."

"*John Strickland was here?*" he asked sharply.

"I wondered how Chilton and Poteet knew I was in town because they seemed to be interested in me and until I was almost ambushed, I couldn't figure it out. It seems that they'd been given warning by Strickland after I arrived."

He then slid the shaded copy of the note from his shirt pocket and handed it to the sheriff and watched his expression as he read it.

"I can't believe it! They had me and Agatha's lawyer convinced," he said quickly before he looked up and asked, "Why didn't they just take the ten thousand and skedaddle? The longer they stayed, the more likely it would be that they'd be exposed."

"I have no idea. I guess there might have been a bit of revenge on the part of Mister Strickland for being denied what he thought was rightfully his. Maybe Agatha really emasculated him before she sent him on his way. It doesn't matter now. How do you want to handle this? I don't believe that they saw me ride into town. As far as they know, I'm dead and probably below the ground by now."

"If you'll come along, let's go and pick them up at the boarding house."

"Um, I don't want to step on your toes, Sheriff, but I don't want to risk any trouble, so why don't you just go find them and tell them that Agatha is waiting with her lawyer in the jail with a new offer. I'll be off to the side with my Colt as you enter."

"You're not stepping on my toes, Mister Manning. It's a much better way to put them behind my bars. I'll head over there and bring them back, and after they're in the cell, we'll take Strickland's carcass to the mortician."

Nate nodded as the sheriff stood, then marched across the office floor, snatched his hat from a peg and left the jail.

Nate didn't expect to see him for at least fifteen minutes and hoped that he wasn't sending the sheriff into a bad situation if they had seen him come into town with their dead partner.

———

While Nate waited for the sheriff to return with the two prisoners who didn't realize they were prisoners, ten-year-old Ellis Laughlin trotted to the front of Nate's office and knocked on the door. He wasn't sure that Mister Hawkins hadn't made a mistake when he interpreted the clicking chatter of the telegraph key because he didn't think that Mister Manning had any women living in his house, much less Ruth Miller.

When the door opened, he gawked at Ruth before wordlessly holding out the telegram.

Ruth had been hoping for a reply but didn't think it would come this quickly yet had pocketed some change in the chance that it would show up before Monday, if at all. She handed him a nickel, then closed the door and locked it again before hurrying to Nate's desk and sitting down.

247

Ellis stayed frozen in front of the door for another thirty seconds before he turned and zipped away.

Ruth quickly opened the message and read:

RUTH MILLER 207 KANSAS ST LARAMIE WY

NEVER HEARD OF HIM

LUTHER GALLOWAY HAYS CITY KAN

"That bastard!" she exclaimed under her breath.

The message was one more confirmation of her almost unshakable belief that she finally understood what had really happened to her. She may not know who Nate Manning really was, but it was secondary now. But she had no desire to go running back to her father to accuse him because she suspected that she wouldn't leave the ranch alive, even if her mother was standing on the porch watching them kill her.

She'd wait until Manning, or whoever he was, returned and confront him. But when she did, she'd have the shotgun he'd left behind. It would have both hammers cocked and pointed at his chest. She'd get the truth out of him and then she'd decide how to best get her revenge. It would mean that she would have to be pleasant toward Ike and that Mary White if she showed up again. Ruth wondered what Manning's designs were with the blonde midwife if he had any. Then she snorted and wondered if he had designs on any woman. Nate had just completed a long fall from the top of Ruth's mountain to the lowest chasm of her mind.

Ruth let out a long breath, then took the telegram, rose and walked back to her room to spend more time reviewing all that she'd discovered.

———

Nate was in position against the wall with his Colt in his hand just seconds after he'd seen the sheriff and the pair of blissfully ignorant frauds approaching the jail. It was a relief knowing that he hadn't been spotted after all.

The door opened and the sheriff let them enter and Nate expected them to notice the absence of Agatha and her lawyer then bolt, but the sheriff had told them the widow and her attorney were in his private office, so they continued past Nate and it wasn't until the sheriff closed the door that they saw him. When they did, their reaction was almost exactly as Nate had imagined it would be.

Both set of eyes exploded and their eyebrows popped into small mountains as they realized they'd been found out and that John Strickland hadn't done his job. The only question each of them had in that brief instant before the sheriff spoke was whether John had confessed or was dead. Either answer spelled disaster.

"Okay, boys," the sheriff said loudly, "Your cell is waiting for you, and I don't think you want to push Mister Manning here to give him any reason to shoot either of you like he did your partner."

"John is dead?" Mac Poteet asked quickly.

"As a doorknob," Nate said as he motioned for them to move with his convincing Colt.

The two men began walking and turned into the first cell before the sheriff clanged the door shut behind them.

Nate slid his pistol back into its holster then walked to the bars and stared at Mac Poteet as he asked, "Do you remember me, Mac?"

"Yeah, I remember you. You broke my nose and then after the deputy conked you out, the sheriff turned around and gave you a badge. I avoided you like the plague after that."

"Was John Strickland kin?"

"Yeah, he was my cousin. I hadn't seen him in years 'til he showed up in town and asked me to help him."

Mister Chilton suddenly snapped, "Shut up! Are you stupid or something?"

Mac didn't answer but suddenly whipped his right fist into his lawyer's face, splattering his nose and dropping him to the floor.

Nate almost laughed before he said, "You've improved, Mac."

"He shouldn't have called me stupid. I was the one who kept tellin' him and John that this was gonna be a mess, but they convinced me that we'd get a lot of money. Then when that widow offered us ten thousand dollars, I couldn't believe that they turned it down. We coulda been outta here before you even showed up."

"You're right, Mac. That would have been the smart thing to do."

The sheriff interrupted them when he said, "Let's get Strickland to the mortician and then we'll come back here and get the rest of the story for my report."

Nate nodded, then followed the sheriff out the back door to start the final stages of the dead foreman's scam.

———

"Why would she act as if she wasn't mad?" Ike asked Alice as Mary sat on the other side of the parlor.

"Maybe she just calmed down after she thought about it more. Besides, you said that she liked Bill Caruthers."

"I don't think that was why she was pleasant before I left, Alice. If she wanted to see Bill, she wouldn't have told me to let him know that she didn't need anyone to watch over her anymore."

Alice looked at Mary and asked, "You know her better than I do, Mary. What do you think?"

"I told you before that I'm sure that she's in love with Nate and when Ike gave her the hint that Nate was trying to interest her in Bill Caruthers, then she took that as a sign that he didn't reciprocate her affection. When I was with them, I could see that she almost hero-worshipped him and that's a bad thing. Once there's anything taken away from the pillar that supports that heroic image, it's in danger of toppling to the ground and shattering."

Alice laughed then said, "Couldn't you just say that she was smitten with Nate and when she believed that he didn't like her, she became jealous off you?"

"Oh, I'm sure that she was jealous before Ike introduced her to Bill Caruthers, but she'd be jealous if she saw Nate smiling at you, Alice. She appears to be very possessive with Nate and I can understand why. He's a remarkable man and he saved her from a terrible fate."

"It sounds as if you're in love with him yourself, Mary," Alice said with a smile.

"I don't matter. My concern is that once Ruth has removed Nate from his pedestal, she may let him keep falling and start to see him as a bad man."

252

"Why would she do that? He still rescued her," Ike said.

"It's just a feeling I got from her. She was hurt by Toby Halvorsen and is probably worried that she's pregnant to add to that stress. She thought she was in love with him and then he betrayed her in the worst way imaginable. I hope she doesn't sink so far as to believe that Nate will do the same thing to her."

Ike replied, "Nate told me that she pretty much invited him into her bed those two nights they were alone, and he made sure that didn't happen. How could she ever think that he would do what Halvorsen did?"

Mary shrugged and answered, "I have no idea. I'm talking over my head right now."

"You talk like a woman who was hurt by someone you loved. Is that true, Mary?" Alice asked.

"No. I've never been hurt by someone I loved."

"Really? Not even after a schoolgirl crush?" Alice asked with wide eyes.

"No, not even that."

Ike then said, "If I were you, I wouldn't make Nate Manning your first one. He's steered away from more than a few young women who set their caps for him."

Mary looked at Ike before she asked, "Ike, what do you know about Nate's life before he arrived in Laramie?"

Ike scratched his stubbled chin before replying, "Well, I know he grew up in a small down on the Iowa side of the Missouri River in a big family, but didn't get along with any of them before he left when he was sixteen. He admits that he was ill-tempered and quick to fight as he worked his way west and it wasn't until he met Sheriff Galloway in Hays City, Kansas that he learned to control that temper and became a much nicer man."

"I heard all of that, but do you think that it's true?"

"What do you mean? Why would he lie about it?" Ike asked sharply.

"I guess it doesn't matter," she replied before looking at Alice and asking, "How are you today, Alice? I don't think you calculated your date of conception correctly because I don't think you have that much longer."

"I hope you're right, Mary. I really want this baby to make her grand entrance into the world so I can walk like a human being again and not an old sow."

Ike laughed and said, "You're still a pretty woman, Alice, but I'll admit that it'll be nice to be able to…"

"Stop!" Alice exclaimed, "Don't say another word!"

Mary smiled as Ike grinned at his wife. She was sure that she was right about Alice's progress and expected to deliver her baby in the next three days. She just hoped that she wasn't wrong about Ruth as she suspected that after the Toby disaster, more disappointment would be much worse and the old saw about a hell having no fury like a woman scorned wasn't a myth. Ruth may not have been scorned, but she had been hurt once and if she believed her newfound affections weren't returned, she might exhibit that hellish fury.

Mary still didn't believe that Ruth would hurt Nate, but she couldn't visit Ruth until Nate had returned to try to help him. She understood that she was the last person Ruth wanted to see right now.

———

Nate rode out of Rawlins in the early evening with an offer for Agatha. After talking to both prisoners, the sheriff had left the jail then returned with the county prosecutor. Both prisoners were offered a plea agreement of two years imprisonment, so Nate would present that offer to Mrs. Swarthmore and return tomorrow but would have to go to the sheriff's house to deliver her answer. It would be Sunday, after all.

As he turned north, he wondered what her reaction would be. She didn't seem to be an overly vindictive woman and he expected that as long as her ranch was safe and they were punished for what they'd done, she'd accept the offer. But he still wasn't sure two years would satisfy her.

He soon passed the halfway shack and glanced behind him at Strickland's mare and her empty saddle. He wasn't sure if he'd keep the black horse or leave her with Agatha. He didn't need another one and she wasn't any better than the buckskin mare he had back in his small barn.

Nate spotted the ranch house after another thirty minutes and soon rode under the large wooden sign decorated with a carved 88 before he continued down the long access road. It still wasn't nearly as long as the highway that led to the Lone Wolf ranch owned by Fred Miller, but it was still impressive, and it would remain as her property.

He pulled up before the porch as Agatha stepped through the door making Nate smile.

"Well?" she asked as he tied off the gelding.

"If you noticed the empty mare I'm trailing, Agatha, you can make the logical assumption that I haven't been arrested for murder."

Agatha laughed as Nate stepped onto the porch then she turned and walked back inside with Nate trailing.

He removed his hat and expected to see her head toward the couch, but she continued straight ahead down the hallway before he remembered that she had promised to have dinner waiting for him when he returned. He hadn't even reached the hallway when the very pleasant aromas wafted over him making his stomach rumble and his mouth water.

When he entered the kitchen, he found that the cook wasn't present and asked, "Did you do your own cooking, Agatha?"

"Of course, I didn't, but I held off eating myself because I knew you'd be back before sunset."

Nate took a seat at the table and let Agatha handle loading the plates with the steaks, boiled carrots and baked potato. There were bowls with butter and sour cream on the table, so as soon as Agatha set the filled plate in front of him, he began dressing his potato with the welcomed additives.

"So," Agatha began as she took her seat, "Are they enjoying the hospitality of Sheriff Blount's hotel?"

"Yes, ma'am. Mac Poteet was very forthcoming with information and none of it was a real revelation. He was your ex-foreman's cousin and he was a bit hesitant to be part of the scheme, but the promise of a lot of money outweighed his concerns. He seemed upset when they turned down your first offer."

"Will all of this come out in the trial?"

"That's what I need to talk to you about, Agatha. After listening to their story, the county prosecutor offered them a plea agreement. I guess he figured that a trial would be a lot of work and if there was just one member of the jury who agreed with your foreman that a woman shouldn't run a ranch, especially one this size, then he'd wind up with a hung jury. They agreed to the plea agreement, but he needs your approval."

Agatha stopped eating and looked at Nate for fifteen seconds before asking, "What do you think, Nate? You'd be able to return to Laramie sooner if there wasn't a trial."

"I know, but that doesn't matter. I don't have any jobs waiting right now and I can afford to stay for a few more days. All that matters is if you think that it's enough punishment for what they tried to do."

"Do you? Strickland tried to kill you."

"I know, but he's dead and I'm alive. I don't believe that Mac Poteet is a bad man, but he is a weak man and agreed to do the job rather than make his cousin mad. What I did find amusing was that as he began talking in the cell, Mister Chilton told him to shut up and then made the mistake of calling him stupid. Now the lawyer had a broken nose just like his client."

Agatha laughed before saying, "Okay. I'll agree to the plea agreement. That attorney won't be able to practice law anymore; will he?"

"Not legally, but I'm sure he'll find some out-of-the-way place and pretend he's an honest lawyer after he leaves prison."

"I'll have to go into town to sign something; won't I?"

"Yes, ma'am. Sheriff Blount said to find him at his house tomorrow and you can sign the papers there."

"Will you be leaving on the evening train to Laramie?"

Nate smiled before replying, "If it's alright with you, Agatha. I'll take the morning train on Monday. It leaves at 8:10 on Mondays, so I'll have to get on the road before sunrise."

"I'll be happy to have you stay even for a few more hours. You are a remarkable young man, Nate Manning."

Nate didn't reply but continued to eat. He hadn't asked her where he'd be sleeping, but the big house was mostly empty, but he wasn't sure if the cook and probably a maid or housekeeper slept. He hadn't had time to explore the big ranch, so there might be a servants' quarters in back of the house.

Agatha seemed to have read his mind when after two minutes of silence, she said, "You can stay in the middle bedroom on this floor. My room is next door."

"Thank you, Agatha. Tomorrow, after we return from Rawlins, maybe you could give me a tour of your ranch that is now securely in your hands."

"That was my plan if you decided to stay. Now, you can tell me about the work you did for Fred Miller."

"Yes, ma'am," he replied before beginning the story.

Nate didn't leave out any details, including Ruth's obvious invitation to her bed and his excused refusal. He expressed his concerns over Fred Miller's reaction to Stubby Nicks' failure and what he might do in the future.

————

After checking Alice's progress one more time, Mary left their bedroom and walked to her temporary bedroom next door. She would stay with them until three days after Alice delivered her first baby.

She closed the door and as she began to change out of her clothes, she thought about the Ruth Miller situation. Ruth had been jealous of her since they'd met and could understand why she felt that way. But she'd never been rejected as Ruth had been, and she believed that Nate had turned her away when he really hadn't even let her in. It was difficult for her to really understand how Ruth felt because she had never experienced that emotion.

She had lost love, but not as Ruth had. Hers was a much longer and much more distant love that she had always thought had little chance of being fulfilled, but now there was a possibility that it finally could be yet there were two major obstacles: one named Ruth Miller and the other named Nate Manning.

————

Nate pulled off his boots as he sat on the edge of the bed and after setting them aside, pulled off his britches and then slipped his socks from his feet before setting them in a pile nearby. He still had one more clean set of clothes and that would get him through tomorrow before he made that early train trip back to Laramie.

After he'd slipped beneath the quilts, he tried to think of anything he'd missed about this case. There was always something, but he couldn't think of a single loose thread. The two living members of the scheme were in jail and Mac Poteet had told them that there weren't any others involved. Agatha had no more worries and trusted her new foreman, who obviously didn't have the arrogance or ambition of John Strickland.

He spent twenty more minutes reviewing the Double 8 case before he shifted his mind back to Laramie and Ruth Miller, who would be waiting for him in his house. He was curious if she'd been smitten by Bill Caruthers. If he was that fortunate, he might even find an empty house when he got there, but Ike would be in the office and he'd explain what had happened even if she was gone. He just didn't think it would be that fast.

If that little ploy failed, he would have a bigger problem than he had when he'd left. She'd miss him and be more likely to expect him to join her in her bed and that couldn't happen. He hated the idea of hurting her again after the Toby Halvorsen fiasco, but he didn't see any way to avoid it if she didn't become enamored of Bill Caruthers.

Why can't Ruth be more like Mary White? If anything, she was prettier than Ruth, but she didn't seem to advertise it. She was a bright, thoughtful young woman who had a large warehouse full of compassion yet still had a wonderful sense of humor. If Ruth had those traits, he might have started to remove some of those bricks in his wall, but she didn't and he didn't know of many women, or men for that matter, that did have them. He was grateful that Mary wasn't interested in him at all because he enjoyed having her around.

CHAPTER 8

It was early that Sunday morning when Nate and Agatha rolled out of the Double 8 in her buggy. He even let her take the reins as it was her buggy and she was probably better at driving it than she was.

As they drove, she asked him about the situation with Ruth Miller and he surprised himself by being more candid with her than he'd been with Ike or anyone else. He told her of his concerns and what might happen when he returned.

"If you need someplace to send her, you can always ask her to come here to live with me."

"No, I don't think that would solve anything, Agatha. It might even make it worse because she'll think that I'm trying to get rid of her."

"Aren't you?" she asked.

Nate sighed and replied, "Yes, I suppose that's exactly what I'm trying to do, but I don't want to hurt her, especially after what happened to her less than a week ago."

"Do you want me to return with you and talk to her?"

"No. I think that wouldn't be any different than if I asked her if she'd like to come here. I'll have to handle it myself."

"I hope you can. Don't you like her?"

"Yes, I like her, but I can't allow her to expect me to love her."

"Why not? Do you have another girlfriend?"

"No, I've never had a girlfriend."

Agatha turned her eyes from the road and asked, "Never? A handsome, smart young man like you has never had a girlfriend?"

"No, ma'am."

"Don't you like girls, you know, as women?"

"I like them very much if you don't mind. I'm not inexperienced with women but being with a woman and loving a woman are two different things."

"I'll grant you that. I loved Leo for as long as I can remember, but I know that he spent time with other women whom he didn't love. As long as he only loved me, I didn't object."

Nate was thrown off balance by her candor but asked, "It didn't bother you at all?"

"Of course, it bothered me, but I didn't let him know that because I loved him. And before you ask, I didn't use that as an excuse to invite other men into my bed."

"I wasn't going to ask, Agatha."

She turned her eyes forward again and laughed before saying, "No, but you were thinking about it."

Nate grinned before replying, "I'll confess that I was."

"I'll confess something to you now, Nate. I was seriously thinking of sneaking into your bedroom last night. It's been too long since I've been with a man and I spent a long night debating doing that."

"Really?"

"Don't think that I'm some old brokenhearted widow, Nate. I'm still a healthy woman with very strong urges. I grieved for my Leo for a long time, and now I'm finished grieving and am ready to get on with my life."

"I didn't say you were old, Agatha. I think you're a very handsome woman."

"Then you won't mind spending some time with me tonight?" she asked as she smiled at him.

"As long as you don't expect me to fall in love with you and beg you to marry me."

Agatha laughed again before she let her hand slip onto his thigh and then said, "I just want you to make passionate love to me as many times as you can before you leave in the morning. I won't make any demands on you at all, other than to satisfy those urges I just mentioned."

Nate picked up her hand, kissed her fingers and said, "I'll see what I can do."

Agatha looked back at him and felt those urges explode. She just hoped she could last long enough to get back to the ranch. Suddenly, the ride of exploration meant a lot more and she knew exactly where their journey would end when they returned to the ranch house.

———

The business in Rawlins didn't take long, but they stayed for lunch before heading back in the buggy. As much as each of them anticipated spending some private time to release their pent-up lust, they managed to just talk on the drive back, although it took less time than the ride into town as Agatha pressed the horse to a fast pace.

After she pulled the buggy to a stop before the house, she stepped out and let one of the ranch hands take the buggy and without acknowledging any change in their business relationship, they walked sedately onto the porch and entered the parlor.

Once the door was closed, sedately didn't describe what happened after they were alone. It was Sunday, and Agatha had told Nate that the house would be empty all day. It wasn't a subtle hint.

Nate forgot about the Double 8 or Ruth Miller as he pulled Agatha close and kissed her passionately. She wasted no time in running her hands over him as he began to almost rip the buttons from her dress.

They waltzed toward her bedroom with their active hands probing and rubbing each other as they kissed in ever-increasing displays of unchecked passion.

By the time they spun and dipped through the bedroom door, Agatha's dress was around her waist and her naked breasts were being kissed and caressed by Nate's sensitive fingers.

Nate had to step out of his britches after Agatha dropped them to his ankles, so he wouldn't trip but she didn't slow in her own excited exploration.

They began tossing off their remaining impediments to their frantic lovemaking until they were fully disrobed, and Nate had her back against his chest as he kissed the back of her neck and massaged her breasts.

Agatha felt him pressed to her back and writhed against him to make him even more excited. She felt so incredibly free as she reveled in his touches and kisses. It had never been like this with Leo, especially in the last few years. She was a woman in need and Nate was fulfilling those needs in spectacular fashion.

For ten more minutes, they lavished their attention on each other at an ever-increasing pace until Agatha thought she'd pass out from the incredible explosion of lust that she was experiencing.

She finally whipped around to face Nate and shoved him back onto her bed and once he was flat, she straddled him and kept her hands on his chest as she took control of the final act in the play of passion.

Nate could only marvel at Agatha's unrestricted behavior and took a moment to wonder if Leo hadn't died trying to please her. She was completely uninhibited in expressing herself and doing anything she could to please him. He'd been with a few women, but none of them compared to Agatha's wildness and fury.

It wasn't long after Agatha had shoved him onto his back before she was writhing in ecstasy as she screamed as if to announce her incredible satisfaction. Nate felt his eyes begin to roll back in his head as she bounced and wiggled above him. She shrieked once more even more loudly before she began to slow and then she dropped down to bed beside him and Nate put his arm around her and pulled her halfway onto his chest.

She bent her knee and laid it across his thigh as she kissed him and whispered, "My God, Nate! How much better would it have been if we were in love?"

Nate may have been enormously happy to have been with Agatha, but he still replied, "I guess we'll never know; will we?"

"No, but that doesn't mean we can't enjoy ourselves for another fourteen hours; does it?"

Nate was relieved she hadn't given him a different answer that might have sent him back to Rawlins right away, so he replied, "No, it means that we may have to forget about exploring the ranch and just continue to explore each other until I have to leave."

"That sounds like a much better idea," she replied softly before kissing him again and then sliding her hand down to his inner thigh again.

"No rest for the weary," Nate said with a smile as he ran his hand across her slippery curves.

———

While Nate and Agatha spent the rest of Sunday in various stages of undress as they mixed normal daily activities like eating with a lot of time spent divining new ways to expend their lust, the stage was being set for an event that would soon occur in Albany County that would have severe repercussions by the time Nate returned to the county seat of Laramie tomorrow.

_____

Ruth spent the day doing nothing more than cooking and preparing for Nate's return. She didn't do anything drastic as most of her planning was in her mind which was trying to fill missing holes in her theory of the despicable collusion Nate with her father and Toby Halvorsen.

If she had known what Nate was doing in Agatha Swarthmore's bedroom as she read one of his books, she would have taken the next train to Rawlins with the shotgun. But she wasn't even sure he was really in Rawlins helping Mrs. Widow. She began to suspect that it was a cover story to get him out of town and away from her so their friend, Bill Caruthers could win her affection. The longer she was alone, the more convinced she became that even Ike and that Mary White were in on the plot.

_____

As the sun was setting, Nate and Agatha were sitting at the kitchen table sharing coffee instead of each other.

"You didn't ask me the one question that I expected, Nate?" she asked with a slight smile.

"You mean, why you asked me to enjoy your favors?"

"Kind of. I thought you'd ask in some convoluted way if I'd had invited a ranch hand or someone from Rawlins to do what we've been doing all day."

"No, I wasn't thinking about that. I was curious why you granted me the privilege."

She laughed before replying, "Aside from your physical desirability, which is very high, I knew shortly after you arrived that you had no ulterior motives and that you wouldn't brag about having me. You're an honest and incredible man, Mister Manning. I'm very happy that you agreed to satisfy me, and trust me, you have done more than simply satisfy me. You sent me to new heavens of unearthly delights."

"Agatha, as much as you seemed to enjoy our romps, how have you managed to maintain your sanity?"

The edges of her eyes crinkled as she smiled and said, "I had a lot of things on my mind since Leo died and in answer to my own question, I wouldn't have allowed anyone on this ranch into my bed and not because they worked for me. Honestly, part of your attraction was that I knew you'd be leaving soon. I'll treasure every second we've spent together and that will make me more, um, lonely than I had been before. You set new standards for me, Nate, and I know I'll never have that experience again."

"Are the memories enough, Agatha?"

271

"I hope so. Now, you've got to promise me something before you go."

"Anything."

"Don't agree until I tell you what I'm going to ask of you."

"Okay. Go ahead and make your request."

"Don't withhold your love from a woman who loves you. I don't know why you feel that you need to keep it bottled up inside you and I don't want to know. But it wasn't just sex that we enjoyed. I could almost feel a deep love within you bursting to be free. You've kept it locked in your heart for too long. Let it out and then you'll really live."

Nate just looked into her dark brown eyes and knew that she was right but knowing that she was right didn't mean that he could so readily tear down those thick walls he'd spent a lifetime building. It would take an extraordinary woman to even chip away at those walls and she would have to truly understand why they had been built before he even gave her a hammer. He couldn't imagine any woman who was capable of understanding.

"I'll try, Agatha. That's all I can offer."

"Tell me that you'll really try and not just pay lip service to that promise."

"I will."

She smiled at him before standing and taking his hand, "Shall we have one last dance before we collapse?"

Nate rose and replied, "I thought you'd never ask."

She laughed before pulling him down the hallway.

————

It was later that night, in Monday's first hours that Mary White was awakened by pounding on her bedroom door.

She hurriedly threw on her robe, opened the door and followed Ike to their bedroom where Alice lay on soggy sheets. She was already having strong contractions, so she immediately took control and ordered Ike to heat some water on the stove before she closed the door behind him.

————

Nate's pocket alarm began chiming at five o'clock and it almost died before he was able to push the button to silence it. He kissed Agatha, who rolled over and went back to sleep before he slid out of bed and snatched his scattered clothes from the floor and then grabbed his boots and left the bedroom.

She'd told him that it was likely that he'd be on his own in the morning, and he hadn't been offended in the least. It was as each of them had expected. Each had satisfied the other's needs and there was no lasting emotional bond.

As he dressed in his own bedroom, he wondered if that was an acceptable way of life. He'd lived his life in that manner and had never thought he'd ever change, which he didn't consider to be a serious problem. But her simple request that he love a woman had made him review his life in a different light.

He particularly recalled Agatha saying how much better their coupling would have been if they loved each other. It wasn't just the act's importance that struck him as the reason that he placed so much emphasis on that simple comment. It was that she made it sound as if love elevated everything about life. If that was true, then he was only living a half-life. He was reasonably successful, enjoyed his work and always thought it would be enough. *But was it?*

He finished dressing and quickly walked outside to the privy before returning to the house to use the washroom. He washed his face and upper body, then brushed his teeth before shaving without having a single nick.

Nate skipped making breakfast as he'd have to be in town early to catch the train, but he should have enough time to visit the café.

He donned his gunbelt and grabbed his hat and saddlebags before walking down the hallway past Agatha's bedroom and was smiling as he left the house.

He saddled his brown gelding, but left Strickland's horse and gear in the barn. After hanging his second set of saddlebags in place, he mounted and rode out of the barn and headed for the access road in the early morning sun.

He glanced behind him before the house disappeared from sight and wasn't surprised to see no one waving to him from the porch. He didn't think he'd hear from Agatha again and wouldn't submit a bill for services either. She'd rewarded him much more than he could ever charge her for what he'd done to keep the ranch in her hands.

He reached Rawlins just after six o'clock and after buying his train ticket and tag for his horse, he headed for the boarding house where he still had his Winchester '76, which he still hadn't fired.

By eight o'clock, he was on the platform waiting for the train that would take him back to Laramie. Even though he had promised Agatha that he'd try to do as she asked, he knew that it couldn't be with Ruth Miller. He simple felt awkward around her for reasons that he couldn't explain. It was almost the same sensation he experienced when he'd found himself in the company of men he couldn't trust.

The train was running a bit late, but by nine o'clock, he had boarded the train and it was rolling out of the station heading into the bright sun.

———

At his destination, the morning arrived with new life about to be brought into the world in one part of town, when just north

275

of the city, another life had ended. Of the two events, it was the second which would cause the far greater convulsions.

As Ike remained at home to provide as much help as he could for Mary as she cared for Alice during her labor, a rider rode quickly to town from the Lone Wolf ranch, his horse leaving a long trail of dust in its wake as it sprinted along the road.

In the sheriff's office, Sheriff Scott and Deputy Caruthers were sharing coffee as the deputy tried to seek the sheriff's advice about what he should do about Ruth Miller, which had little to do with providing the protection that Nate had requested.

Before the sheriff could pass along any of his wisdom, the door burst open and Sheriff Scott saw the panicked look on the man's face before he asked, "What's wrong, Joe?"

Joe Willets exclaimed, "They killed him, Sheriff! They shot the boss!"

"*Somebody shot Fred Miller?*" he all but shouted.

Joe nodded vigorously and then quickly said, "He rode out to look at the herds like he always does and somebody drygulched him. Me and a bunch of the fellers heard the shot and I thought the boss was just shootin' at some varmint, but then we saw him drop onto the horse's neck before fallin' to the ground. By the time we got there, he was dead. Got shot on the left side of his chest, right where the heart is."

"Did you see who took the shot?"

Joe shook his head and said, "No, sir. There were twelve of us who went lookin' for the shooter but all we found was some tracks that headed back to town. We lost 'em on the road."

"Did you recognize the sound of the gunshot?"

"Nope, we weren't payin' attention, but I reckon it was a Winchester."

Sheriff Scott turned to Deputy Caruthers and said, "Do you want to inform Miss Miller, or do you want me to do it?"

"I'll do it. I know she told me that she didn't need me there anymore, but Ike will be there, so it'll be okay."

"Go ahead," he said then turned to Joe Willets and said, "Let's get out to the ranch and I'll take a look around for clues. We'll stop and tell Lou Pendergrass to take his hearse out there."

"Okay, Sheriff," Joe said as the sheriff grabbed his hat then followed Bill Caruthers and Joe out the door.

———

Nate's train was more than halfway back to Laramie when Deputy Caruthers arrived in front of his office and dismounted. After tying off his horse, he walked to the front of the office, stepped onto the small porch and tried to open the door but found it locked.

277

He peeked through the door's window to see if he could spot Ike at his desk, but the office was deserted. He almost turned around but then decided to see if Miss Miller was still there and pounded on the door.

Ruth was in the kitchen cleaning up after a late breakfast when she was startled by the noise. She put the plate down and dried her hands on her dress before taking a deep breath. She had to be pleasant to Ike and assumed he'd forgotten his keys in his rush to get away from her on Saturday. She was smiling as she walked down the hallway and only saw a shadow of a face looking in the window as she entered the office. It wasn't until she was just six feet away when she realized that it wasn't Ike, but Deputy Caruthers.

For a moment, she thought about turning around and going back to the kitchen, but she had to act the part of a pleasant person until Nate returned, so she unlocked the door and swung it open.

"Good morning, Bill," she said cheerfully before she noticed his deathly serious expression.

"Um, Ruth, I need you to sit down."

She was ready to snap at him, but instead, she slowly turned and walked to Nate's desk where she took a seat on his big chair as Deputy Caruthers walked behind her with his hat in his hands.

"Where's Ike?" he asked as he stood in front of the desk.

"I have no idea. I thought you were Ike when you knocked. Why did you need me to sit down, Bill?"

"Oh. Um, yes. We were just notified by Joe Willets that there was a shooting out on the Lone Wolf this morning. Somebody drygulched your father, Ruth. He's dead."

Ruth was stunned. When she first saw his haggard face, she almost expected him to tell her that Nate had been killed in Rawlins, but this news was totally shocking and even as she tried to grasp the improbable, her mind began fitting it into her conspiracy theory. It wasn't difficult to do.

As Bill Caruthers watched, Ruth's face morphed from shock, to confusion then to a growing rage that wasn't unexpected. He thought she was angry because her father had been killed. He had no way of knowing that she was seething because she believed that she knew who had killed him.

She slowly rose to her feet and between her clenched teeth she growled, "That bastard! I know he did this!"

It was the deputy's turn to be stunned as he quickly asked, "You know who did it? Why? Who is it?"

She glared at him before saying more clearly, "It doesn't matter if you know. Only that I know."

"You're not making any sense, Ruth. If you know who did it then tell me and we'll go arrest the son of a bitch."

279

"You won't arrest him because you won't believe me. I'll get him to confess and then you can arrest him."

"Please tell me who you think did it, Ruth. It's no good to hold that back. He might escape."

Ruth looked at Bill Caruthers and almost laughed. She knew that if she told him, he'd go and warn Nate. She suspected that he wasn't in Rawlins and now she was sure. He'd probably gone to the ranch and demanded more money and when her father refused, he shot him in the back. *Who else would have wanted him dead?* Besides, she knew that he had his new Winchester with him, and he was a good shot.

Bill stood there waiting for her reply, but she simply stood, then turned and left the office leaving him standing before the desk. When he heard the bedroom door close, he made his own exit to head back to the office. The sheriff wouldn't be there, but by now, Ed Ledbetter should be in the office, and he could man the desk while he went to Ike's house in the hopes of finding him there. Maybe Ike could explain Ruth's bizarre reaction.

———

Nate was in a great mood as the train began slowing on its approach into the station in Laramie. He'd solved Agatha's problem much sooner than he'd expected and enjoyed his time with her, even if they hadn't spent so much of it in her bed. She was a very impressive woman. She'd be the kind of woman that most men would be grateful to be able to spend their lives with, but he wasn't one of them.

The train was slowing to walking speed as he stood and grabbed his '76 musket and strolled down the almost empty aisle to the door.

He stepped onto the passenger platform while the train was still moving and held onto the steel railing before it lurched to a halt and the cars began their banging stops into each other.

He hopped down onto the platform and headed for the stock corral to pick up his horse and waved at some of the folks who passed by.

Nate reached the corral fence near the gate and watched as the gelding was led from the car by Jack Mumford, the stock manager. He brought the horse to Nate and handed him the reins before opening the gate.

As he stepped up, Jack said, "Glad you're back, Nate. How'd it go?"

"Better than I could have hoped for, Jack," Nate replied before sliding the '76 home then nudging the gelding away from the corral and throwing a quick wave to Jack.

He turned onto Main Street but passed Kansas Street then turned down the back alley so he could ride directly to his small barn and unsaddle the gelding.

Two minutes later, he had dismounted and led the gelding into the barn. Before he unsaddled the horse, he patted the buckskin mare on the neck to let her know they were back, in case she'd missed it. Then he looked at the horse that Ruth had ridden out of her father's ranch and wondered if he should return it. The small barn was getting crowded.

He snickered to himself as he removed his saddlebags and then his two Winchesters. He needed to clean his '73 as he'd been too distracted while he was in Rawlins. He leaned them against the wall then began to strip the gelding. After setting his tack on the wide shelf, he began to brush the horse down. As he worked the gelding's coat, he wondered what Ike would tell him about Ruth and Bill Caruthers. He still didn't hold out too much hope that it would amount to anything, but there was always that possibility.

Nate soon finished the brushing before he checked the feed boxes and trough then he hung one set of saddlebags over each shoulder and grabbed his two Winchesters. He left the barn and headed for the back door just forty feet away. He expected that it might be locked, so when he got there, he set one Winchester down and was pleased to find it unlocked. He opened the door, picked the carbine up again, then entered and set the two repeaters in the rack near the doorway before he lowered the saddlebags to the floor.

After closing the door, he loudly shouted, "Hey, Ike! I'm back and you won't believe what happened!"

Ruth was startled by his shout as she'd been in the depths of concentration trying to piece together the last parts of the puzzle. But his arrival inflamed her anger to volcanic levels as she popped to her feet from the chair and stormed to the door. She yanked it open and threw it against the wall making an enormous bang which stunned Nate just before she blew into the kitchen to stun him much more.

"Ruth?" he asked as she marched close to confront him.

He saw the absolute rage on her face and was about to ask what had happened when she lit into him.

"You bastard! *Why did you shoot him?*" she screamed.

Nate had only shot one man in the past six months and even though he didn't understand the connection between Ruth and John Strickland, he quickly replied, "I had to shoot him, Sissie. He was going to shoot me."

"Liar! You shot him in the back!"

"*How do you know?* You weren't there!" he exclaimed in utter confusion.

Ruth was ready unleash hell on Nate as she loudly asked, "What happened? Didn't he give you enough money?"

"Why would he give me any money? I wasn't about to change sides no matter how much he gave me."

Ruth let her rage blast into him as she snarled, "Wasn't a thousand dollars enough to satisfy you?"

Nate finally just looked back at her still trying to understand what she was saying and asked, "What are you talking about, Ruth? Sit down and we'll have a normal talk."

"What, so you can try to convince me that I'm wrong? You can't fool me any longer, Nate, or whoever you are. I know what you did, and I'll see you hang!"

Nate was totally lost trying to follow her train of thought, so he said, "I have no idea what you mean, Ruth. Why would I hang for what I had to do? The sheriff didn't have any problems with it, so why should you?"

Instead of answering, Ruth reached back and with all the strength she could muster, delivered a massive slap across the left side of Nate's face. Satisfied with the physical release of her disgust, she whipped around and marched into her bedroom where she grabbed her two travel bags then quickly left her room and soon stormed out the front door leaving it open.

Nate stood frozen in the kitchen as his fingers slowly touched his reddened cheek. *What had just happened? Where was Ike?* Nothing that she had screamed at him made a lick of sense. If she knew that he'd shot the ex-foreman, *why would she be mad about it? Where would she be going?*

He stayed in place for almost two minutes without getting a single answer to any of his questions. He finally started walking down the hall and soon exited his office closing the door but not locking it in case she decided to return.

As he walked to Ike's house, he couldn't see where she had gone and that only added to his confusion. It was as if he'd left Rawlins and returned to Mister Carroll's Wonderland, where at least he knew he could find Alice.

He continued his slow walk as he scanned for Ruth without seeing her but figured out that Ike may be at home because Alice went into labor. Hopefully, Ike would be able to answer some of his many questions.

He turned onto Main Street and stepped onto the boardwalk heading west. Everywhere he'd looked, he found people but not Ruth. As strange as their meeting had been, he was worried about her. She was hideously angry with him for shooting a man who she probably didn't even know and that smacked of madness. *How did she even know that he'd had to shoot him?* He simply couldn't stop asking himself questions about the bizarre encounter.

He turned down the street to Ike's house and the sight of the white house with green shutters calmed his troubled mind somewhat.

Nate soon turned onto their short walkway and stepped onto the porch and knocked on the front door.

When the door opened, he wasn't surprised to see Mary White looking back at him, but he was curious about her frazzled appearance.

"Is Ike at home, Mary?" he asked.

She smiled before pushing some loose blonde strands back where they belonged and said, "Come in, Nate. I'm surprised you made it back so quickly. Did you fix the widow's problem that fast?"

"I did, and it's quite a story," he replied as he entered the house and closed the door.

"I'm sure it is, but before you even begin to tell it, you'll have to wait with me in the parlor until Ike finishes saying hello to his new daughter."

Despite the recent attack by Ruth, Mary's pleasant face and the wonderful news of the birth of Ike and Alice's baby was like a soothing balm.

"That's wonderful, Mary. How is Alice doing?"

"She's tired, but very happy and healthy."

"I'm sure Ike is just as happy. Did they already give her a name?"

"Are you ready?" she asked with a smile, "The baby girl is Esmerelda Lydia Parker."

Nate was able to withhold his laugh to a grin as he said, "Well, whatever her name, I'm sure that her parents will love her and raise her right."

"I'm sure they will. Did you hear about it somehow or did you just use your impressive powers of deduction to realize the reason why Ike wasn't at the office?"

"I figured it out, but the reason I had to come by was to talk to Ike about Ruth."

"Oh? What do you need to know? Maybe I can help."

He took her arm and guided her into the parlor where she took a seat on the couch before he joined her.

Nate let out a breath and said, "I just got in from Rawlins a few minutes ago and entered the house through the back door. I called out to Ike to let him know I was back, and Ruth came storming into the kitchen like a bat out of hell and began screaming at me. She called me several profane names and even finished her tirade by viciously slapping me. Then she stormed off, grabbed her travel bags and disappeared. I have no idea where she went or what triggered it."

"What did she scream at you?" Mary asked quietly.

"That was part of the mystery and I was worried that she was slipping into madness. She seemed incredibly angry at me for shooting a man whom she probably didn't even know."

"You shot someone in Rawlins?"

Nate nodded then said, "He was the one who set up the scam to cheat Mrs. Swarthmore out of her ranch. They didn't count on my arrival and part of the problem was that I didn't realize until I talked to the widow that the man claiming to be her long-lost brother-in-law had come from Hays City where I'd been a deputy sheriff for more than a year. That upset their apple cart and the man I shot, who was the disgruntled foreman who'd left the ranch, was planning on eliminating me so they could continue to try to cheat Mrs. Swarthmore."

"And Ruth was mad about it?"

"She was more than just mad, she was furious. But I still can't understand how she could even have found out about it. It only happened on Saturday and Sheriff Blount didn't have any legal problems with the shooting, so why is she so upset?"

"That is odd, but I think what started her down that road was when Ike asked her if she liked Deputy Caruthers and she seemed to think that you were trying to get rid of her."

Nate grimaced before replying, "I guess I was trying to find someone for her so she wouldn't try to latch onto me."

"Why? Ike said that you seemed to push away any potential girlfriends. Was she getting too close to being a girlfriend?"

"No, not really. At least not as far as I was concerned and that was the problem, you see? She expected me to feel the

288

same way about her and I didn't. I tried to explain it to her but no matter how I tried to do it, I guess I wasn't successful."

"Well…" she began to reply when there was a loud knock on the door.

Nate stood and motioned for her to stay seated before he walked to the door and swung it open.

Deputy Caruthers glanced inside before he said, "Can you come with me to the jail, Nate?"

Nate nodded, then turned to Mary and said, "Tell Ike that I'm happy for him and Alice and I'll stop by when I can. I'm going to go to the sheriff's office with Bill."

"I'll tell him, Nate," Mary replied.

Nate then walked onto the porch, closed the door and as he and the deputy stepped to the ground, Bill said, "Ruth came to the office and claims that you admitted to shooting her father."

Nate stopped in mid-stride and with wide eyes, he sharply asked, "*I did what? Her father was shot? When did that happen?*"

"You didn't know? She said that she told you and you said that you had to shoot him because he was getting ready to shoot you. Is that right?"

They resumed walking before Nate replied, "Kind of. She didn't say who had been shot. She just asked me why I shot

289

him. I had a gunfight in Rawlins on Saturday with a man named John Strickland, so I thought that she had somehow heard about it, which was why I answered the way that I did."

"She swears that she asked you why you shot her father."

"She didn't. Bill, when did this happen?"

"Around eight-thirty this morning."

"I was on the train from Rawlins when he was shot. Want to see my ticket? I also had a short chat with Jack Mumford when I claimed my gelding. If you need to corroborate my alibi, wire Sheriff Blount in Rawlins. I dropped the body off with him on Saturday, then Mrs. Swarthmore and I met him and the county prosecutor on Sunday so she could sign a plea agreement for the two men who had tried to swindle her."

"I believe you, Nate, but she's making a lot of noise about it."

"I can understand why she'd be upset, Bill, but why is she so ready to accuse me of doing it?"

"I have no idea, but she was still spitting mad when I left. I don't know if she's still there, but Ed Ledbetter was there. The sheriff is up at the Lone Wolf looking for evidence."

"Nobody saw him get shot in broad daylight?"

They stepped onto the boardwalk on Main Street and turned toward the jail as Bill answered, "The ranch hands heard the shot, but thought Fred was just taking a shot at a varmint. By the time they realized he'd been hit and then rode down to help him, he was already dead."

"Did they do a search for the shooter?"

"Yup. Trailed him to the roadway where they lost him. He's probably still in Laramie, but he might have skipped town by now."

They reached the sheriff's office and walked through the open door where they found Deputy Ledbetter but not Ruth.

"Where did Miss Miller go?" Bill asked as he and Nate approached the desk.

"She took off right after you did. She said she wasn't going to spend another second talking to Nate."

"Do you know where she went?"

"She said she was going to get her horse from Nate's barn and then go to the ranch to talk to her mother. I think she was going to blame Nate for killing him."

"That's what she told me, too. I'm sure that he didn't do it because he was on the train back from Rawlins when Fred was shot."

"I told her that Nate was there, but she said he was lying and that he wasn't even Nate Manning."

"She said that?" Bill asked as he and Nate pulled chairs close to the desk.

Even before Bill had asked his question, Nate felt a knife twist in his stomach. *How had she discovered even that about his past?*

Before he could even think of making an excuse, Bill turned to him and asked, "Do you want us to keep her from leaving town, Nate?"

He shook his head and replied, "No, let her go. She's not a criminal, Bill. If she wants to go and see her mother, we can't stop her."

"Aren't you worried that she might try to shoot you? She was really mad."

"If she was going to do that, she could have used my shotgun when I entered my house, but the only damage I received was a slap in the face."

"What are you going to do?" Bill asked.

"I need to calm this mess that I probably created without even knowing it. I'll go out to the Lone Wolf and talk to her and maybe she'll give me a chance to answer her questions. If not, I'll try to talk to her mother."

"By the time you get out there, she may have convinced that whole crowd that you're a murdering monster."

"I know, Bill, but I've got to try. I'll stop by Ike's house to let him know what's going on before I ride out there. Maybe I'll see the sheriff before I get reach the ranch, and he can tell me the mood of the place."

"Do you want me or Ed to come along, Nate?" Bill asked.

"No. She wouldn't believe anyone but me and even that is no better than a fifty-fifty chance."

"Okay, Nate. Good luck and stop by when you get back."

"If I can, Bill," Nate replied before turning around and leaving the jail through the open door.

He walked more quickly to Ike's house than he'd left. He estimated that Ruth was probably less than a mile out of town and may not even have finished saddling her horse yet, so she wouldn't have that much time to tell anyone before he arrived. She might even bump into Sheriff Scott on the road and spend some time telling him what she believed.

Nate reached Ike's house and knocked loudly at the door hoping that he was finished visiting Alice and Esmerelda Lydia.

A tired, but smiling Ike opened the door and before he could say a word, Nate walked past him into the parlor and waited until he closed the door and joined him.

As Nate pulled off his hat, Mary White rose from the chair where she'd been resting and walked closer.

Ike was confused but still smiling as he asked, "Mary said that you visited. I can't believe how pretty our baby girl is."

"I can, Ike. Alice is a pretty lady. But I need to tell you something quickly before I leave. I have a problem that you need to know about."

"What's wrong, Nate?" Ike asked.

"I took care of Mrs. Swarthmore's case faster than I had expected. I'll fill you in later. Anyway, I returned to the house less than an hour ago and when I entered, I called for you, but you weren't there. But Ruth came out of her room and began screaming at me and accusing me of killing her father."

"What?" Ike exclaimed, *"Fred Miller was murdered?"*

"I didn't know about it when I entered the house, so when she demanded to know why I killed him, I thought she was asking about the man I had to shoot in Rawlins. She was accusing me of one thing, and I was defending my actions for something totally different. I was completely confused and never even knew that her father had been shot out at the Lone Wolf. She hauled off and slapped me and then grabbed her things and left. I didn't know where she'd gone, so I came here to see if you knew. That's when I talked to Mary while you were seeing Alice and your baby. I still had no idea why Ruth was so angry until Bill Caruthers stopped by to find me. It was only then that I understood what had happened."

"But you were in Rawlins when her father was killed; weren't you?"

"I was actually on the train coming back. She doesn't know that and accused me of lying about everything, even demanding money from her father. She asked me if a thousand dollars wasn't enough. It's as if she believes that I took all the money that she stole from her father."

"It's still in the saddlebags under my desk."

"I know that, but she never gave me a chance to explain anything. If she'd even stopped screaming for a few seconds, I might have been able to figure out what she meant."

"Why would she accuse you of killing her father in the first place? You rescued her and have protected her since finding her out at Halvorsen's ranch."

Nate sighed then replied, "I don't know exactly, and I don't have time to try to figure it out right now. I'm going to head back to the house and saddle the buckskin then ride out to the Lone Wolf to try to reason with her and maybe she'll listen."

"You're not going alone; are you?" Ike asked sharply.

"I have to, Ike. She needs to hear the truth from me, and I have to convince her that it is the truth before everything gets out of hand."

"It sounds like she's gone mad and she'll be dangerous, Nate. Don't go out there alone. Take the sheriff along."

"He's already out there and I might run into him on the road. But it doesn't matter if he's with me or not. I've got to get going. I'll stop and see you when I return."

Before Ike could try to object any longer, Nate pulled on his hat, smiled at Mary and said, "Hello, Mary," before he added, "Goodbye, Mary," then turned and quickly left the house.

Ike and Mary both stared at the door after it closed behind him and she said, "He's right, you know. He has to do this alone and he's the only one who can change her mind."

"If she still has one to change," Ike replied.

———

It was forty minutes later when Nate rode away from his house on the buckskin mare and shortly after he turned onto the road to the Lone Wolf he spotted the sheriff returning from the crime scene, so he continued riding for another minute then when Sheriff Scott was just a hundred yards away, he pulled the mare to a stop and waited.

The dust created by the sheriff's arrival hadn't returned to the ground before he loudly asked, "What the hell is going on, Nate? Ruth Miller was claiming that you shot her father and had schemed with Toby Halvorsen to take his money."

Nate was momentarily stunned by the new accusation before he replied, "I already talked to Bill Caruthers about the murder accusation, but the second one is new to me. I don't have time to explain right now, Bart, but I have more than enough proof that I was on my way back from Rawlins when her father was shot. She accused me of everything short of shooting President Lincoln."

"I thought she wasn't making a lot of sense, but after she finished telling me, she headed to the house to talk to her mother."

"I figured that. I have to go there and try to find out what set her off before this gets even worse. Before I do that, can you tell me if you found anything?"

"Just a bunch of tracks where the shooter was hiding and brass from a single .44 rimfire."

"Were all the ranch hands accounted for?"

"Yup. It wasn't anyone on the ranch, which kind of makes Ruth's accusations a bit more believable."

Nate nodded before saying, "I'll stop by the office on the way back, Bart."

"You don't want me to come with you, Nate?"

"No, sir. I want to be able to talk to her privately if I can. I'll be okay."

"I don't know about that. She's really mad and I don't reckon her family will let you get close enough to the ranch house to even talk to her."

"I've stayed alive so far and if I see anyone pointing a gun at me, I'll hightail it outta there."

"Well, if you want to take that risk, go ahead. But when you get back, hunt me down even if the office is close. Got that?"

"Yes, sir," Nate replied as he gave the sheriff a short salute then started the buckskin forward as Sheriff Scott shook his head before heading back to Laramie.

As Nate had the mare moving at a slow trot, he tried to make sense out of the intense confrontation with Ruth. He could understand why she'd be angry at him if she perceived his request to have Bill Caruthers stop by and then stay with her for what it was, a feeble attempt at matchmaking. But what he couldn't understand was why she would even remotely make the leap that he had murdered her father. She also seemed to believe that he'd rescued her solely to take the money that she'd taken from her father. But the worst accusation she'd made in that vicious harangue was when she said that she knew he wasn't Nate Manning at all. That meant she'd either been told by someone who knew his past, or she'd done some investigating on her own while he was gone. Either possibility could be devastating.

It was that one statement that could have the biggest impact on his life, assuming that she didn't shoot him before he even had a chance to talk to her. If she began passing that bit of news around Laramie, he'd have to pull up roots again, which is something he really didn't want to do. All he could hope for was that she meant to say that she didn't understand him.

He was totally immersed in his concerns for Ruth's confused anger and its effect on his own life that he continued heading toward the ranch at a slow pace so he could mentally rehearse what he could say when he arrived. He was completely unaware of his surroundings which was something he never did when he was on a job. He just didn't believe he was on a job. *Besides, he'd spotted that unexpected drygulch attempt on the ride to the Double 8, so what were the odds of it happening again, especially so close to Laramie?*

Nate wasn't fully satisfied with the script he'd developed for when he arrived at the ranch house as much of it depended on who would be waiting. He might not even get a chance to see Ruth if the sheriff was right. But he could change the dialogue depending on the situation, so he shifted his mind to his investigative prowess and began to work on the murder of Fred Miller. It would be a bit difficult because he wasn't exactly a likeable man and his unexpected demise would be helpful for Ruth, but it was still a murder, and one that many people may believe he had committed. Folks loved undiscovered, mysterious plots better than straightforward solutions.

He had just begun to delve into the facts that he knew of the killing when his anxious, but peaceful ride abruptly ended with the sharp crack of a Winchester. Even as his ears registered the unexpected sound, they reported the zipping sound of the .44 slug as it buzzed past inches from the front his chest.

Nate was startled and yanked back on the reins and was reaching for his Colt when a second shot was fired. But he had pulled back so hard on the buckskin's reins that her head was lifted back as she slammed her forelegs into the road. The second bullet that was meant for him slammed into her neck creating a red shower of blood as she screamed and began to buck in pain.

Nate's right hand was on his pistol's grips as he tried to avoid being thrown, but his left hand and clenched thighs weren't enough to keep him in the saddle and as his mare fought to stop the agony, he felt himself leaving her back even as the sound of a third shot mixed with his dying horse's wails.

He flew off her left side and as he arced through the air, he felt as if it was happening to someone else. He'd never been thrown before and he had no idea how hard he would hit. Time seemed to slow which he began to believe was a precursor to his death. Maybe he was supposed to be having his life flash before him, but then he realized he really didn't have a life to review. This entire train of thought rolled through his mind in the few seconds from the time he left the saddle until he impacted on the hard ground and everything stopped.

"Nate! Nate!" he heard through a mist.

His mouth felt like stone, he was sore all over and his left shoulder was the worst as he tried to remember what had happened. Then it came back to him in a flash. *He and his mare had been shot, but why wasn't he dead? Who was calling to him?*

Again, he heard that disconnected voice calling, "Nate! Nate!", then it added, "Wake up, for God's sake!"

Nate recognized the voice and as he slowly opened his eyes, he noticed how late it was. The sky was red, so he must have been lying on the road for hours.

Then he saw the sheriff's concerned face and croaked, "Could I have water, please?"

Sheriff Scott must have been ready to empty his canteen onto his face to wake him, so he didn't leave, but lifted Nate's head then tilted the canteen's spout to his lips.

Nate felt the cool wetness flow across his thick tongue and down his appreciative throat and after three long swallows, the sheriff lowered the canteen and then Nate's head.

"What happened, Nate? Who shot your horse?"

"Three shots, Bart. He took three shots at me. The first one missed but was really close. The second one hit my horse's neck and I got tossed. I don't know where the third one went. What time is it?"

"Around eight-thirty, I'd guess. I was ready to lock up and figured you'd forgotten to stop by, so I headed over to your place and your buckskin wasn't there, so I rode over to Ike's and he said that you hadn't stopped by after telling him about Fred's murder. I figured you might have run into trouble at the ranch, so after I had my supper, I headed this way."

Nate didn't ask why he'd had his dinner before looking for him but asked, "Did you see anybody since you left town?"

"Nope. When I spotted you on the ground not moving and with your shirt all bloody, I thought you were dead. Your horse is dead, but when I checked, you were still breathing, so I looked for a bullet hole and didn't find one. I reckon you hit the ground pretty hard."

"Why didn't the shooter come over and finish me off? He should have at least checked to make sure I was dead. There wasn't anybody around."

"I guess he didn't want to take a chance that I heard the gunshot. Whoever drygulched you must have seen me riding to town and then skedaddled after he let loose with those three shots."

"Can you help me up, Bart? I need to see how I'm doing."

"Let's do that," the sheriff said before standing then bending over and taking Nate's hands.

Nate let Sheriff Scott do most of the work as he rose slowly from the ground until he was vertical. The world was spinning and for a moment, he thought he'd vomit all over the sheriff, but he managed to keep control of his stomach as he gripped the lawman's left shoulder.

The horizons continued to move for another minute as he blinked and wobbled but then his world began to steady.

"It's getting better now, Bart."

"Did you get even a glimpse of the shooter, Nate?"

"Not at all. I wasn't even scanning the area as I always do. I was stupid and almost paid the ultimate price for it."

"Any ideas who pulled the trigger? You don't think it was somebody from the Lone Wolf; do you?"

"No. That doesn't make any sense. Why would they shoot me this far away from the ranch when they could just let me show up, smile and then shoot me and bury me. That ranch is so big no one would ever find my body. If I had to guess, it's the same man who killed Fred Miller."

"That's what I was thinking. Any guesses?"

Nate was feeling steady enough to release his grip on the sheriff before he replied, "I had just started working on that problem when those shots arrived. I'd thought about it some before I left town, and I had narrowed it down to two suspects. Who would have a recent grudge against Fred Miller? Unless someone waited to seek retribution against the man because lord knows that he pissed off a lot of folks, then the most likely suspects would be either Toby Halvorsen or Stubby Nicks."

"Okay. I'm with you so far. Now explain why each of them would want to kill Fred Miller."

"Toby had run off with his daughter and convinced her to take a thousand dollars. He was probably after the money and Ruth was just a side benefit. When I took it away from him, he had nothing. He might have returned and threatened to shoot his wife or someone else unless he gave him money. Trying to coerce Fred Miller wouldn't work, so after he was refused, Toby shot him. Now that's a really flimsy theory because I talked to Toby and I don't think he's got it in him to even confront a man like Fred Miller or the spine to drygulch a man, either."

"I was going to point out those two minor issues with that idea. What about Stubby?"

"We both know that Stubby has the guts to shoot anyone and when I caught him following me, I know that he wasn't happy and not just because I took the Sharps sniper rifle from him. I really got under his skin by suggesting he leave town rather than face Fred Miller's wrath for his failure. He might have returned to Laramie and stewed for a day or two while I was gone, then headed out to the Lone Wolf with some excuse for his failure and to ask Fred to pay him anyway. I believe that his payment was that he'd get to keep the thousand dollars, or at least a good portion of it. Once he lost that opportunity, he may have asked Fred to finance his move to Cheyenne and been refused.

"Stubby isn't the kind of man to take no for an answer but is smart enough to not become a prime suspect in Fred's murder. So, he finds a good place outside the ranch for both an ambush and a hideout. He's got to figure out that if he shoots Fred while he's on the ranch, his cowhands or family will hear the shot, which won't give him time to make an escape all the way to Laramie. So, after he shoots Fred, he leaves the site and disappears into the trees then rides toward town and after riding on the road for a while, he goes to his hideout and lays low for a while."

"That's better than your Toby theory. Okay, so you have Stubby hiding out while the ranch hands search for him then I show up and can't find him. What was he waiting for?"

"If he was watching the road, which would be the smart thing to do, then he would have seen the ranch hand race into town to fetch the law, then he'd see you ride past heading that way. He couldn't risk leaving until you'd gone back into town and things settled down. Then he probably would wait until it was dark before taking a back route into town. I imagine that'd he'd even told a bunch of guys around town before he rode out there that he was moving to Cheyenne, so when you went looking for suspects, you wouldn't be that surprised to find him missing."

Sheriff Scott nodded then after he glanced at the trees on both sides of the road, he said, "So, while he was watching the road to make that I didn't return with my deputies, he spotted you and couldn't resist the temptation to make you pay for taking away his big payday."

"That's what I think anyway."

"Do you think he's still there, watching?"

"Not a chance. He made his plans for killing Fred Miller, but I was just a bonus. Once he put me and my horse on the ground, he probably saw all that blood and lit out through the trees. I just don't know where he went if he did leave his hiding hole."

"We'll talk about that later. Are you up to riding without falling off again?"

"I'll manage. What about my gear?"

"Grab your Winchester and slip it under my slicker once you're on board. Let's get moving."

Nate nodded before walking to his dead horse and slipping his '73 from its scabbard and returning to the sheriff who had already mounted. He handed his repeater to the sheriff, then mounted behind the saddle before he took the carbine back and just pushed it into the rolled-up slicker behind his butt.

As the sheriff walked his horse back to Laramie, Nate felt enormously tired and hoped that he didn't fall off again. It had been a long, exhausting day that had started so well and ended so badly. He'd never had a chance to explain anything to Ruth, and he doubted that he'd be able to go out there tomorrow. He'd need a day to recover and sort out what he'd do now.

Ruth was probably already telling her family and the large number of workers on the ranch that Nate Manning wasn't his real name and he was probably an outlaw. She'd be able to make a compelling case that he had murdered her father as no one on the ranch had heard his side of the story. His hidden walls of privacy had been breached and he wasn't quite sure how he could stay in Laramie much longer.

––––––––

It was dark when he slid from the sheriff's horse in front of his house and said, "Thanks, Bart. I'll stop by in the morning."

"Alright. I'll see if we can't find Stubby Nicks before you show up or at least find out if anyone has seen him."

Nate waved before the sheriff rode off and slowly walked toward his porch and after entering his office, he closed and locked the door before shuffling to his room where he set his

Winchester on his dresser and then tossed his hat on the nearby chair.

He didn't bother lighting a lamp but left his room and after stopping in the kitchen to pump some water into a pitcher, he emptied two glasses of water before heading out the back door to use the privy.

It was almost as if he was dreaming when he reentered the house and closed the door. He meandered through the kitchen, then down the dark hallway and turned into his room where he sat on the bed. He pulled of his boots, then dropped onto his back and shifted until he was in the middle of the mattress and just pulled the quilt over him and closed his eyes.

Nate never had another conscious thought on that unforgettable Monday.

CHAPTER 9

When Nate finally opened his eyes on Tuesday morning, he was confused and felt almost like a stranger in his own bed. It took him a couple of minutes to recall why he hurt so badly and the sequence of startling and upsetting events that had begun shortly after his return to Laramie.

He didn't bother getting out of bed as he reviewed each of them beginning with Ruth's vitriolic and confusing attack in the kitchen before ending with his waking up on the road to the Lone Wolf ranch. Even after he'd recalled each one, he remained lying on his back, staring at the ceiling.

Nate wasn't even sure what time it was as the late spring sun sent blasts of bright sunshine through his window. Then he remembered that he needed to visit Sheriff Scott this morning and hoped he hadn't slept until noon.

He carefully sat up and swung his legs out of the bed and let his feet touch the floor. He rubbed his hand over his head and neck feeling for bruises and was surprised that he didn't feel any added pain. That changed when he pushed on his left shoulder. His back and legs were sore, but he needed to move. They'd be stiff but staying in bed would only make it worse.

Nate pulled on his boots and slowly stood before taking out his pocket watch and found it was only 9:20. It was much later than he usually awakened, but it wasn't as bad as he'd expected.

He slid the watch back into his pocket and walked out of the room with a stiff gait, but not a limp. He reached the kitchen and started a fire in the cookstove before pumping more water into the pitcher and downing two glasses of water.

While the stove heated, he headed out to the privy and was moving better by the time he returned and passed through the kitchen to go to the washroom.

Once he was inside, he pulled off his shirt and inspected his body for damage. It wasn't as bruised as he'd expected which was a positive and as long as he had his shirt off, he thought he'd take the opportunity to wash. He didn't have time for a bath, but he stripped and then after pumping some water into the tub, he soaked a towel and worked some lather with a bar of white soap and washed his upper body before dropping his britches and underpants and washed below the waist. He stayed in that semi-dressed condition while he shaved and thought he was dry enough to pull up his pants when he'd finished.

He carried the blood-stained shirt back to his bedroom and tossed it into the waste bin before donning a clean shirt. He looked at the bed and was surprised that none of the buckskin's blood had been transferred to the quilt, but then again, it had a long time to dry.

Nate didn't bother making a hot breakfast but did put on the coffeepot and then cut some smoked pork and put it on a plate with two biscuits and a tub of butter.

By the time he walked out to the office, it must have been well after ten o'clock and for a moment, he wondered where Ike was, and then remembered Esmerelda Lydia had arrived and was probably keeping him and Alice awake nights. He smiled at the only good news he'd had since his return. He wondered how Mary White was holding up and how she could manage to do her housekeeping jobs when she had to act as a midwife and was curious if she was going to show up tomorrow to clean.

After entering the office, Nate walked to Ike's desk and pulled the saddlebags full of Ruth's cash from underneath and carried it to his bedroom where he put them in his gun cabinet's large bottom drawer with the ammunition. Without Ike in the office, he was uncomfortable just leaving them in the open.

Five minutes later, he'd locked the front door and was walking along Kansas Street to go to the sheriff's office. As he turned onto Main Street, he glanced across at T.F. Green's and his mind made a strange connection...pickles. He suddenly remembered that in the saddlebags that were still on the buckskin were his two wrapped pickles he'd taken with him

311

to Rawlins. He almost giggled when he realized that he'd never had a chance to eat them and had totally forgotten they were there. Considering all of the much more serious things on his mind, it was such a silly memory to make its appearance that it lightened his mood. Pickles: the cure for all that ails him.

He was still smiling as he approached the jail and then turned and walked through the open doorway.

Deputy Ed Ledbetter was at the desk and when he spotted Nate, he said, "There you are. The boss was gonna send me over to your house to find you in a little while."

"Is he in?"

"Yup. He was just about to head out to the Lone Wolf."

Nate nodded then pulled off his hat and walked past the deputy and soon entered the sheriff's office.

"Glad to see you ain't dead, Nate. Sit down and I'll fill you in on what's been going on."

"Yes, sir," Nate replied before taking a seat.

"While I was doing the rounds this morning, I sent Bill and Ed around to ask about Stubby. He's not in town and a few of the folks told them he had gone to Cheyenne, just as you suspected."

"Okay. Did you ask Harvey over at the depot if he took the train?"

"I didn't, but you can ask. I'm getting ready to head out to the Lone Wolf to tell Mrs. Miller what we have so far. I don't think they know that you had a few chunks of lead sent your way yesterday."

"I don't think it'll make any difference anyway, Bart. What I do need you to do for me is to take the saddlebags with the money I got from Toby Halvorsen back to Mrs. Miller. I'll ride bareback with you to pick up my saddle from the buckskin."

"Okay. I'll be leaving in about twenty minutes or so."

"I'll swing by Ike's house to let him know what happened and I'll meet you in the street outside of my place."

"See you there."

Nate stood and quickly walked out of the office, waved to Ed as he passed and was pulling on his hat as he reached the boardwalk. He wouldn't be able to take much time at Ike's, but he needed to at least let him know the basics just in case Stubby, or whoever had shot had taken those shots had another chance and didn't miss this time. At least he'd be a lot more attentive now.

He reached Ike's house and after he knocked on the door, he glanced at both ends of the street in the smallest of chances that he'd spot Stubby riding past, but he only saw normal traffic before the door opened.

"You didn't stop by again yesterday," Mary said as she let Nate enter.

He pulled off his hat and said, "I ran into a few problems. How are you doing, Mary?"

"I'm fine, but you seem a bit worse for the wear. What kind of problems?"

He entered the parlor and was surprised not to see Ike, so he turned to her and asked, "Where is Ike?"

"He's sleeping in the bedroom with Alice and the baby. They were up most of the night."

"Oh. How about you? Did you get any sleep?"

She smiled and replied, "I nap. I'm used to late nights when I have to work as a midwife. You seem anxious. Do you have time to join me for coffee?"

"I wish I could, Mary. I just stopped by to tell Ike what happened when I rode out to the Lone Wolf to talk to Ruth, but I have to leave with the sheriff in a few minutes."

"I'll tell him. What happened?"

"I was heading out to the ranch and someone took a shot at me with a Winchester, the first one missed, the second one

314

killed my mare, then the third went somewhere else. I was thrown from the saddle and knocked out for a while, so I never got a chance to explain anything to Ruth. The sheriff is going to go up there now and talk to the family and I'm just going to retrieve my saddle and then return."

"Who would want to shoot you?"

"A lot of men, I reckon, but my best guess was Stubby Nicks. I think he's the one who shot Fred Miller, too. But Ruth is probably trying to convince everyone out there that I was his murderer, so that rumor may find its way into town, even if we do find the real killer."

"Does that bother you?"

"Parts of it does, and not just because it would hurt my business and make everyone believe I was no better than the worst breed of bounty hunter."

"I know you have to run, but when I come over to your house tomorrow, can we talk more?"

"You don't have to clean the house, Mary. I know how tired you must be. I'll still pay for the job, but you need to rest."

"I'm fine, Nate. You forget that I'm young and resilient."

Nate smiled as he said, "I never forget that you're young, Miss White. And I know that you're much more than resilient. You have character, Mary."

315

"Thank you for the compliment, and I'll still be there tomorrow. Alice and the baby are both doing very well. I'll probably sleep well tonight, and I'll see you tomorrow. You still haven't told us what happened in Rawlins."

"I will. Tell Ike that if he wants to wait until Monday to return to work, that's fine. I'll be busy helping the sheriff track down Fred Miller's killer."

"I'll tell him, but you take care, Nate. I don't want to have to come over to your house as a nurse."

"Well, if I do get shot, that'll make up for it."

"I'd rather you avoid that in the first place, Nate."

"So, would I, Mary," he said before turning then pulling on his hat and leaving the house.

Mary watched him leave and after the door closed behind him, she wondered just how much damage Ruth would cause. Ike had told her that Nate had mentioned that he might have to leave Laramie after Ruth made Nate aware of her affections. She hoped that he wasn't considering it even more seriously now that Miss Miller espoused unadulterated hatred for him.

———

As Nate hustled along the boardwalk to get to his house, he wondered why he had almost been flirting with Mary White. He'd never done that before, yet she had disarmed him

316

somehow. He was still sure that she wasn't trying to take Ruth's place, but deep behind his walled sanctuary, he began to feel that if anyone could get past those strong defenses, it would be Mary White. He'd yet to find a single characteristic in her that wasn't admirable. He was already feeling his only way to keep his life intact, whether it was from Ruth's external onslaught, or Mary's growing fifth column assault was to leave Laramie as soon as Fred Miller's killer was brought to justice.

But before he even made the turn onto Kansas Street, he remembered his promise to Agatha just a few days ago. He'd said that he'd try not to withhold his love from a woman who loved him. The underlying question he'd had for years was whether or not he had any love inside to withhold in the first place. He wasn't even sure he knew what it was.

He turned onto Kansas Street and didn't see the sheriff yet, so he cut into the back alley. When he reached his barn, he put his spare bridle on the brown gelding then led him out of the barn and tied him in back before going inside the house and retrieving the money saddlebags from the gun cabinet. He would be happy to get rid of the damned things.

By the time he rode bareback to the front of the house, he found Sheriff Scott sitting in his saddle out front.

When he reached the sheriff, he handed him the saddlebags and said, "I counted exactly nine-hundred and twenty-eight dollars in here, after I gave fifty to Tory Halvorsen and I guess he and Ruth spent the other twenty-two."

317

"Don't be surprised if they demand you give them the remaining seventy-eight dollars, Nate," he replied as he hung the saddlebags over his own.

"I'd be more than happy to give it to them if they just left me alone. I swear that I never want to hear about the Lone Wolf ranch again."

They turned their horses north and Sheriff Scott replied, "That'll be hard to do if you stay in Laramie."

"I know," Nate said even though he knew the sheriff didn't realize that he was very close to leaving town.

———

It was already after the sun had passed its zenith when Nate slid from the gelding and approached his dead buckskin.

The sheriff held his horse in place as he asked, "Will you be able to get that saddle out of there, Nate?"

"I think so. If I can't, I'll ride back and buy a new rig."

"Well, good luck. Stop by tomorrow and I'll let you know what's going on at the ranch."

"Okay, Bart," Nate replied before the sheriff popped his legs and rode away.

Nate was able to get his saddlebags and scabbard off without a problem, but he found that even removing the cinch was difficult because the carcass had expanded in the heat. He could cut the leather, but then that would need to be repaired and he'd still have to work to get his saddle free.

He stood and glanced toward the Lone Wolf before deciding that it just wasn't worth the effort. Even if he was able to remove the saddle, it would probably smell as bad as the horse's body already did, so he set the saddlebags on the ground and opened the left side. He pulled out his two wrapped pickles and tossed them as far as he could before hanging the saddlebags over the gelding then hopping onto his back.

He was going to head back to Laramie, but then sat on the horse and studied the surroundings; something he hadn't done when he should have. Those three shots came from his right, so he turned the horse in that direction and walked him from the road and soon entered the trees.

He knew that the sheriff hadn't investigated the area, so any hoofprints he found would belong to the shooter. They wouldn't be more than a hundred yards from the road, but he didn't think that Stubby would want to be closer than thirty yards so he wouldn't be seen.

It was dark in among the pines and he was walking the horse slowly as he studied the ground. Having a lot of broken branches and pine needles on the floor of the forest would make it easier to notice where they had been disturbed.

It took him another five minutes before he spotted the first signs of the shooter and he wasn't surprised to find the hoofprints of two horses. He suspected that the second horse belonged to a packhorse because Stubby always worked alone, if the shooter was Stubby. If he was someone else, then the investigation would be much more difficult because he would be out of suspects.

He followed the trail as it wound south through the trees and then after more than an hour of slow, twisting tracking, the trees ended at the east-west road that ran between Cheyenne and Laramie. There had been too much traffic for him to follow the tracks after that, so the question was which direction the shooter had gone.

Nate needed to buy another saddle, so he headed for Laramie and thought about where to look for Stubby. He'd told Stubby to go to Cheyenne and the men that the sheriff and the deputies had interviewed had all said that where Stubby had told them he was headed. That might have been true before he decided to murder Fred Miller, but he doubted if he'd gone there now. It would be too easy for the sheriff to send a telegram to his counterpart in Cheyenne, the seat of Laramie County. It was a bit confusing for Laramie to be in Albany County and Cheyenne in Laramie County. At least they didn't name Cheyenne Albany which would add even more confusion to the mapmakers.

He entered Laramie in Albany County and headed for Rothman & Sons Leather Works just on the eastern end of town. Twenty minutes later, he was riding comfortably in his new saddle as he headed for his house to have some lunch and study his maps to get a better idea of where he would find Stubby Nicks. He already had some thoughts but staring at a map made things more logical.

The first thing he retrieved from his cold room was a sour pickle. He took a big bite and reveled in the tart explosion in his mouth as he picked out more ingredients for what he expected would be his biggest meal of the day.

After building a fire in the cookstove, he filled the coffeepot and set it on the hot plate as he polished off the pickle but didn't go back to get a second. He'd learned that an empty stomach and two of the big sour delights didn't go well.

While the coffee water heated, he walked to his office and took his maps from the bottom drawer and headed back to the kitchen where he spread them out on the table. He studied the area for just a minute before returning to the stove to cook his lunch.

———

After finishing his food, he was working on his third cup of coffee as he traced different paths that Stubby could have taken from the point where he'd reached the road. There were towns all along the railroad in both directions which served as watering and coaling stations for the trains. If Stubby had a packhorse, it may have been just to provide supplies for him

321

while he was hiding after shooting Fred Miller, or he could be planning on going somewhere they wouldn't look.

He folded the maps and finished off his coffee before leaving the kitchen and returning the maps to the drawer.

Without the buckskin, he was down to one horse now, so he wouldn't have a packhorse when he started and didn't want to buy one just for this job. He'd pack later, but right now, he'd ask some questions in town that might give him a better guess as to where he might find the man.

He took his new Winchester, left the house then mounted the gelding and rode down the alley. His first stop was at the train station where he asked if Stubby had used a train to leave town and wasn't surprised that to learn that he hadn't been seen. With that possibility gone, he headed for M&D Livery. They hadn't seen Stubby either and it wasn't until he asked Don Mc Callister at Don's Livery that he got some answers. Don said that Stubby had bought a mule and a pack saddle four days ago but hadn't seen him since.

A trip to T.F. Green's gave him a better idea of Stubby's purpose for buying the mule. Ron Fairly, one of the clerks, told him that Stubby had purchased a large order three days ago including a lot of food and other supplies. He remembered joking with Stubby about it and Stubby had told him that he was going on a job that would keep him out of town for a week or more.

THE NOTHING MAN

After getting a reasonably accurate list of what he'd bought, at least at T.F Green's, Nate left the store and decided he'd make one more stop before he returned to the house before everyone closed for the day.

Five minutes later, he dismounted in front of the gun shop and quickly entered before Jerry closed the doors.

When Jerry spotted Nate he grinned and said, "Well, if isn't the murderer Nate Manning himself."

Nate wasn't amused and snapped, "That's not even remotely funny, Jerry. Where did you hear that?"

"A couple of the boys from the Lone Wolf are in town spreading the word. Curly Davis was the one who came in here to buy a box of .44s and told me."

"Damn! I was hoping to keep that stupid rumor confined to the ranch. I guess I should have realized that it wasn't going to stay there. You know that I was on the train from Rawlins when he was shot; don't you?"

"No, but I knew you were in Rawlins, which is why I thought it was safe to make the bad joke. Sorry."

"That's okay. The reason I stopped by was to ask if Stubby Nicks stopped by to buy anything in the last few days."

"Yup. He came by three days ago and bought a couple of boxes of .44s and a Sharps rifle, one of the Big Fifties. It didn't have a scope like the one you took from him, though."

"Did he say if he knew how to use it? The one he had before looked almost brand new."

"He said he'd used them before, but I'm not sure how good he was."

"Okay. Now, excuse my ignorance, but how is the range of the one he bought versus the one I have?"

"Well, he bought some .50-100 cartridges and you have .45-100s for yours. His has more stopping power, but yours will have more range, but it'll still depend on other factors. Even then, it won't be much, maybe fifty yards or so."

"I don't think it'll matter, but I'll probably take the Sharps with me when I try to find him."

"Why are you looking for Stubby?"

"I think he's the one who shot Fred Miller. When I was on my way to the Lone Wolf to reason with Ruth Miller, I was drygulched. The shooter took three shots at me with a Winchester, not a Sharps. He killed my horse, but not me. I'm pretty sure that Stubby was the one on the trigger then, too. Nobody else makes any sense."

"Well, he's the kind of guy to do those things. He's all temper and no soul."

"That's the right of it, Jerry. I've got to get back to my house to get ready to leave. Anything else you can remember about his visit?"

"Well, he did ask about you."

"That's not surprising. What did he want to know?"

"He said he heard most of the story about how you found Miss Miller but didn't know how you found her so fast. I told him that you just checked the land office and found that his folks used to have a ranch south of Little Laramie."

Nate nodded and said, "Thanks, Jerry. You helped a lot."

"I've gotta make up for that sorry excuse for a joke."

"You more than made up for it, Jerry," Nate said before he turned and left the shop.

After mounting the gelding, Nate headed back toward his house and was almost sure that Stubby was hiding out in the Halvorsen ranch. He wanted to do this alone because he felt responsible for this mess. He let Stubby go and then he tried that stupid matchmaking scheme that set Ruth off.

He pulled the gelding into the empty barn and dismounted. He began removing his new saddle as he remembered the landscape surrounding the abandoned Halvorsen ranch.

There was a lot of open ground around the ranch house and the barn and with Stubby now having that Sharps, it would be almost suicide to try to get near the house during the day. His best bet would be to wait until well after nightfall and that would mean he'd have to be sure that Stubby was in the house.

When he returned to his house, he sat down and poured himself a cup of cold coffee before he took a seat at the table. He sipped on the coffee without really tasting it as he thought about his future after finding Stubby if he returned at all. That rumor he had hoped would be stopped before it left the Lone Wolf would probably continue to thrive even after Stubby was exposed as the real killer. It might even be worse if he wound up shooting the man.

If he was the murderer, then he wouldn't surrender or even talk to Nate. If he chose to hide out on the Halvorsen ranch, then Stubby probably suspected that the sheriff had already tied him to Fred Miller's murder and he probably thought that Nate was dead, too. Maybe that was his best advantage. If Stubby didn't know he was alive, then maybe he could use that to capture Stubby without getting into a gunfight at all.

That line of thought continued and blended with his earlier plan to go into the ranch house at night. The coffee cup in his hands was empty as he continued to develop the idea. Sheriff Scott was probably still at the Lone Wolf ranch, so he'd see him tomorrow to reveal what he'd uncovered about Stubby. Then he'd start out for Little Laramie. He might ask the sheriff to send one of his deputies along as a witness in case he did have to kill Stubby, but even then, he doubted if it would have any serious impact on the rumors that Ruth had planted.

He was still sitting at the table in deep thought when he was startled by a knock on the front door. It was too late for a client and Ike had a key, so he expected that the sheriff had returned with news of what had happened at the Lone Wolf. He rose and walked quickly to the office and soon unlocked then opened the door but didn't find a lawman on his doorstep.

"Ike asked me to come by," Mary said before stepping past him and entering the office.

Nate closed and locked the door before following her into the office where she'd taken a seat in the chair beside his desk. He walked around her and sat in his own chair and waited for her to explain what Ike needed to know.

Mary smiled then said, "He and Alice are worried about you, Nate."

"I appreciate that, but why did Ike send you here instead of taking a little time out of the house and stopping by himself."

"Because I believe that Alice is trying to push me into your life and convinced Ike to send me here to ask how you were doing."

"It's not a surprise because they've been trying almost since I've been here but thank you for letting me know."

327

"You're welcome. So, how are you doing?"

"I suppose I have to tell you that someone, probably the same man you murdered Fred Miller, tried to shoot me when I was headed to the Lone Wolf yesterday. He missed me but killed my horse and I spent some time unconscious on the road. I'm okay now."

Mary was startled but asked, "Did you want me to check your injuries?"

"No. I'm just a little sore. Would you like some coffee?"

She looked at him with a measure of disbelief before replying, "That sounds like a good idea," before she stood and waited for Nate to leave his chair.

When he did, she took his arm and as they walked down the hall, he asked, "I thought you were going to get some sleep. It's already close to sunset."

"I know, but I thought I'd just sleep here. I have to come here in the morning anyway."

As soon as they reached the kitchen, Nate turned and faced her before he said, "I don't have a chaperone, Mary. You can't stay here. It's bad enough that you're in the house and the sun is still up."

"Oh, please. We're both unmarried adults with no family. Besides, I'm already hearing rumors that would probably hurt your reputation much worse."

Nate sighed then turned to pick up the coffeepot as he said, "I know. I've been hearing them already myself."

Mary took a seat and asked, "Can I guess that Ruth is the source?"

"She's the only one who believes that I murdered her father, unless Sheriff Scott has convinced her to change her mind when he went to the ranch around noon."

He emptied and rinsed out the coffeepot before filling it with water and setting it on the cold hotplate. Mary just watched as he added kindling and wood to the firebox and then lit a match and started the blaze before closing the heavy door with a clang.

Nate then walked to the table and took a seat across from Mary who then asked, "Why are you going to try to find the murderer? Isn't that the sheriff's job?"

"He and his deputies are working on it, too, but if I'm right about who did it, then I want to be the one who finds him."

"Is it that Stubby character who you thought was going to kill Ruth and the cowhand?"

Nate stared at her for a few seconds before asking, "Did I tell you that?"

"No, but as soon as I heard that Mister Miller had been shot, he was the only one I could think of with a motive."

"You should be a detective, Mary. It took me a lot longer to make him my choice as the potential killer."

"I can afford to be wrong, Nate. You can't. Do you know where he is?"

"I have a good idea, so I'll talk to Sheriff Scott in the morning and let him know. I need to find out how his visit to the ranch went anyway."

"There's something else that I heard you may need to know."

"About Stubby Nicks?"

"No. It's part of the rumors that are being spread about you. You know about the murder part, but they're also saying how you and Toby Halvorsen conspired with her father and you killed him so you could keep the money she took."

"Now I know that I told you she'd made that accusation while she stood right here, so that shouldn't be a surprise."

"No, it wasn't. But the last part of the accusation that you didn't mention was that they're saying you aren't who you say you are and that you're really an outlaw on the run."

Nate looked up at the ceiling as he blew out his breath. It was the only part of the rumors that he wouldn't be able to dispel without revealing his past. He may not have been an outlaw but being a bareknuckle brawler who had fought his way across several states was bad enough. Before that, he had nothing to prove that he even existed, so there was no way he could fight those rumors.

He lowered his eyes and looked at Mary before he said, "Would you believe me if I told you that that part of the rumor is as untrue as the rest?"

"Of course, I would. Why shouldn't I? Do you recall the first time we spoke just a few days ago in T.F. Green's?"

"Every word, ma'am."

"I may be young, but I've seen the best and worst of people since I left St. Louis. I can look into their eyes and get a pretty good idea of what lurks behind. I've never seen anything but good in yours from that first moment you stood in front of me with the armful of diapers."

"You don't know me at all, Mary. Don't make me into some hero like Ruth did. Look what it did to her after she realized I was just a man with as many faults as any other man."

"I didn't say you were a hero, Nate. I said you were a good man. Are you telling me that I'm wrong and that you have some violent misdeed in your past that makes you think of yourself as unworthy to be considered a good man?"

"No. I've never done anything that approaches bad, but I'm not some sweet, kind gentleman."

"You may not think so, but I think you are all of those things. You told me that I had character, and I believe that you have even more than I do."

"I'm seriously flawed, Mary. Surely, you understand that."

"I understand that you seem to be afraid of letting anyone, especially a woman, get too close to you. Alice didn't have to point it out to me, either. Her efforts to try to find a woman for you aren't a misguided attempt just to marry you off. She believes that you need someone to share your burden, and so do I."

"But you aren't me, Mary, and neither is Alice. Even Ike doesn't really know me. I've only been here three years and all they know of me is what I've done since I've been here."

"Can you tell me about your life before you arrived in Laramie?"

Nate looked at her blue eyes and was almost ready to honestly answer her question before he replied, "No, I'd rather not. It's not something that I'm proud of, even though it was far from criminal."

Mary hadn't really expected him to answer, so she wasn't going to tell him about her history, at least not yet. She would reserve that until it became critical.

"Alright. At least you know it's out there. I was thinking about Stubby Nicks. Why don't you have the sheriff with jurisdiction go and arrest him if you know where he is?"

"I'm not sure he's there and I found out that he bought a long-range rifle before he left, so if they show up with their badges, he'd be able to shoot them before they could get in range."

"But you're not worried about that?"

"No, I know he has it, so I'll be able to plan for it."

Nate then stood and walked to the cookstove and pulled the coffeepot off the hotplate and opened the lid. After pouring in the ground coffee, he took two mugs from the shelf and filled each one before returning to the table.

As she accepted her mug, Mary asked, "So, is it alright if I stay here tonight?"

"I suppose it's okay. At least you'll be able to get that good night's sleep you hoped for."

Mary laughed and said, "I will. I'll admit that I'm a bit worn out and I promise that you won't have to worry about having me sneak into your bedroom in the dark."

"I didn't think you would. I had to almost wrap myself in a cocoon when I was sleeping on the floor in the same room with Ruth even though she was in her bed."

333

"So, what are your plans for tomorrow?"

"I'll visit with Sheriff Scott, then probably come back here and pack for the ride to Little Laramie. I think Stubby is hiding out in the Halvorsen ranch where I found Ruth. He asked the gunsmith where I'd found her and Toby when he bought that long-range rifle."

"Are you taking yours?" she asked before sipping her coffee.

"Yes, ma'am. I'll probably do a few practice shots on the way to get a feel for it. I've never shot one before. I still need to fire my new Winchester, too."

"How long will you be gone?"

"If he's there, probably two or three days. If not, it'll be a lot longer."

"Would you mind if I stayed in your house rather than my small room at the boarding house?"

"I would actually appreciate it if you did. Ike won't be back here until next Monday, so the place will be empty. At least that money is gone. The sheriff took it with him when he went to the ranch."

"I'll still lock the doors at night in case anyone hears that the money was here and comes looking for it."

"That's a good idea. If you want to feel safer, you can take the shotgun out of my room and keep it near your bed. Can you shoot a gun?"

"I've fired a shotgun and a Winchester, but not often."

"That's alright. Keep the shotgun in your room in case some would-be thief breaks in. If you hear glass breaking, just take the shotgun and stay in your room. There are locks on all the doors, so when you're ready to turn in, lock the door. I don't have anything in the house worth stealing now that the saddlebags with the money is gone, so let anyone who breaks in ransack the place. You stay behind that locked door with the shotgun until daybreak. Okay?"

"Yes, sir, but I don't think anyone will do such a thing. They know you live here and are good with your pistol."

"All the same. Please do as I ask."

"I will, but I'm not going to lock the door tonight because I trust you."

"I won't lock mine either because…well, just because."

Mary laughed again before she took a longer sip of her coffee.

Nate was getting decidedly comfortable with Mary and the feeling was alien to him and it was its strangeness that made it uncomfortable to feel comfortable. Her question about his life before Laramie had left its mark when he almost answered it. He'd never been so close, since leaving Kansas after his time with Luther Galloway. No one in Laramie knew that he really didn't even have a name or anything else to document his existence in this world, yet Mary had almost heard his confession after knowing him for a week.

If the timing had been different, he might have even been more worried about the effect she was having on him, but with the shotgun spread of rumors about him racing through Laramie, he expected that he'd be pulling up roots again before the Fourth of July holiday.

―――

They were still talking while Mary made a real dinner and Nate lit some lamps. He'd explained what had happened with the Double 8 case, and although he didn't tell Mary about how he and Agatha had spent his last day on the ranch, he did describe Agatha to her.

After they'd finished eating, the conversation continued in the light of the lamps, yet neither paid attention to the passage of time.

It wasn't until the lamp in the kitchen sputtered and died when it used the last of its kerosene fuel that Nate realized how late it was.

"I'm sorry, Mary. I've kept you from getting your much-needed sleep. At least you can sleep in tomorrow morning."

Mary smiled as she replied, "You forget that I'm a midwife and have the habit of waking early even after just a few hours of sleep. Besides, I thoroughly enjoyed our long talk."

"As did I. Well, at least try to stay under the quilts as long as you can."

"I promise that I'll do that, but don't lose your temper if you see me wandering the house when you wake up."

"I don't think I could ever get angry at you, Mary. You're too good a person."

"I know a few people who would argue that point. At least you don't have to worry about me turning into Ruth."

"In many ways," Nate said as he stood.

He waited for Mary to leave the kitchen and enter the room she'd used when she'd acted as a chaperone. He wondered what she would be wearing to bed as she hadn't brought a travel bag. Maybe she was wearing a nightdress under her dress.

He heard her door close before he stepped into his room and closed the door. He sat on the bed and pulled off his boots as he tried to think about what he needed to do tomorrow, but it was difficult to concentrate. He knew that Mary was an attractive, well-formed young woman, yet he didn't lust after her as much as he expected, and it surprised him. When Agatha had barely suggested that they enjoy each other's company, he was eager to join her in her bed. With Ruth, he understood that he needed to stay away, but that didn't mean it was easy to ignore her offers. He had been tortured for most of the night knowing what he had denied himself. But Mary was lying in bed just a few feet away and may even be naked under the quilts and he only thought of her as someone he wanted to have nearby. He didn't doubt that she could inspire his lust with just a word, but he hadn't even needed a word from the other women he had admired and with whom he had shared intimacy. Mary was just…different. She was different in a good way and he wasn't sure why she was.

But he would be leaving tomorrow for Little Laramie and Mary would be staying in his house while he was gone. He wondered if Alice and Ike knew she'd be staying here rather than returning to her room. He'd be surprised if they didn't.

He eventually let the night take him away and slipped into a deep sleep filled with imaginary images and stories.

CHAPTER 10

Nate was able to wash, dress and even start the fire in the cookstove before Mary walked out of her room wearing a nightdress.

"I see that you presumed that I'd allow you to spend the night, Miss White."

Mary smiled as she passed by and said, "It was just a precaution in case you did, sir," then left the house to use the privy.

Nate had the coffeepot filled and on the hot plate when she returned.

"I'll cook breakfast while you get washed and dressed, ma'am," Nate said when she stopped nearby.

"You need to pack for your trip, Nate. I kept you up too late to do your preparations. I'll cook breakfast unless you're too embarrassed to have me in the kitchen in my nightdress."

"No, I'm not embarrassed in the slightest. I was just trying to maintain my façade of being a good man. But thank you for giving me the chance to get ready to make the ride. It won't take me that long because it's only about four hours to Little Laramie, so I won't need a lot of supplies."

"Just go ahead and start packing while I fix breakfast."

"Yes, ma'am," Nate said before leaving the kitchen and entering his room. He took his empty set of saddlebags and began loading it with a spare set of clothes, two towels and one box of ammunition for his pistol, another for the Winchester '76 and a third of the .45-100s for the Sharps. He set the repeater and the scoped rifle on the bed before pulling on his gunbelt.

As he looked around for anything else that he might need, he snapped his fingers and walked to the bottom drawer of his dresser and after opening it, he pulled out his field glasses. He hadn't needed them in more than six months, but expected they'd be handy when he reached Little Laramie. He could use the rifle's scope, but the field glasses gave him a wider view.

His last act was to check the shotgun load and after he confirmed both barrels were loaded with buckshot, he brought it into Mary's room and set it near her bed before returning to his room where he hung his saddlebags over his shoulder and picked up the two long guns.

He returned to the kitchen and leaned the Sharps and the Winchester against the wall before lowering the saddlebags to the floor nearby.

"All set?" Mary asked as she scraped the scrambled eggs in the skillet.

"All except for some traveling food. I'll add that after breakfast."

"I'll tell you what. How about if I fix you something while you're visiting the sheriff? I'll pack it in some butcher paper, so it'll stay reasonably fresh."

"I'm sure it will be better than what I usually take with me, so I'll gratefully accept your offer."

He poured two mugs of coffee and set them on the table before he put two empty plates on the counter near the cookstove. After placing the tableware before their chairs, he sat down and took a sip of the scalding coffee.

"Did you get a good night's sleep last night, Mary?" he asked.

"A very good night's sleep. I haven't felt so comfortable in, oh, the last time I slept in that bed."

Nate laughed then said, "With Ruth sleeping in the other bedroom."

She began piling the scrambled eggs onto the plates as she asked, "What will you do about Ruth? She lives here and it's only a matter of time before you meet her in town."

"If she still continues to believe that I killed her father, then I may have to move. We'll see. But the strangest thing about the hatred she holds for me in the mistaken belief that I

341

murdered him is that she hated him, or at least that's what I thought when we were at the Halvorsen ranch house. Did you talk about her father with her at all?"

"We didn't talk much because I think she was jealous of me the moment she met me."

"I know, but why would she be so angry at me even if she believed that I'd murdered him if she wanted him gone anyway."

Mary moved the slices of ham onto the plates then walked to the table, set them down before taking a seat and saying, "I don't think that was the reason at all. She was using that as cover for what she was really furious about."

"My poor attempt at matchmaking."

Mary nodded before taking a big bite of scrambled eggs then after she swallowed, she said, "She was hurt and felt rejected, but you already know that."

"I did, and I feel like a heel for even thinking about it."

"Do you think she'd be any less hostile if you told her directly that you weren't thinking of her as a possible mate?"

"No, I guess not."

"How do you think she'll react if she finds out that I stayed here last night or am living here while you're gone?"

"I have no idea. You probably could guess better than I could."

Neither spoke for a couple of minutes but just ate in silence as each imagined Ruth's reaction to that tidbit of gossip. Even when Mary had asked if she could stay the night, he hadn't thought of that unexpected consequence.

Nate finally said, "After I see the sheriff, I'll come back with more information about how she is now. Maybe she calmed down after she had a good night's sleep and Sheriff Scott was able to get her to understand that I did none of the things that she accused me of doing."

"I hope so. I don't want you to leave, Nate, and not just because it would cost Ike his job. I enjoy spending time with you, and I think I can help you."

"I don't want to leave, Mary, but I may not have any choice. I'll make sure that Ike is set before I leave, but I can't stay if Ruth continues to spread her lies."

Mary sighed then said, "Just don't do anything rash. Will you promise me that?"

"I don't do anything rash, at least not for a while. Let's just hope that Ruth has come out of her storm."

"I guess that's all we can do right now."

"Well, I'll go and talk to the sheriff. I should be back within an hour or so."

"I'll have your food ready for you when you get back."

Nate smiled at her before standing and taking his hat before walking out the back door then heading for Main Street.

As he walked, he paid attention to the buildings and people that had become so familiar to him these past three years. He hadn't lived in one place this long since he left that damned bottle factory, if one could call that living. He'd never really had a home, not even in Hays City, until he came to Laramie. Now he'd probably have to leave because he didn't believe that Ruth would change her mind. Even if she didn't and became a friend, which would be nothing short of a miracle, the rumor she had started about him being a fraud would linger and sooner or later, someone would discover the truth.

He turned onto Main Street and hopped onto the boardwalk as he walked west toward the sheriff's office. *How many more times would he be stepping across these wooden paths?*

When he entered the jail a couple of minutes later, he found all three lawmen sitting around the front desk talking, probably about what had happened when the sheriff visited the Lone Wolf. They all turned when they heard his loud footsteps, but none of them passed a word of greeting as Nate pulled off his hat, which was an ominous sign.

Nate looked at the sheriff and asked, "How did it go, Bart?"

"It wasn't as bad as I expected, Nate. Grab a cup of coffee and pull up a chair."

Nate took a cup from a nearby shelf, filled it with coffee, then slid a straight-backed chair closer to the desk and waited for the mixed news from the Lone Wolf.

"Ruth was a lot calmer than the last time I talked with her and everyone seemed to believe that you hadn't murdered Fred and were on the train from Rawlins. Returning the money helped. But strangely enough, once I thought that issue was behind me, when I said that you'd been drygulched on the road to the ranch, Ruth apparently changed her mind again. She asked me for details and when I told her that your horse had been killed and I found you unconscious but unhurt, she asked me I'd found any evidence of the shooter. I said that I had to get you back to town, but it had been a few hours anyway."

"Are you telling me that she thinks that I shot my own horse and then waited for you to find me, so I'd be a victim and not a suspect?" Nate asked in astonishment.

"She didn't come right out and say that, but that was my impression when she asked the question."

"Great. Is that it, or do you have more news?"

"The only other tidbit I found that was different from what I'd first been told was that not all of the ranch hands were accounted for on the day that Fred was shot. Two of them, Art

Stanfield and Curly Davis were out at the eastern line shack. Nobody even thought about it until they rode in for chow that evening."

"Did either of them have a grudge with Fred?"

"Almost all of them had at least one or two run-ins with him over the past couple of years. Fred wasn't an easy man to please and he was pretty unforgiving of any mistakes."

"Did you talk to them while you were there?"

"Nope. I didn't have a chance. Anyway, aside from what I just told you, nothing else has changed. How did your day go after you got back? I noticed you weren't able to get your saddle free."

"I bought a new saddle, then I began asking around about Stubby. He's not in town, as you probably already know, but I found that he'd bought a pack mule then a lot of supplies. He also bought a Sharps rifle, one of those Big Fifties, from Jerry Hare. When I was talking to Jerry, he told me that Stubby asked him where I'd found Toby and Ruth Miller. I think that's where he headed to hide out for a while until things calm down."

"You said it was a Winchester that was used to try to take you down."

"He wouldn't have used a single-shot rifle in that situation. He was reasonably close, about sixty yards from the road, and

I was riding past on a perpendicular path, so hitting me with a Sharps when you have to account for the trees is a very iffy proposition. Besides, he probably would have had his Winchester ready to fire before he even spotted me."

"So, how sure are you that he's on that ranch?"

"Not very. He could have gone to Cheyenne like he told everyone, but why would he let everybody knows he's going there if he's planning to shoot Fred Miller?"

"I'll give you that. I didn't think it was likely he'd let us know where he was. He didn't take the train, either."

Nate nodded then replied, "I know. I found where he'd set up and taken the shots at me. I trailed him to the road to Cheyenne but lost him in the busy traffic prints."

After a short pause, he said, "Bart, I'm planning on going down to that ranch in a little while to see if he's there. If he is, then I'll wait until it's dark and then capture him. I don't want to kill him because I need to have a trial and hopefully a confession. If I am able to capture him, I won't ask him a single question. I'll just truss him up and bring him back here and turn him over to you, so you can do your job."

"I can send Bill or Ed with you, Nate."

"I'd rather do this alone, Bart. I don't want to waste your time if you're wrong and the plan I have in mind will work better with only one, anyway. I feel like I'm responsible because I let Stubby go."

"I can appreciate how you'd feel that way, but that doesn't mean you shouldn't have a backup. Stubby is a tough character and he's facing the noose, so he's not going to come easy."

"I've never had backup, Bart. I'll be fine and hopefully by tomorrow I'll return with Stubby and even Ruth may be convinced that I didn't kill her father."

"Okay, Nate. But if you aren't back in four days, I'll send a deputy down to Little Laramie or come down there myself."

"I don't have a problem with that. I need to get going in case Stubby is already getting ready to leave if he's even there."

"When are you leaving?"

"Within an hour. I should be able to get there with at least an hour of daylight left and take a look."

Nate then stood and shook the sheriff's hand before turning and leaving the jail. As soon as he was outside, he pulled on his hat and headed back to the house. He thought about swinging by and telling Ike but expected that Mary would go there and explain things after he'd gone. They had spent so much time in conversation that she knew as much as he did about events since he'd returned from Rawlins.

Mary had been dominating his thoughts too much since he'd returned. It was an odd conflict that was being waged in his mind. He enjoyed spending time with her almost from that chance meeting in T.F. Green's, and that level of comfort had only been increasing with each minute he'd been with her. At the same time, his well-entrenched concerns about keeping his past hidden and fears of exposure were fighting to keep her from getting too close. He'd worried about others discovering his secrets, but this was different. He wished he could tell her but knew what would happen if he did. Then there was the whole Ruth factor that could explode at any moment. His best and maybe only option would be to do what he had been hoping to avoid and leave Laramie.

He reached his house and rather than go through the office, he walked around to the back and stepped onto the short porch. He was reaching in his pocket for his keys when the door opened, and Mary stepped back to let him enter.

"What did the sheriff say?" she asked as he removed his hat.

She closed the door and Nate replied, "It seems as if everyone on the ranch now believes that I didn't kill Fred Miller, but Ruth questioned the sheriff in such a way as to make it sound that I had staged the drygulch attempt to deflect suspicion. I don't think she's convinced yet."

"Why am I not surprised," she said as they walked to the table and sat down.

349

"I'm going to saddle my horse and then head to Little Laramie."

"I made you some food to take with you and put it into your saddlebags. There are two paper sacks with sandwiches and one heavier one with some fried chicken and biscuits."

"When did you have time to make fried chicken?"

"I made some yesterday because we were expecting you at Ike's. After you left, I went to Ike's house and told them what happened then brought my clothes and the chicken with me when I returned."

"What did Ike say?"

"He was surprised that you had been caught in an ambush but understood the rest of the stories. He said to tell you to be more careful and that he was grateful for the extra days off."

"The sheriff said that if I'm not back in four days, he'd send somebody to find me, but I don't think that'll be necessary."

"You'd better be back before then, mister. Don't forget that Ike will be back to work next Monday."

"What does that have to do with it?"

"We wouldn't be able to continue our private conversations with Ike around; would we?"

Nate felt the skirmish simmering in his mind again, so he replied, "Maybe. I'd better be going."

They both stood and Nate pulled on his hat before picking up the heavy saddlebags and the Sharps. After hanging the saddlebags over his shoulder, he grabbed the Winchester and as he headed for the door, Mary trotted past him and opened it for him.

"Thank you, ma'am," he said as he crossed the threshold.

He expected to hear the door close behind him, but instead he heard her light footsteps on the porch as he hopped to the ground. Nate was about to look behind him when Mary caught up with him and strode beside him as he walked to the barn.

"You don't think you're coming along; do you?" he asked as they passed through the open barn doors.

"Do you have another horse already?"

"No, but I can't think of any other reason for you to come to the barn. All I'm going to do is saddle my horse and ride out of town."

"Are you going to follow the same route you took to get to that ranch the first time?"

"No. I took that path because of where I'd started, and I didn't want to risk having Stubby Nicks try to get behind me again. This time, I'll take the roads to Little Laramie. It's much faster."

He set the Winchester against the wall and as he was about to lean the Sharps next to it, Mary took it from his hands.

He lowered his saddlebags to the barn floor and asked, "Why did you take the Sharps?"

"I just wanted to see how heavy it was. It's pretty impressive."

"Do you want to shoot it when I get back?"

"Heavens, no! I just was curious how difficult it would be to hold a heavy gun like this steady for any length of time."

"It takes practice, but I've never fired one, so I'll have to try it myself when I get out of town."

He began saddling the gelding with his new saddle and would take the occasional glance at Mary as she studied the Sharps. He found it difficult to believe that hefting the big gun was her real reason for coming to the barn with him. He just didn't know what it could be.

He'd just tightened the cinch before taking another quick look and found her blue eyes focused on him rather than the Sharps.

Nate attached the scabbards to the saddle and then took the Sharps from her hands.

"Thank you, Nate. I didn't know if I could hold it much longer."

"You could have rested the butt on the barn floor, Mary," he said as he slipped the rifle into the left scabbard.

Mary handed him his Winchester which he slid into the right scabbard before he picked up his saddlebags and after placing them behind the saddle, tied them down.

When he untied the gelding's reins and began to lead him from the barn, Mary got in step with him again until he stopped just outside the doors.

"Nate," she said before he mounted, "Please don't think about leaving Laramie, even if Ruth starts even more rumors."

Nate sighed then replied, "Mary, I may have to leave even if she suddenly thinks I'm her hero again. I wish I didn't, but it may be the only thing I can do."

"Why? I thought you liked it here?"

"I do. It's my first real home and I wish I could spend the rest of my life here, but that may not be possible."

Before she could say anything else, Nate stepped into the saddle and took the gelding's reins in his hands but didn't set the horse in motion. He looked down at Mary as she stared up at him with her blue eyes shining in the brilliant sunshine.

That earlier skirmish in his mind had erupted into a massive battle as she smiled and said, "Please just come back and talk to me before you even think of making that decision. Okay?"

"I promise," he said before nudging the gelding forward at a walk and headed north down the alley toward Main Street.

Nate didn't look back for fear that he'd weaken even more in his resolve to leave Laramie. Mary White had a sledgehammer and was fracturing his stone walls of protection and he felt as if he was losing the battle.

He turned onto Main Street and had set the gelding to a medium trot as he passed by T.F. Green's where he'd first met Mary, then the sheriff's office. He hoped he hadn't made the wrong decision in not accepting Sheriff Scott's offer to send one of his deputies with him. He'd find out if he had in a few hours.

———

Nate left Laramie behind and had the gelding moving at a fast trot to put some distance between him and the town so he could do some target practice with his two new guns. He didn't expect that much of a change with the upgraded Winchester, but the Sharps was a totally new weapon to him. He knew how it worked and how to load it, but he'd never used a telescopic sight or even shot at anything more than two hundred yards away. He still didn't think he'd need either gun to capture Stubby if he waited until late at night and the man was

354

sleeping in the ranch house. But he didn't want to be caught at a big disadvantage now that Stubby had that new Sharps, and Stubby had claimed that he'd used them before, so that would be to his advantage.

He rode for over ninety minutes before he turned the gelding to the south and left the road. He didn't need to go far, and he needed to eat some of the food that Mary had packed for him. He just hoped she hadn't included some form of love note but didn't think she would. Mary wasn't like that. Ruth, on the other hand, would probably have written him a love sonnet on a pair of her bloomers.

He was snickering as he dismounted and tied off the gelding on a nearby pine branch before taking the Winchester from its scabbard. He expected the bigger .45-95 round to give him another sixty to seventy yards of range and the drop would be less, so he set the step ladder sight to a hundred yards and picked out a target that was around that distance. It was a snapped branch that had fallen to the ground but remained attached to the tree.

He set his sights and squeezed the trigger. The repeater popped against his shoulder with more force than the '73, but not that much more. He missed the branch but saw the impact of the bullet behind it and knew he'd been high. He hit the branch on the second shot and fired three more rounds before he was satisfied with its accuracy and the change in trajectory. He returned to the gelding, reloaded the Winchester and then slid it back into its scabbard before taking four of the .45-100 cartridges for the Sharps.

Even though the range of the rifle was much greater than the Winchester, Nate first selected a target just two hundred yards away and used a thick tree trunk rather than a branch. He needed to see where the bullet hit.

He removed the lens caps from the telescopic sight, then opened the breech and slid the massive cartridge home before closing it and cocking the hammer. He didn't use the adjusting screws on the scope because he wasn't sure how they worked anyway. After bringing the Sharps level, he stared down the scope and had a hard time finding the tree trunk. So, he looked above the optical tube and aligned the muzzle with the trunk, then looked through the scope again. This time he found the crosshairs on the trunk and set them on an unusual coloration in the bark before releasing the first trigger. He held his breath, slowly pulled back on the second and was rewarded when the rifle boomed and slammed into his shoulder. He looked downrange and was impressed that he'd hit just a couple of inches above the spot on the tree.

For another ten minutes, Nate practiced with the long-range rifle and then returned to the horse and slid it home. Before he mounted, he opened his saddlebags and pulled out one of the two smaller paper sacks and opened it. He smiled as he pulled out a tubular-shaped wrapping of butcher paper and after unrolling the paper, took the big pickle in his fingers and took a bite. He was giggling as he unwrapped one of the two sandwiches while holding the pickle between his teeth. He put the bag with its remaining sandwich into the saddlebag and quickly ate the pickle before wolfing down the sandwich. He washed it down with some water from his canteen then mounted the gelding to continue his ride to Little Laramie.

He soon reached the turnoff to the town and headed south. He knew he was just a couple of hours away from the ranch and debated about swinging around the town. Even as that thought occurred to him, he thought it might be wiser to approach the ranch house from the southwest where Stubby wouldn't expect anyone. So, before Little Laramie even came into sight, Nate turned the gelding off the road and headed southwest to skirt the town and then continue in that direction for an hour before turning back east. By then, the sun should be low in the sky and at his back, which would make it difficult for him to be spotted but would illuminate the ranch house for his observation. He'd follow the same path that Toby had used to run away from Ruth, but he'd be going toward the ranch house.

Nate saw the roofs of Little Laramie to his left a little while later and continued to ride until it disappeared behind him and he shifted to the south. The ranch was less than two hours southeast of town at this pace, so he'd make his turn to the east soon. The distant trees that Toby had used as cover would provide him with his path to get closer to the house. He kept glancing to his left as he continued toward the trees but angled slightly in that direction knowing that he'd see the roof of the barn before anyone in the house could see him. He just hoped that Stubby was relaxing in his temporary home. He'd been there for at least three or four days and after the first two, he might be less concerned about the law hunting him down. But even if he was still watching for riders, he couldn't watch in all directions and he couldn't keep it up all day. Nate was counting on Stubby's need to sleep.

He was just about a half a mile from the trees when he spotted the outline of the barn, so he shifted the gelding to the right until it disappeared again. He entered the trees three minutes later and continued into the forest for another hundred yards before turning east.

Even with the late afternoon sun, it was dark among the dense pines, so he'd only get brief glimpses of the buildings of the Halvorsen ranch as he wound his horse through the trunks. When he thought he was as close as he would get, he pulled up then dismounted and tied the reins to a branch.

He took his field glasses from his saddlebags and began walking north toward the ranch house but didn't see any buildings until he'd almost walked past the tree line and had to step back then shift to the side until he had a decent view.

Nate didn't need his field glasses to notice the smoke coming from the stovepipe which meant that someone was in the house. It might be some squatters, but it was much more likely that it was Stubby fixing himself his supper.

THE NOTHING MAN

He put the field glasses to his eyes and focused them on the back of the ranch house. The door was closed, but after almost two minutes, he picked up a shadow moving past the window. He then had to lean against a tree trunk to avoid losing his balance as he continued to monitor the back of the house.

The advantage of choosing this location was that Stubby wouldn't expect him to be here. Of course, Stubby didn't expect him to be breathing either. The disadvantages were that he wasn't able to see into the barn to get a look at the animals inside and he wasn't able to observe the front of the house where Stubby probably spent most of the day watching the road to Little Laramie unless he used the barn loft which would give him another half a mile of visibility.

After about fifteen minutes, Nate lowered the field glasses but continued to keep an eye on the house. If someone came outside, he'd use them to see if it was Stubby.

He spent another forty minutes just watching and was about to return to his gelding to have another sandwich when the back door opened, and he almost rammed his field glasses into his eyes.

Nate was so convinced that he would be seeing Stubby Nicks that he was smiling as he stared through the lenses until he finally recognized the man on the short back porch who was tossing a panful of a dark liquid onto the ground. It was Toby Halvorsen.

"Son of a bitch!" Nate swore under his breath as he continued to watch the house.

Toby then turned and walked back inside leaving a frustrated and angry Nate Manning staring at the closed door through his field glasses.

He lowered the glasses and turned around to head back to the horse already wondering what he should do now that his guess about where Stubby had gone was proven wrong. If anyone other than Toby had been in the house, he would have just mounted his horse and ridden back to Laramie, but he'd told Toby to move on and he'd returned anyway. He suspected that he'd heard that Fred Miller was dead and maybe he thought it was safe to return to Laramie.

As he reached his horse, Nate decided he'd have a chat with Toby and let him know what was happening in Laramie just in case he thought of returning to the town. The last thing he needed was for Ruth to see Toby again, especially if she ever returned to a normal mindset.

He untied the reins, mounted and turned the horse toward the ranch house before taking his new Winchester from its scabbard. He didn't think Toby would try to shoot him, but then he didn't think Toby would come back, either.

Nate walked the horse into the low western sun and kept his eyes focused on the house as he held his uncocked Winchester in his right hand. He'd learned his lesson when he'd almost been ambushed on the way to the Double 8 and then was almost killed during his ride to the Lone Wolf. He wasn't about to fall into that trap again. But then, knowing that he was facing Toby and not Stubby, he slipped the Winchester into its scabbard and pulled his Colt.

But he had made a mental mistake that was much worse than not expecting an ambush. He'd been so convinced that Stubby Nicks was hiding out at the Halvorsen ranch that when he identified Toby, he totally forgot about Stubby. He expected to find one man in the ranch house, and he'd spotted one man. Now he was riding toward the ranch house to talk to that one man and wasn't looking for a second.

In the barn's loft, Stubby Nicks was leaning against one of the support beams with his Winchester across his lap and his new Sharps leaning against the wall twelve feet away as he chewed on a stalk of hay and watched the road to Little Laramie. He was close to finishing his second shift of the day and he was hungry. Toby was cooking supper and he expected to hear from him soon.

———

When he'd arrived at the ranch, he'd been startled to find smoke coming from the cookstove pipe. He had heard that it had been abandoned and he was high strung after his two murders, so he'd pulled his pistol when he walked his horse to the front of the house expecting whoever was inside to be in the kitchen.

361

He'd left his horse and pack mule standing and slowly entered the house with his cocked pistol ready to shoot anyone. But he was actually concerned that there might be a woman doing the cooking, so he wasn't going to shoot anyone until he at least identified the person as a threat.

He made it halfway down the hall before Toby heard a board creek and turned to see what had made the noise, but fortunately for him, he wasn't wearing his gunbelt. When Stubby suddenly appeared with a cocked pistol in his hand, there was just that brief moment where Stubby hesitated and Toby threw his hands into the air.

After that near-death introduction, they talked and discovered they had more in common than either had expected. The strongest was their strong dislike for Nate Manning. Toby had been pleased and relieved when Stubby had told him that he'd killed both Fred Miller and Nate, and Stubby was happy to have a backup while he stayed there as he knew that he couldn't stay alert all the time.

Now he was watching the road and thinking about supper. Toby might be a boring sort, but he could cook. Neither one had seen even a whisper of a rider since Stubby had arrived, and the longer that road stayed empty, the less likely that they would.

He glanced across at the Sharps and wondered what he would do with it now that Nate Manning was dead. It was the only reason he'd bought the gun after Manning took the one

Fred had given him. He didn't want to face Nate even before he had that damned scoped Sharps, but with the added range, Manning would have another advantage that he didn't need. Now his Sharps just sat there unused as protection against a visiting lawman.

Nate hadn't even given a glance at the barn since he'd seen Toby return to the house. He didn't expect Toby to send a .44 his way, but he still focused his attention on that window and door.

He was about forty feet from the back door and another eighty yards from the barn when the door's hinges suddenly squealed, and Toby stuck his head out the door and looked toward the barn without even noticing Nate.

"Hey, Stubby!" he shouted, "Chow's ready!"

What followed was a domino cascade of revelations as Nate was stunned by Toby's call to Stubby and turned his eyes toward the barn where Toby was facing just before Toby shifted his eyes and saw the supposedly dead Nate Manning on his horse just fifteen yards away with his pistol out.

Inside the barn, Stubby popped to his feet with his Winchester and took one long stride to the door to tell Toby he was on his way when he spotted Nate sitting on his horse just fifty feet from Toby. He quickly cocked his Winchester and was bringing it to bear when Nate shifted his Colt's sights to the barn and fired.

363

Nate didn't expect to hit Stubby at that range but needed to at least make him miss with his first shot before he had a chance to get his Winchester free.

Stubby had barely gotten Nate in his sights when he saw Nate fire and quickly pulled his trigger before ducking.

Nate was about to change weapons when he made another mistake that almost cost him his life...he'd forgotten about Toby once he spotted Stubby. He had convinced himself that Toby was a cowhand and wasn't a danger long before he had even known Stubby was there, so he never so much as glanced down at Toby who had pulled his Colt and cocked the hammer.

Nate's pistol was halfway to his holster when he was stunned as he heard a nearby gunshot at the same time that he felt a hot jerk on the left side of his chest. He rocked and twisted in the saddle but didn't drop his Colt. He cocked the hammer and aimed it at Toby, who thought he'd killed Nate and hadn't bothered to prepare for a second shot. He was new at gunfight game.

Nate wasn't a newcomer and as Toby stared at Nate with his pistol still pointed at him, Nate fired. His bullet ripped along Toby's forearm before punching through the ranch house wall. He screamed and dropped his pistol before grabbing his arm and racing back into the house.

Nate quickly turned his eyes back to the barn as he
rammed his pistol home and was reaching for the Winchester
when Stubby fired his next shot.

For the second time in the space of fifteen heartbeats, Nate
felt the burn of a bullet as it passed through his left buttock
and buried itself in his new saddle's seat. He could feel blood
flowing from his chest and now his behind, and knew he
wouldn't have time to get his repeater, so even as Stubby
prepared to make the finishing shot, he dropped to his
gelding's neck, and whipped him to the right before kicking
him into a gallop.

He heard Stubby's shot but didn't know where the bullet
went as he cleared the ranch house and pulled hard on the
reins then quickly turned the horse to the left to put the house
between him and the barn.

Once he felt safe behind the house, he had to start
gambling. He pulled the gelding to a stop and pulled his
Winchester before he painfully dismounted. He had to ignore
his wounds until he stopped Stubby. The biggest gamble was
how he planned to do it. He was depending on Toby's inability
to shoot left-handed and that he was now concentrating on
stopping his own bleeding rather than where he was.

He quickly stepped around to the front of the house which
was out of sight of the barn's doors. He suspected that Stubby
had his Winchester aimed at the far side waiting for him to
either ride past or try to take a shot from the porch. So, he

entered the house as quickly as he dared and headed for the window on the west side of the front room that faced the barn. The sun was so low in the sky that most of the room was in deep shadows, but that window had a bright shaft of sunlight spreading across the floor where he needed to be in order to take the shot.

What made it critical that he make the shot count was that he wasn't in condition to engage Stubby in a long gunfight. If he didn't put him down with that first shot, then he'd have to get to his horse and make a break for Little Laramie to get someone to fix his wounds. Even that would be a problem as Stubby would probably follow him and shoot him in town as he was being treated. *He was a wanted murderer already, so what did he have to lose?*

He stayed out of the sunlight as he slowly stepped toward the west wall but kept his eyes focused on the window as more of the barn came into view. When the edge of the open right door appeared, he slowed down even more. He could hear Toby's grunting and swearing coming from the kitchen, so he knew where he was. After he took his shot, if he was lucky enough to at least take Stubby out of action, he'd have to deal with Toby and do it quickly.

As more of the barn door became visible, he didn't expect to see Stubby. He should be back in the shadows waiting for a target, so when he'd moved another couple of feet closer to the wall, he was gratefully surprised to see Stubby with his

Winchester aimed at the edge of the porch. He was exposed and Nate would have his shot but couldn't afford to miss.

He took a kneeling position to get a better angle but had to remove his hat to get a clear view. He knew it would hurt but he needed to make the shot.

After he'd set the hat on the dusty floor, he cocked his new Winchester and set the sights on Toby hoping he stayed put for another few seconds. Just as his sights settled and his index finger moved to the trigger, Stubby suddenly shifted his sights. For a moment, Nate thought he'd been spotted, but then he realized that Stubby was changing his angle more to the front of the house and not the window.

He didn't waste time wondering why he had done it but held his breath and squeezed his trigger. As the loud report echoed through the almost empty house, his .45 shattered the window and a fraction of a second later ripped through Stubby's chest, sending him stumbling backwards into the dark loft. Nate couldn't afford to waste time to verify his hit but needed to get Toby under control.

He left the Winchester on the floor then stood and pulled his pistol before heading to the kitchen at a fast pace. There was no need for stealth now.

He limped as quickly as he could manage down the short hallway but didn't hear Toby anymore, which didn't surprise him after the gunshot's report had echoes through the house.

Now he needed to know if Toby had his pistol in his left hand or was cowering in the corner with his bloody arm.

He had his Colt cocked and pointed at the kitchen as he slowed and shouted, "Toby, I know you're hurt and if you want me to help you, toss that pistol to the end of the hall. I won't shoot you!"

There was a three or four second delay before he heard a thump and Toby's Colt slid across the floor and stopped at the edge of the hallway.

Nate shuffled into the kitchen hoping that Toby didn't have a second gun but had his Colt ready to fire if he saw him armed.

He cleared the hallway and spotted Toby sitting with his back against the far wall staring at him with a blood-soaked towel wrapped around his right arm.

He lowered his Colt and slid it home before asking, "How bad is it?"

"I can't feel my hand and I'm still bleedin'."

"You shot me first, Toby, but I've got two wounds. I'm going to try to stop my own bleeding then we're going to ride into Little Laramie to get help."

"They probably ain't got a doc there."

"They'll have somebody who will be able to stop the bleeding. You stay there and I'll be back in a minute."

"Don't leave me here!" Toby yelled.

"I'm not going to leave you, Toby. You need to tell me what Stubby was doing here," he replied before turning and making his way back to the front room.

When he reached the porch, he understood what had attracted Stubby's attention. His horse had wandered out from behind the house.

He stepped off the porch and when he reached his gelding, he quickly took the two towels from his saddlebags, then opened his shirt and looked at the wound on the left side of his chest. He folded one of the towels into a long, thick strip then after holding it against the wound, he closed and buttoned his shirt then pulled his knife and cut a piece of his rope and tied it around his chest to keep it in place. It wasn't pretty and it hurt like hell, but it was only temporary.

His butt wound didn't need a rope, but he folded the second towel into a thick pad then slid it under his britches. He tied off the horse before he pulled his Colt and walked to the barn. He was reasonably sure that Stubby was dead, but he had to be sure. He also needed a horse for Toby.

As he entered the barn, the only noises he heard were made by the three horses and one mule inside. He saw blood dripping from between the cracks in the loft floor, but he didn't bother climbing the ladder.

He didn't know why, but Stubby's horse was saddled. Nate didn't spend any time thinking about it but took the horse's reins and led him out of the barn to the front of the house where he tied the horse beside his gelding before heading back through the open doorway.

It took another ten minutes to get Toby into the saddle before he was able to mount his own horse. Toby wasn't armed and Nate wasn't expecting any trouble as they set their horses at a medium trot toward Little Laramie as the sun began to set.

Once underway, Nate asked, "How did you and Stubby get together?"

"After you left me, I rode for a while but didn't have any place to go. I figured you and Ruth would be leavin', so I headed back here the next day to figure things out. I was doin' okay until Stubby showed up and surprised me while I was cookin' my supper. I thought he was gonna shoot me, but we got to talkin' and he told me he killed Fred Miller and then you, so I figured I was okay."

"You weren't worried that he'd killed two men?"

"He seemed right friendly, so we ate supper and talked some more. Then he asked me to help him out 'cause the law might be lookin' for him. So, that's what we've been doin' 'til you showed up."

"Why the hell did you shoot me? I wasn't going to shoot you."

"I got all afraid and that you mighta figured I was in cahoots with Stubby and I guess I kinda lost my head."

"Well, Toby, I won't hold that against you, but I need you to return to Laramie with me and talk to Sheriff Scott. You just tell him the truth and I won't press charges against you. Do you understand?"

"I understand. I guess I'm just stupid. I don't know why Ruth ran off with me in the first place. She really liked me, but she had more money than I'd ever seen before and after a few days with her, it was more important than she was. How is she doin', anyway?"

"I'm not sure. After I got there, I think she kind of was smitten with me, kind of like a schoolgirl crush. I acted as if she wasn't, and I think she felt hurt because of it. I had to go to Rawlins to do a job and when I got back, she just about bit my head off and accused me of killing her father. I didn't even know he'd been shot until after she'd gone back to the ranch."

"She thought you done it?" Toby asked with big eyes.

"Not only that, she accused me of being in league with you to get the money and a few other things."

"How come you ain't dead? Stubby said he shot you and saw you hit the dirt and not movin' before he left."

"He shot my horse and I hit the dirt and was knocked out. He must have seen the blood on my shirt from the horse. Ruth was so mad at me, when Sheriff Scott told her about the ambush, she thought I had faked it myself to deflect suspicion for killing her father."

"What do you reckon she'll do to me if she sees me again?"

"I think you'll be safer than I will."

Toby took a deep breath and looked north hoping to see Little Laramie.

Nate was trying to maintain some level of comfort which was secondary to keeping from falling out of the saddle after losing so much blood. His folded towels were helping, but his shirt and britches were soaked.

———

Two hours later, Nate and Toby were lying on cots in the feed and grain store. When they had ridden into town, Nate had called over the first person he'd spotted who didn't run away and asked him if anyone in town could sew up some gunshot wounds.

The man had led him and Toby to the home of Mrs. Hedda O'Hara, the town's midwife. She hadn't been flustered when

372

she'd been asked to suture the wounds, and Nate expected it was because she'd done more than her share. She'd probably fixed more cuts, wounds and other injuries that men inflict on each other than she'd delivered babies.

She cleaned and sutured Nate's wounds first because his took less time. He was resting on his cot as he watched her spend almost an hour tending to Toby's long gash across his forearm left by Nate's bullet.

After she finished, she told them to rest while she cooked them something to eat.

While she was working on Toby, the mayor of the town, Jim Fletcher, stopped by to ask what had happened, so Nate filled him in and asked him to send a telegram to Sheriff Scott in Laramie. He told the mayor that he'd head back to the ranch in the morning to pick up Stubby Nicks' body.

Toby fell asleep after Hedda left, so Nate had time to think about the repercussions brought on by the onslaught of events that had resulted from that first visit by Fred Miller. He broke it down by problems that awaited him when he returned to Laramie with Toby.

The murder of Fred Miller would be solved, at least to everyone's satisfaction who wasn't named Ruth Miller, but the other rumor, the one that actually worried him more than the murder accusation wasn't going to leave. He suspected that Ruth would probably do more investigations into his past and let everyone know what she discovered. At the very least, it would ruin the reputation that he'd worked so hard to build. He'd lose business if he stayed, but that would be the least of the impacts the revelation would have on his life.

As he lay on his side on the cot, he knew that once the truth was out, people would look at him differently. Those he liked and who had trusted him would have doubts. He wondered if Ike would quit even if he didn't have another job.

He expected that most folks would act as if it didn't matter, but he suspected that Ruth would not only spread the truth, she'd embellish it with a few added sprinkles of lawlessness and violence that would simmer beneath the surface. But despite all of those concerns, the one that bothered him the most was that he believed that once the word was out, Mary would stop visiting and no longer talk to him. He could deal with the lack of respect or even dislike from anyone else, but not from her. That worry was his biggest reason for leaving. He didn't want to see that look of disappointment in her blue eyes.

Mrs. O'Hara brought some stew into the room and had to wake up Toby to get him to eat and drink two glasses of water.

By the time they'd finished, it was well after ten o'clock, and Mrs. O'Hara blew out the lamp and left to return to her bedroom.

Nate was exhausted and his body cried out for sleep, but his mind was too busy dealing with his uncertain future. He stayed awake until almost midnight before finally drifting to sleep.

CHAPTER 11

It was midmorning when Nate rode back out to the Halvorsen ranch. He'd left Toby in Little Laramie under the watchful eye of Hedda O'Hara and his horse under guard by Roddie Trotter at the livery. He didn't want Toby to leave town.

He was sure that the sheriff had received the telegram but didn't expect him to do anything but wait for more information.

His butt was more painful than his chest wound as he tried to stand in the stirrups as much as sit awkwardly in his saddle. He was wearing a clean shirt and a new pair of britches, and that helped to tell him that he wasn't losing any more blood.

He soon spotted the ranch and after another twenty minutes reached the barn. He tied off the gelding then went inside and began saddling the other two horses and the mule which took him much longer than it normally would have. When he finished, he looked up at the ceiling and wondered how he'd get Stubby down then headed for the ladder and climbed to the loft.

After stepping onto the worn boards, he spotted Stubby's corpse lying awkwardly against the wall. He stepped close and removed his gunbelt and then grabbed his ankles and grunted as he slid the body toward the open loft doors. When he reached the edge, he stepped over the body and rolled it off the floor to the ground. He heard the muffled thump, then turned and picked up the gunbelt, his Winchester and the Sharps and headed for the ladder. He couldn't climb with both guns, so he slid the Winchester to the floor and slowly worked his way down the ladder.

After retrieving the Winchester, he slid both guns into their scabbards on Toby's dark red gelding, fashioned a trail rope to the packhorse and mule, then led the two horses and the mule outside where he tied off the gelding to the door latch and looked at Stubby's body. He hadn't loaded the mule as he intended to use it to transport Stubby, but now he wondered if he should do it at all. His stitches in his chest were fresh and might rip open when he lifted the body, so he tried to think of some other way to get it onto the mule, but finally just sighed and bent at the knees and slid his arms under the body and managed to put Stubby face down across the mule's pack saddle. After tying it down, he mounted the red gelding and led the horse and mule to the front of the house and just took his horse's reins before heading north to return to Little Laramie. He planned on staying long enough to thank Mrs. O'Hara and then check to see if the sheriff had sent a reply before taking the road back to Laramie.

As he rode, he remembered that Mary had packed enough food for four meals and he'd only had one, so he slowed down and painfully twisted in the saddle before reaching across to his own horse and pulling the second smaller sack from the saddlebag. He let the reins to his horse drop, then carefully

377

settled back into the saddle and set Stubby's red gelding to a medium trot. He glanced at his brown horse to make sure he was following then opened the bag and took out the pickle. He tossed the butcher paper away and greedily bit into the sour treat and a smile crossed his face as he chewed. He wasn't sure if it was the pickle that made him smile or knowing that Mary had packed it without him even asking, but the reason wasn't important.

He finished the pickle quickly then ate both sandwiches before tossing the bag away. He was still in a reasonable amount of pain, but his stomach was pleased, and he felt as if at least part of the Miller Mess was behind him...literally as Stubby's body bounced on the back of the mule.

When he reached Little Laramie, he pulled up in front of Hedda O'Hara's house and gingerly dismounted. He tied off the red gelding and then when his horse arrived, he lashed it to the hitchrail as well.

Just twenty minutes later, he and Toby were riding out of Little Laramie heading north. He'd given Mrs. O'Hara twenty dollars for all she'd done and although she'd protested, he could tell she was grateful. There hadn't been any telegrams which hadn't surprised him, but it also made him wonder what kind of a reception he'd get when they reached Laramie. While he was gone, who knows what Ruth had been doing.

378

After thirty minutes of silent riding, Toby asked, "How come we didn't stop for chow before we left?"

"I figured you'd get something from Mrs. O'Hara."

"I think she liked you but wasn't all that pleased with me."

Nate was riding his own horse again, so he blindly reached behind him and opened the saddlebag on the left and rummaged around with his fingers until he found the big sack with the fried chicken and pulled it free.

He didn't hand it to Toby in the off chance that Mary had written a note but reached inside and pulled out a drumstick and handed it to him.

Toby snatched the piece of chicken and greedily began chomping it down. Even though he'd recently eaten a pickle and two sandwiches, the aroma of the chicken made Nate decide to take one of the drumsticks himself.

There wasn't a note, but the wonderful flavor of the chicken spoke volumes to him. He wished he had eaten the chicken first as his stomach was already protesting the excessive amount of food.

It didn't matter anyway as he looked over at Toby, who'd just tossed away the clean bone then handed him the bag.

He was still eating when they turned east and picked up the major thoroughfare to between Laramie and Rawlins. They should be in Laramie within three hours.

Nate then turned to Toby and asked, "Why prompted you to run off with Ruth Miller? Was it your idea?"

"Kinda. She's a real pretty gal and we hit it off real good, so I reckoned that if I married her, her pa would fix me up like he did with his other daughter's husband. But after she agreed to marry me, she told me we had to run away because her father wouldn't let us get married. I was a bit put off 'cause I was expectin' more than just gettin' Ruth. So, I told her I couldn't afford to take care of her, and she said she'd get a lot of money before we left, and she did."

"Fred Miller didn't know about it at all? He didn't threaten you that you'd be fired if you spent any more time with her?"

"He knew that we were sweet on each other and all, and he sure didn't make any noise about it which is why I figured he'd give us a house and some cattle of our own."

"Did he even talk to you about Ruth?"

"Yeah, he did and that made me wonder why he sent you after us."

"What did he say when he talked about you and Ruth and why would it make you believe that he approved?"

380

"Not much. He just asked if I liked her and I kinda figured he was happy about it. He even smiled when I told him I was sweet on her."

"When he showed up in my office the first time, he made it sound as if he didn't know anything about it and that you two had snuck off behind his back. When I brought her back to the ranch, he didn't even make a lot of noise about the missing thousand dollars and even paid my bill."

"Do you still have the money?" Toby asked hopefully.

"No, I gave it to Sheriff Scott, and he returned it. Did Stubby tell you who hired him and what he was supposed to do for the money?"

"Yeah. You were right about part of it. He wasn't supposed to shoot me, but he was gonna kill you first and then Ruth. I don't know why he wanted her dead, but I reckon after he killed you, he'd come to the ranch house and kill her and then take the money. Maybe he would have killed me anyway, but he said he wasn't supposed to."

"And you believed him, Toby? Surely, you must know that he had to kill you to keep the secret."

Toby paused then shrugged his shoulders and replied, "Yeah, I suppose."

Nate now had a more complete picture of most of the web spun by Fred Miller, but not all of it, including the motive for

Stubby killing the rancher. He could understand his need to drygulch him, but not why he would kill Fred Miller.

"Did Stubby say why he shot Fred Miller?"

Toby surprised him when he giggled, then looked back at him and answered, "That was kinda funny. After you took his gun and told him to leave town, he figured he'd knock off Mister Miller and then he wouldn't have to worry. He said he went and bought that Sharps, the pack mule and the supplies then waited in the trees to spot Fred. He had the Sharps ready to fire and when he saw Fred leave the house, he had him in his sights at four hundred yards just standing on the porch talkin' to some of the hands. He squeezed the trigger and the Sharps just snapped, but the powder didn't go off. He got real mad and threw it down and pulled his Winchester.

"He had to wait for him to get closer, so he picked up the Sharps again and opened the breech and found that somehow, a beetle had crawled into the breech when he wasn't lookin and the hammer had mashed it against the cartridge. He didn't bother cleanin' the gun but stuck it back in the scabbard and then he took his shot with the Winchester and saw Fred drop."

"Then he made his escape and hid out in the trees until later, expecting that the sheriff would be showing up soon."

"Yup. Then when you showed up after that, he couldn't resist some payback."

"Okay, I think I can see the whole picture now. You just tell the sheriff all of that and then you can ride away."

If he had been surprised by Toby's giggle, he was stunned when Toby then asked, "Now that he's dead, do you reckon that I could see Ruth again?"

At first, Nate was going to laugh and tell him that if he did, he'd be singing like a little girl soon after they met, but then he wasn't sure what she would do anymore. She may just welcome him back with open arms and try to convince him to kill her father's murderer; the same man who had just wounded him.

"What you do is up to you, Toby. I have no idea what she'd say."

Toby nodded and looked down the road as he thought about it.

———

It was late afternoon when the westernmost buildings of Laramie appeared on the horizon and Nate's recent mood of satisfaction over putting the last pieces of the Fred Miller puzzle into place vanished. It was replaced by a more stressful condition when he started thinking about what would be waiting for him when they reached town.

Twenty minutes after that first sighting, they entered Main Street and Nate soon pulled to a stop before the sheriff's office. It had been a long, painful ride back and despite his many concerns, he was glad it was over.

His foot had barely contacted the dirt when Sheriff Scott and Bill Caruthers stepped out of the office.

"How are you, Nate? All the telegram said was that you'd been shot twice."

"I'm okay, just sore. I brought Toby Halvorsen with me to let you know what Stubby told him at the ranch house. Can someone take Stubby's body to the mortician?"

"I'll take care of it, Nate," Bill said as he stepped off the boardwalk and untied the corpse-laden mule from the trail rope.

After Toby dismounted, they followed Sheriff Scott into the jail and after the sheriff sat down, Toby took a seat, but Nate remained standing.

"One of those shots was in my backside, Bart," Nate said to explain why he had stayed on his feet.

"I reckoned as much. That shooting was close to Carbon County, so I sent a telegram to Sheriff Blount to let him know about it as a courtesy and he asked if you could come by and let him know the particulars. He added that he had more information about those two scoundrels you uncovered that might interest you, too."

"I'll go there in two or three days, depending how I feel. Did he tell you what they said?"

"Nope. I won't keep you long, so just give me the quick version and then I'll stop by your place later for the rest of it."

"Thanks, Sheriff," Nate said as he braced himself on the desk and began telling the sheriff what had happened when he arrived at the ranch.

It didn't take long, but when he finished, Nate said, "I'm not going to charge Ned for shooting me, but I do want you to keep him here and write down what he tells you about all that happened at the Lone Wolf and what Stubby had told him while they were together on his parents' abandoned ranch. Some of it will surprise you as much as it did me. When you visit my office tomorrow, I'll see if it matches what he told me on the way back."

Sheriff Scott glanced at Toby before replying, "Okay, Nate. You head home and rest up."

"I'm going to leave you the pack horse and the mule along with Stubby's guns, including his Sharps. I'll take the red gelding with me to replace my buckskin."

"Thanks again, Nate."

Nate nodded then turned and walked awkwardly out of the jail and after detaching the packhorse, he mounted his brown gelding and headed east trailing his new red horse.

He thought about stopping to tell Ike what had happened but was anxious to tell Mary and to find out if Ruth had come into town. He could have asked the sheriff, but he suspected that if she did visit Laramie, she'd head to his office and try to see him or shoot him.

He rode past Kansas Street and then cut down the back alley, so he'd be able to get to the barn. He felt his anxiety growing as he approached his house as things had seemed to be happening almost too fast to keep everything straight since Fred Miller had made his request.

Whatever else happened, he knew that his simple days of bounty hunting and finding signs of infidelity were gone.

He reached his barn, carefully stepped down and led the two horses inside. After each of them began drinking at the long trough that ran alongside the wall, he started unsaddling the red gelding keeping mindful of his recently sutured chest wound.

He was just sliding the saddle from the horse's back when he heard someone entering the barn and hoped it was Mary and not Ruth as he turned.

"I was told that you were coming back today, Nate. How badly were you hurt?" Mary asked as she examined him for blood stains.

"Not bad. They've both been sutured and cleaned, but they're a bit sore."

"Where were you hit?"

"The first one is on the left side of my chest and the second is on the left side of my butt. Neither was very deep, though."

"I'll look at them when you come inside. Do you want me to help unsaddling the horses? You can tell me what happened while we do that."

"No, I'll handle the horses, but I can talk to you while I do it."

"Alright."

"Before I start, can I ask if you heard anything else about Ruth? Has she stopped by or even come into town?"

"Not that I know of, but you've only been gone two days and other than a couple of visits to Ike and Alice, I've stayed inside the house behind locked doors."

"How are they? Do they know about my escapades at the Halvorsen ranch?"

"They were the ones who told me that you'd been shot and were returning with Toby Halvorsen, which created some questions."

"I imagine so. His presence at the ranch was what almost got me killed. I made a lot of mistakes over the past couple of weeks, Mary. I should have been killed in Rawlins, then on the road to the Lone Wolf and then yesterday. I've never even been close to being shot before, yet now it seems to happen with regularity."

Nate had finished with the red gelding and moved onto his brown horse as he began telling Mary what had happened when he arrived at the Halvorsen ranch.

"That must have been a shock when you spotted him instead of Stubby," she said when he paused.

"It was, but then I got stupid and assumed he was alone and stopped scanning for Stubby. If Toby hadn't stepped out to tell Stubby that supper was ready, I have no idea what would have happened."

"You might not have been shot at all."

"Maybe," he replied as he moved the second saddle to the shelf.

After unsaddling both horses, Nate slid the Winchester out of its scabbard and handed it to Mary before taking the Sharps. He then hung his saddlebags over his shoulder and started walking out of the barn with Mary striding beside him.

"Is Ike going to stop by later?" he asked.

"I'm sure he will as soon as he hears that you're back."

"The sheriff is coming tomorrow to let me know what Toby told him for his official report."

"What did he tell you?" she asked as they entered the kitchen.

"I'll be happy to tell you if you'll give me some coffee."

"I have a fresh pot ready. It's the third pot I've made today in anticipation of your return," she said before placing the Winchester in the wall rack then walking to the cookstove.

Nate put the Sharps in the lower rack and after setting the saddlebags on the floor, he walked to the table and carefully lowered himself onto the chair with only the right side of his behind on the wood.

After Mary set the two cups of coffee on the table, she sat in the chair next to him.

He took three sips of the hot coffee before he began repeating what Toby had told him as Mary listened intently and ignored her own coffee as she asked questions and expressed surprise at what he related.

When he finished, she asked, "So, do you think that Ruth will finally believe that it was Stubby who killed her father?"

"Honestly? I don't think she ever believed what she was saying in the first place. If not then, she surely realized that I couldn't have committed the crime after Sheriff Scott told her I was on the train."

"You think she's still going to try to ruin your reputation?"

"I don't know, but I have to assume that even if she doesn't say another word, those rumors that she started will have a lingering effect."

She finally took a sip of her lukewarm coffee before she quietly asked, "What are you going to do to change everyone's minds?"

"I don't think I can do anything to get them to disbelieve all of what she said. I'm thinking that it might be time to leave Laramie and go somewhere else."

"You can't give in so quickly, Nate! If she wants to hurt you as much as she believes that you hurt her, then leaving will give her that satisfaction."

"Maybe she'd be able to return to normal after I'm gone. I don't know, Mary. I just can't guess what will happen. I just know that even now, there are whispers and rumors about me that I can't fight."

"Why not? When I arrived in Laramie, your reputation was impeccable. When I first heard of you, it wasn't as a bounty hunter but as an exceptional investigator. I've heard nothing but good things about you ever since."

Nate smiled at her before saying, "I'm sure it's just because you spent most of that time with Ike and Alice."

"No. You forget that I do cleaning, and I've only been Alice's nanny for a couple of months. I was here for four months before I met them."

Nate then asked, "Ike told me that you didn't charge them for all that you did to help Alice and not even for your midwife duties. How can you afford that, Mary? You aren't exactly well situated."

"I haven't been robbing banks, if that's what has you worried."

Nate smiled as he shook his head then replied, "No, I wasn't worried that you had some dark criminal past, Mary. I was just curious why you didn't charge Ike and Alice."

Mary stared at her half-full coffee cup for a few seconds before lifting her eyes and saying, "I liked Alice. I felt she was my friend more than a client. How could I charge a friend for helping her?"

"You'd better charge me, Miss White."

"Maybe I will, but how can I charge you if you're not here? Please don't leave without telling me."

Nate wanted to ask if it mattered to her whether he stayed or not but knew the answer. He was getting close to revealing his sad past to her again, but for the same reason he didn't want to be in town when she heard the truth from someone else, he held back. He couldn't bear to see the disappointment in those expressive blue eyes.

"I promise that I won't leave without letting you know."

Mary stared intensely at him as she said, "I don't want you to think that you can leave me a note, either. You will not pack a bag or saddle a horse without talking to me. Is that clear?"

"Yes, ma'am."

"Now, let's go into your bedroom and I'll check your wounds."

Nate had forgotten she'd mentioned it in the barn and quickly said, "That's okay. I'll go see the doctor tomorrow."

"I'm a nurse, Nate. Or have you forgotten? Let's go," she said firmly as she stood and waited for him to get off his half-butt.

Nate sighed then slowly stood and tried to minimize the pain from the wound to his bottom left cheek by walking with as little a limp as possible.

When they entered his bedroom, he turned and asked, "Mary, can you limit your examination to the chest wound? The one on my behind isn't bad at all."

"Oh, please! I'm sure that you've allowed other women to inspect more of you than just your posterior."

"Yes, but this is different."

"Why? Is it because you don't know me well enough?"

Agatha Swarthmore's image flashed in his mind before he let out his breath and began unbuttoning his shirt. He couldn't tell her the real reason he preferred that she not see his naked butt.

Mary stepped to his front as he pulled back his shirt revealing the recently bandaged wound. When his shirt was off, she carefully pulled the bandage and saw the scar. It was over an inch long and she guessed that the bullet had left a good quarter-inch gap in the skin over the ribs. But the sutures were well done, so she approved of the treatment and replaced his bandage.

"Another midwife did this?" she asked as he donned his shirt.

"Yes, ma'am. Mrs. O'Hara down in Little Laramie. She's a widow and probably almost three times your age."

"Then she's experienced which is why they looked so good. Now, let's see the other one."

Nate was about to protest but realized he would lose, so he began unbuckling his belt and then popping the buttons free on his britches.

"I'll be very circumspect, Mister Manning. Lay on the bed on your stomach."

"Yes, ma'am," he replied and slowly prostrated himself on his bed and closed his eyes.

Mary just pulled back his underpants on the left side exposing the second gunshot wound. It was deeper than the first, but actually shorter. It was swollen more too, which surprised her, but the sutures were still tight after all the riding and she was pleased with what Mrs. O'Hara's work.

But when he'd taken off his shirt, and now that she was examining his lower torso, she could see the scarring from multiple blows but understood that he wouldn't explain them because they were all very old and she understood that he wasn't about to give her an honest answer if she asked. At least not yet, and when he did decide to tell her how he'd gotten them, it had to be his choice to explain the damage.

She pulled his underdrawers back up and stepped back.

Nate slid back to his feet and quickly pulled his britches up and after buttoning the fly, he buckled his belt.

"Both wounds should heal well as long as they don't get infected, but I'll keep an eye on them for the next few days."

Nate quickly said, "But I have to go to Rawlins to meet Sheriff Blount. He said he has more information from those two men I caught and wants me to tell him what happened at the Halvorsen ranch, too."

"Okay, but you don't have to go right away; do you?"

"No, I can wait a while."

"Good. Before you go, I'll check those wounds for any sign of infection."

"That might be another two or three days. What about your other jobs? Don't you have all those cleaning jobs? What about other ladies who may need you as a midwife?"

"I can do my jobs while I act as your nurse, Nate. Are you trying to get rid of me?"

"No, but I don't want to make a mess of your life any more than I already have."

Mary smiled before saying, "You haven't messed up my life at all, Nate. You've made it much better."

Nate felt his walls closing in on him again as he thought about making a confession again almost in the hope of driving her away, but he couldn't do it.

He was still looking at her when the front door opened, and he heard Ike shout, "Nate, are you in here?"

"In my room, Ike," he yelled back before stepping out into the hallway with Mary walking behind him.

The moment Ike spotted Mary walking out of Nate's bedroom, he broke into a grin but didn't comment.

"What happened? I only got the word that you'd been shot twice and was returning with Toby Halvorsen after shooting Stubby Nicks."

Nate nodded then said, "Let's go out to the office. I just finished telling Mary, so she doesn't need to suffer through it again."

Mary quickly said, "I don't mind hearing it again, Nate."

"Alright," Nate replied before they walked to the office.

———

Ike left the office more than an hour later but like Mary, he hadn't heard a word about Ruth Miller. She may have come into Laramie, but he hadn't seen her but hadn't asked about her either.

After he'd gone and the sun was dropping low in the sky, they returned to the kitchen and Nate took his offset seat at the table while Mary started a fire in the cookstove.

"I never did get a chance to thank you for the food you sent along, Mary. The pickles were an unexpected treat."

Mary laughed as she lit the fire and replied, "It's not as if it was a big secret, Nate."

After she closed the firebox door, she set a skillet on the hot plate and began gathering fixings for their supper as Nate watched.

Why was he so comfortable being with her? It had taken him months to get comfortable with Sheriff Galloway and even then, had never been this relaxed around him or his family. He'd known her less than two weeks and he felt as if he'd known her for years. He had no answer and just accepted it for what it was.

While she cooked, they talked about everything that had transpired since they'd first met and what Ruth might do or say. Neither talked about anything that had happened in their lives more than six months earlier when Mary had arrived in Laramie.

She didn't ask him about his family or background, and he didn't ask her because he didn't want to trigger that topic of conversation.

But the conversations that they did share again lasted until well after the dirty dishes had been washed and dried and the cookstove was completely cold.

It was close to midnight when they mutually decided they needed some sleep, so after wishing each other a pleasant night, they adjourned to their bedrooms.

397

After he'd stripped down to the bare minimum, Nate slid under the quilts just to see how sore he was and found it wasn't that bad as long as he stayed on his right side.

He had a lot on his mind and all of them revolved around Mary and how much she had wormed her way into his life and into his heart and soul. She was becoming addictive and like the recovering alcoholic who understood the consequences of taking up the bottle, he knew that he shouldn't spend so much time with her. When he left, it would only make things worse.

He tried to shift his thoughts to other subjects, but they were all secondary now. He also noticed that now he was thinking of Mary as a woman as well as a companion, and that only added to his concerns. She was a very pretty woman with a good figure, but it was her personality that made her so welcoming. He still couldn't understand why she hadn't married or even why she chose to come to Laramie, but he wasn't about to ask.

She was still on his mind when he finally slipped into slumber.

CHAPTER 12

During the midmorning the next day, Sheriff Scott arrived as expected and met with Nate in his office while Mary sat nearby.

He gave the sheriff his own statement that he'd written that morning before he took the sheriff's official record. Nate read the lawman's report that had been prepared with the testimony provided by Toby Halvorsen and nothing had been missed, not even the confusing behavior by her father before he and Ruth eloped.

When he finished reading, he handed the report back to the sheriff then said, "It's exactly what he told me, Bart. You can let him go, but just a word of warning. He asked me if I thought it would be okay to go the Lone Wolf and see Ruth. I told him it was his decision, but it could cause you some grief if he does."

"I agree with you, but if you're not going to press charges, then he can go wherever he wants. I'll add my recommendation that he avoids the place. But as you just said, it's his choice."

"I may not make it to Rawlins as soon as I'd like. Can you notify Sheriff Blount that I'll get there sometime next week? My nurse, who is sitting beside me, has laid down some rules and one of them is that I can't leave until she gives her permission."

He glanced at Mary and smiled before he said, "I wouldn't argue with her, Nate. I'll let Mitch Blount know. Besides, having a woman around your house will do you some good."

Nate didn't reply to his insinuation but said, "If you want to give Toby one of those pack animals and saddles, that's okay. I would prefer that you keep the Sharps and the Winchester."

"I had no intention of letting him have either, but I was going to let him take the mule and whatever he's carrying that doesn't go bang."

"Bart, have you heard anything about Ruth recently? Has she come into town or has she stayed out at the ranch?"

"As far as I know, she's stayed out at the ranch. Are you worried that she might come in here and give you two barrels of buckshot?"

"Maybe not that, but I'll admit that I'm concerned about her. If I met her and we had a normal conversation, then I'd feel a lot better, but I don't see that happening."

"You never know. If Toby goes out there, she may shift all that anger at him and forget all about you."

"I doubt it, but if you hear that she's in Laramie, can you let me know?"

"Sure. I have to go out there right after I let Toby out anyway. I need to update them on Stubby's death and what you just read. I may stop by if I see any change in her behavior."

"I'd appreciate it, Bart," Nate said as he slowly stood and shook the sheriff's hand.

Sheriff Scott smiled at Mary then turned and left the office.

After he'd gone, Nate carefully took his seat as Mary said, "You should go and lie down for a while, Nate. You lost a lot of blood two days ago and you're not close to full strength yet."

"I'm all right, Mary. What are you going to do today?"

"I planned to take care of you. I don't have any jobs today or tomorrow and Ike will be back on Monday to watch over you while I handle the Butlers' house."

"Ah, yes. The lecherous Maurice and his long-suffering wife, Jeanette. After I'd been in town for a while, I expected that she would have asked me to document his womanizing but found that she didn't seem to care as long as he bought her things. I've met a few women that didn't mind what their husbands did as long as they provided them with a home and put food on the table."

"Would you be that kind of a husband, Nate?"

"I wouldn't know because I don't believe I'll ever have a wife to cheat on."

Nate expected to see some measure of disappointment in her eyes, but he didn't see it before she asked, "Why is that? You never have given me an answer."

"It's just that, well, I just can't see it."

"If you can't see yourself as a husband and father, then what do you see in your future?"

Nate looked into her blue eyes for a few seconds before he quietly replied, "Nothing."

Mary was momentarily stunned by his answer but could understand why he gave it. After the way he described his time with Ruth and her reaction, she was sure that he was exactly the man she thought he was, and his answer confirmed that suspicion. Her real concern now was that, promise or not, he might leave Laramie without talking to her. If that happened, she'd have to start all over again.

———

After Toby happily left the jail with his right arm heavily bandaged, he mounted his horse and told the sheriff he'd pick up the mule and supplies on his way back.

Sheriff Scott watched him ride east and hoped he wasn't going to the Lone Wolf, but he'd be heading that way after lunch and he expected that if Toby had visited, he'd know about it as soon as he arrived.

Toby had his horse moving at a fast trot as he turned onto the road that led to the Lone Wolf. He knew the road and the ranch well and hoped that at the very least, he'd be able to get his job back. He didn't believe he'd hurt Ruth at all but had just disappointed her. But now that her father wasn't there anymore, he could tell her what really happened and why he was afraid of being tracked down and shot, which almost did happen. He suspected that the reason that Nate Manning had suggested he stay away from Ruth was that he was smitten with her. The sheriff's admonition was just because he was Nate's pal.

He rode for another hour before he passed the rotting and picked apart carcass that had once been Nate's buckskin mare and held his good hand over his nose and mouth as he passed by.

He hadn't seen anyone on the road which kind of surprised him. He expected that the boys would be heading into town to waste some of last month's pay. Maybe they'd already gone but he hadn't seen any of them when he was there, but he'd spent all that time in the jail.

Toby still hadn't seen anyone until he was just a mile away from the ranch house and spotted some of the boys milling around near the chow house. At least that explained why they weren't on the road.

403

Then he turned his eyes to the house and suddenly his optimistic expectations vanished as he almost imagined Fred Miller walking onto the porch with his cocked Winchester to make him pay for what he'd done to Ruth. He pulled up and stared at the ranch house for two minutes before wheeling his horse around and heading back to Laramie.

After he'd ridden for twenty minutes, he picked up a rider coming from Laramie and figured it must be the sheriff as he told him that he'd be coming to the ranch after he had lunch. Toby relaxed and continued to ride south.

When he and the sheriff met on the road, each pulled up and Sheriff Scott asked, "I thought you were going to the Lone Wolf. Why are you heading back?"

"I figured it was a stupid thing to do."

"I thought so myself, but now that I'm almost there, you'll turn your horse around and come with me to see Miss Miller."

"*Why would I want to do that?* I just told you it was a bad idea and you said it was, too!" Toby exclaimed.

"Because she still might not believe me, but I reckon she'll believe you about what happened down there when she sees your arm. You're going to explain how you got that bullet wound."

"But she hates me!"

"She can't shoot you while I'm there. You may as well get it over with, Toby."

Toby sighed then nodded and said, "Okay."

He turned his horse around and soon both were trotting north for a date with the irrational Ruth Miller.

————

In the enormous Lone Wolf ranch house, the irrational Ruth Miller had been returning to earth since the sheriff's last visit when he'd told her of the drygulch attempt that almost killed Nate.

Ever since he'd gone to Rawlins, she'd been alone and left to construct her own theory that would explain his rejection of her affections. There had to be another reason because he said that he liked her, and he knew that she was in love with him. Once she started down that illogical path, the idea kept expanding until she began to seriously believe it. The telegram from Hays City seemed to confirm her growing suspicions.

By the time he'd come through the kitchen door, she was convinced that he'd played her for a fool even more than Toby had done. When she'd accused him, and he'd all but admitted to everything, she'd screamed at him then finally lashed out with her hand and stalked off, still believing she was right.

After she'd returned to the ranch, she had to convince them that she was right and felt some level of gratification when they started to agree with her.

Then things began happening to shake the foundations of that well-constructed theory.

Sheriff Scott arrived and told everyone that Nate had been on the train from Rawlins when her father had been murdered and had witnesses and had seen his ticket. That was the first crack in her dam. But she had to keep it from collapsing or admit that none of what she believed was true and argued her point despite the beginnings of doubt in her mind.

When the sheriff arrived to tell them that Nate had been drygulched enroute to the ranch to talk to her, she had exploded in an even more outlandish explanation to maintain a token of support for her alternate view. Even as she'd shouted her new accusation, she knew it was a last gasp effort just to salve her wounded heart.

After the sheriff had gone, she'd gone to her room and cried for what seemed like hours. Some of the tears were for her shattered hopes but most were for Nate as she pictured him lying in the road beside his dead horse. He could have been killed just because he was coming to talk to her to make things better.

Since then, she'd stayed in the ranch house but simply existed without living. She was miserable and didn't know how to escape the dark mood.

Ruth was sitting in the parlor reading a book whose title she didn't even know just to keep anyone from talking to her. There was a knock at the door and when her mother answered it, Ruth was shaken when she heard one of the ranch hands tell her that the sheriff was approaching with another man who appeared to be Toby Halvorsen.

She tossed the book onto the side table, stood and walked quickly across the parlor as her mother walked out the front door onto the porch. She wondered if the sheriff had arrested Toby for what he'd done to her and the anger that she'd held for so long for Nate refocused onto the man who had pushed her over the cliff.

When she stepped onto the porch, the sheriff and Toby were just a hundred feet away and Ruth wished that she had a pistol but then noticed that Toby had a big bandage that covered most of his right forearm.

She stood beside her mother and waited for them to arrive.

"Why is he with the sheriff?" she asked her mother as she stared at the approaching riders.

"I don't know, but he doesn't look happy."

The sheriff and Toby pulled up and both slowly stepped down and tied off their horses before walking to the porch steps where they stopped.

"Mrs. Miller, Toby has some things that he needs to tell you and Miss Miller. I have the official report of what he explained to me, but I believe that you should hear it directly from him."

Mabel glanced at Ruth's face before saying, "Of course, Bart. Come into the parlor."

Ruth didn't say anything but glared at Toby who didn't have the courage to even look at her. She turned and entered the house first and marched across the parlor and took a seat. She was trying to control her anger by massaging the backs of her hands, but it wasn't helping much. She did want to hear what was so important that the sheriff had to drag Toby all the way to the ranch.

Sheriff Scott and Toby followed Mrs. Miller into the parlor, and each took a seat. Toby chose one that was as far away from Ruth as possible.

Once seated, the sheriff said, "Yesterday, Nate Manning rode into town escorting Toby and two horses and a mule that was carrying Stubby Nicks' body. He'd been shot twice but is going to be all right. I'll let Toby explain what happened beginning with what happened here before he and Miss Miller left."

Before Toby could even manage to get a word out, Ruth unleashed a Gatling gun series of questions when she asked, *"Nate was shot? Who shot him? Where was he hit? How bad was it?"*

Bart replied, "He'll be fine, ma'am. You'll get all your answers from Toby."

She shifted her eyes to Toby who looked as if he was attending his own funeral.

Sheriff Scott looked at the terrified ranch hand and said, "Toby, tell them everything you told me and do not leave anything out."

Toby nodded before he took a deep breath and said, "I first wanna say I'm real sorry for what I did, Ruth. I guess it was the stupidest thing I ever did and that's sayin' somethin'."

He didn't wait for an acceptance of his apology because he knew there wouldn't be one, so he immediately began his long confession.

Sheriff Scott listened to him as he spoke and could hear the deep sadness in his voice. He wasn't making any excuses for his behavior nor was he attempting to push the blame onto Nate or even Stubby Nicks. Despite all that he'd done, the lawman was impressed with Toby Halvorsen's honesty.

Ruth listened to his narrative with ever-shifting emotions. When he described the conversations that he'd had with her father, the intense dislike she had held for years for the man who had sired her was rekindled. Then when he talked about being more interested in the money than her, she refocused her disgust on Toby again. But through the entire lengthy story, the one common thread was the decent and still heroic behavior of Nate Manning. He may not love her, yet despite all of her vitriol and lies, he had still risked his life to find the man who had murdered her father for the sole reason of proving to her that he hadn't been the one who had killed him.

What made it worse was knowing that he'd only chased after Stubby Nicks and almost been killed again because he was trying to convince her that he hadn't done any of those things she'd accused him of doing. She may have been sulking since she arrived at the ranch, but now she was genuinely disgusted with herself. Nate had rescued her and treated her with respect and kindness since he'd found her, and she hadn't earned one moment of it.

First, she'd put him in a terrible position by expecting him to join her in her bed and then sulked because he hadn't. Once they returned to Laramie, he'd protected her, yet all she cared about was herself and her feelings. She'd become jealous of Mary White for no reason at all and then made those horrible accusations that almost resulted in his death.

As Toby reached the shootout, she was startled when he said that he'd shot Nate before Nate returned fire. But by then, she'd been drained of anger and hate and only felt an enormous need to set things right.

When Toby finally finished, he finally raised his eyes to Ruth and was surprised to find her not even looking at him. She was staring at the sheriff.

Sheriff Scott had been watching Toby, so when he stopped talking, he turned to Ruth and was surprised to meet her eyes.

"Well, Miss Miller, are you satisfied that Nate Manning wasn't your father's killer?"

In a firm voice, Ruth replied, "Yes, I am, Sheriff. I'm sorry for ever doubting Nate. I have no excuse for my behavior and was wondering if I could come with you back to Laramie. Do you think that Nate would allow me into his office?"

Bart was relieved and a bit taken aback by her sudden shift even though he'd been hoping that it would happen.

"Of course, you may. I'm sure that Nate would be pleased to see you again. He was worried about you."

"I could understand why he might want to shoot me, but knowing him, he'll just smile and then apologize."

She smiled and stood as she said, "I'll get changed and then get my horse saddled," before leaving the parlor.

After she'd gone, Mabel said, "Thank you for coming, Bart. I'm glad that you brought Toby along. I suspected that Fred had a part in all of this as soon as they left. I'll run this ranch the way it should be run and make sure that my sons understand that's how it will always be if they want to inherit it after I'm gone. I'll be sure that my girls get their share as well. Let's go into the kitchen and have some coffee while Ruth is getting ready. I'd like to talk to you about Mister Manning."

"Yes, ma'am," the sheriff replied before all three rose and left the parlor.

————

Nate had finally acquiesced to Mary's insistence that he lay down to rest because he hated to admit that she was right. So, he was lying on his bed on his side as Mary sat in chair in front of him.

He tried not to look at her just three feet away, but it would have been rude for him to look elsewhere while they talked. The longer they conversed, the more he felt the urge to tell her the truth about why he couldn't marry or have children. It was difficult enough for him to understand without having to explain it. His empty life and the hole it left in his soul would be impossible for anyone to understand, especially a woman as whole as Mary. She seemed almost without flaws as opposed to his own deeply entrenched defects. Maybe that was why he was so comfortable with her.

"It'll be interesting to hear what the sheriff says when he returns after visiting Ruth," Mary said.

"It would be more interesting if Toby actually went out there to try to see her again. I hope he wasn't that foolish, but then again, he buddied up to the man who was sent to kill him."

"Why do you think Stubby didn't shoot him as soon as he walked into that house?"

"The only reason I can think of is that he needed to have a backup, at least for a few days until he felt safe. I wonder if Toby realized that once that happened, he wouldn't live much longer."

"You said that this was the first time that you've been shot. How did you manage that for so long in your line of work? How long have you been a bounty hunter and detective?"

"I wasn't always a bounty hunter, but I've been doing this kind of work for a while now. I guess I've just been lucky a lot of the times, but usually I avoid taking a bullet because of my suspicious nature. Ike always tells me that it's why I'm good at the job."

"Then how did you almost get shot in Rawlins, then on the way to the Lone Wolf before you were shot twice at the Halvorsen ranch?"

"In the first two cases, it was because I was woolgathering because I didn't think I was in a dangerous situation. It was just pure luck that I wasn't hit. My luck ran out when I was so convinced that Toby was alone and not a threat that I didn't even look elsewhere. That was a real mistake."

413

"Why were you distracted? Was it because of Ruth?"

Nate had to recall the details in each of them before replying, "The first one was only partially because I was worried about what would happen when I returned to Laramie. I knew that she was hoping that something would happen between us and I didn't know how to let her know that it wasn't. But the bigger reason was that I was happy to be able to tell Mrs. Swarthmore that her ranch was safe because I'd identified the fake brother-in-law. The second one, when I was riding to the Lone Wolf, was all about my concerns for Ruth. After she'd made those accusations, I was trying to find the right words to convince her that I wasn't her father's killer and wasn't in cahoots with Toby. The third time, where I was shot, was just a bad mistake on my part."

"If Ruth doesn't believe the sheriff this time, what will you do?"

Nate sighed and answered, "I'll get on the train to Rawlins to see Sheriff Blount then return and start shutting down my office before I figure out where I'll go."

"Just because she'll continue to spread lies that will have been disproven?"

Nate almost said that one of her accusations wasn't a lie but replied, "You forget that she's still a Miller and that family has a lot of influence in this county."

"But if she admits she was wrong, you'll stay?"

"Yes, ma'am. I just wouldn't hold your breath."

Mary then stood and said, "You get some rest. I'll be out in the kitchen if you need anything."

"Thank you for being here, Mary. I know that I'm a pain in the behind, but I do appreciate it."

Mary smiled as she replied, "You aren't a pain in the behind, Nate. You have a pain in the behind," then left the room.

Nate was still smiling as he closed his eyes. Each minute he spent with Mary was torture knowing that he was letting her get too close and should try to keep her away, but he was getting more addicted and didn't know how to break the habit.

————

Nate didn't know how long he'd been napping but when there was a loud knocking at the front door, his eyes popped open and he felt his heart pounding almost as loudly.

He rolled off the quilts and stood before his butt reminded him of its wound then he walked around the bed and out the bedroom door.

He'd just reached the office when Mary opened the front door and he froze when he saw Ruth framed by the afternoon light.

As he stood at the end of the hall, Mary smiled at Ruth and said, "Hello, Ruth. Won't you please come in?"

Ruth had been anxious from the moment she'd left the ranch but after the sheriff and Toby continued down Main Street and she'd turned onto Kansas Street, she thought she wouldn't be able to make it from the street to the door before collapsing. That fear vanished with Mary's friendly greeting.

She smiled in return and as she entered, she said, "Thank you, Mary. How are you?"

Mary closed the door and replied, "I'm fine. As you can see, Mister Manning isn't doing as well."

Ruth stepped across the office slowly with Mary walking behind as she looked at Nate's concerned face.

But before she could say anything, that face broke into a big smile and he said, "It's good to see you again, Sissie."

What remained of her anxiety melted away as she quietly said, "Toby told us what happened, Nate. May we talk?"

"Toby told you?" he asked before answering her question by saying, "Of course, we can talk. Let's go to the kitchen where I can sit a bit more comfortably."

"I'll stay here," Mary said.

"No, I need you to listen as well, Mary," Ruth quickly replied.

Nate waited until Ruth and Mary passed by before following them down the hallway. He already knew that Ruth believed that he hadn't killed her father or was in league with Toby, but he needed to know if she was going to tell them how she'd learned that he was only Nate Manning for three years. He hoped that she had meant something different when she'd said that she didn't know who he was, but didn't want to be the one to broach the subject.

After they were seated around the table, Ruth quickly said, "Nate, I am so sorry for my behavior and making those ludicrous and unfounded accusations. I knew you were in Rawlins, but all I did while you were gone was to try to hurt you."

"I can understand why you would, Sissie. I hurt you and you were just reacting to what I did. I'm sorry for that and I hope you can forgive me."

Ruth smiled and said, "I told the sheriff that would be your reaction. But before we put aside apologies, I'd like to give one to Mary for being jealous of her with no cause."

Mary said, "There's no reason to apologize, Ruth. I wasn't offended."

"I just wanted you to know that if you and Nate decide to marry, then I'll be happy for you both."

Nate had anticipated some measure of regret, but this was something that was completely unexpected, but Mary didn't seem flustered at all by the comment and that surprised him just as much.

Mary simply smiled at Ruth as she said, "I'm sure that Nate isn't interested in marrying me or anyone else, Ruth."

"He told you that, too? Then it wasn't just me?"

"No, it wasn't. We've talked a lot since I moved into his house to take care of his wounds and he's expressed his lack of interest in marriage a number of times. He may not have given me a sufficient reason for that decision, but it wasn't about you. It's about our Mister Manning."

Ruth looked at Nate and after a short pause, she just said, "Oh," before continuing and saying, "Let me tell you what happened when the sheriff arrived with Toby."

Nate was still trying to absorb their brief conversation as he replied, "Okay. I still find it hard to believe that he rode out there."

Ruth laughed before she started telling them about the visit.

As she talked, Nate listened and hoped she'd explain her final and most dangerous accusation, but all she talked about was what Toby had told them. He was a bit amazed that Toby had the courage to tell her about her father's involvement, but he guessed that it helped that the sheriff was sitting nearby and would probably tell her anyway.

He glanced at Mary every so often as she stared at Ruth and wondered what she was thinking. Most of what they heard from Ruth was close to what she already knew, so the rapt attention on her face was a bit out of place.

When Ruth finished, she looked at Nate and asked, "So, can we be friends again, Nate?"

Nate smiled back and replied, "We were always friends, Sissie, or I'd be calling you Ruth or Miss Miller."

Ruth felt much lighter when she saw Nate's smile and knew that he meant what he'd said.

Then she asked him to tell her about what had happened since he'd been drygulched on the road to the Lone Wolf, so Nate took control of the conversation for a while.

Mary simply listened to another story that she knew well but didn't complain as she hoped to hear details she'd missed before. She had gleaned new information as Ruth spoke, now she was curious if she'd learn more from Nate. She was especially interested if he'd venture into the explanation of why Ruth had said that he wasn't Nate Manning at all. She hadn't mentioned it and although she hoped that Nate might ask about it, she was almost certain that he would keep that topic out of any part of the discussion. He had never even talked about his past and whatever Ruth had discovered obviously worried him.

419

They spent another hour and a half talking and most of it was by Nate, but it was getting late and Ruth had to return to the ranch.

"I'm not about to ask if I can stay," Ruth said as she stood, "but I do hope you don't mind if I visit whenever I'm in town."

"I'd be happy for you to visit, Sissie. But before you go, may I ask one more question?"

Mary quickly looked at Nate in anticipation of the critical inquiry about that last accusation.

She was disappointed when he asked, "What are you going to do about Toby?"

"I'm not going to shoot him, but we're not hiring him back either. I don't imagine he'll stay in town very long."

"I don't think so either," Nate said as he rose slowly from his seat.

Mary stood and said, "I'll walk with you to your horse, Ruth. Nate needs to lay down on his side before his bottom falls off."

Ruth laughed, then she and Mary left the kitchen and walked down the hall as Nate walked to the cookstove to pour himself one more cup of bitter coffee.

He heard the door close and as he stood at the cookstove sipping his coffee and looking out the back window to his small barn that now housed two horses again, Mary entered.

"Ruth seems even better than when I first met her," she said as she walked closer.

Nate didn't turn but replied, "I'm relieved that she is and happy for her."

"What about you, Nate? Are you better now?"

"Not until my bottom is healed or falls off."

Mary laughed then asked, "When are you going to Rawlins?"

"I don't need your permission, Nurse White?"

"No, sir. You haven't shown any signs of infection and the healing is progressing nicely, but I will examine both wounds before you leave."

"As I expected, ma'am," he said before looking into his cup and grimacing.

He turned and dumped the cup's contents back into the coffeepot before carrying the coffeepot to the back door and emptying the stale coffee onto the ground and returning.

As he set the coffeepot into the sink, Mary asked, "You aren't thinking of moving now; are you?"

"I'll let you know before I decide. That's the best I can do."

"Is it because Ruth didn't explain that charge that you weren't who you said you were?"

Nate was about to make another excuse but replied, "Yes. It's just another rumor that could cause trouble. She may have forgotten she ever said it."

"Then why didn't you ask about it?"

Nate felt his walls closing in with every one of Mary's questions and his fortress was now being crushed into a closet.

"I forgot," he blurted out before saying, "I need to follow your suggestion and get some rest."

"I'll cook supper while you do."

"Okay," Nate said before he quickly left the kitchen then entered his room and closed the door.

Mary was angry with herself for asking because she knew that she was pushing him too fast and too far. She had to be patient, or he would leave without telling her. After he returned from Rawlins, she wouldn't have any excuse for remaining in the house. She'd have to return to room at the boarding house and her cleaning and midwife duties. That was if he returned from Rawlins at all. All she could hope was that he'd keep his promise to tell her before he left if she couldn't find some way to get him to tell her of his past and then make him stay.

Nate lay on his bed almost in a fetal position, grateful that both wounds were on the same side. Now that Mary was asking those questions, the battle that had been ongoing in his mind about telling her or just leaving Laramie had escalated to a no-holds-barred war.

He began to look at the trip to Rawlins as an opportunity to calmly evaluate the situation. Maybe it wasn't as bad as he thought. Maybe Ruth didn't really know anything, and Mary was just concerned. He knew he couldn't lie to her, but he needed to at least explain his name change.

———

The remains of the day were somewhat normal as neither he nor Mary talked much about Ruth's visit. Nate found that talking about Toby was a good distraction.

By the time they turned in that night, Nate was much calmer than he'd been earlier.

In the next room, Mary was still concerned, but thought that Nate seemed more content than he'd been immediately after Ruth left. She just hoped that he'd forgotten about leaving.

CHAPTER 13

Sunday morning arrived with a heavy overcast and the threat of rain. Before he dressed, Mary inspected Nate's wounds and told him that he was doing well before she left to cook breakfast.

Before he'd fallen asleep, Nate had decided what to say when he talked to Mary, so as they were eating breakfast, Nate said, "You know, Mary. I'm going to just stop worrying about what people think. If they want to believe that I'm the boogeyman or a creature that swoops out of the sky at night, let them. I'm just going to be me and do my job."

Mary was surprised but pleased by the change and replied, "That's good to hear, Nate. You were just worrying too much. You think too much and don't spend enough time enjoying yourself."

"I've been told that before, so I'll try to start enjoying myself more as soon as my stitches are removed, and my nurse give me permission."

Mary laughed before she said, "Don't forget that I'll be the one taking them out either."

"No, ma'am," Nate replied with a grin.

"How do you want to enjoy yourself on this cloudy and rainy day? You can't go out riding or shooting."

"Can you play chess?"

"No, but I'll learn if you want to show me."

"We'll do that in a little while."

Mary nodded then continued to eat, still happy with the improvement in his demeanor.

———

The rest of the day was pleasant and the house echoed with laughter often as Nate tried to teach Mary the intricacies of chess which was made more difficult because he never played before but only knew the moves and how the game ended.

After dinner, Nate said that after Ike arrived in the morning, he'd be heading to Rawlins to meet Sheriff Blount but should be back in two days.

Mary was surprised but told him because she'd already checked his wounds, she wouldn't need to look again in the morning, so Nate spent the evening hours preparing for the trip.

He'd be taking his new red gelding and just the Winchester '73 as he was just riding into town, but if he had time, he'd visit Agatha to see if she had any troubles with anyone on the ranch after he'd gone. He wasn't intending to stay this time and for some reason, he felt as if he'd be cheating on Mary if he did visit her in her bedroom. It was an odd sensation.

He had his saddlebags packed and was ready to leave by the time he slipped into bed and his now normal sleeping position on his right side. He couldn't wait to be able to sleep on his back again.

Mary was under her quilts and wondered if Nate really had decided that what the folks in town thought of him didn't matter. It was such a radical change from everything he'd said since she'd known him that it was difficult to believe. But at least he wouldn't be leaving and that meant she'd be able to spend more time with him when he returned. Maybe he'd finally tell her of his past life and she'd be able to confess her own history.

————

After Ike arrived earlier than usual the next morning, Nate barely had time to tell him that he was leaving for two days to go to Rawlins and that Mary would tell him about Ruth's visit and everything else that had happened.

A perplexed Ike Parker watched as Nate disappeared down the hallway then turned to Mary and asked, "What's the rush?"

"His train leaves in forty minutes."

"Oh. I suppose we need to talk."

"You might say that," she replied before taking a seat beside Ike's desk.

———

As Nate's train pulled out of Laramie, he was sitting on a cushion he'd brought from the house. He hadn't been dishonest with Mary when he'd told her that he would disregard the rumors but had decided that the one rumor that would cause him to lose much more than clients was now dead. Whatever reason Ruth had for saying that he wasn't Nate Manning didn't seem to be resurfacing. Ruth didn't mention it after her long explanation of what she'd told the sheriff and except for Mary's questions, it hadn't come up again anywhere else.

So, as the train hurtled westward, Nate believed that his past would remain buried. With that issue behind him, Nate began to think about Agatha, but not about that extraordinary time they'd spent together. He recalled what she'd asked of him and extracted a promise. She'd asked him not to withhold his love from a woman who loves him. He wasn't sure if what he felt for Mary was love because it was so alien to him, but he'd never felt this way about any woman. But she was just a close friend, so he supposed that it didn't matter how he felt.

At least he'd be able to talk to her now that he wasn't going to have to leave Laramie, but he was still concerned about hiding his past from her.

Nate had no idea what awaited him in Rawlins, and it wasn't just Sheriff Blount or even Agatha Swarthmore.

———

Nate stepped off the train and walked across the platform to the stock corral to claim the red gelding. Once he mounted his horse and rode out to the street, he thought about getting some lunch, but decided to get his visit with Sheriff Blount out of the way, so he would be able to ride out to the Double 8.

He pulled up before the jail and dismounted. After he tied off the gelding, he stepped across the boardwalk and passed through the open front door and spotted Deputy Klipsch at the desk.

"Howdy, Deputy. Sorry it took so long, but I need to talk to the boss about my shootout south of Little Laramie and he said he had some information for me."

"Go on back, Mister Manning."

Nate waved as he walked past the front desk and soon entered the sheriff's office.

"I didn't think I'd see you this soon after getting shot twice, Nate, but I'm glad to see you on your feet. Where did you get hit?"

Nate remained standing after the train ride and replied, "I took a glancing hit on the left side of my chest and then

428

another .44 found its way through the left side of my butt. The slug is still in my saddle by the way."

Sheriff Blount snickered then said, "I wondered why you were still standing. So, tell me what happened."

Nate began his practiced explanation beginning with his decision to look for Stubby at the Halvorsen ranch.

After he finished, he wound up having to sit anyway after the sheriff asked him about the other drygulch attempt he'd heard about.

Nate wound up spending more than forty minutes with the sheriff, and the discussion finally ended when the sheriff finally said, "Okay, about what those two said that I thought you might want to know. Actually, it wasn't what they both said, it was what the lawyer said that might cause you some grief. I didn't want to put it in a letter because you'd probably have questions."

"Okay. What did Mister Chilton tell you?"

"Well, before the guards came to take him and Mac to prison last Monday, he told me that he'd be sending letters to the *Laramie Bugle* and some officials in town, including Bart Scott with information he'd gotten from Poteet. He said that those letters would expose you as a fraud and all sorts of other shady things. He'd been grousing about a bunch of things while he was our guest, so I didn't pay him much mind. I just figured you might want to know so you can tell 'em the truth before those letters started showing up."

Nate nodded then weakly smiled before he replied, "Thanks, Sheriff. I'll keep an eye out for them. Just when I figured that mess was behind me, too."

"Well, now you know. It was probably just an idle threat anyway. I'm gonna head home and get some lunch."

Nate nodded as the sheriff stood then stepped past him and left his office.

Nate listened to his bootsteps as they faded away and tried to wrestle with the terrifying news. Just when he thought the whole matter had been put to bed, he learns that it had awakened with a vengeance.

He slowly turned and left the sheriff's office and headed for the door. As he passed the deputy, he gave him a short wave to try to appear normal, but he was in a daze.

He left the jail and after untying the horse, he mounted and just sat in the saddle as he tried to think of what he could do. It had been nine days since he'd uncovered their plot and he hadn't heard of any letters arriving in Laramie, at least not yet.

The next eastbound train wasn't until late and it was a hundred miles to Laramie. He turned the gelding away from the jail and rode to the nearest eatery to fill his stomach while he decided what he should do.

As he ate his baked ham lunch, he was torn about acting before any letters even arrived. *What if the man was bluffing?* He wouldn't gain anything by doing it and wouldn't even know what impact it would have if he was in prison. But if he did write the letters, Nate was sure that he'd mix facts with sordid embellishments and that would be a true disaster. His real history that he'd taken great pains to hide was just a story of an angry nothing of a boy who became a nothing of a man. It wasn't anything that he was proud of, but it wasn't criminal or even antisocial. Bareknuckle fighting was frowned upon by polite society, but he'd seen men of substance in the audience who had more money to wager than the dirty men. It may have been ignored, but it wasn't illegal.

Nate finished his meal, left fifty cents on the table and left the diner. After mounting his gelding, he turned him east and thought about riding to the Double 8 to talk to Agatha. Maybe it would be better if he told her the truth first. He knew that she wouldn't judge him, and he wasn't worried about driving her away. He decided that rather than waste a couple of hours and tiring the gelding even more, he'd just ride to Laramie.

He wouldn't get in until after midnight, but he felt an urgency to get home and start packing. He needed to get away before that first letter arrived.

After he rode out of town at a medium trot, he picked up the pace and hoped that the red gelding had the stamina for the long ride. He began calculating how long it would be for the

431

letters to arrive, assuming that the lawyer hadn't been just making idle threats.

He had been taken to prison seven days ago, so he arrived two days later, which would put him in his new home five days ago. If he wrote those letters that day and posted them, they could arrive in the next day or two. He wasn't familiar with how the mail system in the prisons worked, so maybe they held the mail and only posted it once a week, which could give him more time.

He could have been drygulched a dozen times by the time the sun set, and he was more than halfway to Laramie. He couldn't care less if someone shot him as he lived in his mind thinking about the lawyer, the mail, and where he would go. He thought about telling Sheriff Scott about the possibility that the lawyer may send a letter to him making wild accusations, but he didn't want to have to explain what he thought was in the letter.

Then there was the promise he'd made to Mary and that bothered him more than the thought of being exposed. She would be back in her room at the boarding house by now, so he'd be able to pack and talk to Ike before he had to talk to her again. *But what would he say? Would he tell her the real reason and see the disappointment in her eyes?* The thought of that being the last image he would have of her was chilling.

He'd given the horse a few breaks and let him have water, but none were very long as he rode through the night. He hadn't even paid attention to the pulsing pain in his backside as he sat in the bouncing saddle. Nor was he even the least bit tired as the full moon traced its path overhead giving him a good view of the roadway.

He didn't know or care what time it was when he picked up the shadowed outline of Laramie on the eastern horizon. He wasn't planning on going to bed or even making something to eat. He'd start packing right away, so when Ike arrived, he'd be ready to leave. He hadn't made any plans to take care of Ike, but he'd leave him six months' pay, which should hold him over until he found another job. He was a good man and well-respected, so he shouldn't be idle for long.

He reached Main Street and slowed the tired gelding to a walk as he passed the jail and then T.F. Green's. Melancholy began to grow inside him as he looked at the moonlit buildings of the only town that he'd really called home.

Nate passed Kansas Street then turned into the back alley as he always did. The houses were all dark and he estimated that it was after three o'clock in the morning when he reached his small barn and dismounted. His butt reminded him of the abuse it had suffered when his boot reached the ground, but it didn't matter anymore.

That sharp pain did remind him that he'd need to have the sutures removed from his wounds and if he left, he'd either have to do it himself or find a doctor wherever he wound up.

He began unsaddling the gelding as it began to munch on the oats in the feed box. As he removed the tack, he set them on the shelf and tried to calm down. He was an emotional disaster and he didn't like it. *He was a damned bounty hunter, for God's sake!*

He finished clearing the gelding and in a form of repentance, he started brushing the horses coat. He could have just gone to the house, but he owed it to the horse.

Each stroke of the brush seemed as if it was a second hand and was counting down the time he would be spending in Laramie.

He finally tossed the brush aside, then patted the gelding on the flank and didn't bother taking his saddlebags or his Winchester as he turned to leave the barn.

When he was outside again, he stopped and looked at his empty house and then closed his eyes. He felt as empty as he ever had before, and he didn't think it was possible.

Nate opened his eyes, took a breath and headed for his short porch. When he reached for the door, he found it locked and almost laughed. He then reached for his keys and unlocked the door before stepping inside. He took off his hat and hung it on the peg near the back door before removing his gunbelt. He used the buckle to hang it on another peg then walked to the kitchen table and struck a match which he used to light the lamp.

After he closed the chimney, he was about to pick it up and go to his bedroom when he heard a noise from the hallway. He wasn't sure if his ears had deceived him because it didn't repeat, so he took a step toward his bedroom and then heard another one, but it wasn't coming from his bedroom. It was coming from the bedroom where Mary had stayed.

He thought about returning to get his pistol, but instead he stopped where he was and called out, "Who's there? This is my house and I've got a Colt in my hand!"

He'd barely finished when he heard a loud thump which was immediately followed by Mary's reply, "Is that you, Nate?"

"Mary?" he asked loudly before saying, "Yes, it's me. What are you still doing here? I thought you were moving back into your room?"

He heard the bedroom door unlock, then he saw Mary step out of the room in her nightdress.

"I was waiting for you, Nate. I didn't want you to return and change your mind about leaving."

As she walked closer Nate said, "I promised you that I wouldn't leave without telling you first."

"Why are you back so soon? I didn't think the next train arrived for another couple of hours."

"It doesn't. I rode back after seeing Sheriff Blount."

"Why? What happened?"

"Mary, take a seat and I'll tell you."

"Alright," she replied before walking slowly to the table and sitting down while Nate followed and set the lamp on the inner edge of the table.

After he sat next to her, he let out a long breath to steady his nerves. It was time to tell her the truth and maybe because it was in the lamplight, he wouldn't see the effect that the revelation would have on her.

"Mary, this is very difficult for me. I've been holding a secret for so long that it's almost painful to talk about it."

"You don't have to tell me, Nate. It doesn't matter."

"Yes, it does. I need you to know."

"Why?"

He took in a long breath before saying, "Because you've become such a good friend that I don't want to hear things after I'm gone that are worse than the truth."

"Ike is a good friend, why didn't you tell him?"

"Because, well, he's my friend and you're more important to me now."

"Do you love me, Nate?" she asked quietly.

"I don't know what love is, Mary. I honestly haven't felt it before, but I feel something very new that makes me very happy and comfortable when I'm with you. I think about you when we're apart and want to come back to you as soon as I'm away. It could be love, but I'm not sure. But it doesn't matter how I feel."

"Why doesn't it matter?"

Nate was struggling as he searched for the right words to talk about a subject that was a mystery to him.

"Because it doesn't. It's kind of complicated because I don't know about such things."

"You mean about love?"

"Yes. When I was in Rawlins the first time to help Agatha Swarthmore, she was so happy when I told exposed the fraudulent brother that she asked me to stay the night and we were intimate. I knew it wasn't love and she said the same thing. But before I left, she asked me to make a promise. She said that I shouldn't hold back my love from a woman who loved me. How would I know if a woman loved me if I didn't even know what it was?"

"You could ask the woman."

"No, I couldn't. Look what happened with Ruth and I never even thought of asking her that because I knew that she did and that I didn't feel that way about her."

"Why don't you practice and ask me?"

Nate stared at her in the lamplight for a few seconds before he swallowed and in a low voice asked, "Do you love me, Mary?"

"Yes, Nate. I love you."

Her answer surprised him to the point where he thought she was just acting the part, so he quickly said, "Okay. I understand that you're just pretending because you don't know me at all."

"I meant every one of those three words, Nate. I know you a lot more than you realize."

"You can't, Mary. No one does. It's what I was going to confess to you and now it's going to be a lot harder."

"I'll understand whatever you tell me, Nate, and I promise you that I'll still love you when you've finished."

"You can't understand, Mary. You're so perfect and so complete that despite your immense amount of compassion, you will only be able to feel pity if not scorn."

"Just tell me what you're so afraid to tell me."

Nate slowly nodded, then began his confession by saying, "I'm not really Nate Manning. I guess that's not really true because it's the name I go by now, but until I left Hays City more than three years ago, I went by the name of Ned Boyd."

He paused as he expected a question or gasp, but Mary sat quietly as she waited for him to continue.

"But even Ned Boyd wasn't my real name. I had no real name. I don't know what day I was born, so I don't even know my real age. I don't know my parents name or where they lived."

He paused again but Mary still said nothing, which surprised him, so he resumed his life's tale.

"My first memory was when I was in an orphanage outside of St. Louis. They gave me a name, but I don't remember what it was. I think it began with a J, but it doesn't matter. I was always an angry, troublesome boy, so when I was around six, the orphanage sold me to a local bottle factory. They didn't give me a name either but gave me a number. I was #207.

"My behavior didn't change and actually got worse. I got into fights with the other boys and found that I had the skills that were necessary to fight. I wasn't bothered by the big boys by the time I was eight. I hated that factory. Every morning, they would march us out of the dormitories onto the floor and made us work until it was dark with only short breaks. They said that giving us food, raggedy second-hand clothes and a place to sleep was our pay.

"I was so much trouble that the began giving me harder and more dangerous jobs in the factory until I was around sixteen and I lost my temper and almost killed the supervisor. If it hadn't been for the two guards, I would have. When they threw me out into the night, the supervisor pointed at me and told me that I was nothing and would always be nothing."

Mary finally spoke when she quietly asked, "What did you do after you left?"

"I used those fighting skills that I'd discovered at the factory and began going to gyms, halls and back rooms where they paid me to fight. I was a bareknuckle fighter and after I learned more about real fighting, I got a manager and became very good at beating up other men. I chose the name Ned Boyd because I remembered that the supervisor had told me that I would always be nothing and so I used the name as a pseudonym for Nothing Boy.

"But my manager got greedy and set me up to lose against a fighter who had no business being in the ring with me. I quit and as I left, he told me that I was nothing without him, just like the bottle factory manager had thought of me when I was tossed out of his place.

"I fought my way across Missouri and most of Kansas as Ned Boyd and no one questioned anything about my past as I was just a transient fighter. That changed when I arrived in Hays City and met Sheriff Luther Galloway. I actually pushed him and was about to hit him when his deputy popped his Colt's barrel into my head and dropped me to the floor. When I woke up in the jail, I was still mad, but the sheriff told me that being angry all the time wasn't a good way to spend your life. He offered me a job as a deputy, and I accepted.

"I stayed there for more than a year until he retired then I moved on. When I did, I was a completely different person. I wasn't angry any longer, so I decided to change my name to Nate Manning, which I understood to mean Nothing Man. That's how I see myself, Mary. I have no real history and no family. Over the years, I've built a wall inside me that keeps anyone from getting too close and since I met you, you've been smashing your way through that wall. It's a very unnerving idea."

"I understand, Nate. It's not such a horrible history. In fact, it's probably a lot better than the ones that most men could tell about their lives. You have nothing to be ashamed of."

"It's not that, Mary. I'm not ashamed of it, I just feel like a phony by acting as if I'm a normal person. I've made up a complete fictitious life history with an imaginary family living in Iowa to keep people from either looking down at me or pitying me."

"Anyone who really knows you wouldn't do either of those things, Nate. Do you honestly believe that Ike or Alice would think less of you if you told them? I know that Ruth wouldn't and if anything, I think more of you now than I did before just because you told me. So, please stay here with me. Marry me, Nate. I won't care what you write on the marriage license."

Nate wanted this more than he'd ever wanted anything, but he still believed that Mary didn't know him well enough to spend the rest of her life with him. They'd only known each other for two weeks and he'd been gone for a few of those days.

"Mary, you've only known me for two weeks. How can you be sure that you feel that way?"

"You aren't thinking about leaving anyway; are you?"

"I have to go, Mary. Those letters might arrive, and I'll become a pariah."

Mary looked at him for fifteen seconds, then stood and stepped away from the table as she said, "Can I ask you to do a job for me before you make that decision?"

"A job?" he asked.

"Yes. A job that needs your skills as an investigator."

"Of course, I will. What do you need?"

Mary turned until her back was to him and untied the knot on the front of her nightdress's drawstring then loosed the neckline.

Nate stared at her and thought she was going to offer herself to him to keep him in Laramie almost like Ruth had done, but he hadn't expected it from Mary. It just wasn't like her.

442

She lowered the top of the nightdress and held it at her waist letting Nate see her naked back.

Nate stared at her back and saw two long welts that ran at an angle from the top of her left shoulder down to the middle of her spine.

"I want you to find a man for me," she said softly.

Nate felt his old anger well up inside him as growled, "I'll find the man who did this to you and make him wish he had never been born."

"No, Nate. I don't want you to find him. I want you to find the man who stopped him from hurting me even worse."

"Why do you want me to find him?"

She pulled her nightdress back over her shoulders and as she tied the drawstring, she turned and smiled at him.

"Because in my entire life, he was the only person who cared about me. I don't believe I ever said more than ten words to him, but when I needed him, he protected me even though he could have been killed by doing it."

"When did that happen?"

"When I was just a girl of eleven. I had knocked over a bottle from my table and it had shattered on the floor. When I went to pick up the pieces, the supervisor yelled at me and

443

began to whip me. The pain was so bad that I thought he was going to beat me to death.

"Then he suddenly stopped, and I didn't know why until I looked to my right and saw the teenaged boy I only knew as #207 come charging across the floor with his fists clenched. I watched as the supervisor hit him as hard as I'd seen him whip any of us, but the boy kept coming as if he wasn't touched. Then he began beating the bigger supervisor and knocked him onto glass.

"When the guards came and grabbed him, all I could do was to look into his eyes and thank him. I expected to see anger and hate in those eyes, but I didn't. I saw compassion and loneliness. I'll never forget the short time when I shared that look with #207."

Nate stared at Mary as she stood just three feet in front of him then quietly asked, "That was you? I never even knew your name. Why did you come here?"

"I've been following you since I became a nurse. Finding out your new name, Ned Boyd, wasn't difficult as one of the guards had mentioned that he'd seen you fight under that name. Just as you did, I worked my way across Missouri and Kansas, but I didn't take as long. I finally reached Hays City, where I was told you moved on, but they didn't know your new name. That cost me some time until I reached Laramie."

"Why didn't you tell me when you got here?"

"At first, I wasn't sure if it was really you. Everyone I asked said you'd arrived three years ago, but the rest of the information was all wrong, which complicated things. I had to be sure."

She finally took her seat as Nate asked, "But you must have figured it out before long."

"I did, and when I found out that Ike worked for you and Alice was expecting, I offered to be her midwife at no cost. I wanted to learn more about you from the people who were closest to you. When I finally had the chance to spend some time with you, it didn't take long to understand that you didn't want anyone to know about your past for some reason that I couldn't understand."

"But if you'd told me, then I would have explained everything."

"I'm sure you would have, but I felt it was important that you make the decision to tell me without knowing that I was that girl you kept from being hurt."

"I was just angry at the supervisor, Mary."

"You were angry because he was beating a defenseless girl, not because he was a vicious man. I noticed that you didn't beat him when he whipped you a few times for your many offenses that left all those scars on your back."

"No, it just didn't matter what he did to me. I was nothing. If he killed me, they'd toss me in a hole the ground and no one would ever know that I existed."

"I think that's why you're afraid of anyone knowing your history, Nate. It's not that it's terrible or scary, but it's because you're afraid to take that step out of your nothing world and become someone who matters. You need a wife and children to become that man, Nate."

Nate quietly asked, "Do you really believe it works that way, Mary?"

"Yes, I do."

"Have you ever loved anyone before?"

"Just you, Nate. And like you, I didn't know my parents or when or where I was born. I just stayed in the orphanage a lot longer and knew the name they'd given me. But after I was sent to the factory, I saw even more cruelty. Yet even though you thought of yourself as an angry troublesome boy, I saw you much differently.

"I've loved you ever since you were #207. Not because I saw you as a hero or my rescuer as Ruth did, but because of what I saw when I looked into your eyes as you were being led away. Of course, I've had many men tell me that they loved me and wanted to marry me after I left the factory, but they just wanted to have me, not love me."

"Then how do you know what it is?"

"I wish I could explain it to you, but I can't. I just know. Do you know what was my biggest worry as I followed you across the plains? I was afraid that when I found you, you would already be married."

Nate smiled as he said, "I guess there was a reason for my decision not to get married that I didn't know about."

He then asked, "Mary, why are you so whole? It's the one thing that struck me the most about you. Since that first meeting that we had at T.F. Green's, it was your completeness of character that almost scared me away."

"I don't see myself that way, but I wasn't ashamed or even paid any attention to my past. But the biggest difference, I believe, is that I knew that I loved you and that kept me going and gave me hope as I crossed half the country."

"Weren't you afraid of being hurt?"

"Of course, I was. But I was more worried that I wouldn't find you or that you might be married when I did."

"Even if you did find me unmarried, how could you know that I'd love you in return and want to marry you?"

She smiled before she replied, "I never questioned that both would happen. It was probably just an overzealous hope that drove that certainty, but I was convinced by just that one short

447

look on the factory floor as Mister Bristol screamed at you before the guards hauled you away. Call me a silly romantic girl, but I knew."

Nate glanced at the lightening sky as the predawn arrived, then asked, "Are you going to get some more sleep? I'm just going to bring my gear inside and clean up for the day before Ike arrives."

"No, I'm finished sleeping. I'll go visit the small house and then get dressed. Oh, and you can take the shotgun out of my bedroom now. I don't think I'll need it anymore."

She stood and smiled at Nate before crossing the kitchen and then exited the back door.

Nate rose and followed her out the door leaving it open and once in the soft light of the predawn, he stopped on the short back porch and watched her enter the privy and then scanned the same alley he'd passed through an hour or so earlier. It seemed different now. He had been almost despondent when he was approaching the barn, but now it was nothing like it was earlier and it wasn't because of the light. Now was home, and he wasn't leaving.

He stepped down and soon entered the barn where he gathered his saddlebags and his Winchester before returning to the house.

———

By the time Ike arrived in the office, he was surprised to find Nate waiting for him after leaving for Rawlins yesterday. While the rapidity of his return surprised him, finding Mary sitting beside him on the couch pushed it to a higher level.

"Back so soon, Nate?" he asked as he hung his hat on the coat rack.

"Have a seat, Ike. I have a long story to tell you. But before I start, I want to apologize for not telling you earlier…much earlier."

Ike nodded, then pulled one of the client chairs closer to the couch and took a seat.

"When I Sheriff Blount yesterday, he mentioned that the lawyer who was involved in that scheme to defraud Mrs. Swarthmore said that he was going to send letters to the *Laramie Bugle* and others in town exposing me as a fraud."

Ike snapped, "That bastard! We wouldn't believe any of his lies, Nate."

"They wouldn't all be lies, Ike. Since I've been here, whenever I was asked about my home and family, I described a large family in Iowa that simply never existed. Let me tell you the truth about my past."

As Ike listened intently, Nate began his true-life story from being taken from the uncaring orphanage to the bottle factory where they had assigned him a number and how he'd been tossed out into the night without a penny. He didn't tell him that Mary was the girl that was been being punished but left that to her.

He ended his history when he arrived in Laramie, then tried to explain why he was so intent on keeping his past private.

Ike asked, "You could have told us, Nate. It wouldn't make any difference."

"I know that now, but once I started down that path after leaving Fort Hays, I couldn't change. The longer I kept that story alive, the more protective I became of my past life."

"Why did you suddenly decide to tell me? Is it because of the letters that the lawyer threatened to send?"

"That was why I rode back so quickly, but not why I decided to stay and tell you and a few others the truth. I was going to leave Laramie when I walked into the house and found Mary here. She is the reason that I'm staying and why I am telling you the real story."

Ike looked at Mary who was smiling and said, "Thank you for convincing him, Mary. How did you do it?"

"I told him my own life. You see, I was the girl who he had prevented from being beaten on the factory floor. I knew when I looked into his eyes that I would have to find him no matter how long it took. After I became a nurse, I left St. Louis and I've been searching for him for two years."

Ike blinked as he looked at Mary then turned to Nate and asked, "Is this permanent then? You're not going to think about leaving again; are you?"

"No, Ike. I'm staying and Mary isn't going to live in the boarding house any longer. She's staying here and not as my nurse."

"*You two are getting married?*" Ike asked in astonishment.

Nate glanced at Mary then back to Ike before he replied, "I haven't asked her yet, but when I do, I have a good idea she might accept me. But before I ask her, we need to talk a bit more, so why don't you take one more day off and tell Alice that she can stop her attempts at matchmaking."

Ike's face was split by a giant grin as he popped to his feet and quickly dragged the chair back to his desk then hurried to the coat rack, snatched his hat and reached for the door. Before he opened it, he turned back to Nate and Mary and opened his mouth to say something but then just giggled and left.

After the door closed, Mary turned to Nate and said, "I told you that no one would care one bit about your mysterious past."

"I feel like an idiot for keeping it locked up inside. When I look back now, I can't even understand why I thought it was so important to hide those years before I arrived in Laramie. I told

Sheriff Galloway about my life and it didn't bother me then, so why did it become so critical to me after I left Hays City."

Mary took his hand and said, "You just need to step back and look at yourself from the outside. You thought you were nothing before you arrived in Hays City as Ned Boyd and met Sheriff Galloway, and you still thought that way when you arrived in Laramie as Nate Manning. You felt as if your life was empty and would always be that way. You believed that if you started a new life as Nate Manning and discarded your life as Ned Boyd, you could start filling that void. But it didn't make a difference; did it?"

"No, it didn't. Personally, I'd rather stop trying to figure out why I was that way and just focus on the future for once. You once asked me what I saw in my future if I didn't see myself as a husband and father. Do you recall my answer?"

"Perfectly because it was so brief. You simply replied, 'nothing'. It was what made me realize just how much you needed me."

"I do need you, Mary. You are my future. Will you marry me, Miss White?"

Mary smiled then kissed him gently before quietly replying, "Yes, I'll marry you, Number 207."

EPILOGUE

Over the next couple of days, Nate and Mary were never apart as they visited acquaintances to tell them their story. The empty past that Nate had spent three years trying to hide became a fairytale love story because of Mary's search and devotion.

They were married on June 15th. The small ceremony was attended by their friends which included Ruth and a visitor from Rawlins. Nate had sent her a telegram letting her know that he had kept his promise to her. She not only was present at the marriage ceremony but gave them a wedding gift of a thousand dollars because he had failed to send her a bill for the very satisfactory services he had provided.

When they had completed the marriage license paperwork, both had written 'unknown' in many of the form's spaces and even Nate thought it was funny.

They bought a larger house two doors down from the office when Mary announced her pregnancy in September.

On April 7th, Mary gave birth to their daughter, Lauren Marie Manning. She was the first of six children they would have together, and none would ever face any of the loneliness or hardships that their parents had endured.

Ruth married another ranch hand, Walter Lipscomb, in October that year, but it wasn't a happy marriage and he left in May of 1888. She never remarried.

Toby Halvorsen left Laramie and was never heard from again.

None of the threatened letters ever arrived but wouldn't have mattered even if any of the recipients opened the envelopes.

Agatha Swarthmore ended her days as a widow in November and let her new husband believe that he was in charge, so she was content in her new life.

Mr. and Mrs. Manning visited Hays City and the Galloway family in October before she became noticeably pregnant and it was only then that Nate discovered that Ruth had telegrammed his old boss to ask about Nate Manning. By then, it was nothing more than a humorous anecdote.

Nate continued his work as a bounty hunter and detective, but as Laramie grew, most of his work was as a private investigator. He never had to engage in a gunfight again.

In late May in 1898, as Nate and Mary sat on the porch in their swing watching the traffic and listened to the sounds of their children playing nearby, she looked over at her husband whom she had loved for almost all of her life even before she found him. He was smiling as he looked down at their children and Mary could see his contentment and knew he was whole now without any emptiness in his soul.

When he turned his smiling face to her, she leaned across the short gap and kissed him before saying, "Nate Manning, you are really something."

1	Rock Creek	12/26/2016
2	North of Denton	01/02/2017
3	Fort Selden	01/07/2017
4	Scotts Bluff	01/14/2017
5	South of Denver	01/22/2017
6	Miles City	01/28/2017
7	Hopewell	02/04/2017
8	Nueva Luz	02/12/2017
9	The Witch of Dakota	02/19/2017
10	Baker City	03/13/2017
11	The Gun Smith	03/21/2017
12	Gus	03/24/2017
13	Wilmore	04/06/2017
14	Mister Thor	04/20/2017
15	Nora	04/26/2017
16	Max	05/09/2017
17	Hunting Pearl	05/14/2017
18	Bessie	05/25/2017
19	The Last Four	05/29/2017
20	Zack	06/12/2017
21	Finding Bucky	06/21/2017
22	The Debt	06/30/2017
23	The Scalawags	07/11/2017
24	The Stampede	07/20/2017
25	The Wake of the Bertrand	07/31/2017
26	Cole	08/09/2017
27	Luke	09/05/2017
28	The Eclipse	09/21/2017
29	A.J. Smith	10/03/2017
30	Slow John	11/05/2017
31	The Second Star	11/15/2017
32	Tate	12/03/2017
33	Virgil's Herd	12/14/2017
34	Marsh's Valley	01/01/2018
35	Alex Paine	01/18/2018
36	Ben Gray	02/05/2018

Made in the USA
Monee, IL
10 July 2020